THE
Brand-X Anthology of Fiction

≫≫≫≫≪≪≪≪≪≪≪≪≪≪≪≪≪≪≪≪≪≪≪≪≪≪≪≪≪≪≪

BURNT NORTON EDITION

THE
Brand-X Anthology
of Fiction

BURNT NORTON EDITION

WILLIAM ZARANKA
UNIVERSITY OF DENVER

APPLE-WOOD BOOKS, INC.
Cambridge • Watertown

To My Wife, Ruth

Contents

>❯❯❯·❯❯❯·❯❯❯·❮❮❮

Foreplay

The Brand-X Anthology of Fiction provides an alternative to traditional literature and should be read simultaneously with (perhaps even at the same time as) its companion volume, *The Brand-X Anthology of Poetry*. The avowed purpose of both is the same: to fool the sophomores. This was, of course, Plato's purpose in banishing the poets from *his* anthology. While I did not ban a single poet from my first anthology, I have banned them all from the second, but for more subtle reasons than Plato's, which I have neither time nor space enough to go into here. Suffice to say, poets are difficult. They say one thing and mean another. They keep company together and make dreary intellectual talk. They drink and keep late hours. Ignored, they complain. Praised, they preen. Criticized, they mewl and puke and write letters to the editor. Advertised, they don't sell. I'm terribly fond of poets but must admit they are subversive; they write little things and demand big remuneration.

On the other hand. I have friends who are fiction writers, and I find that they are easier to work with and are more modest. They are not nearly as paranoid as poets, which is reflected in their work. The best ones write for the fun of it and prefer good liquor to intellect. Generally, they shun company in favor of good talk. Best, they write long pieces and give permission to reprint for nothing. That is why the reader will find *The Brand-X Anthology of Fiction* full of fiction writers.

The reader will note that the volume is arranged chronologically for convenience, often in accordance with the actual dates. The type is large to prevent eye strain (a common problem for students of the rival *Ed Norton Anthology*) and to fulfill a swollen page count. While it may seem strange that Edmund Gosse and Edna Ferber are accorded space here at the expense of such American masters as Hawthorne or Fitzgerald, it is not. Always, the student is encouraged to read, on his own, synopses of any work not included here and to present a copy of this book as a gift to every friend and parent.

William Zaranka, poet
University of Denver
Winter, 1983

BEGINNINGS

Richardson's *Shamela* Through Auden's *Enema*

1707: W. C. Fielding born.
1722: Defoe's *Journal of the Plague Year*; first study of plagiarism in 18th century.
1748: Richardson swears "fidelity to hormone experience."
1755: Johnson's *Dictionary*; first masterpiece of dislexicography.
1759: Voltaire's *Candide*; first nikonoclastic fiction.
1781: Johnson frees mind of Kant.
1790: Burke's *Symbolic Action in a Revolution by the French*.
1805: Scott's *Lay of the Last Menstrual*.
1815: End of Neoplatonic Whores.
1816: Auden's *Enema*.

FIDELITY TO HORMONE EXPERIENCE

Any survey of literary fiction must take into account the social mildew. There can be no minimizing the effect of Bubonic Plagiarism on the birth of the eighteenth-century novel. This dread disease dessicated the population of London between 1664-1665 and has been compared favorably by historians to the Writing Pogroms of America for sheer kill-power. Furthermore, it is much more interesting than the fiction of the period, which concerned itself with such ridiculous things as "holding the mirror up to Mother Nature" and Aristotle's "emetic theory," which held that for a work of literature or art to be successful it must be possessed of a beginning, a midwife, and a wedding. Richardson's *Shamela* is an imperfect novel because it lacks a midwife; on the other hand, it includes a beginning and a wedding. Indeed, Madame Wartly Montague (the "coy mattress" of Swift's *A Modest Proposition*) called *Shamela* a "comic epoch in prose" and it soon became the joy of chamberpots of all nations. Thus, it is superior to Defoe's *A Journal of the Plagiarism Year* and his beat epic, *Robinson Corso*, neither of which ever pleased a chamberpot. What's more, if Realism is what Ian Twat has called "fidelity to hormone experience," then Richardson, treating as he does incipient fornication and sex, is the more realistic.

THE WILLING SUSPENDERS OF DISBELIEF
Hard on the heels of so-called hormone literature come the so-called "tales of terror," written in Gothic and translated by Thelonius Monk Lewis. These "sickly and stupid German travesties," as Wordsworth called them in the "Foreplay to *Lyrical Bellows*," evoke a vaguely futile past, a trick they no doubt learned from Roethke's *The Sores of Young Werther*. Replete with beautiful heroins, clanking amour, closet *homo-fatals*, underground catamarans, and other melodramatic stage-crappings, these fictions are less terrifying than amusing for the testimony they bear on the gullibility of our four fathers, who saw in the falling hemlocks of Foulpole's *Castle of Amontillado* the foreshadowing of the flying buttocks of the modern haunted house.

STORMY MOORS VS. ENGLISH GENTILE FOLK
The lingering influence of the Gothic language persisted during the nineteenth century. Emily Brontë's tale of passion between Catherine Hensure and Heathcliffe, for instance, conforms nicely to the Gothic formula of pitting a beautiful maidenhead against an obsessed and haggard *homo-fatal*.

On the other hand, Jane Auden seems less Gothic in temperature than might be expected. In *Northamber Abbey*, for instance, she pokes fun at the dark vaginal side of human nature. This was the side which appealed to Romantics such as Mary Shelley Frankenstein (the great grandmother of Barbara Herford Herrnstein), though not to Walter Scott, whose work is peppered with dangerous adventures about missing hairs and feuding clams. In *Sensual Sensibility* and *Friendly Persuasion*, she dispenses marital advice to young, leisure-class lady virgins. Her crowning achievement, of course, is *Enema*. The engaging story of a young anorexic's meddling in the affairs of provincial English gentile-folk, it gives the lie to criticism of her work as being uncircumcised by her own limited experience.

DANIEL DEFOE
(1659-1731)

From Robinson Crusoe

"Behold," says I, "how depraved these devils are, for surely these are gobbets of human flesh they are about to eat up and devour, such food as I never in all my life have eaten. No one," says I, "on my island shall indulge tastes so foreign to me. These devils must be reformed, if it takes my last ounce of powder, for they are not of my way of thinking."

With that I took aim upon these unsuspecting villains, for I had concealed myself in a sort of ambuscado upon my first discovery of them, and at the first shot I killed three and wounded two more. Again I fired upon them with my other gun and many more were hit and, all bloody and wounded, ran about with devilish outcry, so that it was diverting to watch them. The rest fled to their boats, nor was I able to finish the good work completely, being somewhat mazed in strong drink, but not so as to prevent me from despatching the wounded with my cutlasses and a hatchet, they being, by the mercy of Heaven, unarmed. And, though a few escaped, it was not a bad day's work, since I had to my bag no less than thirteen.

"Now," says I, when I had done, "let this be a lesson to thee. For this devouring of human flesh is not orthodox nor well esteemed by Englishmen and all who indulge in such unholy practices are rightly to be reformed in this manner."

With which advice, I left the dead devils where they lay and was returning homeward, when I beheld one other that had fled unobserved to the woods.

By this time the strength of my potations was ebbing and I saw that this was no demon, but a blackamoor. I was first of a mind to reform him also, but, perceiving what a lusty strong-made fellow he was, and, by his gestures, that he was inclined to yield himself a prisoner, it came to me that here was one that might be converted into a Christian and a good servant or slave withal. My natural piety prompted me to this generous thought, much to my profit, as it turned out.

Marching him before me as a prisoner, I brought him to my

cavern and there made him safe and secure with ropes, but, as it appeared, the fellow had no thought to leave me, being much in awe of me, no doubt, as an angel from another and better world.

My first care was to make clothes for him of goatskin. Also I contrived for him a great cap of the same and made him wear these.

I was not long in teaching him to talk, instead of jabbering in his heathenish manner, and thus I raised him from his brute condition to that of a human being, for, though it may be these savages and other foreigners can understand their own barbarous lingo, it cannot be gainsaid that the English tongue is the only right human language.

When he had thus come upon a civil footing in the manner of his speaking, I made to go forward with his instruction in the Christian religion and the manners and customs of true believers.

"Friday," says I, for so I called him, "Thy body having been fed and clothed, it is time thy soul be nourished with the truth and clad in the garments of righteousness. Though thou art a miserable degraded wretch and a blackamoor into the bargain, I must believe that we are sprung from a common origin, children of the same first parents, wherefore it is my duty, painful and disgustful though it be, to call thee brother."

"Yassuh, Mista Crusoe," says he, "dat's ve'y nice an' Ah'm 'bleeged to you, suh, but, ef dat's de case, how come you all done shot all de rest of yo' family an' chopped 'em up wid a hatchet? Dat's what Ah wants to heah about, Mista Crusoe, suh."

"Brother Friday," says I, "never in all my life have I eaten so much as the little finger of any human being, having a disgust for such food and esteeming it indigestible, so when I found thee and thy fellows in the very act of such debauchery, what should I do but kill them?"

"Mista Crusoe," says he, "you sho'ly got dis all wrong. Dat wasn't no 'bauchery. Dat wasn't nuthin' but me an' my fambly havin' a picanic an' we wasn't eatin' no little fingers nur nuthin', but des only cookin' a few turkles we don cotched on de shoah. Nen 'long comes you an' goes a shootin' an' a choppin' an' a killin' ev'ybody, mah ole grandpap an' mah pappy an' a lot o' mah brudders an' uncles, des havin' a fambly pahty an' eatin' a few turkles. Seem like scan'lous conduck to me, it sho' did."

"Well, Brother Friday," says I, "if that is the case, then I admit the joke is on me. But I am willing to forgive and forget and to let bygones be bygones, as a Christian should, and we will say no more about it."

"Mista Crusoe," says he. "Kin Ah ax you one moah question? Whaffoah Ah gotta weah dis heah ole goat suit in all dis hot weathah? Lawd knows it's hot 'nuff heah 'thout no clo'es 'tall an', 'sides, dese heah gahments got awful rough seams inside of 'em. Scratch mah hide all to pieces, dey do, an' make me pow'ful soah."

"Brother Friday," says I, "no true-born Englishman can look upon bare flesh without a shock, from which I conclude that nakedness is an offense against religion. Did not our common ancestors when they first had knowledge of good and evil clothe themselves? This then is the first law of Heaven. And as to the climate of this island, such as it is, was it not ordained by the Creator? Well, then, both clothes and heat are of divine origin and, though the one chafe and bruise thee and the other make thee to sweat mightily, the laws of Heaven must be obeyed, even unto the mortification of the flesh."

"Well, Mista Crusoe," says he, "ef you say so, Ah spose, Ah gotta weah 'em. All Ah gotta say is dey dam' uncomf'table."

"Now, Brother Friday," says I, "thou hast learned the first duty of the Christian, obedience. The prime virtue of the lower classes, Brother Friday, is obedience—obedience and humility. We will now pass to the second lesson, which is the bearing of one another's burdens. The one must bear the other's burdens. Setting thee an example in humility, I denominate thee the one, I accept the secondary position of the other. Therefore it appears that the labor of sustaining us both must be borne by thee."

"You mean me gotta do all de wuhk?" says he.

"That, Brother Friday," says I, "appears to be the law."

"Whah at you git dat law?" says he, with some truculence.

"That, Brother Friday," says I, "is a law of Nature."

"How come me 'lected to be one an' you de othah?" says he.

"A fair question, Brother Friday," says I, "and it shall have a fair answer. Thou wert born the one and I the other, for I am of the dominant, thou of the servient race. These Brother

Friday, are facts of Nature, which—alas!—neither of us can alter, though we try our best. Be resigned to thy lot, Brother Friday, as I am to mine, for from such resignation springs contentment and, from contentment, happiness."

"How 'bout ef Ah doan do all de wuhk? What you all gwine do den?" says he.

"In that case, Brother Friday, thou wouldst not only be flying in the face of Heaven and of Nature, but I would be regretfully obliged to blow thy black head off, dear Brother Friday."

With that he looked at me earnestly and then sat for a long time in deep thought, his eyes fixed upon the ground. Then says he suddenly, "Mister Crusoe, is you all gwine teach me how to shoot a gun?"

"Certainly, Brother Friday," says I. "If thou art faithful, industrious and obedient in the meantime, then, when I am so old that I have lost all my senses, I will teach thee to shoot a gun. Until then I shall relieve thee of that part of the work, dear Brother Friday."

With a mighty sigh, he arose and went about his duties and from that time forward he was, indeed, a useful sort of workaday Christian, as the saying is.

—Christopher Ward

JONATHAN SWIFT
(1667-1745)

From Book V Of *Gulliver's Travels*:
A Voyage To Cynosuria

I inquired if I might not visit on this day's travels one of the places of education in this remarkable country. My guide assented, and we set off across the hills, presently emerging from the forest into the clearing of a University. A number of Cynosures were engaged in scratching with their claws on wax, busily criticising the mediocre verses of a successful poet. I remarked that in my country pupils were not expected to learn criticism, but applause; and that their appreciation of good poetry and art was all the stronger because they had always been assured of their goodness, without being confounded by examples of inferior productions.

Several pupils would from time to time cease from work, and, lifting one leg, relieve themselves against a tree. My guide could not comprehend my horror at what he stated to be a normal function; on the other hand, acquired tastes such as art, he pursued, were restricted to youth, and even hedged round with some suggestion of indecency, so that the young Cynosures might become addicted to them in later life.

Poetry and smelling, the two greatest of the arts, were strictly forbidden to all Cynosures under nine months of age. Accordingly, continued my guide, the public smelling glades were visited by great numbers, unharassed in their youth by constant praises of arts they could not understand. The treasures of these glades were placed among inferior productions, to heighten the pleasure of a critical faculty. I confess I found it strange to conceive a public bold enough to find its pleasures for itself; and I was much puzzled at a system of education which did not result in that complete removal of curiosity and lust for knowledge which is the chief glory of our own.

—Frank Adams

SAMUEL RICHARDSON
(1689-1761)

From Shamela

LETTER I.

SHAMELA ANDREWS *to Mrs.* HENRIETTA MARIA HONORA ANDREWS *at her lodgings at the* Fan *and* Pepper-Box *in Drury-Lane.*

Dear Mamma,

This comes to acquaint you, that I shall set out in the wagon on Monday, desiring you to commodate me with a ludgin, as near you as possible, in Coulstin's-Court, or Wild-Street, or somewhere thereabouts; pray let it be handsome, and not above two stories high: for Parson Williams hath promised to visit me when he comes to town, and I have got a good many fine clothes of the old put my mistress's, who died a wil ago; and I beleve Mrs. Jervis will come along with me, for she says she would like to keep a house somewhere about Short's-Gardens, or towards Queen-Street; and if there was convenience for a *bannio*, she should like it the better; but that she will settle herself when she comes to town.——*O! How I long to be in the balconey at the Old House!*——so no more at present from

Your affectionate Daughter,
SHAMELA.

LETTER II.

SHAMELA ANDREWS *to* HENRIETTA MARIA HONORA ANDREWS.

Dear Mamma,

O What news, since I writ my last! the young squire hath been here, and as sure as a gun he hath taken a fancy to me; Pamela, says he, (for so I am called here) you was a great favourite of your late mistress's; yes, an't please your Honour, says I; and I believe you deserved it, says he; thank your Honour for your good opinion, says I; and then he took me by the hand, and I pretended to be shy: Laud, says I, sir, I hope you don't intend to be rude; no, says he, my dear, and then he kissed me, 'till he took away my breath——and I pretended to be angry, and to get away, and then he kissed me again, and breathed very short, and looked very silly; and by ill-luck Mrs. Jervis came in, and had like to have spoiled sport.—*How troublesome is such interruption!* You shall hear now soon, for I shall not come away yet, so I rest,

Your affectionate Daughter,
SHAMELA.

LETTER III.

HENRIETTA MARIA HONORA ANDREWS *to* SHAMELA ANDREWS.

Dear Sham,

Your last letter hath put me into a great hurry of spirits, for you have a very difficult part to act. I hope you will remember your slip with Parson Williams, and not be guilty of any more such folly. Truly, a girl who hath once known what is what, is in the highest degree inexcusable if she respects her *digressions*; but a hint of this is sufficient. When Mrs. Jervis thinks of coming to town, I believe I can procure her a good house, and fit for the business; so I am,

Your affectionate Mother,
HENRIETTA MARIA HONORA ANDREWS.

LETTER IV.

SHAMELA ANDREWS *to* HENRIETTA MARIA HONORA ANDREWS.

Marry come up, good madam, the mother had never looked into the oven for her daughter, if she had not been there herself. I shall never have done if you upbraid me with having had a small one by Arthur Williams, when you yourself—but I say no more. *O! What fine times when the kettle calls the pot!* Let me do what I will, I say my prayers as often as another, and I read in good books, as often as I have leisure; and Parson Williams says, that will make amends.—So no more, but I rest

Your afflicted Daughter,
S—.

LETTER V.

HENRIETTA MARIA HONORA ANDREWS *to* SHAMELA ANDREWS.

Dear Child,

Why will you give such way to your passion? How could you imagine I should be such a simpleton, as to upbraid thee with being thy mother's own daughter! When I advised you not to be guilty of folly, I meant no more than that you should take care to be well paid before-hand; and not trust to promises, which a man seldom keeps, after he hath had his wicked will. And seeing you have a rich fool to deal with, your not making a good market will be the more inexcusable; indeed, with such gentlemen as Parson Williams, there is more to be said, for they have nothing to give, and are commonly otherwise the best sort of men. I am glad to hear you read good books, pray continue to do so. I have inclosed you one of Mr. Whitefield's sermons, and also the dealings with him, and am

Your affectionate Mother,
HENRIETTA MARIA, &c.

LETTER VI.

SHAMELA ANDREWS *to* HENRIETTA MARIA HONORA ANDREWS.

O Madam, I have strange things to tell you! As I was reading in that charming book about the dealings, in comes my master—to be sure he is a precious one. Pamela, says he, what book is that? I warrant you Rochester's poems.—No, forsooth, says I, as pertly as I could; why how now saucy chops, boldface, says he—Mighty pretty words, says I, pert again.—Yes (says he) you are a d—d, impudent, stinking, cursed, confounded jade, and I have a great mind to kick your a—. You, kiss—says I. A-gad, says he, and so I will; with that he caught me in his arms, and kissed me till he made my face all over fire. Now this served purely, you know, to put upon the fool for anger. O! What precious fools men are! And so I flung from him in a mighty rage, and pretended as how I would go out at the door; but when I came to the end of the room, I stood still, and my master cried out, hussy, slut, saucebox, boldface, come hither—Yes, to be sure, says I; why don't you come, says he; what should I come for, says I; if you don't come to me, I'll come to you, says he; I shan't come to you, I assure you, says I. Upon which he run up, caught me in his arms, and flung me upon a chair, and began to offer to touch my under-petticoat. Sir, says I, you had better not offer to be rude; well, says he, no more I won't then; and away he went out of the room. I was so mad to be sure I could have cried.

O what a prodigious vexation it is to be a woman to be made a fool of!

Mrs. Jervis, who had been without, harkening, now came to me. She burst into a violent laugh the moment she came in. Well, says she, as soon as she could speak, I have reason to bless myself that I am an old woman. Ah child! if you had known the jolly blades of my age, you would not have been left in the lurch in this manner. Dear Mrs. Jervis, says I, don't laugh at one; and to be sure I was a little angry with her.—Come, says she, my dear honeysuckle, I have one game to play for you; he shall see you in bed; he shall, my little rosebud, he shall see those pretty, little, white, round, panting—and offered to pull off my handkerchief.—Fie, Mrs. Jervis, says I, you make me blush, and upon my fackins, I believe she did. She went on thus: I know the squire likes you, and notwithstanding the awkwardness of his proceeding, I am convinced hath some hot blood in his veins, which will not let him rest, 'till he hath communicated some of his warmth to thee, my little angel; I heard him last night at our door, trying if it was open; now tonight I will take care it shall be so; I warrant that he makes the second trial; which if he doth, he shall find us ready to receive him. I will at first counterfeit sleep, and after a swoon; so that he will have you naked in his possession: and then if you are disappointed, a plague of all young squires, say I.—And so, Mrs. Jervis, says I, you would have me yield myself to him, would you; you would have me be a second time a fool for nothing. Thank you for that, Mrs. Jervis. For nothing! marry forbid, says she, you know he hath large sums of money, besides abundance of fine things; and do you think, when you have inflamed him, by giving his hand a liberty with that charming person; and that you know he may easily think he obtains against your will, he will not give anything to come at all?—This will not do, Mrs. Jervis, answered I. I have heard my mamma say (and so you know, Madam, I have) that in her youth, fellows have often taken away in the morning what they gave over night. No, Mrs. Jervis, nothing under a regular taking into keeping, a settled settlement, for me, and all my heirs, all my whole lifetime, shall do the business—or else crosslegged is the word, faith, with Sham; and then I snapt my fingers.

Thursday Night, Twelve o'Clock.

Mrs. Jervis and I are just in bed, and the door unlocked; if my master should come—Odsbobs! I hear him just coming in at the door. You see I write in the present tense, as Parson Williams says. Well, he is in bed between us, we both shamming a sleep; he steals his hand into my bosom, which I, as if in my sleep, press close to me with mine, and then pretend to awake.—I no sooner see him, but I scream out to Mrs. Jervis, she feigns likewise but just to come to herself; we both begin, she to becall, and I to bescratch very liberally. After having made a pretty free use of my fingers, without any great regard to the parts I attacked, I counterfeit a swoon. Mrs. Jervis then cries out, O sir, what have you done! you have murthered poor Pamela; she is gone, she is gone.——

O what a difficulty it is to keep one's countenance, when a violent laugh desires to burst forth!

The poor Booby, frightened out of his wits, jumped out of bed, and, in his shirt, sat down by my bed-side, pale and trembling, for the moon shone, and I kept my eyes wide open, and pretended to fix them in my head. Mrs. Jervis applied lavender water, and hartshorn, and this for a full half hour; when thinking I had carried it on long enough, and being likewise unable to continue the sport any longer, I began by degrees to come to myself.

The squire, who had sat all this while speechless, and was almost really in that condition which I feigned, the moment he saw me give symptoms of recovering my senses, fell down on his knees; and O Pamela, cried he, can you forgive me, my injured maid? by heaven, I know not whether you are a man or a woman, unless by your swelling breasts. Will you promise to forgive me? I forgive you! D—n you, says I; and d—m you, says he, if you come to that. I wish I had never seen your bold face, saucy sow—and so went out of the room.

O what a silly fellow is a bashful young lover!

He was no sooner out of hearing, as we thought, than we both burst into a violent laugh. Well, says Mrs. Jervis, I never saw anything better acted than your part: but I wish you may not have discouraged him from any future attempt; especially since his passions are so cool, that you could prevent his hands going further than your bosom. Hang him, answered I, he is not quite so cold as that, I assure you; our hands, on neither side, were idle in the scuffle, nor have left us any doubt of each other as to that matter.

Friday Morning.

My master sent for Mrs. Jervis, as soon as he was up, and bid her give an account of the plate and linen in her care; and told her, he was resolved that both she and the little gipsy (I'll assure him) should set out together. Mrs. Jervis made him a saucy answer—which any servant of spirit, you know, would, tho' it should be one's ruin—and came immediately in tears to me, crying, she had lost her place on my account, and that she should be forced to take to a house, as I mentioned before; and that she hoped I would, at least, make her all the amends in my power, for her loss on my account, and come to her house whenever I was sent for. Never fear, says I, I'll warrant we are not so near being turned away as you imagine; and, i'cod, now it comes into my head, I have a fetch for him, and you shall assist me in it. But it being now late, and my letter pretty long, no more at present from

Your Dutiful Daughter,
SHAMELA.

LETTER X.

SHAMELA ANDREWS *to* HENRIETTA MARIA HONORA ANDREWS.

... I had not been long in my chamber before Mrs. Jewkes came to me, and told me, my master would not see me any more that evening, that is, if he can help it; for, added she, I easily perceive the great ascendant you have over him, and to confess the truth, I don't doubt but you will shortly be my mistress.

What, says I, dear Mrs. Jewkes, what do you say? Don't flatter a poor girl; it is impossible his Honour can have any honourable design upon me. And so we talked of honourable designs till supper-time. And Mrs. Jewkes and I supped together upon a hot buttered apple-pie; and about ten o'clock we went to bed.

We had not been a-bed half an hour, when my master came pit-a-pat into the room in his shirt as before; I pretended not to hear him, and Mrs. Jewkes laid hold of one arm, and he pulled down the bed-clothes and came into bed on the other side, and took my other arm and laid it under him, and fell a-kissing one of my breasts as if he would have devoured it; I was then forced to awake, and began to struggle with him; Mrs. Jewkes crying Why don't you do it? I have one arm secure, if you can't deal with the rest I am sorry for you. He was as rude as possible to me; but I remembered, Mamma, the instructions you gave me to avoid being ravished, and followed them, which soon brought him to terms, and he promised me, on quitting my hold, that he would leave the bed.

O Parson Williams, how little are all the men in the world compared to thee!

My master was as good as his word; upon which Mrs. Jewkes said, O sir, I see you know very little of our *sect*, by parting so easily from the blessing when you was so near it. No, Mrs. Jewkes, answered he, I am very glad no more hath happened; I would not have injured Pamela for the world. And to-morrow morning perhaps she may hear of something to her advantage. This she may be certain of, that I will never take her by force; and then he left the room.

What think you now, Mrs. Pamela? says Mrs. Jewkes; are you not yet persuaded my master hath honourable designs? I think he hath given no great proof of them to-night, said I. Your experience I find is not great, says she, but I am convinced you will shortly be my mistress, and then what will become of poor me?

With such sort of discourse we both fell asleep. Next morning early my master sent for me, and after kissing me, gave a paper into my hand which he bid me read; I did so, and found it to be a proposal for settling 250*l.* a year on me, besides several other advantageous offers, as presents of money and other things. Well, Pamela, said he, what answer do you make me to this? Sir, said I, I value my vartue more than all the world, and I had rather be the poorest man's wife, than the richest man's whore. You are a simpleton, said he; that may be, and yet I may have as much wit as some folks, cried I; meaning me, I suppose, said he; every man knows himself best, says I. Hussy, says he, get out of the room, and let me see your saucy face no more, for I find I am in more danger than you are, and therefore it shall be my business to avoid you as much as I can; and it shall be mine, thinks I, at every turn to throw myself in your way. So I went out, and as I parted, I heard him sigh and say he was bewitched.

Mrs. Jewkes hath been with me since, and she assures me she is convinced I shall shortly be mistress of the family, and she really behaves to me as if she already thought me so. I am resolved now to aim at it. I thought once of making a little fortune by my person. I now intend to make a great one by my vartue. So asking pardon for this long scroll, I am,

Your dutiful Daughter,
SHAMELA.

—Henry Fielding

JOHN CLELAND
(1709-1789)

The Elegant English Epistolary Eroticism

Mr. N . . . chanc'd to offer a bout of dalliance and disport. My blush serv'd but to inflame the young gentleman's ardours, and a heart-fetch'd sigh at the size of his remarkable fouling piece banish'd all reserve. Canting up my petticoats and unlacing my stays, I fell supine on the settee, my exquisite treasures at his disposal. Thus embolden'd, he took in hand the prodigious engine and, abandoning restraint, remm'd the rubid cleft where grows the wanton moss that crowns the brow of modesty, but to naught avail. Thrice again the frightful machine assail'd the region of delight which, with maidenhead's sweet mant'ling, celebrates the triumph of roses o'er the lily, but that delicious cloven spot, the fairest mark for his well-mettl'd member, quell'd and abash'd the gallant intruder. Mustering his ferbour, once more didst Cupid's capt'n 'tempt to brunt the fierce prow of his formidable vessel past the shoals of luxuriant umberage which garland'd my rutt'd charms and into that uncloy'd cove where humid embars blaz'd on visitation, yet was, e'en so, repulst. Tho' toss'd 'twixt profusion and compliance, my hand crept softly to the sturdy lad's ripen'd tussle and roam'd the sprout'd tufts, whilst he my hillocks wander'd, then rekindl'd his nobly stock'd conduits, distend'd the proud steed, where'pon I near swoon'd of extasy's bright tumult as the sturdy stallion, his exhaultations fir'd, gallop'd o'er ev'ry hedge and thicket, spending the jetty sprig, won the sally, and gain'd a lodgement. Encircl'd in the pleasure-girst, ingorg'd by dissolution's tender agony, each 'fusive stroke stirr'd my in'most tendrils, devolv'd my dewy furrow of its secrets, which I, flush with straddl'd frolik, was far from disrelishing, 'til, somewhat appeas'd, his quiv'ling extremity, twin'd by unquench'd appetite, durst 'frock the fury of unflagg'd inspersions, yet homeward play'd my rake the plenteous protraction, redoubl'd his endeavours that joy's thrust might soon drink deep at rapture's well, then didst, at last, sheath, to the churl'd hilt, his massy weapon, and so suffer'd me to bliss.

I am
  Madam
    Yours, etc, etc, etc.

—*Michael O'Donoghue*

MARQUIS DE SADE
(1740-1814)

From Algolagnia

The Comte was in the formal gardens whipping his linoleum when he was joined by the Bishop. Ceasing his exertions, he greeted the prelate, and said:

"You are undoubtedly curious why I am whipping my linoleum. And yet, on closer examination, nothing could be more natural . . . or might I say 'unnatural,' as they are the same thing. Man, it goes without saying, is intrinsically evil, bearing in mind, of course, that good and evil, vice and virtue, exist only within the confines of society. It is the laws which cause crime, for, without law, there is no crime. Nature capriciously destroys the fools who forsake their instinctual lust and hunger in the name of virtue, as Nature does us all. Man is an animal with a soul that exists only through sensations. Although man must not limit his actions, there is no free will, therefore he is not responsible for his actions. Quite obviously, the more disgusting the act, the greater the pleasure, and since pleasure, or might I say 'pain,' as pleasure is but pain diminished, remains the chief aim of all human existence, it should be enjoyed at any cost, particularly at the expense of other people, that is to say, not only is there joy in whipping my linoleum, but there is also joy in reflecting upon those who are not allowed to whip their linoleum. Hence, cruelty is nothing more than man's life force uncorrupted by civilization. As we are pawns to misery, so must we dispense misery to pawns. Since pain is the absolute, it is essential that I, as a philosopher, pursue this absolute. So it seems that the question, my dear Bishop, is not 'Why do I whip my linoleum?' but rather, 'Why doesn't everyone whip his linoleum?'"

—Michael O'Donoghue

SIR WALTER SCOTT
(1771-1832)

The Bra' La'

The bra' la' sta'r'd, an' sta'r'd. Bein' but a bra' la', he went on sta'rin', though naething at a' was there to sta'r' a'.

"Wad be ye sta'rin a', ye fa' head'd bra' la'?" demanded his mother, finally, impatient to be at the sweeping of the floors. She stood for all the world like a soldier ready to fire, broom in hand, hands on hips, head akimbo, mouth open, eyes fixed, tongue flapping, hair disheveled, feet tapping, skirt twitching.

He only nodded, out across the wild expanse of green lawn. He did not speak: in those days, bra' la's were not given much to words: it was deeds that mattered, to bra' Scots hearts, thaen.

"Wad? Do ye see sumthin'?" his mother insisted. But her attention was fixed so exclusively on her son, that she could not follow his sta'r', could not see what, in all innocence, the bra' boy was seein'. "Wad? Tell me, ye poor fule ye?"

He giggled, a manic sound that echoed and re-echoed in their humble cot.

"What think ye," he said softly, slapping his bra' thigh and bending his bra' knees, "of the fire on yon bonny hill? Nice fire, nice fire," he chuckled, stamping his bra' feet and giggling.

His mother, impatient to be at her matutinal labors, lifted him bodily and set him in a bra' wee chair that the husband and father had built for him, out of bra' Scots wood, shortly after his poor birth had occurred. It was but a poor object, na mair thaen six or sev'n feet across, na mair thaen four or five feet deep, and weighing but a scant three or four hundred pounds. But in their humble cot, it fitted, it served.

"Sait ye thair," she directed, "and mind tha' tongue of thine, th' whil I make this raeum all clean and sweet, 'gaint the coming haem of tha' bra' fathir of thine."

He giggled cheerily.

"Nice fire, nice fire."

But she was too occupied with her cleaning and sweeping, too utterly absorbed with humble duties, to pay him even scant heed. He sat watching, even from his distant perch, the fire sweeping down the bra' hill, and across the wild green lawn, and ever closer to their poor abode. How brightly it flared! How keenly he relished the hum and then the roar of it, as it swept ever closer! And how steadily, how furiously, his mother swept and cleaned, polished and scrubbed, swept and polished and scrubbed, then swept and polished and cleaned and scrubbed yet again, and again, and again, until the very boards of the floor bled with the pain of it, and the walls wept with the heavy touch of her coarse hands, and the oriental carpets that hung on those walls and half covered those floors curled in horror and cringed in fear. But on she swept, on and on and on, over and over and over.

And when, at the last, the fire had raced to their very door, and into their very door, and into the very room where, all absorbed and unseeing, she swept and swept and swept, he giggled most happily still, welcoming its cheery heat and knowing it would release him fra' this grim, weary life.

"Nice fire, nice fire," he laughed.

And without looking up, his mother, sweeping even more frantically, said, her bra' voice rough with love,

"Is tha' ye naw, faither?"

And hot with bra' Scots lust, the nice fire ate them baith.

—Burton Raffel

JANE AUSTEN
(1775-1817)

From Raskolnikov

"Are not you happy in Hertfordshire, Mr. Raskolnikov?" said Elizabeth.

Raskolnikov looked into her beautiful dark eyes. His own shone with feverish brilliance.

"Would you be happy," he said, "if you had killed a miserable pawnbroker?"

Elizabeth turned away to hide a smile. "I hope I am not so deficient in sense and feeling as either to be capable of the attempt, or to remain in spirits when the crime was accomplished," said she. "But they are not within the range of my acquaintance—pawnbrokers are safe from me."

"She was only a louse, a miserable insect," murmured Raskolnikov. "But I was wrong to kill her—and to kill Lizaveta too."

"How easily may a bad habit be formed!" cried Elizabeth; and with this in mind, though she hoped he was not in earnest, she very soon afterwards took leave of him.

—Gwen Foyle

From Unpleasantness At The OK Corral

The next morning was fair, and Earp almost expected another attack from the assembled posse. With Dr. Halliday to support him he felt no dread of the event: but he would gladly be spared a shootout, where victory itself was painful; and was heartily rejoiced therefore at neither seeing nor hearing anything of them.

The Clantons arrived at the appointed time; and no new difficulty arising, no sudden recollection, no unexpected summons, no impertinent intrusion to disconcert their measures, our heroes were most unnaturally able to fulfil their engagement. They determined on walking round the OK Corral, that ignoble enclosure, whose isolated position renders it so striking an object from almost every opening in Tombstone.

—*David Watkin*

THE NINETEENTH CENTURY

Godine's Lady's Book Through Rube, The Obscure

1815: Rotten burros replace Houyhnhnms.
1830: Godine's Lady's Book founded.
1841: Melville sets sail for Enchiladas.
1844: Hawthorne's "Paganini's Daughter," first short-story masterpizza.
1844: Poe invents sinoidseizure.
1846: Corn Dogs repelled.
ca. 1850: English High-bra, Middle-bra, Low-bra audiences homogenized.
1859: Arthur Condom Doyle born.
1861: Dickens' Great Expectorations.
1865: Polyglot multitudes bring sharp increase of people to America.
1875: James leaves America for deep soil in which to write.
1895: Hardy, Rube, the Obscure.

CEREAL TECHNIQUE IN THE NOVEL

When Henry James said that the novels of Charles Dickens were "quintesexually Victorian," he was referring to Dickens's cereal technique of novel writing, a technique popular among poor, grub-eating Victorian writers who published in magazines such as Blackbeard's and Cornhole. According to James, what these novels share in common is a certain slopdash quality due to the exigencies of writing for a deadlock. However, if what he says is true about Dickens's early Sketches by Boz Scaggs and Oliver Twit, is it true of such later works as Great Expectorations or Bleep House? Surely there is nothing "loose or buggy" (James's electrocution) about the chronicle of Pip's friendship for the escaped convict, Muggeridge, which eventually develops into fatherhood.

Meanwhile, Pip develops a bad case of swollen *hubris*, which is only partially deflated by the spasms of unrequited love he suffers at the hands of Estella. Rejecting even the advances of those who "brought him up by hand," Pip becomes, by the climax, Dickens's ideal of a gentleman. By common consent, *Great Expectorations* is a masterpiece, and the positive feedbag Dickens got from his vast reading public between installments must have hearkened him, while it dramatizes for us the homo-genius nature of that public: it did not yet suffer from the present day division of readers into high-bra, middle-bra, and low-bra.

FROM *THE SLEEPY HOLLOW MEN* THROUGH *GODINE'S LADY'S BOOK*

But let us leave for a moment Dickens's fag-bound London and travel across the ocean to America. While England was busy developing the novel tradition, America was discovering in its midst the deflowering of the short story. Indeed, the short story may have been the only form which the young republic, preoccupied with nudeness and wonder, yearning toward its boarders (both its physical frontiers and those knocked up inside the human heart), may have been capable of. During the years between 1820 and perhaps 1860 (while Eli Whitney was discovering how to make gin out of cotton), the short story four-flushed in America. Although the country remained sparsely populated, with only a thin rural populist spread over its millions of square miles, the short story developed with extraordinary rapacity, found an audience, and bred a host of imitators (such as Rip Van Winkle's "The Legend of the Sleepy Hollow Men," which George Eliot later rewrote for a more cynical gerontion), who were published in such "anals" (yearly gift books) as *Godine's Lady's Book*, the fourflusher of today's "schlock" magazines. However, while many of these imitators cluttered their work with predictable romantic stage-crappings, such artists as Poe and Hawthorne (and later Melville) were perfecting art of an altogether higher ordure.

DEVELOPMENT OF A CENTRAL THUMB

Inasmuch as I have written elsewhere of Poe's use of onomatopotato and sinoidseizure (stimulation of all five scent glands by squanching) in foreplay with women, and have been scolded by certain Nude Critics for bringing Poe's life to bare in his fiction, let me simply offer a *mea caca* and suggest that Poe's attention to craft is nowhere more apparent than in his review of Hawthorne's *Twice Cold Tales*, in which he praised Hawthorne's use of a detached, unobtrusive stylus, his rounded development of a central thumb, and his meaningful integration of pork in his stories—qualities Poe used to codify short story theory for half a century.

EVIL AS A POSITIVE FARCE

Not for Nathaniel Hawthorne the innate gooiness and lack of depravity of men like Ralph Waldorf Emerson and Paul Thoreau. Against their ubiquitous optimism, Hawthorne pitted a grim, marble vision of evil as a positive farce in the world. A far cry from Thoreau's experiments with the wattles and beanrows of the lady of the lake, Hawthorne's portraits of the humid condition in such works as *The Scarlet Ledger*, a brooding tale of a CPA's fall from corporate grace, or "The Minister's Black Ball," in which a clergyman seeks to expurgate a missing testicle, are considered to be birthmarks in the history of the short story. "Paganini's Daughter," meanwhile, is considered to be the first minor masterpizza of the gender.

BEYOND THE ENCHILADAS

If the work of Hawthorne, the deeply pessimistic allegorist who comes out of a deep-throated Puritan hermitage, and the work of Poe, the rootless, erotic student of dental castration and immature burial, were responsible for putting America on the European literary map, Herman Melville helped make America a household tern in such faraway places as Typoe, Bemidgi, and Tashtego. Born in Massachusetts Bay, Melville jumped ship in the Enchiladas in order to learn about Poe's indomitable Cannibal-Lee and Blue Booby. There he authored his metaphysical fish-epic, *Moby Slick*. In *Billy Bug* he vastly reduces his scope, which he regains in such subsequent works as *Redbone* and *Lucky Pierre*. That Melville's novels went largely unread in his time (or any other) is less an indictment of Melville's talent than it is an endorsement of Poe's accurate gauging of the level of the American reading public, which preferred toilet reading that could be got through at one sitting.

FROM CALAVERAS TO YUCKNAPOOCACA

After the Civil War, the influx of polyglot multitudes from Europe brought with it a sharp increase of people. An air of neuralgia for the good old days pervaded fictional circles, while the bygone error turned to amber. It was against this backdrop that such local-cholera writers as Bret Harte and Mark Twain accomplished the synthesis which brought colorful racist language and eyeball-gouging together in such a way as to appeal to Eastern Brahmas. Harte's otherwise vulgar and reprehensible characters were polished and sweetened with a coating of sediment to make them acceptable to the tender polyps of the virgin daughters of the refined readers of his day.

Twain took the other tack, taking by the horns the obvious chromos and brandie alexanders of James Fennimore Copperfield, and proposing instead a "calaveras county of the mind," where the tall tale could be wedded to the manners of James Nincomb Riley. The notion may seem absurd, yet Twain's *Huckleberry Finn* (which Hemingway regarded as the father of Sherlock Anderson) brings to triumphant fulfillment the gentile, didactic stories of the Anti-Bella Absug South. Obviously, it is only a short hop from Twain's Calaveras to Faulkner's Yucknapoocaca.

WANTED: DEEP SOIL IN WHICH TO WRITE

Henry James brought together two different *Weltanschlongs*: that of the ugly American and the deeply-fertilized European. As Leon Edsel has pointed out, such unions are doomed to fail. For James, most Americans were like Edith Wharton, who died of intercourse with the older, more deeply soiled culture. Like Poe, James knew that "terror was the soul's Germany," and his poor Americans are doomed to leave their encounters with the Daisy Müllers of this world sadder but weimar. While James never used four-letter words in his works, his heavily chaparraled characters nevertheless fairly reek of sex. It is no wonder that James has been hailed as a genius of sensensibility.

THE NATURAL HAIR OF GEORGE ELIOT

Nothing could be further from the innuendo-like delicacies of James's style than was the style of Thomas Hardy, who wrote on dead leaves and fragments of slate instead of paper. His novels he composed under the greenwood tree of his father's beloved Sexsex estate, amid the mooing cattle and sheep which sprang from the same yeoman stock as George Eliot. Taking on Eliot's mantle, Hardy published *Tress of the D'Urbervilles*, and at once established himself as her natural hair. While Hardy composed other novels—most notably *Rube, the Obscure*, about a peasant's rise from the furry and mire of human excrement to a position of obscurity in his village, and *The Molar of Casterbridge*, a story of the same bucolic extraction—it was *Tress* that rescued the modern novel from the camp of the athletes of "the art fart's sake movement." After the hostile critical reaction to his *Rube*, Hardy turned to poetry, where he makes use of the same graceless infelicities as endeared him to Theodore Dreiser, who believed that poetry should be at least as well written as prose.

JAMES FENIMORE COOPER
(1789-1851)

From Muck-A-Muck

A MODERN INDIAN NOVEL.

Chapter IV.

Genevra had not proceeded many miles before a weariness seized upon her fragile limbs, and she would fain seat herself upon the trunk of a prostrate pine, which she previously dusted with her handkerchief. The sun was just sinking below the horizon, and the scene was one of gorgeous and sylvan beauty. "How beautiful is Nature!" murmured the innocent girl, as, reclining gracefully against the root of the tree, she gathered up her skirts and tied a handkerchief around her throat. But a low growl interrupted her meditation. Starting to her feet, her eyes met a sight which froze her blood with terror.

The only outlet to the forest was the narrow path, barely wide enough for a single person, hemmed in by trees and rocks, which she had just traversed. Down this path, in Indian file, came a monstrous grizzly, closely followed by a California lion, a wild-cat, and a buffalo, the rear being brought up by a wild Spanish bull. The mouths of the three first animals were distended with frightful significance; the horns of the last were lowered as ominously. As Genevra was preparing to faint, she heard a low voice behind her.

"Eternally dog-gone my skin ef this ain't the puttiest chance yet."

At the same moment, a long, shining barrel dropped lightly from behind her, and rested over her shoulder.

Genevra shuddered.

"Dern ye—don't move!"

Genevra became motionless.

The crack of a rifle rang through the woods. Three frightful yells were heard, and two sullen roars. Five animals bounded into the air and five lifeless bodies lay upon the plain. The well-aimed bullet had done its work. Entering the open throat of the grizzly, it had traversed his body only to enter the throat of the California lion, and in like manner the catamount, until it passed through into the respective foreheads of the bull and the buffalo, and finally fell flattened from the rocky hillside.

Genevra turned quickly. "My preserver!" she shrieked, and fell into the arms of Natty Bumpo, the celebrated Pike Ranger of Donner Lake.

Chapter V.

The moon rose cheerfully above Donner Lake. On its placid bosom a dug-out canoe glided rapidly, containing Natty Bumpo and Genevra Tompkins.

Both were silent. The same thought possessed each, and perhaps there was sweet companionship even in the unbroken quiet. Genevra bit the handle of her parasol and blushed. Natty Bumpo took a fresh chew of tobacco. At length Genevra said, as if in half-spoken revery:—

"The soft shining of the moon and the peaceful ripple of the waves seem to say to us various things of an instructive and moral tendency."

"You may bet yer pile on that, Miss," said her companion, gravely. "It's all the preachin' and psalm-singin' I've heern since I was a boy."

"Noble being!" said Miss Tompskins to herself, glancing at the stately Pike as he bent over his paddle to conceal his emotion. "Reared in this wild seclusion, yet he has become penetrated with visible consciousness of a Great First Cause." Then, collecting herself, she said aloud: "Methinks 't were pleasant to glide ever thus down the stream of life, hand in hand with the one being whom the soul claims as its affinity. But what am I saying?"—and the delicate-minded girl hid her face in her hands.

A long silence ensued, which was at length broken by her companion.

"If you mean you're on the marry," he said, thoughtfully, "I ain't in no wise partikler!"

"My husband," faltered the blushing girl; and she fell into his arms.

In ten minutes more the loving couple had landed at Judge Tompkins's.

Chapter VI.

A year has passed away. Natty Bumpo was returning from Gold Hill, where he had been to purchase provisions. On his way to Donner Lake, rumors of an Indian uprising met his ears. "Dern their pesky skins, ef they dare to touch my Jenny," he muttered between his clenched teeth.

It was dark when he reached the borders of the lake. Around a glittering fire he dimly discerned dusky figures dancing. They were in war paint. Conspicuous among them was the renowned Muck-a-Muck. But why did the fingers of Natty Bumpo tighten convulsively around his rifle?

The chief held in his hand long tufts of raven hair. The heart of the pioneer sickened as he recognized the clustering curls of Genevra. In a moment his rifle was at his shoulder, and with a sharp "ping," Muck-a-Muck leaped into the air a corpse. To knock out the brains of the remaining savages, tear the tresses from the stiffening hand of Muck-a-Muck, and dash rapidly forward to the cottage of Judge Tompkins, was the work of a moment.

He burst open the door. Why did he stand transfixed with open mouth and distended eyeballs? Was the sight too horrible to be borne? On the contrary, before him, in her peerless beauty, stood Genevra Tompkins, leaning on her father's arm.

"Ye'r not scalped, then!" gasped her lover.

"No. I have no hesitation in saying that I am not; but why this abruptness?" responded Genevra.

Bumpo could not speak, but frantically produced the silken tresses. Genevra turned her face aside.

"Why, that's her waterfall!" said the Judge.

Bumpo sank fainting to the floor.

The famous Pike chieftain never recovered from the deceit, and refused to marry Genevra, who died, twenty years afterwards, of a broken heart. Judge Tompkins lost his fortune in Wild Cat. The stage passes twice a week the deserted cottage at Donner Lake. Thus was the death of Muck-a-Muck avenged.

—Bret Harte

EDGAR ALLAN POE
(1809-1849)

The House of Usher

Sole surviving male representative of well-known ancient family, much attached to his old Gothic mansion (well off beaten track, with most distinctive atmosphere, a veritable voice from the dead past) is prepared to receive a few paying guests of the right sort before the fall. Special treatment for nervous disorders; family physician constantly in attendance. No jollifications. Commodious, lofty, airy rooms. Lake (not suitable for bathing). Recherché cuisine. Own fungi grown on premises in great profusion and variety. Unique cellar. Those who genuinely wish to bury themselves in the country should apply to R. Usher, House of Usher.

—Leslie Johnson

CHARLES DICKENS
(1812-1870)

From Holden Caulfield

My father's family name being Caulfield, and my christian name Holden, my infant tongue could make of both names nothing longer or more explicit than Holden Caulfield. So, I called myself Holden Caulfield, and came to be called Holden Caulfield. It might be well to add at this point that the children of my family have, since time immemorial, been noted for precocity.

I give Caulfield as my father's name on the authority of the signature which appeared on the monthly cheques which I received regularly and on the knowledge of my mother's existence, verified by a small, white card which came by mail each year on the occasion of my birthday. Having been trundled off to public school at an early age, I could never remember having seen my mother and father and could not boast of having any likeness of either of them. My first fancies regarding what they were like were unreasonably derived from the character of their signatures. From the squat, short characters which appeared on my father's cheques, I envisioned him as a squat, short character who was associated with a bank. The thin, spidery lines of my mother's handwriting which appeared on the small, white birthday cards impressed upon my childish mind the conclusion that she was a small, thin, spidery woman who was also quite pale and who sat constantly before a table where rested a cake with many candles, six candles which I held as sacred to myself, to my brother D.B., to my younger sister Phoebe, and to the memory of three little brothers of mine—who gave up without a kick trying to gain possession of the puntabout in the vast universal rugby scrum—to whom I am indebted for a belief I religiously entertained that they had been born with their heads down and their arms linked together, and that they had somehow resembled both rugby balls and candles, candles which had never sputtered with the thud of a good, swift wick and which, indeed, had never varied from this appearance. . . .

—R. S. Gwynn

CHARLOTTE BRONTË
(1816-1855)

From Miss Mix

Chapter III.

The crash startled me from my self-control. The housekeeper bent toward me and whispered:—

"Don't be excited. It's Mr. Rawjester,—he prefers to come in sometimes in this way. It's his playfulness, ha! ha! ha!"

"I perceive," I said calmly. "It's the unfettered impulse of a lofty soul breaking the tyrannizing bonds of custom." And I turned toward him.

He had never once looked at me. He stood with his back to the fire, which set off the herculean breadth of his shoulders. His face was dark and expressive; his under jaw squarely formed, and remarkably heavy. I was struck with his remarkable likeness to a Gorilla.

As he absently tied the poker into hard knots with his nervous fingers, I watched him with some interest. Suddenly he turned toward me:—

"Do you think I'm handsome, young woman?"

"Not classically beautiful," I returned calmly; "but you have, if I may so express myself, an abstract manliness,—a sincere and wholesome barbarity which, involving as it does the naturalness—" But I stopped, for he yawned at that moment,—an action which singularly developed the immense breadth of his lower jaw,—and I saw he had forgotten me. Presently he turned to the housekeeper:—

"Leave us."

The old woman withdrew with a courtesy.

Mr. Rawjester deliberately turned his back upon me and remained silent for twenty minutes. I drew my shawl the more closely around my shoulders and closed my eyes.

"You are the governess?" at length he said.

"I am, sir."

"A creature who teaches geography, arithmetic, and the use of the globes—ha!—a wretched remnant of femininity,—a skimp pattern of girlhood with a premature flavor of tea-leaves and morality. Ugh!"

I bowed my head silently.

"Listen to me, girl!" he said sternly; "this child you have come to teach—my ward—is not legitimate. She is the offspring of my mistress,—a common harlot. Ah! Miss Mix, what do you think of me now?"

"I admire," I replied calmly, "your sincerity. A mawkish regard for delicacy might have kept this disclosure to yourself. I only recognize in your frankness that perfect community of thought and sentiment which should exist between original natures."

I looked up; he had already forgotten my presence, and was engaged in pulling off his boots and coat. This done, he sank down in an arm-chair before the fire, and ran the poker wearily through his hair. I could not help pitying him.

The wind howled dismally without, and the rain beat furiously against the windows. I crept toward him and seated myself on a low stool beside his chair.

Presently he turned, without seeing me, and placed his foot absently in my lap. I affected not to notice it. But he started and looked down.

"You here yet—Carrothead? Ah, I forgot. Do you speak French?"

"*Oui, Monsieur.*"

"*Taisez-vous!*" he said sharply, with singular purity of accent. I complied. The wind moaned fearfully in the chimney, and the light burned dimly. I shuddered in spite of myself. "Ah, you tremble, girl!"

"It is a fearful night."

"Fearful! Call you this fearful, ha! ha! ha! Look! You wretched little atom, look!" and he dashed forward, and, leaping out of the window, stood like a statue in the pelting storm, with folded arms. He did not stay long, but in a few minutes returned by way of the hall chimney. I saw from the way that he wiped his feet on my dress that he had again forgotten my presence.

"You are a governess. What can you teach?" he asked suddenly and fiercely thrusting his face in mine.

"Manners!" I replied, calmly.

"Ha! teach *me!*"

"You mistake yourself," I said, adjusting my mittens. "Your manners require not the artificial restraint of society. You are radically polite; this impetuosity and ferociousness is simply the sincerity which is the basis of a proper deportment. Your instincts are moral; your better nature, I see, is religious. As St. Paul justly remarks—see chap. 6,8,9, and 10—"

He seized a heavy candlestick, and threw it at me. I dodged it submissively but firmly.

"Excuse me," he remarked, as his under jaw slowly relaxed. "Excuse me, Miss Mix—but I can't stand St. Paul! Enough—you are engaged."

Chapter V.

My pupil was a bright little girl, who spoke French with a perfect accent. Her mother had been a French ballet-dancer, which probably accounted for it. Although she was only six years old, it was easy to perceive that she had been several times in love. She once said to me:—

"Miss Mix, did you every have the *grande* passion? Did you ever feel a fluttering here?" and she placed her hand upon her small chest, and sighed quaintly, "a kind of distaste for *bonbons* and *caromels*, when the world seemed as tasteless and hollow as a broken cordial drop."

"Then you have felt it, Nina?" I said quietly.

"O dear, yes. There was Buttons,—that was our page, you know,—I loved him dearly, but papa sent him away. Then there was Dick, the groom, but he laughed at me, and I suffered misery!" and she struck a tragic French attitude. "There is to be company here tomorrow," she added, rattling on with childish *naïveté*," and papa's sweetheart—Blanche Marabout—is to be here. You know they say she is to be my mamma."

What thrill was this shot through me? But I rose calmly, and, administering a slight correction to the child, left the apartment.

Blunderbore House, for the next week, was the scene of gayety and merriment. That portion of the mansion closed with a grating was walled up, and the midnight shrieks no longer troubled me.

But I felt more keenly the degradation of my situation. I was obliged to help Lady Blanche at her toilet and help her to look beautiful. For what? To captivate Him? O—no, no,—but why

this sudden thrill and faintness? Did he really love her? I had
seen him pinch and swear at her. But I reflected that he had
thrown a candlestick at my head, and my foolish heart was
reassured.

It was a night of festivity, when a sudden message obliged
Mr. Rawjester to leave his guests for a few hours. "Make
yourselves merry, idiots," he added, under his breath, as he
passed me. The door closed and he was gone.

An half-hour passed. In the midst of the dancing a shriek was
heard, and out of the swaying crowd of fainting women and
excited men a wild figure strode into the room. One glance
showed it to be a highwayman, heavily armed, holding a pistol
in each hand.

"Let no one pass out of this room!" he said, in a voice of
thunder. "The house is surrounded and you cannot escape.
The first one who crosses yonder threshold will be shot like a
dog. Gentlemen, I'll trouble you to approach in single file, and
hand me your purses and watches."

Finding resistance useless, the order was ungraciously
obeyed.

"Now, ladies, please to pass up your jewelry and trinkets."

This order was still more ungraciously complied with. As
Blanche handed to the bandit captain her bracelet, she
endeavored to conceal a diamond necklace, the gift of Mr.
Rawjester, in her bosom. But, with a demoniac grin, the
powerful brute tore it from its concealment, and, administering a hearty box on the ear of the young girl, flung her aside.

It was now my turn. With a beating heart I made my way to
the robber chieftain, and sank at his feet. "O sir, I am nothing
but a poor governess, pray let me go."

"O ho! A governess? Give me your last month's wages, then.
Give me what you have stolen from your master!" and he
laughed fiendishly.

I gazed at him quietly, and said, in a low voice:

"I have stolen nothing from you, Mr. Rawjester!"

"Ah, discovered! Hush! listen, girl!" he hissed, in a fierce
whisper, "utter a syllable to frustrate my plans and you die; aid
me, and—" But he was gone.

In a few moments the party, with the exception of myself,
were gagged and locked in the cellar. The next moment
torches were applied to the rich hangings, and the house was

in flames. I felt a strong hand seize me, and bear me out in the open air and place me upon the hillside, where I could overlook the burning mansion. It was Mr. Rawjester.

"Burn!" he said, as he shook his fist at the flames. Then sinking on his knees before me, he said hurriedly:—

"Mary Jane, I love you; the obstacles to our union are or will be soon removed. In yonder mansion were confined my three crazy wives. One of them, as you know, attempted to kill me! Ha! this is vengeance! But will you be mine?"

I fell, without a word, upon his neck.

—Bret Harte

EMILY BRONTË
(1818-1848)

Wuthering Heights

Anybody seeking comfort, soft scenery and polite conversation should keep away, for we are rough here and live near to the earth. Outsiders are invited only because their presence makes it possible for me to go on living here. So there is neither pretence of welcome nor hiding of my satisfaction when your stay is over. This said, nobody can claim to have been misled if the routine at the house is not to his taste. This is a small unfenced farm won from the moor. It is too bleak for cattle, but there is goat milk, bread and potatoes. Baggage can be sent by the Wednesday provision cart from Haworth. Guests walk. No dogs, or women. Heathcliff, Proprietor.

—*Royston Millmore*

GEORGE ELIOT
(1819-1880)

From Middlemarch

XV.

FROM PROFESSOR FORTH TO THE REV. MR. CASAUBON.

The delicacy of the domestic matters with which the following correspondence deals cannot be exaggerated. It seems that Belinda (whose Memoirs we owe to Miss Rhoda Broughton) was at Oxford while Mr. and Mrs. Casaubon were also resident near that pleasant city, so famed for its Bodleian Library. Professor Forth and Mr. Casaubon were friends, as may be guessed; their congenial characters, their kindred studies, Etruscology and Mythology, combined to ally them. Their wives were not wholly absorbed in their learned pursuits, and if Mr. Ladislaw was dangling after Mrs. Casaubon, we know that Mr. Rivers used to haunt with Mrs. Forth the walks of Magdalen. The regret and disapproval which Mrs. Casaubon expresses, and her desire to do good to Mrs. Forth, are, it is believed, not alien to her devoted and exemplary character.

Bradmore-road, Oxford, May 29.

Dear Mr. Casaubon,—In the course of an investigation which my researches into the character of the Etruscan "Involuti" have necessitated, I frequently encounter the root *Kâd*, *k²âd*, or *Qâd*. Schnitzler's recent and epoch-making discovery that *d* in Etruscan = b^2, has led me to consider it a plausible hypothesis that we may convert *Kâd* or *Qâd* into *Kab²*, in which case it is by no means beyond the range of a cautious conjecture that the Involuti are identical with the *Cab-iri* (Cabiri). Though you will pardon me for confessing, what you already know, that I am not in all points an adherent to your ideas concerning a "Key to All Mythologies" (at least, as briefly set forth by you in Kuhn's *Zeitung*), yet I am deeply impressed with this apparent opportunity of bridging the seemingly impassable gulf between Etrurian Religion and the comparatively clear and comprehensible systems of the Pelasgo-Phœnician peoples. That *Kâd* or *Kâb* can refer either (as in *Quatuor*) to a four-footed animal (quadruped, "quad") or to a four-wheeled vehicle (*esseda*, Celtic *cab*) I cannot for a moment believe, though I understand that this theory has the support of Schrader, Penka, and Baunder.[1] Any information which your learning can procure, and your kind courtesy can supply, will be warmly welcomed and duly acknowledged.—

---

[1]Mr. Forth, we are sure, is quite wrong, and none of the scholars he quotes has said anything of the kind.

Believe me, faithfully yours,

JAMES FORTH.

P.S.—I open this note, which was written from my dictation by my secretary, Mrs. Forth, to assure myself that her inexperience has been guilty of no error in matters of so much delicacy and importance. I have detected no mistake of moment, and begin to hope that the important step of matrimony to which I was guided by your example may not have been a rash experiment.

FROM THE REV. MR. CASAUBON TO JAMES FORTH, ESQ., PROFESSOR OF ETRUSCAN, OXFORD.

Dear Mr. Forth,—Your letter throws considerable light on a topic which has long engaged my earnest attention. To my thinking, the *Cab* in *Cabiri* = CAV, "hollow," as in *cavus*, and refers to the Ark of Noah, which, of course, before the entrance of every living thing according to his kind, must have been the largest artificial hollow or empty space known to our Adamite ancestors. Thus the Cabiri would answer, naturally, to the Patæci, which, as Herodotus tells us, were usually figured on the prows of ships. The Cabiri or Patæci, as children of Noah and men of the "great vessel," or Cave-men (a wonderful anticipation of modern science), would perpetuate the memory of Arkite circumstances, and would be selected, as the sacred tradition faded from men's minds, as the guides of navigation. I am sorry to seem out of harmony with your ideas; but it is only a matter of seeming, for I have no doubt that the Etruscan Involuti are also Arkite, and that they do not, as Max Müller may be expected to intimate, represent the veiled or cloudy Dawns, but rather the Arkite Patriarchs. We thus, from different starting-places, arrive at the same goal, the Arkite solution of Bryant. I am aware that I am old-fashioned—like Eumæus, " dwell here among the swine, and go not often to the city." Your letters with little numerals (as k^2) may represent the exactness of modern philology; but more closely remind me of the formulæ of algebra, a study in which I at no time excelled.

It is my purpose to visit Cambridge on June 3, to listen to a most valuable address by Professor Tösch, of Bonn, on Hittite and Aztec affinities. If you can meet me there and accept the hospitality of my college, the encounter may prove a turning point in Mythological and Philological Science.—Very faithfully yours,

J. CASAUBON.

P.S.—I open this note, written from my dictation by my wife, to enclose my congratulations on Mrs. Forth's scholarly attainments.

FROM PROFESSOR FORTH TO REV. MR CASAUBON.

(Telegram.)
Will be with you at Cambridge on the third.

FROM MRS. FORTH, BRADMORE-ROAD, OXFORD, TO DAVID RIVERS, ESQ., MILNTHORPE, YORKSHIRE.

He goes on Saturday to Cambridge to hear some one talk about the Hittities and the Asiatics. Did you not say there was a good Sunday train? They sing "O Rest in the Lord" at Magdalen. I often wonder that Addison's Walk is so deserted on Sundays. He stays over Sunday at Cambridge.[2]

FROM DAVID RIVERS, ESQ., TO MRS. FORTH, OXFORD.

Dear Mrs. Forth,—Saturday is a half-holiday at the Works, and I propose to come up and see whether our boat cannot bump Balliol. How extraordinary it is that people should neglect, on Sundays, the favourite promenade of the Short-faced Humourist. I shall be there: the old place.—Believe me, yours ever,

D. RIVERS.

FROM MRS. CASAUBON TO WILLIAM LADISLAW, ESQ., STRATFORD-ON-AVON.

Dear Friend,—Your kind letter from Stratford is indeed interesting. Ah, when shall I have an opportunity of seeing these, and so many other interesting places! But in a world where duty is *so much*, and so *always* with us, why should we regret the voids in our experience which, after all, life is filling in the experience of others? The work is advancing, and Mr. Casaubon hopes that the first chapter of the "Key to All Mythologies" will be fairly copied and completed by the end of

---

[2]"He" clearly means, not Addison, but Professor Forth, the lady's husband.

autumn. Mr. Casaubon is going to Cambridge on Saturday to hear Professor Tösch lecture on the Pittites and some other party, I really forget which;[3] but it is not often that he takes so much interest in mere *modern* history. How curious it sometimes is to think that the great spirit of humanity and of the world, as you say, keeps working its way—ah, to what wonderful goal—by means of these obscure difficult politics: almost unworthy instruments, one is tempted to think. That was a true line you quoted lately from the "Vita Nuova." We have no books of poetry here, except a Lithuanian translation of the Rig Veda. How delightful it must be to read Dante with a sympathetic fellow-student, one who has also loved—and *renounced!*—Yours very sincerely,

DOROTHEA CASAUBON.

P.S.—I do not expect Mr. Casaubon back from Cambridge before Monday afternoon.

FROM WILLIAM LADISLAW, ESQ., TO THE HON. SECRETARY OF THE LITERARY AND PHILOSOPHICAL MECHANICS' INSTITUTE, MIDDLEMARCH.

My Dear Sir,—I find that I can be in your neighbourhood on Saturday, and will gladly accept your invitation to lecture at your Institute on the Immutability of Morals.—Faithfully yours,

W. LADISLAW.

FROM WILLIAM LADISLAW, ESQ., TO MRS. CASAUBON.

Dear Mrs. Casaubon,—Only a line to say that I am to lecture at the Mechanics' Institute on Saturday. I can scarcely hope that, as Mr. Casaubon is away, you will be able to attend my poor performance, but on Sunday I may have, I hope, the pleasure of waiting on you in the afternoon?—Very sincerely yours,

W. LADISLAW.

P.S.—I shall bring the "Vita Nuova"—it is not so difficult as the "Paradiso"—and I shall be happy to help you with a few of the earlier sonnets.

[3]It was not Asiatics, but Aztecs; not Pittites, but Hittites! Woman cares little for these studies!— A.L.

FROM MRS. CASAUBON TO MRS. FORTH.

June 5,

Dear Lady,—You will be surprised at receiving a letter from a stranger! How shall I address you—how shall I say what I ought to say? Our husbands are not unknown to each other, I may almost call them friends, but we have met only once. You did not see me; but I was at Magdalen a few weeks ago, and I could not help asking who you were, so young, so beautiful; and when I saw you so lonely among all those learned men my heart went out to you, for I know what the learned are, and how often, when we are young, we feel as if they were so cold, so remote. Ah, then there come *temptations*, but they must be conquered. We are not born to live for ourselves only, we must learn to live for others—ah! not for *Another!*

Some one[4] we both know, a lady, has spoken to me of you lately. She too, though you did not know it, was in Magdalen Walk on Sunday evening when the bells were chiming and the birds singing. She saw you; you were *not alone!* Mr. Rivers (I am informed that is his name) was with you. Ah, stop and think, and hear me before it is too late. A word; I do not know—a word of mine may be listened to, though I have no right to speak. But something forces me to speak, and to implore you to remember that it is not for Pleasure we live, but for Duty. We must break the dearest ties if they do not bind us to the stake—the stake of all we owe to all! You will understand, you will forgive me, will you not? You will forgive another woman whom your beauty and sadness have won to admire and love you. You *will* break these ties, will you not, and be free, for only in Renunciation is there freedom? He *must not* come again, you will tell him that he must not.—Yours always,

DOROTHEA CASAUBON.

—Andrew Lang

---

[4]The editor has no doubt that some one was—Miss Watson. Cf. "Belinda."

HERMAN MELVILLE
(1819-1891)

From Barthelme, The Scribbler

I am a man who has come to believe that moral fiction of the more or less traditional realistic sort is the best. Avant-garde, experimental fiction, fiction as word-sculpture, and so on, I have never suffered to invade my comfortable aesthetic. With cool determination I have invented characters possessed of motivation and involved in humanly understandable conflicts, many of them domestic and unsensational, some of them, I would hope, moral in communicable theme. These preferences—nay, standards—it has been my practice to insist on in the pages of...*Dead Letters*, which name, I admit, is a forgery, for it is a snug business of reputation, this editor's business, nor do I sully my own or another's reputation without great care.

Thus, my consternation may be imagined when, over the transom, so to speak, of my *Dead Letters* office, came Barthelme, manuscript in hand, with a notion, I supposed, toward publication. Engaged by his failed existential manner, generally favorable reviews, and unstamped SASE, I bid Barthelme sit and wait while I perused his photocopies. After an expanse of time spent reading—the man's work could not be dismissed outright—I stood up and gazed at him for a while. What ought I to do? Here was talent; indeed, a quirky inventiveness matched with a certain ironic verbal constraint —which, nevertheless, one would rather not see in print. I decided to offer him a bit of advice.

"Barthelme," I said, "these stories of yours. They seem to lack traditional plot. As prerequisite to publication in the pages of *Dead Letters*, I'm afraid they will have to be revised in the direction of a more traditional plot structure. Is that acceptable to you?"

"No way, José," replied Barthelme.

I moved back a step, cocked my ear, and repeated my request.

"No way, José," again was his response.

A wrinkle of scorn overwhelmed my upper lip as I stared at this forlorn mother's son, sitting like a bust of Lincoln on the floor of my *Dead Letters*, refusing to make his plotless tomfooleries aright.

"You refuse, then?" I asked. "In that case, it behooves me to tell you that your plotting is not your only weakness in these stories. Your characters are motiveless sandwich boards. You must motivate them in some way."

"Up your nose with a rubber hose," was Barthelme's answer. I felt the slow scrape of my testicles on the wooden floor as a feeling of self-righteous anger rather than one of fraternity overcame me.

"Not only do your stories lack plot and sufficient character motivation, they often lack understandable human conflict— the verb of fiction—and a consistent point of view. Surely, you agree."

"Not a chance, Vance," came his curt rejoinder.

I closed the window on the neck of an eavesdropping publication intern and advanced toward Barthelme with, I must confess, murderous intent. I felt now that rage, not sympathy for the human predicament, was probably man's fate; my unlimited responsibilities for the world's bag-ladies and vent-men were quickly getting the best of my limited resources.

"Exposition, complication, rising action, climax, denouement—these are Latin to you?" I fairly spit at him.

"Say it, don't spray it," Barthelme vouchsafed to answer.

"You insist on writing non-stories, or anti-stories, as is fashionable to call them? In your right mind, you choose instead of realistic fiction with implied larger import these genderless allegories without payoffs? In the name of decency, man, I demand you reconsider!"

"Take a hike, Mike. Suck a duck, Huck..."

Revolving all these things, it was natural that something broke inside me. Both I and Barthelme knew that it was the bond of common humanity, always a fragile one between men, dissolving now like a pill to cure dyspepsia. Almost before I knew it my right hand—about which my mortal left hand had always been in ignorance—had snatched out of a bookcase my leatherbound *Helen Grendler*, and had begun beating the hapless Barthelme about the head. With shame I admit that the job was finished by my *On Moral Fiction*, also in hardback.

Ah, Barthelme! Ah, ad nauseam!

—*William Zaranka*

LEO TOLSTOY
(1828-1910)

From Anna Kremlinina

BOOK 23, PART 14, CHAPTER 71

Looking at himself in a mirror, Ledin stroked his beard, and his eyes glistened benignly with a newly discovered realisation of the goodness and purpose of life.

"Yes," he said softly, "the masses are right. They are already toiling before the snipe are astir. Even the cows on the *kolkhozes* yield purer milk, free from the poisonous bacilli of decadent western pastures, because they rise at dawn. Yes, that is our goal—the Brotherhood of the Udder. The moment I take up my pen at nine o'clock I shall whisper, 'Flow on, little fountain of ink! You are an image of my new resolution. Black though you be as the bourgeois midnight, you stand for the dignity of labour, the natural morning stream of life newly awakened, the noble excellence of an early rise'."

—J. R. Till

LOUISA MAY ALCOTT
(1832-1888)

From Little Swinging Women

'These are capital boots, so boyish and comfortable' cried Jo. 'What did Marmee say about your new mini-dress, Meg?'

Meg's cheeks grew rosy as she answered thoughtfully, 'Mother said it was neat and well made, but she wondered if I was wise to use a kingsize crochet hook.'

'It would look nicely over my body stocking,' said Jo. 'You might have it, but it's laddered. Mercy, what are you painting, Amy?'

'A psychopathic experience I had at the party last night,' returned Amy with dignity.

'If you mean psychedelic, I'd say so,' advised Jo, laughing, while Meg looked at the little picture and said gently, 'If that's his beard, dear, it was auburn, not red.'

'Mercy, I must fly,' exclaimed Jo. 'I'm meeting Laurie for a demonstration.'

'Let me come too,' coaxed Amy. 'I'd dearly love to see him pull a policeman off a horse.'

'Stop bothering,' scolded Jo. 'You'll be frightened of the crowds, Laurie will have to put his arm round you and protect you, and that will spoil our fun. How happy Beth looks!'

'She's hearing heavenly music,' said Amy.

'Christopher Columbus, look at the cats!'

'She shares her LSD with them,' whispered Meg, 'the little saint.'

—Gwen Foyle

LEWIS CARROLL
(1832-1898)

From Alice In Orgie Land

'Off with her clothes!' roared the Queen.

'How very strange!' exclaimed Alice.

'Who is that impertinent young girl?' demanded the Queen, 'and why is she wearing so many clothes?'

'Chimneys are her thing,' leered the white rabbit, 'she likes putting her foot up them.'

'*Chacun à son flue,*' remarked the Queen, and began to do things with a hedgehog which Alice did not altogether like.

'What curious people!' Alice could not restrain herself from saying out loud. The King who had been looking at Alice with vigorous interest since the white rabbit's remark, murmured to her: 'I am a curious fellow. And while we're on the subject, how do you like the look of those soldiers over there?' Alice saw a soldier, doubled-up, and moving his head against the midriff of another soldier.

'The croquet hoops have become tangled up!' said the King and absently began to play croquet with himself...

—*J. Y. Watson*

SAMUEL LANGHORNE CLEMENS
(1835-1910)

Pro Malo Publico

It had been a hotly contested campaign, and Senator _____ invited me to try the barley water with him before I began the dusty return. Snug in a booth out of earshot of the general rabble, and flushed with victory, my companion sketched a little history of his triumphal rise up from the squalid obscurity of a Missouri small town. The quality of the barley water, a superior lubrifacient in every way, may have contributed to his openness, but the prime mover seemed to me to be the human need for appreciation, the need of even the most humble to look at the sky just once and get his piece aired.

I'll append the Senator's tale about as he told it, merely ironing a phrase here and there, so it'll lie straight, and sponging out a few of the more colorful bits of diction.

"It was early in my career, really before I had any career. I'd just finished a day's work—foreclosed a couple of homesteads, saw to the removal of a widow and her litter from a shack set picturesquely across from the city dump, connived at putting aside a will in favor of a n'er-do-well nephew, and informed on a small-time sneak thief to curry favor with the sheriff—and was heading for the local watering hole, when the sun seemed to go into eclipse. As there'd been no warning, I took the trouble to glance up, and instead of the sky saw a big, rawboned, skinny individual in flannel and levis standing between me and the light. As he seemed disinclined to step out of my way, I chose to try to go around him; but he wasn't there, I gathered, by mere happenstance.

"Well, standing out there with a crowd just gradually seeping into place around us, I learned his history, at least the parts most relevant to *us*, and the rest of the town learned a good deal too. He'd left for the gold fields about thirty months before, promising the little woman silks and coach-and-four and whatever else his limited imagination could rake out of the scratchy ground of his dreams. In the natural course of things, he'd been gone longer than expected, her money had run out, and she'd thrown herself on my mercy (as the saying goes) mentioning sundry tykes dependent on her, and so forth.

"My inclination had been to help, but I exacted some slight recompense. One thing led, as it usually does, to another, and, in this case, it led her into the local bordello, where, as I recall, she became something of a favorite. (For this I claim no credit, by the by. The lady had talent. If I put her in the way of using it, she made the toss. It was with considerable sorrow that, some time later, I learned of her demise at her own hand.)

"I had heard invective before; still that fellow's rage helped him plumb depths entirely outside my parochial experience. Invective? He inveighed against my family tree, my friends, savaged any dog or cat I might chance to own, took dead aim at my personal habits, and went methodically through my appearance, work, manner of talk, and general demeanor. My, but he was thorough! Just when I thought he'd run down, he revved up again and began to root around the crannies of my character, snuffing out tidbits of meanness which, I blush to admit, came as a surprise. I learned a lot from that fellow. There's no end of difference between being sunk in depravity and being winched up enough to get to know the neighborhood. I'm a deal better for him, for until a man *knows what he is*, how is he to polish himself into all-around perfection?

"At any rate, once I knew where I was, I knew my way, and set about making myself over from self-indulgence and general wickedness to something above the run of ordinary villainy. It took perseverance, I won't deny it! I had to beat out rivals so ornery a toad wouldn't spit on them, had to live with trepidations that if I wasn't lynched, shot, or stomped by some more-than-usually perturbed citizenry, I might be dirked by a boon companion or poisoned by the inamorata of the evening.

"These problems, I'm pleased to say, vanished soon after I became a politician. As I sank lower, paradoxically, I rose higher. What had been reprehensible in a common lickspittle, was, I discovered, respectable in a senator. Then, too, I no longer needed to besmirch myself. There proved to be a perfect fly hatch of fellows willing to do the dirty work. Besides which, we have committees here at the capitol which set standards for iniquity a Roman emperor'd give his favorite's eyeteeth to approach.

"Frankly, there's only one way for me to better my record. With luck, the inaugural ball four years hence will enlighten you, along with the steaming hordes."

Whatever else the Senator said, then, if anything, dissolved in that superior barley water. I've been waiting and watching, though, counting the days passing into weeks and the weeks adding up to months and lo-and-behold the inaugural ball's not so very far away, mighty suddenly. Senator _____'s the odds-on-favorite. I keep hoping for some dark horse to gallop over the horizon, eyes ablaze and mane slick as snake juice. I keep hoping, but I remember to say hello to the Senator when he nods my way. A body can't be too careful these days, and can't have too many friends.

—*Stuart J. Silverman*

BRET HARTE
(1836-1902)

A Hero Of Tomato Can

Mr. Jack Oak-hearse calmly rose from the table and shot the bartender of Tomato Can, because of the objectionable color of his hair. Then Mr. Oak-hearse scratched a match on the sole of his victim's boot, lit a perfumed cigarette and strolled forth into the street of the camp to enjoy the evening air. Mr. Oak-hearse's face was pale and impassive, and stamped with that indefinable hauteur that marks the professional gambler. Tomato Can knew him to be a cool, desperate man. The famous Colonel Blue-bottle was reported to have made the remark to Miss Honorine-Sainte-Claire, when that leader of society opened the Pink Assembly at Toad-in-the-Hole, on the other side of the Divide, that he, Colonel Blue-bottle, would be everlastingly "——ed if he didn't believe that that ——ed Oak-hearse would open a ——ed jack-pot on a pair of ——ed tens, ——ed ef he didn't." To which Miss Ste.-Claire had responded:

"Fancy now."

On this occasion as Mr. Jack Oak-hearse stepped in the cool evening air of the Sierras from out of the bar of the hotel of Tomato Can, he drew from his breast pocket a dainty manicure set and began to trim and polish his slender, almost feminine finger nails, that had been contaminated with the touch of the greasy cards. Thus occupied he betook himself leisurely down the one street of Tomato Can, languidly dodging an occasional revolver bullet, and stepping daintily over the few unburied corpses that bore mute testimony to the disputatious and controversial nature of the citizens of Tomato Can. He arrived at his hotel and entered his apartments, gently waving aside the half-breed Mexican who attempted to disembowel him on the threshold. The apartment was crudely furnished as befitted the rough and ready character of the town of Tomato Can. The Wilton carpet on the floor was stained with spilt Moet and Chandon. The full-length portrait of Mr. Oak-hearse by Carolus Duran was punctured with bullet-marks, while the teakwood escritoire, inlaid with buhl and jade, was encumbered with bowie knives, spurs, and Mexican saddles.

Mr. Oak-hearse's valet brought him the London and Vienna papers. They had been ironed and scented with orris-root, and the sporting articles blue-penciled. "Bill," said Mr. Oak-hearse, "Bill, I believe I told you to cut out all the offensive advertisements from my papers; I perceive, with some concern, that you have neglected it. Your punishment shall be that you will not brush my silk hat next Sunday morning."

The valet uttered an inarticulate cry and fell lifeless to the floor.

"It's better to stand pat on two pair than to try for a full hand," mused Mr. Oak-hearse, philosophically, and his long lashes drooped wearily over his cold steel-blue eyes, like velvet sheathing a poignard.

A little later the gambler entered the dining-room of the hotel in evening dress, and wearing his cordon of the Legion of Honor. As he took his accustomed place at the table, he was suddenly aware of a lustrous pair of eyes that looked into his cold gray ones from the other side of the catsup bottle. Like all heroes, Mr. Jack Oak-hearse was not insensible to feminine beauty. He bowed gallantly. The lady flushed. The waiter handed him the menu.

"I will have a caviar sandwich," affirmed the gambler with icy impassivity. The waiter next handed the menu to the lady, who likewise ordered a caviar sandwich.

"There is no more," returned the waiter. "The last one has just been ordered."

Mr. Oak-hearse started, and his pale face became even paler. A preoccupied air came upon him, and the lines of an iron determination settled upon his face. He rose, bowed to the lady, and calmly passed from the dining-room out into the street of the town and took his way toward a wooded gulch hard by.

When the waiter returned with the caviar sandwich he was informed that Mr. Oak-hearse would not dine that night. A triangular note on scented mauve paper was found at the office begging the lady to accept the sandwich from one who had loved not wisely but too many.

But next morning at the head of the gulch on one of the largest pine trees the searchers found an ace of spades (marked) pinned to the bark with a bowie knife. It bore the following, written in pencil with a firm hand:

Here lies the body of
JOHN OAK-HEARSE
who was too much of a gentleman
to play a Royal-flush
against a Queen-full.

And so, pulseless and cold with a Derringer by his side and a bullet in his brain, though still calm as in life lay he who had been at once the pest and the pride of Tomato Can.

—Frank Norris

THE TWENTIETH CENTURY

Sado-Marxism Through *The Sump Also Rises*

1900: Freud holds first Oedipus Contest.
1903: Julie London, *The Call of Oscar Wilde.*
1922: Joyce becomes Enema of the People.
1925: *The Great Gretsky*, Fitzgerald's *la dolce velveeta.*
1929: Hemingway publishes *A Farewell to Alms*, first anti-solicitation novel.
1962: Faulkner completes Yucknapoocaca.

SADO-MARXISM AND THE OEDIPUS CONTEST
Nowhere do the clichés of the college literary survey run so rampant as in a discussion of the twentieth century. Almost as appalling are the number of overused expressions. Let us avoid such expressions, while at the same time we grant that a tremendous Edna St. Vincent Malaise was created in the wake of the twentieth-century watershed. No longer was man in control of his own free will, as he was in Shakespeare's time. Now, economic and sexual farces came together in the form of Sado-Marxism, which denied man his central place in the gross natural product. Psychological and Darvonian revolutionary farces also came together in Freud's theories of The Oedipus Contest, which placed man in a blackboard jungle. Man was an animal; his behaviorism could be plotted on a cartesian plane, like the results of a deuteronomy experiment. Product of his heresy and environment, man was doomed to spend his holidays in a test tube.

FRACTURED ADAMS
The application of this sort of scientific imperialism to literature is called Naturalism, a glum vision of humanity as at the mercy of feces beyond its control. Most writers were heavily influenced by Hardy's lines, many of which can be

looked up in his poetry. "As flies to won-ton boys/are we to the gods:/they kill us for their soup," he writes, lines echoed by Hamlin Garlic, who compared his privates to "some minute, stingless variety of fly." Small and powerless—is this not what Dreiser's Clyde feels when he drowns his three-months repugnant Roberta, or what Cather's Paul feels when he throws himself prostate at the foot of an on-coming train? From the crown of things to what Eliot called "fractured Adams"—that is how far the human race had fallen.

THE HARDY LIFE OF SEMEN

Joseph Conrad forsook those fractured Adams for the bounding main and the hardy life of semen. His youthful travels took him from Melville's Enchiladas to Tono's Bungay aboard the good ship Cosa Nostromo. In his *Wopshot Chronicles*, Conrad speaks as his own altar-ego in relating the adventures of a picturesque hero, Rudyard Kipling. In *Lord Kim*, Rudyard jumps ship with Gunga Din and sets up house in the brooding atmosphere of Omoo. There these secret sharers live the hardy life of semen, the toast of the island girls, until the Jacobian massacre at the end of the book puts an end to their ménage a twat.

MODERNISM'S WIDESPREAD VITALIS

A component of D.H. Lawrence's Modernism is his willingness to let animals speak for him. In "Snake," for instance, a Bavarian gentleman surprises a snake in the act of impersonating an albatross. Enraged, the gentleman hoves a log at the poor serpent. (An action, no doubt, suggested to him by Samuel Butler Coleridge.) The snake writhes in horror at the gentleman's "accursed humid education," and beats a retreat. The same thing happens to the huge sea turtles who fornicate in a Lithuanian poem of that name. While the persona of "Snake" goes on to pastures new, these poor primitive sea turtles cannot. They are reduced to empty shells by what poet Anthony Hecht calls their "blundering blood." It is not that there is anything wrong with sex. Far from it. Lawrence was at home with all that was elemental and deep-throated in man and nature. A pioneer of erotic punctuation and a revel versus conventions to the last, Lawrence died, leaving behind him a body of work which charted with uncarney precision what poet Hecht has called "the relief map of our blundering blood."

CLOSING THE GERONTION GAP

Unlike Lawrence, who wrote with rectal abandon, Joyce wrote carefully, in finely-horned multiple punt clusters. Unlike Conrad, who wrote of far-away adventures among the Enchiladas, Joyce wrote about his home town of Dubliners. Against the fallen-away religious belief and spiritual mayonnaise of Conrad, Joyce set the great Dedalus mist and the mist of Ulysses. Against the rapid evaporation of time moving in a horizontal cartesian plane of Lawrence, Joyce pitted time as vertigo. (A man's whole life became a constant flow rather than a series of separate *Bulldungsromans*, a theory he borrowed from Marcel Prude, who held that a man is his mammaries.) Finally, against the old notions of consciousness, Joyce pitted his stream-of-concubines techniques.

AN ENEMA OF THE PEOPLE

These were, of course, evolutionary ideas, and like Henrik Ibsen, Joyce considered himself to be an enema of the people. After leaving his home town of Dubliners for a broad (an uneducated Galway Kinnell girl), Joyce assumed the athletic distance of the writer as a kind of God, at a remove from common humid experience, paring his fingernails in support of the dramatic mode. Indeed, a tremendous *in medias wreck* characterizes his *A Portrait of the Artist*, which points the way to the *romans-fleuves* of Joyce's later novels, *Ulysses* and *Finnegan's Wok*. In *Portrait*, we follow Stephen's career through his pronunciation of his first labias, while in *Wok*, Western and Accidental philosophies are juxtaposed in a system of enormous reverberating punts on the road Joyce took into exile. Surely there can be no doubting the cunnilinguistic virtuosity of the genius of Modernism, James Joyce.

LA BELLA ABSUG SANS MERCI

Across the ocean, meanwhile, three young new writers were busily at work forging the smithy of twentieth-century America out of the soul of the age. F. Scott Fitzgerald was the first to break silence with his *La Dolce Velveeta*, a novel about party-goers who swam nude in public taxis and danced all the way to the jazz age. Essentially, they were harpless romantics like himself and Zelda, a Southern Bella Absug Sans Merci, with whom he fell in love when he was undergoing one of his shy, youthful crack-ups. Like protagonist Jay Gretsky, Fitzgerald was a romantic suffering from latent realism. While it was possible to live a life of romantic idealism, staring at Daisy's duck from the safe haven of Easter Egg, he knew that what remained after the gaudy parties, the sexual trombones and stairways to New Haven, was the dreaded visit to Tai Babylonia in pursuit of his Lost Honorarium. Alas, Fitzgerald was doomed to never fully attain his Judy Jugs, a symptom of the creative imagination. It is no wonder that by the time of his death Fitzgerald was hailed as the stepfather of "the lost gerontion" by Gertrude Stein, who was its mother.

MARGARINE AFFIRMATIONS

Hemingway arrived by other means than did Fitzgerald. Where Fitzgerald's language was often florid, Hemingway's was simplified almost to the point of reticence—a falsie economy in a writer. However, his media served him well in such works as *A Farewell to Alms* (an anti-solicitation novel) and *For Whom The Bull Tolls*. In the latter, Hemingway dwells on such obsessive concerns as are allowed by the machismo Hemingway code. According to the rules, heroes conform to three cardinal tenants:

1. They maintain amazing grace under pressure;
2. they smoke only the opium of the people;
3. they pray in Spanish.

The true hero is like the old waiter in "A Clean Well-Lighted Place," who rejects the outworn *arroz con pollo* of his youth for the *de nada* of the present. It may be all too easy for the student to dismiss Hemingway as something of a boar, yet in the vacuum of the twentieth-century watershed, Hemingway's thinly-clad, Papa look-alikes dying of terminal gangrene and grazing on the heights of Machu Pichu continue to have lasting appeal.

FAULKNER'S SPOTTED WHORES

William Faulkner is perhaps best known for fashioning the microcosm of the American South into the larger "calaveras county of the mind" he called Yucknapoocaca. Everything Faulkner wrote is part of this great microcosm, from the autobiological "Spotted Whores" of his youth to *The Omelette* of his later years.

However, it is not merely through creating big, hulking microcosms that novelists succeed. The sophisticated modern reader craves also something of the panorama of life. Faulkner manages to give this illusion by adopting the personal point of view of the idiot in all of us. *The Mound and the Furry*, for instance, is an extraordinary tour de farce of retarded action, until the idiotic point of view is given meaning by the dildo section at the end. Similarly, in *As I Lay Drooling*, Faulkner puts the action in the mouths of some fifteen odd idiots in order to illustrate the great sin of the South, which was slavering. This is in keeping with his theme, the decline of the South concurrent with the rise of mean-spirited modern men like Ike Snopes and Oscar Wilde, whom he portrayed as crass materialists with a thirst for revenge in the short story "Bunburrying." It is a vision at once terrifying and comforting, ugly and beautiful, depressing and exhilarating, awful and wonderful, brutal and gentle, and served to propel Faulkner into the forefront as well as the backdrop of the avant gourd for all time.

THOMAS HARDY
(1840-1928)

From The Youthful Indiscretions
My Summer Vacation

In the holidays I went to stay on my godmother's farm. It was near the church, I often went there in the afternoon and made rubbings of the brasses, the Vicar showed me how. In the evening I often walked back through the churchyard, it was so ghostly, when the sun set it made all the windows red like fire and the shadows on the grey stones were all purple. My godmother said the grass grew greener in the churchyard than anywhere else. I often wondered if the dead people worried about their farms and things they had left behind them, or if it didn't matter to them any more.

There weren't many other boys, the ones on the farm were always busy and they were older than me except Crazy Dick who shouted at the crows. There were four children and their mother and father came to stay in Mrs. Webb's cottage, they were lodgers, but they wouldn't play, they said their father was miserable because they were too many. It made me feel queer to see them. They went soon after, in the middle of the night my godmother said.

One of the dairymaids told me stories sometimes. She had dark brown hair the same colour as a field which has just been ploughed, and her eyes were blue. She said that her people were great lords and she nearly always seemed to be thinking to herself instead of speaking or laughing. I liked to watch her milking the cows and churning the butter. Once she told me that Bob the ploughman tried to sell his wife on a Fair day.

I read some books as well, Fox's Book of Martyrs, the Seasons, a poem by Thomson which had some good parts about the country and the Mysteries of Udolpho.

That is how I spent my holidays.

—*G. De Vavasour*

HENRY JAMES
(1843-1916)

The Mote In The Middle Distance

It was with the sense of a, for him, very memorable something that he peered now into the immediate future, and tried, not without compunction, to take that period up where he had, prospectively, left it. But just where the deuce *had* he left it? The consciousness of dubiety was, for our friend, not, this morning, quite yet clean-cut enough to outline the figures on what she had called his "horizon," between which and himself the twilight was indeed of a quality somewhat intimidating. He had run up, in the course of time, against a good number of "teasers"; and the function of teasing them back—of, as it were, giving them, every now and then, "what for"—was in him so much a habit that he would have been at a loss had there been, on the face of it, nothing to lose. Oh, he always had offered rewards, of course—had ever so liberally pasted the windows of his soul with staring appeals, minute descriptions, promises that knew no bounds. But the actual recovery of the article—the business of drawing and crossing the cheque, blotched though this were with tears of joy—had blankly appeared to him rather in the light of a sacrilege, casting, he sometimes felt, a palpable chill on the fervour of the next quest. It was just this fervour that was threatened as, raising himself on his elbow, he stared at the foot of his bed. That his eyes refused to rest there for more than the fraction of an instant, may be taken—*was*, even then, taken by Keith Tantalus—as a hint of his recollection that after all the phenomenon wasn't to be singular. Thus the exact repetition, at the foot of Eva's bed, of the shape pendulous at the foot of *his* was hardly enough to account for the fixity with which he envisaged it, and for which he was to find, some years later, a motive in the (as it turned out) hardly generous fear that Eva had already made the great investigation "on her own." Her very regular breathing presently reassured him that, if she *had* peeped into "her" stocking, she must have done so in sleep. Whether he should wake her now, or wait for their nurse to wake them both in due course, was a problem presently solved by a new development. It was plain that his sister was now watching him between her eyelashes. He had half expected that. She really was—he had often told her that she really was—magnificent; and her magnificence was never more obvious than in the pause that elapsed before she all of a sudden remarked "They so very indubitably *are*, you know!"

It occurred to him as befitting Eva's remoteness, which was a part of Eva's magnificence, that her voice emerged somewhat muffled by the bedclothes. She was ever, indeed, the most telephonic of her sex. In talking to Eva you always had, as it were, your lips to the receiver. If you didn't try to meet her fine eyes, it was that you simply couldn't hope to: there were too many dark, too many buzzing and bewildering and all frankly not negotiable leagues in between. Snatches of other voices seemed often to intertrude themselves in the parley; and your loyal effort not to overhear these was complicated by your fear of missing what Eva might be twittering. "Oh, you certainly haven't, my dear, the trick of propinquity!" was a thrust she had once parried by saying that in that case, *he* hadn't—to which his unspoken rejoinder that she had caught her tone from the peevish young women at the Central seemed to him (if not perhaps in the last, certainly in the last but one, analysis) to lack finality. With Eva, he had found, it was always safest to "ring off." It was with a certain sense of his rashness in the matter, therefore, that he now, with an air of feverishly "holding the line," said "Oh, as to that!"

Had *she*, he presently asked himself, "rung off"? It was characteristic of our friend—was indeed "him all over"—that his fear of what she was going to say was as nothing to his fear of what she might be going to leave unsaid. He had, in his converse with her, been never so conscious as now of the intervening leagues; they had never so insistently beaten the drum of his ear; and he caught himself in the act of awfully computing, with a certain statistical passion, the distance between Rome and Boston. He has never been able to decide which of these points he was psychically the nearer to at the moment when Eva, replying "Well, one does, anyhow, leave a margin for the pretext, you know!" made him for the first time in his life, wonder whether she were not more magnificent than even he had ever given her credit for being. Perhaps it was to test this theory, or perhaps merely to gain time, that he now raised himself to his knees, and leaning with outstretched arm towards the foot of his bed, made as though to touch the stocking which Santa Claus had, overnight, left dangling there. His posture, as he stared obliquely at Eva, with a sort of beaming defiance, recalled to him something seen in an "illustration." This reminiscence, however—if such it was, save in the scarred, the poor dear old woe-begone and so very beguilingly *not* refractive mirror of the moment—took a peculiar twist from Eva's behaviour. She had, with startling suddenness, sat bolt upright, and looked to him as if she were overhearing some tragedy at the other end of the wire, where, in the nature of things, she was unable to arrest it. The gaze she fixed on her extravagant kinsman was of a kind to make him wonder how he contrived to remain, as he beautifully did, rigid. His prop was possibly the reflection that flashed on him that, if *she* abounded in attenuations, well, hang it all, so did *he*! It was simply a difference of plane. Readjust the "values," as painters say, and there you were! He was to feel that he was only too crudely "there" when, leaning further forward, he laid a chubby forefinger on the stocking, causing that receptacle to rock ponderously to and fro. This effect was more expected than the tears which started to Eva's eyes and the intensity with which "Don't you," she exclaimed, "see?"

"The mote in the middle distance?" he asked. "Did you ever, my dear, know me to see anything else? I tell you it blocks out everything. It's a cathedral, it's a herd of elephants, it's the whole habitable globe. Oh, it's, believe me, of an obsessiveness!" But his sense of the one thing it *didn't* block out from his purview enabled him to launch at Eva a speculation as to just how far Santa Claus had, for the particular occasion, gone. The gauge, for both of them, of this seasonable distance seemed almost blatantly suspended in the silhouettes of the two stockings. Over and above the basis of (presumably) sweetmeats in the toes and heels, certain extrusions stood for a very plenary fulfilment of desire. And, Since Eva *had* set her heart on a doll of ample proportions and practicable eyelids—*had* asked that most admirable of her sex, their mother, for it with not less directness than he himself had put into his demand for a sword and helmet—her coyness now struck Keith as lying near to, at indeed a hardly measurable distance from, the border-line of his patience. If she didn't *want* the doll, why the deuce had she made such a point of getting it? He was perhaps on the verge of putting this question to her, when, waving her hand to include both stockings, she said "Of course, my dear, you *do* see. There they are, and you know I know you know we wouldn't, either of us, dip a finger into them." With a vibrancy of tone that seemed to bring her voice quite close to him, "One doesn't," she added, "violate the shrine—pick the pearl from the shell!"

Even had the answering question "Doesn't one just!" which for an instant hovered on the tip of his tongue, been uttered, it would not have obscured for Keith the change which her magnificence had wrought in him. Something, perhaps, of the bigotry of the convert was already discernible in the way that, averting his eyes, he said "One doesn't even peer." As to whether, in the years that have elapsed since he said this either of our friends (now adult) has, in fact, "peered," is a question which, whenever I call at the house, I am tempted to put to one or other of them. But any regret I may feel in my invariable failure to "come up to the scratch" of yielding to this temptation is balanced, for me, by my impression—my sometimes all but throned and anointed certainty—that the answer, if vouchsafed, would be in the negative.

—Max Beerbohm

James At An Awkward Age

THE NBC-TV SERIES "JAMES AT 16" WILL SHORTLY RESUME IN A NEW FORMAT. THIS IS THE FIRST EPISODE.

SEGMENT 1: Interior, the Berkeley Institute, a boys' school in Newport, Rhode Island. The Reverend William Leverett has just finished lecturing on "Cicero As Such." Boys stream from the classroom into the hall. JAMES and his only friend, SARGY, meet in front of James's locker.

SARGY: James, my man! *(They shake hands.)* Isn't Leverett something else?

JAMES: As to what, don't you know? else he *is*—! Leverett is of a weirdness.

SARGY: Say, my man, what's going down?

JAMES: Anything, you mean, different from what is usually up? But one's just where one *is*—isn't one? I don't mean so much in the being by one's locker—for it does, doesn't it? lock and unlock and yet all unalterably, stainlessly, steelily glitter—as in one's head and what vibes one picks up and the sort of deal one perceives as big.

SARGY: Don't sweat it.

JAMES: If one might suppose that in the not sweating it one should become—what do you fellows call it?—*cool*—!

SARGY: Hey, your manners pull it off.

JAMES: Would they "pull off" anything, then?

SARGY: I didn't *say* anything.

JAMES: It's what, isn't it? *he* can say.

SARGY: Leverett?

JAMES: Oh, Leverett! You must tell me all about the so more or less poor old Leverett.

SARGY: That's not what you mean?

JAMES: All the same, I wonder about *his* idea of him—Leverett's.

SARGY: *Him*?

JAMES: There it is! Precisely one's own father.

SARGY: They say your pop's a friend of Emerson's.

JAMES: Ah, they! But *they*—! If one's to belong, in the event, to a group of other kids, without giving the appearance—so apparent beyond the covering it, in any way, up—of muscling at all in—! And if, under pressure of an ideal altogether American, one feels it tasteless and even humiliating that the head of one's little family is not "in business"—!

SARGY: I can dig it. But hasn't your dad associated with Greeley and Dana?

JAMES: Ah, associated—! But we don't know, do you know? what he *does*.

SARGY: I heard your old man played a large part in the spiritual reformation of the Forties and Fifties.

JAMES: Yes, but after all, you know, Sargy, exactly what the heck, all the while, do you think, like, *is* he?

SEGMENT 2: Interior, the Sweet Shoppe, JAMES is alone at a table. ENTER his cousin MINNY.

MINNY: May I join you?

JAMES: Oh, immensely!

(*WAITRESS comes over*)

MINNY: A Coke, please.

JAMES: Well, perhaps just a thing so inconsiderable as—the hamburger? Of a medium rarity?

MINNY: Are you doing anything Saturday night? Want to go to a show?

JAMES: Would it be a, then, kept date? I mean, the charm of the thing half residing in the thing itself's having been determined in advance and, in consequence, all intentionally and easily and without precipitant hassle or bummer, taking finally, in fact, place?

MINNY: Are you all right?

JAMES: Oh, *all*—!

(*WAITRESS brings their orders. JAMES takes a bite of his burger.*)

JAMES: This is, on the whole, exactly not medium rare. And *you*—you're so stupendously neat-o! I say—do you think I *had* better keep it?

MINNY: Our date?

JAMES: The little hamburger.

MINNY: Listen, I can put you in touch with this really great teenage drug rehabilitation center—

JAMES: Oh, it's not, I mean, you know—no way!—*drugs*. Unless *it's* one.

MINNY: The hamburger? Oh, never mind! See you around. (*Leaves.*)

JAMES: (*Calls after her.*) No, the wondering, can you hear me? in respect to (*despondently*) oh, wow! *him!*

SEGMENT 3: Interior. James's house. JAMES looks into the sitting room, where his brothers, WILLY, WILKY, and BOB, and his sister, ALICE, are gathered before dinner, chaffing each other and debating Fourierism. JAMES goes down the hall and meets his MOTHER.

JAMES: Only *do* say, Mom, how I'm not to fail in the finding of him—

MOTHER: In his study. Hurry up—some of his Swedenborgians are coming for dinner.

(*JAMES goes to Father's study.*)

FATHER: Come in, son. I was just corresponding with Carlyle and Mill.

JAMES: Ah, but it's all so quite buggingly on *that* point, if I might for a moment be allowed to be prefatory no less than interrogatory and interrogatory no less than up, as it were, front, with regard to your little interlocutor's—that is to say, myself's—becoming, in the not grossing the other boys altogether out at least as much as in the not blowing it in getting what they nowadays call "along" with girls, in any way proficient—and oh! if Minny might feel me up, do you see? to *her* level—that now, while I'm too so almost palpably hot to have your answer—and am I not, though, in my own pyrotechnics, fairly cooking!—would I put to you my minuscule question:—

MOTHER (*appearing in doorway*): Dear, the Swedenborgians are here.

JAMES: *There* pokes at me the stick, as well as beckons to me the carrot, of acceleration. Oh, Dad!—poor Dad—you work, you *do* work, I think—do you?—that's my question. Do tell me. I dare say *you* know what it is you, um, "do"? Or only give me the small dry potato-chip-crumb of a hint. For if it's even a matter of your not declining to say what you aren't, then doesn't it follow, don't you see? that you needn't say what you *are*?

FATHER: Why, son! Say I'm a philosopher, say I'm a seeker for truth, say I'm a lover of my kind, say I'm an author of books if you like. Or best of all, just say I'm a student.

(*MOTHER and FATHER leave.*)

JAMES: Ah, but he's too so very freakingly *much*!

SEGMENT 4: The Sweet Shoppe. JAMES is sitting at a table with SARGY and MINNY. OTHER TEENAGERS are at tables around the room.

JAMES: *We're* all of us students, aren't we? And if each of *us* is one of us, then *he* must naturally be!

SARGY: Far out, man.

JAMES: Yet one *has* seen great big grown-up dudes, well encumbered, one might surely have thought, with the inertest of ponderousnesses, put, by one's little crowd, down as positively not, on the social scales as rigged by *them*, sufficiently heavy.

MINNY: *I* haven't.

JAMES: But there *he* is!

SARGY: *There*—?

MINNY: At the door!

(James's FATHER enters Sweet Shoppe and comes over to James's table. The OTHER TEENAGERS gather, all curiously, all convivially, around and everyone is soon friends and dancing to James's favorite song, "Come On, Baby, Don't Hang Fire.")

NEXT WEEK: A harrowing mix-up occurs until it is discovered that James and his father are both named Henry.

—*Veronica Geng*

EDMUND GOSSE
(1849-1928)

A Recollection

"And let us strew
Twain wreaths of holly and of yew."
*   –Waller*

One out of many Christmas Days abides with peculiar vivid-
ness in my memory. In setting down, however clumsily, some
slight record of it, I feel that I shall be discharging a duty not
only to the two disparately illustrious men who made it so very
memorable, but also to all young students of English and
Scandinavian literature. My use of the first person singular,
delightful though that pronoun is in the works of the truly
gifted, jars unspeakably on me; but reasons of space baulk my
sober desire to call myself merely the present writer, or the
infatuated go-between, or the cowed and imponderable young
person who was in attendance.

In the third week of December, 1878, taking the
opportunity of a brief and undeserved vacation, I went to
Venice. On the morning after my arrival, in answer to a most
kind and cordial summons, I presented myself at the Palazzo
Rezzonico. Intense as was the impression he always made
even in London, I think that those of us who met Robert
Browning only in the stress and roar of that metropolis can
hardly have gauged the fullness of his potentialities for
impressing. Venice, "so weak, so quiet," as Mr. Ruskin had
called her, was indeed the ideal setting for one to whom
neither of those epithets could by any possibility have been
deemed applicable. The steamboats that now wake the echoes
of the canals had not yet been imported; but the vitality of the
imported poet was in some measure a preparation for them. It
did not, however, find me quite prepared for itself, and I am
afraid that some minutes must have elapsed before I could, as
it were, find my foot in the torrent of his geniality and high
spirits and give him news of his friends in London.

He was at that time engaged in revising the proof-sheets of
"Dramatic Idylls," and after luncheon, to which he very kindly
bade me remain, he read aloud certain selected passages. The

yellow haze of a wintry Venetian sunshine poured in through the vast windows of his *salone*, making an aureole around his silvered head. I would give much to live that hour over again. But it was vouchsafed in days before the Browning Society came and made everything so simple for us all. I am afraid that after a few minutes I sat enraptured by the sound rather than by the sense of the lines. I find, in the notes I made of the occasion, that I figured myself as plunging through some enchanted thicket on the back of an inspired bull.

That evening, as I was strolling in Piazza San Marco, my thoughts of Browning were all of a sudden scattered by the vision of a small, thick-set man seated at one of the tables in the Café Florian. This was—and my heart leapt like a young trout when I saw that it could be non other than—Henrik Ibsen. Whether joy or fear was the predominant emotion in me, I should be hard put to it to say. It had been my privilege to correspond extensively with the great Scandinavian, and to be frequently received by him, some years earlier than the date of which I write, in Rome. In that city haunted by the shades of so many Emperors and Popes I had felt comparatively at ease even in Ibsen's presence. But seated here in the homelier decay of Venice, closely buttoned in his black surcoat and crowned with his uncompromising tophat, with the lights of the Piazza flashing back wanly from his gold-rimmed spectacles, and his lips tight-shut like some steel trap into which our poor humanity had just fallen, he seemed to constitute a menace under which the boldest might well quail. Nevertheless, I took my courage in both hands, and laid it as a kind of votive offering on the little table before him.

My reward was in the surprising amiability that he then and afterwards displayed. My travelling had indeed been doubly blessed, for, whilst my subsequent afternoons were spent in Browning's presence, my evenings fell with regularity into the charge of Ibsen. One of these evenings is for me "prouder, more laurel'd than the rest" as having been the occasion when he read to me the MS. of a play which he had just completed. He was staying at the Hôtel Danieli, an edifice famous for having been, rather more than forty years previously, the socket in which the flame of an historic *grande passion* had finally sunk and guttered out with no inconsiderable accompaniment of smoke and odour. It was there, in an upper room, that I now made acquaintance with a couple very different from George Sand and Alfred de Musset, though destined to become hardly less famous than they. I refer to Torvald and Nora Helmer. My host read to me with the utmost vivacity, standing in the middle of the apartment; and I remember that in the scene where Nora Helmer dances the tarantella her creator instinctively executed a few illustrative steps.

During those days I felt very much as might a minnow swimming to and fro between Leviathan on the one hand and Behemoth on the other—a minnow tremulously pleased, but ever wistful for some means of bringing his two enormous acquaintances together. On the afternoon of December 24th I confided to Browning my aspiration. He had never heard of this brother poet and dramatist, whose fame indeed was at that time still mainly Boreal; but he cried out with the greatest heartiness, "Capital! Bring him round with you at one o'clock tomorrow for turkey and plum-pudding!"

I betook myself straight to the Hôtel Danieli, hoping against hope that Ibsen's sole answer would not be a comminatory grunt and an instant rupture of all future relations with myself. At first he was indeed resolute not to go. He had never heard of this Herr Browning. (It was one of the strengths of his strange, crustacean genius that he never had heard of anybody.) I took it on myself to say that Herr Browning would send his private gondola, propelled by his two gondoliers, to conduct Herr Ibsen to the scene of the festivity. I think it was this prospect that made him gradually unbend, for he had already acquired that taste for pomp and circumstance which was so notable a characteristic of his later years. I hastened back to the Palazzo Rezzonico before he could change his mind. I need hardly say that Browning instantly consented to send the gondola. So large and lovable was his nature that, had he owned a thousand of those conveyances, he would not have hesitated to send out the whole fleet in honour of any friend of any friend of his.

Next day, as I followed Ibsen down the Danielian water-steps into the expectant gondola, my emotion was such that I was tempted to snatch from him his neatly-furled umbrella and spread it out over his head, like the umbrella beneath which the Doges of days gone by had made their appearances in public. It was perhaps a pity that I repressed this impulse. Ibsen seemed to be already regretting that he had unbent. I could not help thinking, as we floated along the Riva Schiavoni, that he looked like some particularly ruthless member of the Council of Ten. I did, however, try faintly to attune him in some sort to the spirit of our host and of the day of the year. I adumbrated Browning's outlook on life, translating into Norwegian, I well remember, the words "God's in his Heaven, all's right with the World." In fact I cannot charge myself with not having done what I could. I can only lament that it was not enough.

When we marched into the *salone*, Browning was seated at the piano, playing (I think) a Toccata of Galuppi's. On seeing us, he brought his hands down with a great crash on the keyboard, seemed to reach us in one astonishing bound across the marble floor, and clapped Ibsen loudly on either shoulder, wishing him "the Merriest of Merry Christmases."

Ibsen, under this sudden impact, stood firm as a rock, and it flitted through my brain that here at last was solved the old problem of what would happen if an irresistible force met an immoveable mass. But it was obvious that the rock was not rejoicing in the moment of victory. I was tartly asked whether I had not explained to Herr Browning that his guest did not understand English. I hastily rectified my omission, and thenceforth our host spoke in Italian. Ibsen, though he understood that language fairly well, was averse to speaking it. Such remarks as he made in the course of the meal to which we presently sat down were made in Norwegian and translated by myself.

Browning, while he was carving the turkey, asked Ibsen whether he had visited any of the Venetian theatres. Ibsen's reply was that he never visited theatres. Browning laughed his great laugh, and cried, "That's right! We poets who write plays must give the theatres as wide a berth as possible. We aren't wanted there!" "How so?" asked Ibsen. Browning looked a little puzzled and I had to explain that in northern Europe Herr Ibsen's plays were frequently performed. At this I seemed to see on Browning's face a slight shadow—so swift and transient a shadow as might be cast by a swallow flying across a sunlit garden. An instant, and it was gone. I was glad, however, to be able to soften my statement by adding that Herr Ibsen had in his recent plays abandoned the use of verse.

The trouble was that in Browning's company he seemed practically to have abandoned the use of prose too. When, moreover, he did speak, it was always in a sense contrary to that of our host. The Risorgimento was a theme always very near to the great heart of Browning, and on this occasion he hymned it with more than his usual animation and resource (if indeed that were possible). He descanted especially on the vast increase that had accrued to the sum of human happiness in Italy since the success of that remarkable movement. When Ibsen rapped out the conviction that what Italy needed was to be invaded and conquered once and for all by Austria, I feared that an explosion was inevitable. But hardly had my translation of the inauspicious sentiment been uttered when the plum-pudding was borne into the room, flaming on its dish. I clapped my hands wildly at sight of it, in the English fashion, and was intensely relieved when the yet more resonant applause of Robert Browning followed mine. Disaster had been averted by a crowning mercy. But I am afraid that Ibsen thought us both quite mad.

The next topic that was started, harmless though it seemed at first, was fraught with yet graver peril. The world of scholarship was at that time agitated by the recent discovery of what might or might not prove to be a fragment of Sappho. Browning proclaimed his unshakable belief in the authenticity of these verses. To my surprise, Ibsen, whom I had been unprepared to regard as a classical scholar, said positively that they had not been written by Sappho. Browning challenged him to give a reason. A literal translation of the reply would have been "Because no woman ever was capable of writing a fragment of good poetry." Imagination reels at the effect this would have had on the recipient of "Sonnets from the Portuguese." The agonised interpreter, throwing honour to the winds, babbled some wholly fallacious version of the words. Again the situation had been saved; but it was of the kind that does not even in furthest retrospect lose its power to freeze the heart and constrict the diaphragm.

I was fain to thank heaven when, immediately after the termination of the meal, Isben rose, bowed to his host, and bade me express his thanks for the entertainment. Out on the Grand Canal, in the gondola which had again been placed at

our disposal, his passion for "documents" that might bear on
his work was quickly manifested. He asked me whether Herr
Browning had ever married. Receiving an emphatically
affirmative reply, he inquired whether Frau Browning had
been happy. Loth though I was to cast a blight on his interest
in the matter, I conveyed to him with all possible directness
the impression that Elizabeth Barrett had assuredly been one
of those wives who do *not* dance tarantellas nor slam front-
doors. He did not, to the best of my recollection, make further
mention of Browning, either then or afterwards. Browning
himself, however, thanked me warmly, next day, for having
introduced my friend to him. "A capital fellow!" he exclaimed,
and then, for a moment, seemed as though he were about to
qualify this estimate, but ended by merely repeating, "A
capital fellow!"

Ibsen remained in Venice some weeks after my return to
London. He was, it may be conjectured, bent on a specially
close study of the Bride of the Adriatic because her marriage
had been not altogether a happy one. But there appears to be
no evidence whatsoever that he went again, either of his own
accord, or by invitation, to the Palazzo Rezzonico.

—*Max Beerbohm*

GEORGE MOORE
(1852-1933)

From Rebecca Gins

Rebecca Gins walked down the lane putting her feet forward alternately. There were hedges on both sides; one on the left, one on the right. The young leaves were a pale green. Overhead ran the telegraph wires. The poles were about thirty-five yards apart. A thrush sat on a spray of blackthorn, which moved under its weight, now down, now up. Rain had fallen and the ground was wet, especially in the ruts. The second-hand feather in Rebecca's hat drooped a little over her left ear; and the third button of her off boot was wanting. Smoke went up from the chimneys, taking the direction of the wind. All these essential details (including the feather, which was out of sight) escaped Rebecca's notice. She was not gifted with that grasp of actuality which is the sign of an artistic nature.

—*Owen Seaman*

OSCAR WILDE
(1854-1900)

From The Green Carnation.

He frankly admired himself as he watched his reflection, occasionally changing his pose, presenting himself to himself, now full face, now three-quarters face, leaning backward or forward, advancing one foot in its silk stocking and shining shoe, assuming a variety of interesting expressions. In his own opinion he was very beautiful, and he thought it right to appreciate his own qualities of mind and of body. He hated those fantastic creatures who are humble even in their self-communings, cowards who dare not acknowledge even to themselves how exquisite, how delicately fashioned they are. Quite frankly he told other people that he was very wonderful, quite frankly he avowed it to himself. There is a nobility in fearless truthfulness, is there not? and about the magic of his personality he could never be induced to tell a lie.

It is so interesting to be wonderful, to be young, with pale gilt hair and blue eyes, and a face in which the shadows of fleeting expressions come and go, and a mouth like the mouth of Narcissus. It is so interesting to oneself. Surely one's beauty, one's attractiveness, should be one's own greatest delight. It is only the stupid, and those who still cling to Exeter Hall as to a Rock of Ages, who are afraid, or ashamed, to love themselves, and to express that love, if need be. Reggie Hastings, at least, was not ashamed. The mantel-piece in his sitting-room bore only photographs of himself, and he explained this fact to inquirers by saying that he worshipped beauty. Reggie was very frank. When he could not be witty, he often told the naked truth; and truth, without any clothes on, frequently passes for epigram. It is daring, and so it seems clever. Reggie was considered very clever by his friends, but more clever by himself. He knew that he was great, and he said so often in Society. And Society smiled and murmured that it was a pose. Everything is a pose nowadays, especially genius....

—*Robert Hichens*

JOSEPH CONRAD
(1857-1924)

Mystery

I hadn't seen Burleigh for some five years or more when I found him waiting for me that fine light evening in the long low-roofed room with the red curtains—all sailormen know it—at the back of "The Ebb Tide." The front rooms of the tavern of course look out on the square grey shipping offices of the Ultramarine Company, just where the tramway forks—I never could make out, by the way, where that tramway goes to—but Robinson keeps his upstairs room with the bay-windows, the one that looks out over the docks, for a few favoured customers, amongst whom I am privileged to count myself.

Robinson didn't seem to have altered much, I thought. The same white puffed-out cheeks like an elderly cherub in need of fresh air, and the thick black eyebrows that seemed to wave and rustle as if in some invisible wind. Mrs. Robinson was much the same too—angular, moving obscurely in the background, with those thin lips and that faint everlasting smile.

The first part of Burleigh that I noticed when I went upstairs and opened the door was his broad back, encased as usual in a frock-coat of No. 1 sailcloth, the tails of which fell slightly apart as he bent downwards to light his pipe at the fire with a long twist of old newspaper. When he stood up and turned round I was relieved to see that he had not altered either. The ring of fine curly hair that ran round the crown of his otherwise bald head was thinner than it had been, but there was the same lugubrious drollery in his grey eyes and the same gentle murmuring voice that came so incongruously from his deep stalwart chest as though through a sort of syrup. He had that old trick too of his of smiling so that one end of his mouth ran up suddenly against the barrier of his heavy moustache, like the curl of a wave on a spit of reef. The large white-cotton umbrella, badly rolled up, that he always carried when ashore, was still hanging by its crook from his huge right arm.

"Have a——" he said quizzically, and I signified assent in

the usual manner. As we sat down at the gleaming mahogany table and looked at each other smiling across it, he knew, of course—how could he help knowing?—that I wanted to hear all about that remarkable cruise of the "Albatross" away in the Southern ice floes about which the whole water-side was talking and about which nobody surely was likely to know more than he did. But equally of course he wasn't going to tell me all at once, for that wasn't Burleigh's way. Instead he tugged dreamily at one of his big moustaches and smiled up into the end of the other as we looked out at the lighted tideway beneath. Lamps shone high, shone low there, shone with single eyes, shone in rows, were reflected in glittering ladders broken by the shadows of hawsers along the oily inquietude of the stream. Congregated and at rest, the ships seemed to cast gentle inquiring glances at one another, to ask how each had fared in the vast incalculable tangle of wet mysteriousness which passes under the name of the sea.

Burleigh gave a final tug at last and spoke.

"I've asked another man in here to-night to meet you in a kind of way," he said with a sort of depreciatory wave of his big hand as though it was a species of liberty to ask one man to meet another. And then, clearing his throat and twisting his smile again—"Man called Allotson, Jim Allotson"; and, as if with a sudden effort of memory and dragging the words up from some deep recess of his vast interior—"second mate."

"Not on the——" I began, but he stopped me at once with the heavy emphatic nod characteristic of him.

"First man up the berg-side," he cooed in that surprisingly gentle voice. "Girl on it. Sicilian dancer, I believe. Derelict. Polar bears too. Good man, Jim Allotson. I'll tell you about him before he comes."

And bit by bit I came to piece out, between the nods of Burleigh's head and the tuggings of that moustache of his and his quick sideways smile, the history of Allotson's youth up to the day when, by one of those extraordinary coincidences that sailors call chance, he became second officer of the "Albatross"—became second officer and so had his share of the tragi-comedy that was to happen to the crew of about the most adventurous tramp that was ever beaten out of the trade routes into the frozen seas.

He had been the son of a rather superior ship's chandler, I gathered, of a pious disposition, who settled down in East Croydon of all places after retiring from the sight and smell of salt water as they came to him on the quay-side at Singapore. Neither a gravel subsoil nor excessive church-going was able to ward off malaria for long. He soon went under—his wife had died some years before—and left the child to the care of his only surviving relative, a sister named Ann. I can see her now as Burleigh described her to me, with her tight lips, expressionless eyes, grey coils of hair and the black alpaca dress she always inhabited, checking, reproving, forbidding and instilling, endless moral axioms into this touzle-headed waif who had the rover's blood so inalienably in his veins.

He ran away, of course. He was bound to run away, had always dreamed and thought of nothing but ropes and rigging and tar, had seen the alley-ways of his snug suburban home as tidal inlets hung with tropical vegetation; ran away and got a berth as ship's boy, and at fifteen had seen as much of the strange places of the world as many of us achieve in a life-time. He had frizzled in pestilential mud-flats, been driven under stormsails by the stark spite of typhoons, opened up hidden creeks, the passionless offshoots of unknown estuaries, at a time when other lads were grinding away at their Rule of Three.

Somehow or other, Burleigh did not exactly know how, he had managed to get his second-mate's certificate. But what he did know was that all through those wanderings the young man had preserved a sort of simple charming piety that came perhaps from the early lessons of that vigorous uncompromising old lady in Croydon, intolerable though her maxims had seemed.

"Good man, Jim Allotson," cooed Burleigh once more at the end of all this, as though it were a kind of refrain. And just then the door opened and a man came in. He was dressed in a blue reefer suit, stooped slightly and walked a little lame. So much I saw as I gradually drew my eyes upward from the bright spot of light at the bottom of Burleigh's grog glass, where they had been fixed with a sort of fascination while he spoke. Raised now to the level of the stranger's own, they blinked a little, and I held my breath for a moment at the contrast between that fresh ruddy face with slight black whiskers and the crop of hair that surmounted it, white as a bank of snow. He had the grey eyes that seem to be searching out the eternal riddle of heaven and sea, even when they have no further to look than the end of a room. Down the left cheek ran a broad whitey-brown scar that shocked almost as though it were unnatural and had been painted on. I did not need Burleigh's purred introduction to the second mate of the "Albatross" to have my curiosity, already pretty lively, as you know, whipped up to fever-point; and my friend's, "This young man is very anxious to hear——" could have been read without trouble in my eyes.

"But how much have you told him already?" he asked, speaking with a slight stammer as he raised his glass and held it out a little stiffly in front of him, as though this was a necessary preliminary before putting it to his lips. I found out later that this was an invariable trick of his. "Have you told him how I got my second-mate's certificate?"

Burleigh shook his head. He didn't, of course, as I was aware, know.   "About fourteen years ago," began Allotson, and I sighed a little; but before he had said another word the door opened again.   There was something horribly uncanny about that opening of the door, not followed by the appearance of a body but only of a face, as if it had been cut off at the neck——

"Time, gentlemen, please," said the voice of Robinson.

—E.V. Knox (Evoe)

ARTHUR CONAN DOYLE
(1859-1930)

Maddened By Mystery: Or, The Defective Detective

The Great Detective sat in his office.

He wore a long green gown and half a dozen secret badges pinned to the outside of it.

Three or four pairs of false whiskers hung on a whisker-stand beside him.

Goggles, blue spectacles and motor glasses lay within easy reach.

He could completely disguise himself at a second's notice.

Half a bucket of cocaine and a dipper stood on a chair at his elbow.

His face was absolutely impenetrable.

A pile of cryptograms lay on the desk. The Great Detective hastily tore them open one after the other, solved them, and threw them down the cryptogram-shute at his side.

There was a rap at the door.

The Great Detective hurriedly wrapped himself in a pink domino, adjusted a pair of false black whiskers and cried, "Come in."

His secretary entered. "Ha," said the detective, "it is you!" He laid aside his disguise.

"Sir," said the young man in intense excitement, "a mystery has been committed!"

"Ha!" said the Great Detective, his eye kindling, "is it such as to completely baffle the police of the entire continent?"

"They are so completely baffled with it," said the secretary, "that they are lying collapsed in heaps; many of them have committed suicide."

"So," said the detective, "and is the mystery one that is absolutely unparalleled in the whole recorded annals of the London police?"

"It is."

"And I suppose," said the detective, "that it involves names which you would scarcely dare to breathe, at least without first using some kind of atomiser or throat-gargle."

"Exactly."

"And it is connected, I presume, with the highest diplomatic consequences, so that if we fail to solve it England will be at war with the whole world in sixteen minutes?"

His secretary, still quivering with excitement, again answered yes.

"And finally," said the Great Detective, "I presume that it was committed in broad daylight, in some such place as the entrance of the Bank of England, or in the cloak-room of the House of Commons, and under the very eyes of the police?"

"Those," said the secretary, "are the very conditions of the mystery."

"Good," said the Great Detective, "now wrap yourself in this disguise, put on these brown whiskers and tell me what it is."

The secretary wrapped himself in a blue domino with lace insertions, then, bending over, he whispered in the ear of the Great Detective:

"The Prince of Wurttemberg has been kidnapped."

The Great Detective bounded from his chair as if he had been kicked from below.

A prince stolen! Evidently a Bourbon! The scion of one of the oldest families in Europe kidnapped. Here was a mystery indeed worthy of his analytical brain.

His mind began to move like lightning.

"Stop!" he said, "how do you know this?"

The secretary handed him a telegram. It was from the Prefect of Police in Paris. It read: "The Prince of Wurttemberg stolen. Probably forwarded to London. Must have him here for the opening day of Exhibition. £1,000 reward."

So! The Prince had been kidnapped out of Paris at the very time when his appearance at the International Exposition would have been a political event of the first magnitude.

With the Great Detective to think was to act, and to act was to think. Frequently he could do both together.

"Wire to Paris for a description of the Prince."

The secretary bowed and left.

At the same moment there was slight scratching at the door.

A visitor entered. He crawled stealthily on his hands and knees. A hearthrug thrown over his head and shoulders disguised his identity.

He crawled to the middle of the room.

Then he rose.

Great Heaven!

It was the Prime Minister of England.

"You!" said the detective.

"Me," said the Prime Minister.

"You have come in regard to the kidnapping of the Prince of Wurttemberg?"

The Prime Minister started.

"How do you know?" he said.

The Great Detective smiled his inscrutable smile.

"Yes," said the Prime Minister. "I will use no concealment. I am interested, deeply interested. Find the Prince of Wurttemberg, get him safe back to Paris and I will add £500 to the reward already offered. But listen," he said impressively as he left the room, "see to it that no attempt is made to alter the marking of the prince, or to clip his tail."

So! To clip the Prince's tail! The brain of the Great Detective reeled. So! a gang of miscreants had conspired to—but no! the thing was not possible.

There was another rap at the door.

A second visitor was seen. He wormed his way in, lying almost prone upon his stomach, and wriggling across the floor. He was enveloped in a long purple cloak. He stood up and peeped over the top of it.

Great Heaven!

It was the Archbishop of Canterbury!

"Your Grace!" exclaimed the detective in amazement—"pray do not stand, I beg you. Sit down, lie down, anything rather than stand."

The Archbishop took off his mitre and laid it wearily on the whisker-stand.

"You are here in regard to the Prince of Wurttemberg."

The Archbishop started and crossed himself. Was the man a magician?

"Yes," he said, "much depends on getting him back. But I have only come to say this: my sister is desirous of seeing you. She is coming here. She has been extremely indiscreet and her fortune hangs upon the Prince. Get him back to Paris or I fear she will be ruined."

The Archbishop regained his mitre, uncrossed himself,

wrapped his cloak about him, and crawled stealthily out on his hands and knees, purring like a cat.

The face of the Great Detective showed the most profound sympathy. It ran up and down in furrows. "So," he muttered, "the sister of the Archbishop, the Countess of Dashleigh!" Accustomed as he was to the life of the aristocracy, even the Great Detective felt that there was here intrigue of more than customary complexity.

There was a loud rapping at the door.

There entered the Countess of Dashleigh. She was all in furs.

She was the most beautiful woman in England. She strode imperiously into the room. She seized a chair imperiously and seated herself on it, imperial side up.

She took off her tiara of diamonds and put it on the tiara-holder beside her and uncoiled her boa of pearls and put it on the pearl-stand.

"You have come," said the Great Detective, "about the Prince of Wurttemberg."

"Wretched little pup!" said the Countess of Dashleigh in disgust.

So! A further complication! Far from being in love with the Prince, the Countess denounced the young Bourbon as a pup!

"You are interested in him, I believe."

"Interested!" said the Countess. "I should rather say so. Why, I bred him!"

"You which?" gasped the Great Detective, his usually impassive features suffused with a carmine blush.

"I bred him," said the Countess, "and I've got £10,000 upon his chances, so no wonder I want him back in Paris. Only listen," she said, "if they've got hold of the Prince and cut his tail or or spoiled the markings of his stomach it would be far better to have him quietly put out of the way here."

The Great Detective reeled and leaned up against the side of the room. So! The cold-blooded admission of the beautiful woman for the moment took away his breath! Herself the mother of the young Bourbon, misallied with one of the greatest families of Europe, staking her fortune on a Royalist plot, and yet with so instinctive a knowledge of European politics as to know that any removal of the hereditary birth-marks of the Prince would forfeit for him the sympathy of the French populace.

The Countess resumed her tiara.

She left.

The secretary re-entered.

"I have three telegrams from Paris," he said, "they are completely baffling."

He handed over the first telegram.

It read:

"The Prince of Wurttemberg has a long, wet snout, broad ears, very long body, and short hind legs."

The Great Detective looked puzzled.

He read the second telegram.

"The Prince of Wurttemberg is easily recognised by his deep bark."

And then the third.

"The Prince of Wurttemberg can be recognised by the patch of white hair across the centre of his back."

The two men looked at one another. The mystery was maddening, impenetrable.

The Great Detective spoke.

"Give me my domino," he said. "These clues must be followed up," then pausing, while his quick brain analysed and summed up the evidence before him—"a young man," he muttered, "evidently young since described as a 'pup,' with a long, wet snout (ha! addicted obviously to drinking), a streak of white hair across his back (a first sign of the results of his abandoned life)—yes, yes," he continued, "with this clue I shall find him easily."

The Great Detective rose.

He wrapped himself in a long black cloak with white whiskers and blue spectacles attached.

Completely disguised, he issued forth.

He began the search.

For four days he visited every corner of London.

He entered every saloon in the city. In each of them he drank a glass of rum. In some of them he assumed the disguise of a sailor. In others he entered as a soldier. Into others he penetrated as a clergyman. His disguise was perfect. Nobody paid any attention to him as long as he had the price of a drink.

The search proved fruitless.

Two young men were arrested under suspicion of being the Prince, only to be released.

The identification was incomplete in each case.

One had a long wet snout but no hair on his back.

The other had hair on his back but couldn't bark.

Neither of them was the young Bourbon.

The Great Detective continued his search.

He stopped at nothing.

Secretly, after nightfall, he visited the home of the Prime Minister. He examined it from top to bottom. He measured all the doors and windows. He took up the flooring. He inspected the plumbing. He examined the furniture. He found nothing.

With equal secrecy he penetrated into the palace of the Archbishop. He examined it from top to bottom. Disguised as a choir-boy he took part in the offices of the church. He found nothing.

Still undismayed, the Great Detective made his way into the home of the Countess of Dashleigh. Disguised as a housemaid, he entered the service of the Countess.

Then at last the clue came which gave him a solution to the mystery.

On the wall of the Countess' boudoir was a large framed engraving.

It was a portrait.

Under it was a printed legend:

The Prince of Wurttemburg

The portrait was that of a Dachshund.

The long body, the broad ears, the unclipped tail, the short hind legs—all was there.

In the fraction of a second the lightning mind of the Great Detective had penetrated the whole mystery.

The Prince was a dog!!!!

Hastily throwing a domino over his housemaid's dress, he rushed to the street. He summoned a passing hansom, and in a few moments was at his house.

"I have it," he gasped to his secretary, "the mystery is solved. I have pieced it together. By sheer analysis I have reasoned it out. Listen—hind legs, hair on back, wet snout, pup—eh, what? does that suggest nothing to you?"

"Nothing," said the secretary; "it seems perfectly hopeless."

The Great Detective, now recovered from his excitement, smiled faintly.

"It means simply this, my dear fellow. The Prince of Wurttemburg is a dog, a prize Dachshund. The Countess of Dashleigh bred him, and he is worth some £25,000 in addition to the prize of £10,000 offered at the Paris dog show. Can you wonder that——"

At that moment the Great Detective was interrupted by the scream of a woman.

"Great Heaven!"

The Countess of Dashleigh dashed into the room.

Her face was wild.

Her tiara was in disorder.

Her pearls were dripping all over the place.

She wrung her hands and moaned.

"They have cut his tail," she gasped, "and taken all the hair off his back. What can I do? I am undone!"

"Madame," said the Great Detective, calm as bronze, "do yourself up. I can save you yet."

"You!"

"Me!"

"How?"

"Listen. This is how. The Prince was to have been shown at Paris."

The Countess nodded.

"Your fortune was staked on him?"

The Countess nodded again.

"The dog was stolen, carried to London, his tail cut and his marks disfigured."

Amazed at the quiet penetration of the Great Detective, the Countess kept on nodding and nodding.

"And you are ruined?"

"I am," she gasped, and sank down on the floor in a heap of pearls.

"Madame," said the Great Detective, "all is not lost."

He straightened himself up to his full height. A look of inflinchable unflexibility flickered over his features.

The honour of England, the fortune of the most beautiful woman in England was at stake.

"I will do it." he murmured.

"Rise, dear lady," he continued. "Fear nothing. I will

impersonate the dog!!!"

That night the Great Detective might have been seen on the deck of the Calais packet boat with his secretary. He was on his hands and knees in a long black cloak, and his secretary had him on a short chain.

He barked at the waves exultingly and licked the secretary's hand.

"What a beautiful dog," said the passengers.

The disguise was absolutely complete.

The Great Detective had been coated over with mucilage to which dog hairs had been applied. The markings on his back were perfect. His tail, adjusted with an automatic coupler, moved up and down responsive to every thought. His deep eyes were full of intelligence.

Next day he was exhibited in the Dachshund class at the International show.

He won all hearts.

"*Quel beau chien!*" cried the French people.

"*Ach! was ein Dog!*" cried the Spanish.

The Great Detective took the first prize!

The fortune of the Countess was saved.

Unfortunately as the Great Detective had neglected to pay the dog tax, he was caught and destroyed by the dog-catchers. But that is, of course, quite outside of the present narrative, and is only mentioned as an odd fact in conclusion.

—Stephen Leacock

H.G. WELLS
(1866-1946)

The Peculiar Bird

"'Eng!" said Mr. Bottleby, addressing the eighteenth milestone with intense bitterness: "'Eng!"

The bright windy sunshine on that open downland road, the sense of healthy effort, of rhythmic trundling speed, the consciousness of the nearly new ready-to-wear gent's cycling costume which draped his limbs—it had been ticketed "Enormous Reduction," and, underneath that again, "Startling Sacrifice, 25/6", in Parkinson's great front window on the South Parade—none of these things had availed to dissipate the gradual gloom which had been settling like a miasma on Mr. Bottleby's mind through the whole of that morning of May. Various causes, historical, social as well as physiological, had contributed their share towards that tenebrous exhalation which already seemed to hang about him like a tangible and visible cloud. But undoubtedly its immediate origin and the cause of his hasty flight was the state of the Breakfast Bacon. Greasy. Uneatable. Tck! How many times had he told Ann, a hundred times if he had told her once, that he liked it in little crisp hard pieces and the eggs poached separately on toast? He was Fed Up. That was it. Absobloominglutely Fed. Tck!

If some well-meaning social philosopher had attempted to explain to Mr. Bottleby the exact processes whereby a wasteful and ill-organized civilization had condemned him to struggle Laocoon-like in the coils of the retail ironmongery and the embraces of an uncongenial spouse, it is doubtful whether Mr. Bottleby would have clearly understood. But his resentment against fate was none the less profound because it was largely inarticulate and because he would probably have summed up all this mismanagement and stupidity and carelessness and insensate cruelty in some simple epigram like "A bit too thick." Vaguely, in the recesses of his being, Mr. Bottleby knew that in some way or other there ought to have been for him a more beautiful and gracious existence, a life somehow different from the drudgery and pettiness that he endured. . . .

The shop... How he hated it! How he did hate it! Ironmongery! Fast bound—What was it they had said in that church he had strayed into one evening? Misery and iron? Yes, that was it. Fast bound in misery and iron. That was him. And Ann. Sometimes when he thought of Ann... Skinny. Complaining. And why the doose did she cook like that?... There were other things too. In fact, there was One Thing after Another.

"'Eng!" repeated Mr. Bottleby to the nineteenth milestone; "'Eng"!

And having come now to the rather precipitous winding lane which leads down into Fittlehurst village he placed his feet on the rests—it was long before the luxurious days of the free-wheel—folded his arms and began to coast. Perilously, but with a certain sense of satisfaction in his extreme recklessness, to coast....

One figures him, a slightly rotund shape of about three-and-thirty years of age, attired in the check knickerbocker suit which had meant such an earth-shaking sacrifice to Mr. Parkinson; one figures him, I say, with his freckled face, pleasant brown eyes and that large tuft of hair which continually escaped the control of his cap peak, rushing rapidly, worried, tormented by destiny, between those tall hedges on which the hawthorn had already made patches of scented, almost delirious, bloom, rushing downwards—on....

Whuck!

I come now upon a difficulty. I find it exceedingly hard to describe to you the nature of that surprising existence to which Mr. Bottleby awoke when, having caught the fallen telegraph wire—fallen in yesterday's gale so that it blocked the Fittlehurst road like a piece of paddock fencing—having caught this wire exactly under his chin, he was projected out and away into the Ultimate Beyond.

His first impression was agreeable enough. It was one of amazing lightness. And, looking down with those pleasant brown eyes of his, he found that there was indeed good reason for this. For all that lower corporeal part of Mr. Bottleby, that envelope of complicated tubes and piping which had been the source of so much of his trouble, that foundation for the altruistic sartorial efforts of Mr. Parkinson, had completely disappeared. The bicycling suit, and all that therein was, had ceased to be. It had been even more Greatly Reduced. It had been Sacrificed Entirely. And simultaneously Mr. Bottleby was conscious of a kind of soft and feathery growth to right and left of him, a faint iridescent fluffiness a little way behind each of his ears. At the same moment he also became conscious of the fact that he was not alone. All about him, floating, if I may so put it, though the phrase is a singularly inapt one, were thousands of similarly bodiless beings with bright and tiny wings attached to their necks. There was a sound, too, as of a mighty chattering. All these beings were talking, talking hard, talking with a shrill pleasant chirrup like that of song-birds at dawn.

"Queer go," muttered Mr. Bottleby. "Sort of cherribim. Tck."

And instantly he found himself twittering too.

But around and over and under and interpenetrating these more immediate impressions of his a tremendous alteration had come over the mentality of Mr. Bottleby, an alteration that I almost despair of making intelligible. For he was now Out of Time and Out of Space. He was conscious of the Eternal, of the Infinite. The universe as a concrete fact and the universe as a process of change were for him merged into one. The barriers separating history, biology, astronomy, were broken down.

I can perhaps give a faint hint of that new strange consciousness of his when I say that a simultaneous and precisely equivalent impact was now being made on Mr. Bottleby's optical retinæ by the emergency of a huge plesiosaurus from a bog of slime, the murder of JULIUS CÆSAR, and the efforts of a morose and scowling Ann to remove the remnants of bacon grease from a broken willow-pattern plate.

There was also the Future. . . .

One would have thought that this expansion of vision, this sudden opening, as it were, of a thousand intellectual flood-gates, would have suffused Mr. Bottleby's brain with a sense of ineffable beatitude. But it was not so. Whether it was because he was not really fitted for so rapid a translation from the terrestrial to the supernal environment—he was, as a matter of fact, still wearing his bicycling cap,—I cannot say; but the fact remains that in the secret places of his ego Mr. Bottleby was bored, abominably bored. And quite soon, if I may use this inaccurate temporal expression, he made up his mind that, if it were possible, he would abscond.

"Vamoose," he twittered. "Clear. Get out of it."

Curiously enough, he found that he could. By holding his breath very hard till both cheeks and eyes bulged, he found that the infinite consciousness began mysteriously to recede, whilst the terrestrial in some peculiar way enhanced itself. The winged head of Mr. Bottleby began to sink; I should rather say to emerge. Infinity, like a slow sunset, like the memory of a dream, faded. Speaking again in temporal phraseology, Mr. Bottleby became a sort of meteorite, a flying fragment, a detached chip of immortality.

* * *

The question of who was really the first to see the Strange Bird is still hotly debated in the bar parlour of "The Blue Pig" at Fittlehurst. It was certainly seen at ten o'clock by the young man who was dressing the window of Hipley the haberdasher, because his testimony is confirmed by that of the Doctor, who saw it at the same time and said so afterwards to the Vicar. And undoubtedly at half-past ten or thereabouts it perched on one of the great branches of the village oak, for two small boys saw it there and threw stones at it. Equally certain that just before noon it was seen making for the gap in the downs by old Marley the hedger.

"Girt bumblesome thing," he reports it to have been. And then, scratching his head, "Sure-ly."

In any case it was a chance visitor to Pipley-on-Sea, a man named Herringshaw, who wantonly fired at it from the sands near the big breakwater by the bathing-huts at 2.45 p.m. and winged it. Flopping heavily and cumbrously, it dipped down to the waves, rose unsteadily, flopped back and was seen for some time tossing from sunlit crest to crest before it passed out with the tide. It was never heard of again.

Nobody thought of connecting it with the headless body of Mr. Bottleby, the retail ironmonger, which was found entangled with his wrecked bicycle two-thirds of the way down Fittlehurst lane.

—*E.V. Knox (Evoe)*

HILLAIRE BELLOC
(1870-1953)

Of Christmas

There was a man came to an Inn by night, and after he had called three times they should open him the door—though why three times, and not three times three, nor thirty times thirty, which is the number of the little stone devils that make mows at St. Aloesius of Ledera over against the marshes Gué-la-Nuce to this day, nor three hundred times three hundred (which is a bestial number), nor three thousand times three-and-thirty, upon my soul I know not, and nor do you—when, then, this jolly fellow had three times cried out, shouted, yelled, holloa'd, loudly besought, caterwauled, brayed, sung out, and roared, he did by the same token set himself to beat, hammer, bang, pummel, and knock at the door. Now the door was Oak. It had been grown in the forest of Boulevoise, hewn in Barre-le-Neuf, seasoned in South Hoxton, hinged nowhere in particular, and panelled—and that most abominably well—in Arque, where the peasants sell their souls for skill in such handicraft. But our man knew nothing of all this, which, had he known it, would have mattered little enough to him, for a reason which I propose to tell in the next sentence. The door was opened. As to the reasons why it was not opened sooner, these are most tediously set forth in Professor Sir T. K. Slibby's "Half-Hours With Historic Doors," as also in a fragment at one time attributed to Oleaginus Silo but now proven a forgery by Miss Evans. Enough for our purpose, merry reader of mine, that the door was opened.

The man, as men will, went in. And there, for God's sake and by the grace of Mary Mother, let us leave him; for the truth of it is that his strength was all in his lungs, and himself a poor, weak, clout-faced, wizen-bellied, pin-shanked bloke anyway, who at Trinity Hall had spent the most of his time in reading Hume (that was Satan's lackey) and after taking his degree did a little in the way of Imperial Finance. Of him it was that Lord Abraham Hart, that far-seeing statesman, said, "This young man has the root of the matter in him." I quote the epigram rather for its perfect form than for its truth. For once,

Lord Abraham was deceived. But it must be remembered that he was at this time being plagued almost out of his wits by the vile (though cleverly engineered) agitation for the compulsory winding-up of the Rondoosdop Development Company. Afterwards, in Wormwood Scrubbs, his Lordship admitted that his estimate of his young friend had perhaps been pitched too high. In Dartmoor he has since revoked it altogether, with that manliness for which the Empire so loved him when he was at large.

Now the young man's name was Dimby—"Trot" Dimby—and his mother had been a Clupton, so that—but had I not already dismissed him? Indeed I only mentioned him because it seemed that his going to that Inn might put me on track of that One Great Ultimate and Final True Thing I am purposed to say about Christmas. Don't ask me yet what that Thing is. Truth dwells in no man, but is a shy beast you must hunt as you may in the forests that are around about the Walls of Heaven. And I do hereby curse, gibbet, and denounce *in execrationem perpetuam atque aeternam* the man who hunts in a crafty or calculating way—as, lying low, nosing for scents, squinting for trails, crawling noiselessly till he shall come near to his quarry and then taking careful aim. Here's to him who hunts Truth in the honest fashion of men, which is, going blindly at it, following his first scent (if such there be) or (if none) none, scrambling over boulders, fording torrents, winding his horn, plunging into thickets, skipping, firing off his gun in the air continually, and then ramming in some more ammunition anyhow, with a laugh and a curse if the charge explode in his own jolly face. The chances are he will bring home in his bag nothing but a field-mouse he trod on by accident. Not the less his is the true sport and the essential stuff of holiness.

As touching Christmas—but there is nothing like verse to clear the mind, heat the blood, and make very humble the heart. Rouse thee, Muse!

One Christmas Night in Pontgibaud
   (*Pom-pom, rub-a-dub-dub*)
A man with a drum went to and fro
   (*Two merry eyes, two cheeks chub*)
Nor not a citril within, without,
But heard the racket and heard the rout

And marvelled what it was all about
(*And who shall shrive Beelzebub?*)

He whacked so hard the drum was split
(*Pom-pom, rub-a-dub-dum*)
Out lept Saint Gabriel from it
(*Praeclarissimus Omnium*)
Who spread his wings and up he went
Nor ever paused in his ascent
Till he had reached the firmament
(*Benedicamus Dominum*).

That's what I shall sing (please God) at dawn to-morrow,
standing on the high, green barrow at Storrington, where the
bones of Athelstan's men are. Yea,

At dawn to-morrow
    On Storrington Barrow
I'll beg or borrow
    A bow and arrow
And shoot sleek sorrow
    Through the marrow.
The floods are out and the ford is narrow,
The stars hang dead and my limbs are lead,
    But ale is gold
    And there's good foot-hold
On the Cuckfield side of Storrington Barrow.

This too I shall sing, and other songs that are yet to write. In
Pagham I shall sing them again, and again in Little Dewstead.
In Hornside I shall rewrite them, and at the Scythe and Turtle
in Liphook (if I have patience) annotate them. At Selsey they
will be very damnably in the way, and I don't at all know what I
shall do with them at Selsey.

Such then, as I see it, is the whole pith, mystery, outer
form, common acceptation, purpose, usage usual, meaning
and inner meaning, beauty intrinsic and extrinsic, and right
character of Christmas Feast. *Habent urbs atque orbis
revelationem.* Pray for my soul.

—*Max Beerbohm*

HECTOR HUGH MUNRO (SAKI)
(1870-1916)

"Q." A Psychic Pstory of the Psupernatural

I cannot expect that any of my readers will believe the story which I am about to narrate. Looking back upon it, I scarcely believe it myself. Yet my narrative is so extraordinary and throws such light upon the nature of our communications with beings of another world, that I feel I am not entitled to withhold it from the public.

I had gone over to visit Annerly at his rooms. It was Saturday, October 31. I remember the date so precisely because it was my pay day, and I had received six sovereigns and ten shillings. I remembered the sum so exactly because I had put the money into my pocket, and I remember into which pocket I had put it because I had no money in any other pocket. My mind is perfectly clear on all these points.

Annerly and I sat smoking for some time.

Then quite suddenly—

"Do you believe in the supernatural?" he asked.

I started as if I had been struck.

At the moment when Annerly spoke of the supernatural I had been thinking of something entirely different. The fact that he should speak of it at the very instant when I was thinking of something else, struck me as at least a very singular coincidence.

For a moment I could only stare.

"What I mean is," said Annerly, "do you believe in phantasms of the dead?"

"Phantasms?" I repeated.

"Yes, phantasms, or if you prefer the word, phanograms, or say if you will phanogrammatical manifestations, or more simply psycho-phantasmal phenomena?"

I looked at Annerly with a keener sense of interest than I had ever felt in him before. I felt that he was about to deal with events and experiences of which in the two or three months that I had known him he had never seen fit to speak.

I wondered now that it had never occurred to me that a man whose hair at fifty-five was already streaked with grey, must have passed through some terrible ordeal.

Presently Annerly spoke again.

"Last night I saw Q," he said.

"Good heavens!" I ejaculated. I did not in the least know who Q was, but it struck me with a thrill of indescribable terror that Annerly had seen Q. In my own quiet and measured existence such a thing had never happened.

"Yes," said Annerly, "I saw Q as plainly as if he were standing here. But perhaps I had better tell you something of my past relationship with Q, and you will understand exactly what the present situation is."

Annerly seated himself in a chair on the other side of the fire from me, lighted a pipe and continued.

"When first I knew Q he lived not very far from a small town in the south of England, which I will call X, and was betrothed to a beautiful and accomplished girl whom I will name M."

Annerly had hardly begun to speak before I found myself listening with riveted attention. I realised that it was no ordinary experience that he was about to narrate. I more than suspected that Q and M were not the real names of his unfortunate acquaintances, but were in reality two letters of the alphabet selected almost at random to disguise the names of his friends. I was still pondering over the ingenuity of the thing when Annerly went on:

"When Q and I first became friends, he had a favourite dog, which, if necessary, I might name Z, and which followed him in and out of X on his daily walk."

"In and out of X," I repeated in astonishment.

"Yes," said Annerly, "in and out."

My senses were now fully alert. That Z should have followed Q out of X, I could readily understand, but that he should first have followed him in seemed to pass the bounds of comprehension.

"Well," said Annerly, "Q and Miss M were to be married. Everything was arranged. The wedding was to take place on the last day of the year. Exactly six months and four days before the appointed day (I remember the date because the coincidence struck me as peculiar at the time) Q came to me late in the evening in great distress. He had just had, he said, a premonition of his own death. That evening, while sitting with Miss M on the verandah of her house, he had distinctly seen a projection of the dog R pass along the road."

"Stop a moment," I said. "Did you not say that the dog's name was Z?"

Annerly frowned slightly.

"Quite so," he replied. "Z, or more correctly Z R, since Q was in the habit, perhaps from motives of affection, of calling him R as well as Z. Well, then, the projection, or phanogram, of the dog passed in front of them so plainly that Miss M swore that she could have believed that it was the dog himself. Opposite the house the phantasm stopped for a moment and wagged its tail. Then it passed on, and quite suddenly disappeared around the corner of a stone wall, as if hidden by the bricks. What made the thing still more mysterious was that Miss M's mother, who is partially blind, had only partially seen the dog."

Annerly paused a moment. Then he went on:

"This singular occurrence was interpreted by Q, no doubt correctly, to indicate his own approaching death. I did what I could to remove this feeling, but it was impossible to do so, and he presently wrung my hand and left me, firmly convinced that he would not live till morning."

"Good heavens!" I exclaimed, "and he died that night?"

"No, he did not," said Annerly quietly, "that is the inexplicable part of it."

"Tell me about it," I said.

"He rose that morning as usual, dressed himself with his customary care, omitting none of his clothes, and walked down to his office at the usual hour. He told me afterwards that he remembered the circumstances so clearly from the fact that he had gone to the office by the usual route instead of taking any other direction."

"Stop a moment," I said. "Did anything unusual happen to mark that particular day?"

"I anticipated that you would ask that question," said Annerly, "but as far as I can gather, absolutely nothing happened. Q returned from his work, and ate his dinner apparently much as usual, and presently went to bed complaining of a slight feeling of drowsiness, but nothing more. His stepmother, with whom he lived, said afterwards that she could hear the sound of his breathing quite distinctly during the night."

"And did he die that night?" I asked, breathless with excitement.

"No," said Annerly, "he did not. He rose next morning feeling about as before except that the sense of drowsiness had apparently passed, and that the sound of his breathing was no longer audible."

Annerly again fell into silence. Anxious as I was to hear the rest of his astounding narrative, I did not like to press him with questions. The fact that our relations had hitherto been only of a formal character, and that this was the first occasion on which he had invited me to visit him at his rooms, prevented me from assuming too great an intimacy.

"Well," he continued, "Q went to his office each day after that with absolute regularity. As far as I can gather there was nothing either in his surroundings or his conduct to indicate that any peculiar fate was impending over him. He saw Miss M regularly, and the time fixed for their marriage drew nearer each day."

"Each day?" I repeated in astonishment.

"Yes," said Annerly, "every day. For some time before his marriage I saw but little of him. But two weeks before that event was due to happen, I passed Q one day in the street. He seemed for a moment about to stop, then he raised his hat, smiled and passed on."

"One moment," I said, "if you will allow me a question that seems of importance—did he pass on and then smile and raise his hat, or did he smile into his hat, raise it, and then pass on afterwards?"

"Your question is quite justified," said Annerly, "though I think I can answer with perfect accuracy that he first smiled, then stopped smiling and raised his hat, and then stopped raising his hat and passed on."

"However," he continued, "the essential fact is this: on the day appointed for the wedding, Q and Miss M were duly married."

"Impossible!" I gasped; "duly married, both of them?"

"Yes," said Annerly, "both at the same time. After the wedding Mr. and Mrs. Q——"

"Mr. and Mrs. Q," I repeated in perplexity.

"Yes," he answered, "Mr. and Mrs. Q—for after the wedding Miss M took the name of Q—left England and went out to Australia, where they were to reside."

"Stop one moment," I said, "and let me be quite clear—in going out to settle in Australia it was their intention to reside there?"

"Yes," said Annerly, "that at any rate was generally understood. I myself saw them off on the steamer, and shook hands with Q, standing at the same time quite close to him."

"Well," I said, "and since the two Q's, as I suppose one might almost call them, went to Australia, have you heard anything from them?"

"That," replied Annerly, "is a matter that has shown the same singularity as the rest of my experience. It is now four years since Q and his wife went to Australia. At first I heard from him quite regularly, and received two letters each month. Presently I only received one letter every two months, and later two letters every six months, and then only one letter every twelve months. Then until last night I heard nothing whatever of Q for a year and a half."

I was now on the tiptoe of expectancy.

"Last night," said Annerly very quietly, "Q appeared in this room, or rather, a phantasm or psychic manifestation of him. He seemed in great distress, made gestures which I could not understand, and kept turning his trouser pockets inside out. I was too spell-bound to question him, and tried in vain to divine his meaning. Presently the phantasm seized a pencil from the table, and wrote the words, 'Two sovereigns, to-morrow night, urgent.'"

Annerly was again silent. I sat in deep thought. "How do you interpret the meaning which Q's phanogram meant to convey?"

"I think," he announced, "it means this. Q, who is evidently dead, meant to visualise that fact, meant, so to speak, to deatomise the idea that he was demonetised, and that he wanted two sovereigns to-night."

"And how," I asked, amazed at Annerly's instinctive penetration into the mysteries of the psychic world, "how do you intend to get it to him?"

"I intend," he announced, "to try a bold, a daring experiment, which, if it succeeds, will bring us into immediate connection with the world of spirits. My plan is to leave two sovereigns here upon the edge of the table during the night. If they are gone in the morning, I shall know that Q has contrived to de-astralise himself, and has taken the sovereigns. The only question is, do you happen to have two sovereigns? I myself, unfortunately, have nothing but small change about me."

Here was a piece of rare good fortune, the coincidence of which seemed to add another link to the chain of circumstance. As it happened I had with me the six sovereigns which I had just drawn as my week's pay.

"Luckily," I said, "I am able to arrange that. I happen to have money with me." And I took two sovereigns from my pocket.

Annerly was delighted at our good luck. Our preparations for the experiment were soon made.

We placed the table in the middle of the room in such a way that there could be no fear of contact or collision with any of the furniture. The chairs were carefully set against the wall, and so placed that no two of them occupied the same place as any other two, while the pictures and ornaments about the room were left entirely undisturbed. We were careful not to remove any of the wall-paper from the wall, nor to detach any of the window-panes from the window. When all was ready the two sovereigns were laid side by side upon the table, with their heads up in such a way that the lower sides or tails were supported by only the table itself. We then extinguished the light. I said "Good night" to Annerly, and groped my way out into the dark, feverish with excitement.

My readers may well imagine my state of eagerness to know the result of the experiment. I could scarcely sleep for anxiety to know the issue. I had, of course, every faith in the completeness of our preparations, but was not without misgivings that the experiment might fail, as my own mental temperament and disposition might not be of the precise kind needed for the success of these experiments.

On this score, however, I need have had no alarm. The event showed that my mind was a media, or if the word is better, a transparency, of the very first order for psychic work of this character.

In the morning Annerly came rushing over to my lodgings, his face beaming with excitement.

"Glorious, glorious," he almost shouted, "we have succeeded! The sovereigns are gone. We are in direct monetary communication with Q."

I need not dwell on the exquisite thrill of happiness which went through me. All that day and all the following day, the sense that I was in communication with Q was ever present with me.

My only hope was that an opportunity might offer for the renewal of our inter-communication with the spirit world.

The following night my wishes were gratified. Late in the evening Annerly called me up on the telephone.

"Come over at once to my lodgings," he said. "Q's phanogram is communicating with us."

I hastened over, and arrived almost breathless. "Q has been here again," said Annerly, "and appeared in the same distress as before. A projection of him stood in the room, and kept writing with its finger on the table. I could distinguish the word 'sovereigns,' but nothing more."

"Do you not suppose," I said, "that Q for some reason which we cannot fathom, wishes us to again leave two sovereigns for him?"

"By Jove!" said Annerly enthusiastically, "I believe you've hit it. At any rate, let us try; we can but fail."

That night we placed again two of my sovereigns on the table, and arranged the furniture with the same scrupulous care as before.

Still somewhat doubtful of my own psychic fitness for the work in which I was engaged, I endeavoured to keep my mind so poised as to readily offer a mark for any astral disturbance that might be about. The result showed that it had offered just such a mark. Our experiment succeeded completely. The two coins had vanished in the morning.

For nearly two months we continued our experiments on these lines. At times Annerly himself, so he told me, would leave money, often considerable sums, within reach of the phantasm, which never failed to remove them during the night. But Annerly, being a man of strict honour, never carried on these experiments alone except when it proved impossible to communicate with me in time for me to come.

At other times he would call me up with the simple message, "Q is here," or would send me a telegram, or a written note saying, "Q needs money; bring any that you have, but no more."

On my own part, I was extremely anxious to bring our experiments prominently before the public, or to interest the Society for Psychic Research, and similar bodies, in the daring transit which we had effected between the world of sentience and the psycho-astric, or pseudo-ethereal existence. It seemed to me that we alone had succeeded in thus conveying money directly and without mediation, from one world to another. Others, indeed, had done so by the interposition of a medium, or by subscription to an occult magazine, but we had performed the feat with such simplicity that I was anxious to make our experience public, for the benefit of others like myself.

Annerly, however, was averse from this course, being fearful that it might break off our relations with Q.

It was some three months after our first inter-astral psychomonetary experiment, that there came the culmination of my experiences—so mysterious as to leave me still lost in perplexity.

Annerly had come in to see me one afternoon. He looked nervous and depressed.

"I have just had a psychic communication from Q," he said in answer to my inquiries, "which I can hardly fathom. As far as I can judge, Q has formed some plan for interesting other phantasms in the kind of work that we are doing. He proposes to form, on his side of the gulf, an association that is to work in harmony with us, for monetary dealings on a large scale, between the two worlds."

My reader may well imagine that my eyes almost blazed with excitement at the magnitude of the prospect opened up.

"Q wishes us to gather together all the capital that we can, and to send it across to him, in order that he may be able to organise with him a corporate association of phanograms, or perhaps in this case, one would more correctly call them phantoids."

I had no sooner grasped Annerly's meaning than I became enthusiastic over it.

We decided to try the great experiment that night.

My own worldly capital was, unfortunately, no great amount. I had, however, some £500 in bank stock left to me at my father's decease, which I could, of course, realise within a few hours. I was fearful, however, lest it might prove too small to enable Q to organise his fellow phantoids with it.

I carried the money in notes and sovereigns to Annerly's room, where it was laid on the table. Annerly was fortunately able to contribute a larger sum, which, however, he was not to place beside mine until after I had withdrawn, in order that conjunction of our monetary personalities might not dematerialise the astral phenomenon.

We made our preparations this time with exceptional care,

Annerly quietly confident, I, it must be confessed, extremely nervous and fearful of failure. We removed our boots, and walked about on our stockinged feet, and at Annerly's suggestion, not only placed the furniture as before, but turned the coal-scuttle upside down, and laid a wet towel over the top of the wastepaper basket.

All complete, I wrung Annerly's hand, and went out into the darkness.

I waited next morning in vain. Nine o'clock came, ten o'clock, and finally eleven, and still no word of him. Then feverish with anxiety, I sought his lodgings.

Judge of my utter consternation to find that Annerly had disappeared. He had vanished as if off the face of the earth. By what awful error in our preparations, by what neglect of some necessary psychic precautions, he had met his fate, I cannot tell. But the evidence was only too clear, that Annerly had been engulfed into the astral world, carrying with him the money for the transfer of which he had risked his mundane existence.

The proof of his disappearance was easy to find. As soon as I dared do so with discretion I ventured upon a few inquiries. The fact that he had been engulfed while still owing four months' rent for his rooms, and that he had vanished without even having time to pay such bills as he had outstanding with local tradesmen, showed that he must have been devisualised at a moment's notice.

The awful fear that I might be held accountable for his death, prevented me from making the affair public.

Till that moment I had not realised the risks that he had incurred in our reckless dealing with the world of spirits. Annerly fell a victim to the great cause of psychic science, and the record of our experiments remains in the face of prejudice as a witness to its truth.

—Stephen Leacock

STEPHEN CRANE
(1871-1900)

The Green Stone Of Unrest

A Mere Boy stood on a pile of blue stones. His attitude was regardant. The day was seal brown. There was a vermilion valley containing a church. The church's steeple aspired strenuously in a direction tangent to the earth's center. A pale wind mentioned tremendous facts under its breath with certain effort at concealment to seven not-dwarfed on an un-distant mauve hilltop.

The Mere Boy was a brilliant blue color. The effect of the scene was not un-kaleidoscopic.

After a certain appreciable duration of time the Mere Boy abandoned his regardant demeanor. The strenuously aspiring church steeple no longer projected itself upon his conscious-ness. He found means to remove himself from the pile of blue stones. He set his face valleyward. He proceeded.

The road was raw umber. There were in it wagon ruts. There were in it pebbles, Naples yellow in color. One was green. The Mere Boy allowed the idea of the green pebble to nick itself into the sharp edge of the disc of his Perception.

"Ah," he said, "a green pebble."

The rather pallid wind communicated another Incompre-hensible Fact to the paranthine trees. It would appear that the poplars understood.

"Ah," repeated the Mere Boy, "a Green Pebble."

"Sh-o," remarked the wind.

The Mere Boy moved appreciably forward. If there were a thousand men in a procession and nine hundred and ninety-nine should suddenly expire, the one man who was remnant would assume the responsibility of the procession.

The Mere Boy was an abbreviated procession.

The blue Mere Boy transported himself diagonally athwart the larger landscape, printed in four colors, like a poster.

On the uplands were chequered squares made by fields, tilled and otherwise. Cloud-shadows moved from square to square. It was as if the Sky and Earth were playing a tremendous game of chess.

By and by the Mere Boy observed an Army of a Million Men. Certain cannon, like voluble but non-committal toads with hunched backs, fulminated vast hiccoughs at unimpassioned intervals. Their own invulnerableness was offensive.

An officer of blue serge waved a sword, like a picture in a school history. The non-committal toads pullulated with brief red pimples and swiftly relapsed to impassivity.

The line of the Army of a Million Men obnubilated itself in whiteness as a line of writing is blotted with a new blotter.

"Go teh blazes b'Jimminey," remarked the Mere Boy. "What yeh's shooting fur? They might be people in that field."

He was terrific in his denunciation of such negligence. He debated the question of his ir-removability.

"If I'm goin' teh be shot," he observed; "If I'm goin' teh be shot, b'Jimminey—"

*   *   *

A Thing lay in the little hollow.

The little hollow was green.

The Thing was pulpy white. Its eyes were white. It had blackish-yellow lips. It was beautifully spotted with red, like tomato stains on a rolled napkin.

The yellow sun was dropping on the green plain of the earth, like a twenty-dollar gold piece falling on the baize cloth of a gaming table.

The blue serge officer abruptly discovered the punctured Thing in the Hollow. He was struck with the ir-remediableness of the business.

"Gee," he murmured with interest. "Gee, it's a Mere Boy."

The Mere Boy had been struck with seventy-seven rifle bullets. Seventy had struck him in the chest, seven in the head. He bore some resemblance to the top of a pepper castor.

He was dead.

He was obsolete.

As the blue serge officer bent over him he became aware of a something in the Thing's hand.

It was a green pebble.

"Gee," exclaimed the blue serge officer. "A green pebble, gee."

The large Wind evolved a threnody with reference to the seven un-distant poplars.

—*Frank Norris*

THEODORE DREISER
(1871-1945)

Compiling an American Tragedy

Chapter I

Up East Division Street, on a hot day in late July, walked two men, one five feet four, the other, the taller of the two, five feet six, the first being two inches shorter than his more elongated companion, and consequently giving the appearance to passers-by on East Division Street, or, whenever the two reached a cross street, to the passers-by on the cross street, of being at least a good two inches shorter than the taller of the little group.

Walking up East Division Street they came, in two or three minutes, to Division Street proper, which runs at right angles and a little to the left of East Division Street, but not so much to the left as Marcellus Street, or Ransome Street, for that matter. As the two continued strolling, in that fashion in which two men of their respective heights are likely to stroll, they came in succession to—

(Note to printer: *Attached find copy of Thurston's Street Guide. Print names of every street listed therein, beginning with East Division and up to, and including, Dawson.*)

Chapter II

That these two men, presented in the last chapter, would eventually stop walking up Division Street and enter a house of some sort or description, might well be anticipated by the reader, and, in fact, such was the case.

It was, indeed, the house of the shorter of the two, of the one whom we have seen in the last chapter to have been five feet four, if, indeed, he was. It was a typical dwelling, or home, of a man of the middle class in a medium-sized city such as the one in which these men found themselves living.

(Note to printer: *Attached find insurance inventory of household effects and architect's specifications. Reproduce in toto.*)

Chapter III

Reaching the living room described above, Tom Rettle, for such was the name of the shorter of the two—the one to whom the house, or home, or dwelling, belonged—was greeted by his wife, Anna, a buxom woman of perhaps thirty-four or thirty-five, certainly not *more* than thirty-five, if one were to judge by her fresh, wholesome color and the sparkle of her brownish-gray eyes, or even by her well-rounded form, her—

(Print attached passport description of Anna Rettle.)

"Well, hello, Anna," said Tom, pleasantly, for Tom Rettle was, as a matter of fact, a very pleasant man unless he were angered, and his blue eyes smiled in a highly agreeable manner.

"Well, hello, Tom," replied Anna, for it was indeed Anna who spoke, in a soft, well-modulated voice, too, giving the impression of being an extremely agreeable sort of a woman.

"Anna, I want you to meet a very good friend of mine, Arthur Berolston, a very good friend of mine," said Tom, politely, looking, at the same time, at both Anna and Berolston.

"I'm very happy to meet Mr. Berolston," added Anna, genially, although one could see that in her heart she wished that Tom would bring a little different type of friend home, a thing she had often spoken to him about when they were alone, as they often were.

"Dat's very good of yer ter say, Missus Rettle," replied Berolston, in modern slang, which made him sound even more uncouth than he looked, which was uncouth enough. "For de love o' Mike!"

At this indication of a rough bringing-up on the part of her husband's acquaintance, Anna Rettle winced slightly but showed no other sign of her emotions. Tom was such a kind-hearted fellow! So good! So kind-hearted! Tom was.

"What is there for supper tonight, Anna?" asked Tom, when the wincing had died down. "You know how well I like cole slaw, and have always liked it."

"I certainly do know your fondness for cole slaw, Tom," replied his wife, but with a note of regret in her voice, for she was thinking that she had no cole slaw for supper on the particular night of which we are speaking. "But you will remember that we had cole slaw last night with the cold tongue, and night before last with the baked beans and—"

(*Run attached "Fifteen Midsummer Menus for Cole Slaw Lovers."*)

Chapter IV

Prepared as Tom was not to have cole slaw for supper, he could not hide his disappointment. Anna had been a good wife to him.

But somehow tonight, when he had brought Arthur Berolston home to supper, his disappointment was particularly keen, for he and Arthur had been discussing cole slaw all the way up East Division Street, across Division Street and through to the southwest corner of Dawson and Margate, where Tom lived, and each had said how much he liked it.

Should he strike Anna for failing him at this juncture? He, Tom Rettle, strike his wife, Anna Rettle? And, even if he should decide to strike her, *where* should he direct the blow? Tom's mind was confused with all these questions.

(*Reprint the above paragraph twenty-five times.*)

Chapters V-LXXXII Inclusive

To printer: *With the above copy you will find a briefcase containing newspaper clippings giving the complete testimony of Anna Rettle, Thomas Rettle and Arthur Berolston in the case of "Anna Rettle vs. Thomas Rettle," tried in the Criminal Court of Testiman County, September 2-28, 1925. There is also a transcript of the testimony of three neighbors of the Rettles' (Herman Nordquist, Ethel Nordquist and Junior Nordquist), and of Officer Louis M. Hertzog of the Fifth Precinct. Reprint all these and, at the bottom of the last page, put "THE END."*

—Robert Benchley

MARCEL PROUST
(1871-1922)

King Lear, Act Five, Scene Two

That "ripeness is all" was a sentiment of which Edgar even now scarcely believed the truth, and which, until a few days before, his character, formed but secreted, as in the rough milkweed pod the seeds lie like the plated and lapped armor of some hero of antiquity said by peasants to be not dead but asleep and awaiting a resurrection, would not perhaps have permitted him to utter. It may indeed have been that this not particularly distinguished young man (for good breeding and ancient lineage do not necessarily provide their possessors with those other qualities of mind and heart which age and much experience of the world may possibly come to consider valuable) had attained all at once to the making of this epigram more or less by chance, a means no doubt despised by persons in society but not—for he knows too well how many of the most sublime effects, strokes of wit such as, for example, the small hole in the cloud portrayed by Tintoretto in his Ascension of Elijah in the Palazzo Mocenigo, which is a real hole in the canvas, are reached rather by luck than judgment—by the artist. So Edgar was able, but only after having delivered himself of his remark, to perceive at once something of its strangeness and truth, qualities to which, so long as he was no more than the elegant sprig of nobility who had seen, in the spectacle of the three Lear girls, Goneril, Regan, and Cordelia, no more than a single organism proliferating in an anonymous ambience of blond hair and flashing smiles, he could have been at best indifferent. We are taught by sufferings, in this world, and, as when the members of a charitable committee decide to subscribe a certain sum to a hospital, not pausing to reflect that one of them may lately have been ruined by an unfortunate speculation, no one asks us whether or no we can afford the lessons. So that perhaps Edgar's profound remark depended, after all, upon a very simple circumstance: that the sight of his father the aged Duke, in the blind helplessness of the very old or of earliest childhood, his now useless binoculars swinging at his side as, in an allegorical painting of the Middle Ages, saints are depicted as holding the instruments of their martyrdom, Lawrence his gridiron, Catherine her wheel, appealed to the son as holding something of that wealth of irony and strangeness which we feel even through our anger when, for example, our mistress, having pleaded indisposition when we know quite well—but do not dare to say—that she attended the Opera in the company of the Duke of Cornwall, gains, in our eyes, something of the character of fatal necessity itself. So true is it that the profundities of our moral nature occur, for the most part, by accident, of which we may or may not realize entirely the mathematical implications before being overtaken by the last accident, death.

It is also the effect of our perpetual masqueradings and disguisings, effect of which Edgar more than most had in the past days been made to feel the force, to induce in us wavering uncertainties, unstable though golden as the reflexion of sun on running water, concerning the reality, not merely of other people (which we continually suspect without being able finally to disprove) but of ourselves also, and even of life and the world itself; so that Edgar, not absolutely assured to what degree, in playing the fool over so prolonged a period, he had in fact been a fool, or whether, as his grandmother long ago told him it might, the momentary grimace had frozen and become the habitual expression of his face, felt in his own words, without at this time being able to solve the riddle of their meaning, a flickering illumination, fluid and dark as are said to be the waters of Acheron or Styx, lighted by the fires of hell, upon his own character. As he dragged from the field the old lord, whose infirmities gave him something of the look of a drunken person who has disgraced himself at a house to which he will never again be permitted to go, he reflected that the Duke, who had always been remarkable rather for the greatness of his name and the depth to which it could be traced in tradition than for any particular power of intellect or, indeed, perception, would very probably reply by some trivial but fashionable phrase indicative simultaneously of boredom and agreement, such as "very likely", or "that's true", and Edgar's satisfaction at having more or less exactly anticipated this rejoinder, when it at last came, for the moment quite obscured his sense of the larger disaster to which they were a party. So it is, however, with each one of us; the momentary sense of superiority inspired in us by our own wit, however slight, makes bearable (though not, it is true, palatable) the most tragic defeat, by the same process of reasoning as that which makes the bankrupt, giving a dinner for his creditors, take care that the food should be particularly exquisite on this occasion in the course of which he hopes to mitigate the shame of his failure by what will perhaps pass among people of fashion as a courageous wit.

—Howard Nemerov

SOMERSET MAUGHAM
(1874-1965)

From Pussy Pictures

It was just before the war. I was working in the garden at Cap
Ferrat on the stories in *The Mixture As Before*. Beverley, who
was understandably a little nervous about the effect of sunlight
on his peaches-and-cream complexion, had chosen to work
indoors. He too was engaged upon a task that stretched his
creative powers to their uttermost—the compilation of his
Annual Cat Calendar. I finished the first draft of "The Three
Fat Women of Antibes"—a deliciously adroit tale, although I
say it myself—and wandered contentedly indoors.

"Martini time, Beverley," I said, poking my head into his
room.

The poor dear was enisled by literally hundreds of full-plate
pussy-pictures. He had to choose 12, garlanding each with a
paragraph of his inimitably breathless prose. Most of them
were calculatedly endearing, but there was also one of an
alley-cat—scarred, predatory, malignant.

Beverley held it up. "I think I shall call this one Gerald," he
said, with a feline smirk.

I mixed him a really *filthy* cocktail.

—*Martin Fagg*

GERTRUDE STEIN
(1874-1946)

Gertrude Stein

Oh, oh dog biscuit. And when he is happy he doesn't get snappy. Please please to do this. Then Henry, Henry, Frankie, you didn't meet him. You didn't even meet me. The glove will fit, what I say. Oh! Kai-Yi, Kai-Yi. Sure, who cares when you are through? How do you know this? Well then, oh cocoa know, thinks he is a grandpa again. He is jumping around. No hoboe and phoboe I think he means the same thing. . . . Oh mamma I can't go on through with it. Please oh! And then he clips me. Come on. Cut that out. We don't owe a nickel. Hold it instead hold it against him. . . . How many good ones and how many bad ones? Please I had nothing with him. He was a cowboy in one of the seven days a week fights. No business no hangout no friends nothing. Just what you pick up and what you need. . . . This is a habit I get. Sometimes I give it up and sometimes I don't. . . . The sidewalk was in trouble and the bears were in trouble and I broke it up. Please put me in that room. Please keep him in control. . . . Please mother don't tear don't rip. That is something that shouldn't be spoken about. Please get me up, my friends, please look out, the shooting is a bit wild and that kind of shooting saved a man's life. . . . Please mother you pick me up now. Do you know me? No, you don't scare me. They are Englishmen and they are a type I don't know who is best they or us. Oh sir get the doll a roofing. You can play jacks and girls do that with a soft ball and play tricks with it. No no and it is no. It is confused and it says no. A boy has never wept nor dashed a thousand kim. And you hear me? . . . All right look out look out. Oh my memory is all gone. A work relief. Police. Who gets it? I don't know and I don't want to know but look out. It can be traced. He changed for the worst. Please look out. My fortunes have changed and come back and went back since that. . . . They dyed my shoes. Open those shoes. . . . Police mamma Helen mother please take me out. I will settle the indictment. Come on open the soap duckets. The chimney sweeps. Talk to the sword. Shut up you got a big mouth! Please help me get up. Henry Max come over here. French Canadian bean soup. I want to pay. Let them leave me alone.

—Arthur Flegenheimer[1]

[1]Alias "Dutch Schultz," who in the early thirties was the most powerful racketeer and bootlegger in New York City. The above are some of his dying words after he was shot, with three others of his gang, in a Newark bar on October 23, 1935. They were taken down in the city hospital by F. J. Long, stenographer of the Newark Police Department, and were later printed in *Gang Rule in New York*, by Craig Thompson and Allen Raymond (Dial Press, 1940).

ZANE GREY
(1875-1939)

The Lone Rider Of Tarnation Gulch
(The Cowboy Story)

"Put 'em up, thar!"

The crisp command rang out above the tinny rattle of the cheap piano in "Ye Olde Lavender Kettle" Saloon, and forty pairs of hands shot into the air, with a deafening report.

Forty pairs of eyes watched the masked stranger in the doorway.

"Drap them thar shootin' irons," continued the even voice, sighting down the cold muzzle of his gun, "or I'll empty the contents of this magazine (*adv.*)." And by his tone the dissolute crowd of cattle-rustlers knew that he meant what he said.

"What you want of us-all, pardner?" whined Saunders.

"I come fer Prairie Rose," the stranger replied, "her with a voice like a nightingale, whut come out o' nowhere to warm our hearts with song—Gawd bless 'er."

The beaded curtains parted, and the beautiful dancer stared at the bearded stranger in wide-eyed surprise. Gently he reached down inside his dust-stained shirt and drew forth a tiny locket on a gold chain.

"Mother," said the stranger simply.

—*Corey Ford*

SHERWOOD ANDERSON
(1876-1941)

Hello Yourself, Sherwood

DISCORD: A STORY

It was dark. He was coming home alone. The man was coming home alone.

He came to the door of his home, 67 South Hickory Street, and he took out his key. Such a time. He could not find the lock. That is, he could not find *which* lock. There were between one hundred and seventy-five and two hundred locks on that door. You know how it was. Besides, he had the wrong key anyway.

He knocked at the door.

He said: "Oh, Ethel dear."

His wife, Mrs. Stoops, opened the door. "Llewellyn!"

Years of bitterness welled up within her. Years of struggle. Years of pain. No, tears of pain. Tears of pain and bitterness. Why had he stayed so late? Where had he been? "Where have you been?" "Nowheres, m'dear." "Oh, yeah?"

Years of desertion. That time he was playing the swell blonde, for example. Sometimes he didn't come home for a week at a time. Said he was working at the office. "I've been working late at the office, dear, and I won't get home to-night." Sure, sure. A likely story. She thought of that, too.

"Let me in, dearest."

He had been drinking. She could smell his breath. Suddenly she hated him. Her fist swings out. She hits him.

Then they go inside.

God knows, God knows.

SARAH BLEEPLEY'S LOVERS: A STORY

She was only the town milliner.

She was plain, nay, ugly. Her hair was stringy. Her shoes sagged at the heels. She had no appeal for men.

But men came. Night after night men came to visit her house. There was a different man almost every night. There was the town banker last Thursday. Yesterday there was the minister.

What do they see in Sarah? neighbors asked.

Her dining-room window is on a level with the street. Once she forgot to lower the shade. She was sitting in the lap of the local grocer, in her chemise, with her arms around his neck. He was kissing her.

Is this the Sarah we know? people asked. They wondered what her secret was.

"Sarah, I love you," said the grocer. He had forgotten his wife, his children, his home. She had charmed him like a Lorelei. "I love you not for your charm, not for your beauty, God knows. I love you because——"

People stood on tiptoe.

Then he noticed that the shade was up, and he pulled it down. No one knows why the town grocer loves the milliner. It is just life.

—Corey Ford

WILLA CATHER
(1876-1947)

A Call on Mrs. Forrester

I dropped off a Burlington train at Sweet Water one afternoon last fall to call on Marian Forrester. It was a lovely day. October stained the hills with quiet gold and russet, and scarlet as violent as the blood spilled not far away so many years ago along the banks of the Little Big Horn. It had been just such a day as this when I was last in Sweet Water, fifteen years before, but the glory of the earth affected me more sharply now than it had when I was midway through my confident thirties. October weather, once a plentiful wine, had become a rare and precious brandy and I took my time savoring it as I walked out of the town toward the Forrester house. Sweet Water has changed greatly since the days when Frank Ellinger stepped down from the Burlington and everybody in the place knew about it. The town is large and wealthy now and, it seemed to me, vulgar and preoccupied. I was afflicted with a sense of having come into the presence of an old uncle, declining in the increase of his fortune, who no longer bothered to identify his visitors. It was a relief to leave the town behind, but as I approached the Forrester house I felt that the lines of my face were set in grave resolution rather than in high anticipation. It was all so different from the free, lost time of the lovely lady's "bright occasions" that I found myself making a little involuntary gesture with my hand, like one who wipes the tarnish from a silver spoon, searching for a fine, forgotten monogram.

I first met Marian Forrester when I was twenty-seven, and then again when I was thirty-six. It is my vanity to believe that Mrs. Forrester had no stauncher admirer, no more studious appreciator. I took not only her smallest foible but her largest sin in my stride; I was as fascinated by the glitter of her flaws as by the glow of her perfections, if, indeed, I could tell one radiance from the other. There was never anything reprehensible to me in the lady's ardent adventures, and even in her awfulest attachment I persisted in seeing only the further flowering of a unique and privileged spirit. As I neared her home, I remembered a dozen florid charities I had invented to cover her multitude of frailties: her dependence on money and position, her admiration of an aristocracy half false and half imaginary, her lack of any security inside herself, her easy loneliness. It was no use, I was fond of telling myself, to look for the qualities of the common and wholesome morning glory in the strange and wanton Nicotiana. From the darkest earth, I would add, springs ever the sweetest rose. A green isle in the sea, if it has the sparkling fountain, needs not the solemn shrine, and so forth and so on.

I had built the lady up very high, as you see. I had commanded myself to believe that emotional literacy, a lively spirit, and personal grace, so rarely joined in American females, particularly those who live between Omaha and Denver, were all the raiment a lady needed. As I crossed the bridge, with the Forrester house now in full view, I had, all of a sudden, a disturbing fancy. There flashed into my consciousness a vivid vision of the pretty lady, seated at her dressing table, practicing in secrecy her little arts, making her famous earrings gleam with small, studied turnings of her head, revealing her teeth for a moment in a brief, mocking smile, and unhappiest picture of all, rehearsing her wonderful laughter.

I stopped on the bridge and leaned against the rail and felt old and tired. Black clouds had come up, obscuring the sun, and they seemed to take the mushroom shape of atomic dust, threatening all frail and ancient satisfactions. It began to rain.

I wondered what I would say to Marian Forrester if she appeared at the door in one of her famous, familiar postures—*en déshabillé*, her hair down her back, a brush in her hand, her face raised in warm, anachronistic gaiety. I tried to remember what we had ever talked about, and could think only of the dreadful topic of grasping women and eligible men. We had never discussed any book that I could recall, and she had never mentioned music. I had another of my ungallant fancies—a vision of the lovely lady at a concert in the town, sitting with bright eye and deaf ear, displaying a new bonnet and gown, striving, less subtly than of old, to capture the attention of worried and oblivious gentlemen. I recalled with sharp clarity a gown and bonnet she had once worn, but for the life of me I could not put a face between them. I caught the twinkle of earrings, and that was all.

The latest newspaper lying open on a chair, a note stuck in a milk bottle on the back porch, are enough to indicate the pulse of a living house, but there would not even be these faint signs of today and tomorrow in Marian Forrester's house, only the fibrillation of a yesterday that had died but would not stay dead. There would be an old copy of *Ainslee's* on the floor somewhere, a glitter of glass under a broken windowpane, springs leaking from a ruptured sofa, a cobweb in a chandelier, a dusty etching of Notre Dame unevenly hung on the wall, and a stopped clock on the marble mantel above a cold fireplace. I could see the brandy bottle, too, on a stained table, wearing its cork drunkenly.

Just to the left of the front door, the big hall closet would be filled with relics of the turn of the century—the canes and guns of Captain Forrester, a crokinole board, a diavolo, a frivolous parasol, a collection of McKinley campaign buttons, a broken stereopticon, a table-tennis net, a toppled stack of blue poker chips and a scatter of playing cards, a wood-burning set, and one of those large, white, artificial Easter eggs you put to your eye and, squinting into it, behold the light that never was, in a frosty fairyland. There would be a crack in the crusty shell, and common daylight would violate the sanctuary of the yellowed and tottery angels. You could find, in all the litter, as measuring sticks of calamity, nothing longer than an envelope firmly addressed in a gentleman's hand, a cancelled check, a stern notice from the bank.

The shade of one upstairs window was pulled all the way down, and it suddenly had the effect of making the house appear to wink, as if it were about to whisper, out of the corner of its door, some piece of scandal. If I went in, I might be embarrassed by the ungainly sounds of someone moving about upstairs after the lady had descended, sounds that she would cover by riffling nervously through a dozen frilly seasons of her faded past, trying, a little shrilly, to place me among the beaux in some half-remembered ballroom. I was afraid, too, that I might encounter in some dim and dusty mirror a young man frowning disapproval of an older self come to make a judgment on a poor lady not for her sake and salvation but, in some strange way, for his own. And what if she brought out, in the ruins of her famous laughter, what was left of the old disdain, and fixed me shrewdly for what I was, a frightened penitent, come to claim and take away and burn the old praises he had given her? I wouldn't succeed, of course, standing there in my unbecoming middle years, foolishly clutching reasons and arguments like a shopper's husband loaded down with bundles. She would gaily accuse me of being in love with another and, with the ghost of one of her poses of charming bewilderment, would claim a forfeit for my cruelty and insist that I sit down and have a brandy. I would have one—or several—and in the face of my suspicions of the presence of a man upstairs, my surrender would compromise the delicacy of my original cool intentions, and the lost individual would be, once again, as always in this house, myself. I wondered, standing there in the rain, how it would all come out.

She would get the other lady's name out of me easily enough when the brandy began to ebb in the bottle, and, being Marian Forrester, for whom jealousy was as simple as a reflex, she would be jealous of the imaginary relations of a man she could not place, with a woman she had never heard of. I would then confess my love for Mme. de Vionnet, the lady of the lilacs, of Gloriani's bright Sunday garden, of the stately house in the Boulevard Malesherbes, with its cool parlor and dark medallions. I would rise no doubt to the seedy grandiloquence of which I am capable when the cognac is flowing, and I could hear her pitiless comment. "One of those women who have something to *give*, for heaven's sake!" she would say. "One of those women who save men, a female whose abandon might possibly tiptoe to the point of tousling her lover's hair, a woman who at the first alarm of a true embrace would telephone the gendarmes." "Stop it!" I heard myself shout there in the rain. "I beg you to remember it was once said of Mme. de Vionnet that when she touched a thing, the ugliness, God knows how, went out of it." "How sweet!" I could hear Mrs. Forrester go on. "And yet, according to you, she lost her lover, for all her charm, and to a snippet of an applecheek from New England. Did the ugliness go out of *that*? And if it did, what did the poor lady do with all the prettiness?"

As I stood there in the darkening afternoon, getting soaked, I realized sharply that in my fantasy I had actually been handing Marian Forrester stones to throw at the house in Paris, and the confusion in my viewpoint of the two ladies, if up to that moment I had had a viewpoint, overwhelmed me. I figured what would happen as the shadows deepened in the Forrester house, and we drank what was left of the brandy out of ordinary tumblers—the *ballons* of the great days would long since have been shattered. Banter would take on the sharp edge of wrangling, and in the end she would stand above me, maintaining a reedy balance, and denounce the lady of the lilacs in the flat terms she had overheard gentlemen use so long ago over their cigars and coffee in the library. I would set my glass down on the sticky arm of the chair and get up and stalk out into the hall. But though she had the last word, she would not let me have the last silence, the gesture in conclusion. She would follow me to the door. In her house, by an ancient rule, Marian Forrester always had the final moment—standing on the threshold, her face lifted, her eyes shining, her hand raised to wave goodby. Yes, she would follow me to the door, and in the hall—I could see it so clearly I shivered there on the bridge—something wonderful would happen. With the faintest of smiles and the slightest of murmurs, I would bow to my hostess, open the door, and walk not out into the rain but into that damn closet, with its junk and clutter, smashing the Easter egg with my shoe, becoming tangled in the table-tennis net, and holding in my hand, when I regained my balance, that comic parasol. Mme. de Vionnet would ignore such a calamity; she would pretend not to see it, on the ground that a hostess is blind—a convention that can leave a man sitting at table with an omelet in his lap, unable to mention it, forced to go on with the conversation. But Marian would laugh, the lost laugh of the bright occasions, of the day of her shameless passion in the snow, and it would light the house like candles, reducing the sounds upstairs, in some miraculous way, to what they really were, the innocent creaking of the old floor boards. "What's all this about saving men?" I would cry. "Look who's talking!" And, still holding the parasol, I would kiss her on the cheek, mumble something about coming back some day, and leave, this time by the right door, finding, as I went to rejoin myself at the bridge, a poker chip in the cuff of my trousers.

It seems like a long time ago, my call on Mrs. Forrester. I have never been back. I didn't even send her a valentine last February. But I did send a pretty book of impeccable verses to Mme. de Vionnet, writing in the inscription something polite and nostalgic about *"ta voix dans le Bois de Boulogne."* I did this, I suppose, out of some obscure guilt sense—these things are never very clear to any man, if the truth were told. I think the mental process goes like this, though. Drinking brandy out of a water glass in the amiable company of a lady who uses spirits for anodyne and not amenity, a timid gentleman promises his subconscious to make up for it later on by taking a single Malaga before *déjeuner à midi* with a fastidious lady, toying with aspic, discussing Thornton Wilder, praising the silverpoint in the hall on the way out, and going home to lie down, exhausted but somehow purified.

I will carry lilacs, one of these summers, to the house on the Boulevard Malesherbes, and take Mme. de Vionnet to a matinée of "Louise," have a white port with her at one of the little terraces at the quietest corner of the Parc Monceau, and drop her at the door well before the bold moon has begun to wink at the modest twilight. Since, in the best Henry James tradition, I will get nothing out of this for myself, it ought to make up for something. I could do worse than spend my last summers serenely, sipping wine, clop-clopping around town, listening to good music, kissing a lady's hand at her door, going to bed early and getting a good night's sleep. A man's a fool who walks in the rain, drinks too much brandy, risks his neck floundering around in an untidy closet. Besides, if you miss the six-fifteen, the eastbound Burlington that has a rendez-vous with dusk in Sweet Water every day except Sundays and holidays, you have to wait till midnight for the next train east. A man could catch his death, dozing there in that cold and lonesome station.

—James Thurber

HERMANN HESSE
(1877-1962)

Sad Arthur

Go Hesse, Young Man

One morning, Sad Arthur, the banker's son, rose and garbed himself. Softly and lovingly the bedroom Mazdas bathed him as, supple-limbed, he drew on the new costume of his decision. Over his baggy BVD gaiters Sad Arthur put on his resplendent Belstaff Riding Suit with its storm-proof pockets, storm-cuff sleeves, heavy-duty zipper, snapdown pockets, and buckled mandarin-style collar. Sad Arthur bent and stepped into his Beau Geste Rough Rider boots with full-zippered backs, adjustable heel and instep straps, and imbedded front-and-back steel friction plates. Sad Arthur pulled on his Leathertogs genuine-leather jacket with transverse zipper and heavy-duty wrist snaps, and strapped on his stud wristbands and seven-inch stud belt. Delicately Sad Arthur balanced his yellow Foster Grants above his lofty brow and then picked up his flocked fuchsia Fury Helmet. Sad Arthur's mirror, which loved him unquenchably, watched in sad surprise as Sad Arthur left the bedroom forever. Then the mirror fell into a reflective mood, wondering once again how it had ever lost Altman's.

Sad Arthur entered the veranda and stood behind the chair where his father, the banker, was catching a few z's. The good banker, who that week had taken a bath in Leasco, was having a troubled dream about unholy ablutions. In time, he awoke, aware of the presence of leather. "Is that you, Sad Arthur?" he said.

Sad Arthur remained silent, his arms folded. Long ago, he had learned the lesson of the closed yap, the magic of the monosyllable. In the sullen, downward-hanging head, the lidded eye, the unheeding ear, there lay invulnerable peace. There was strange power in this youthful demeanor that willed nothing. Faced with it, the others—the teachers and talkers —became irritated, then flustered, then enraged, then placating, then suppliant. Like a flock of bees, they gave up their golden treasure to him who merely seemed to doze by the hive.

So Sad Arthur stood unmoving. Sunbeams meditated in the unshorn locks on his neck.

"What is it already?" the banker demanded. "Come around here where I can see you." He sighed. "No—on second thought, don't."

"You know what is in my mind," Sad Arthur said at last. "I would leave home and join the Holy Terrors. Like."

"I don't get it," confessed the good banker. "My son the bike freak."

"With the Holy Terrors I will make Vegas," Sad Arthur said. "I wish to attain Nevada."

The banker fell silent. In his secret heart he, too, had seen himself joyful at Vegas, strolling The Sands. Several hours passed in silence, like skipped pages in a meaty volume. In time, the banker gave a start, opened his eyes, yawned, and rose from his chair. "Let me know if you attain Nevada," he said to his son. "Call us collect." He could deny nothing to this young man. Like the Mazdas and the mirror and the sunbeams, like everything and everybody, he loved Sad Arthur, though often it was hard to know why.

Sad Arthur left his home. Near the garage, his faithful companion Irving was waiting with the bikes.

"You have come," Irving said.

"I have come," said Sad Arthur, smiling.

"He was faked out," Irving said.

"He was faked out," said Sad Arthur.

"We can split," Irving said.

"We can split," said Sad Arthur.

They split.

Wandering westward, Sad Arthur and Irving found the Holy Terrors in a blighted grove near Leonia, N.J. They recognized the leader of the band, the fabled Guttheimer, and drew near. This good buddy was known for his teachings and his freaky vines. His ancient bombardier's jacket was encrusted with many a graffitic virtu and many a mottoed malediction, now all faded by wind and dust, that depicted the pain and suffering of the pilgrim's way. The Illustrated One, at ease astride his ancient Harley two-stroke banger, listened to Sad Arthur's and Irving's joyful plea to get their heads together as novitiates in the Holy Terrors, heard their deep desire to attain Nevada. He subjected them to certain rites and then, well pleased, grunted the wished-for grant. Sad Arthur and Irving were Holy Terrors at last!

Happy among brothers, boot to boot with these heavy-footed disciples and their Old Ladies, Sad Arthur wandered westward (and sometimes eastward and ditchward) on the ancient paths of Jersey. Together, the Holy Terrors bombed Bogota, deafened Dumont, horrified Hoboken, outraged Oradell, paralyzed Palisades Park, piqued Parsippany, ravaged Rahway, and were busted in Boonton. Here, within a rustic slammer, Sad Arthur drew near Guttheimer and spoke what was in his mind.

Sad Arthur said: "Hear me, O Illustrated One, for I am, you know, like troubled. I have heard your teachings and learned much. You show the world unbroken, like a well-lubed chain. From you I have learned the Eightfold Path to hop a Honda 90cc SL to a sassy quarter in thirteen with a stroker kit, trochoid pump, overboring, and velocity stacks. From you I have learned the Fivefold Path to dirty up a square Moto Guzzi 750cc Ambassador by means of laid-on chromed riser bars, extended forks, sissy bar, and STP decals. From you I have learned the Fourteenfold Path to cowboy-roll a joint while drafting on a downhill Greyhound at eighty per. All this have I learned, O Good Buddy, yet what do I see? I see this band still mucking about here in upper Jersey, no nearer Vegas than the day I fell in. So what are teachings, what is knowledge, what are dead eardrums and dropped kidneys if they do not take me to Nevada? Are you not, then, the same as my father the good banker, a mere workahubby?"

The Illustrated One's eyes were lowered, his furred mouth set in an unfathomable half-smile of understanding. He was stoned. "You are some punkins, O Sad Arthur," he said. "You are a real smart-ass. I would enlighten you with still another lesson, the Onefold Path to a bust in the mouth, only right now I gotta crash."

The next morning, Sad Arthur took his leave of the pokey. He bade farewell to the Holy Terrors. He bade farewell to the faithful Irving, who was crying. Alone, he wandered westward on his Kawasaki Three. He saw many things. He saw a small boy at a Carvel stand who had dripped chocolate ripple all over his mother's handbag. He saw a man in madras Bermudas who had just been bilked by a used-lawnmower salesman. He saw a young opossum that had just been mashed by a teen-ager in a magenta Corvette. He saw a drunken housewife weeping in front of her Sylvania color console. He saw an elderly pastor playing miniature golf in a black hairpiece. He saw a Fruehauf twelve-wheel rig lying on its side, with its cargo of disposable diapers scattered across the highway. The world was beautiful when seen this way—alone and without questions or meaning. It was beautiful to go through the world like this in childlike cool. The Illustrated One was right, Sad Arthur thought. Sad Arthur, you are some punkins.

In a sun-dappled launderette in Nutley, N.J., but a short distance from the holy ruins of the Nutley Velodrome, Sad Arthur encountered the fair Lambie, whose lips were like unto a melting Tootsie Roll. At one sight of her, he plugged in his Fender and, without thought or further ado, sang this song:

"For love of the fair Lambie,
The pilgrim Sad Arthur,
Sad Arthur the erstwhile Terror,
The fabled rubber-layer,
Would forget Nevada
And stay
Here in Nutley Enn Jayyy!"

"O Sad Arthur, how marvie!" cried the entranced Lambie.
"Yes," said Sad Arthur without unbecoming modesty. "Please note the rhyme."
"O Sad Arthur, c'mere." She drew him to her, placing one heel on his instep and one hand on his ear in the position of love that is known as "Opening the Deck Chair." Then she kissed him with her lips that were like unto a melting Tootsie Roll.

Thus it was that Sad Arthur put away his boots and helmet, put away Nevada, put away his dreams and his Kawasaki to stay in Nutley and groove with the fair Lambie. He cut his hair and went to work for Lambie's father, a merchant, the owner of the Nutley Kwik Kleen Dry Cleaners. He went among the people and took on the people's way. With Lambie, he bought six-packs and electric back-yard rotisseries, he wore His-'n-Hers flowered at-home jams, he joined the Thursday Evening

Swingin' Couples League at Nutley Bowlorama. Lambie's father was pleased with him and said, "You have learned much from me, Sad Arthur."

"No," said Sad Arthur. "All that I have learned I have taught myself. I have learned to deliver a suit on Friday that was promised for Wednesday. I have learned to deliver size forty-two pants to the size thirty-four next door. I have learned to mislay ladies' dress belts, to anneal zippers, and to loosen buttons so that they will pop off upon being buttoned. I have learned to starch alpaca sweaters and imprint indelible rust stains on dress evening shirts. Most of all, I have learned the imperious Brahmin's manner that elicits abject thanks and excessive tips. Thus do I add injury and interest to the lives of these sad schnooks. It is you, rather, who have learned from me."

Lambie's father looked on Sad Arthur with admiration and surprise. "The mouth, O Sad Arthur," he said. "That mouth will get bust wide open one of these days."

Sad Arthur saw that it was time for him to resume his questing. The merchant's message, so like the parting words of Guttheimer, told him that he had come full circle. He had learned the people's ways, their business and their pleasures, and now his soul was sickened, as the soul of one who has played thrice at tick-tack-toe. He went to the fair Lambie and imparted unto her what he had decided.

"O no, Sad Arthur!" cried the fair Lambie. She placed her elbow in his abdomen and her knee against his back, in the position that is known as "Putting Away the Ironing Board," but he pushed her rudely aside.

"Tough darts, Lambie," Sad Arthur said. "It's Nevada for me. Bye now."

Why did her lips, curved in sorrow, remind him of a Cat's Paw heel?

Sad Arthur turned westward once more. On foot now, he wandered with thumb lifted; riding with any who heeded his disdainful summons. Riding silent in high cab beside some trusting trucker, Sad Arthur smiled and commended himself for having put aside still more knowledge, more habits, more mere humans. Within his stomach he felt the tiny gerbil of his Self stirring once again, heard it remount its squeaky little wheel.

Closer to Vegas at last, Sad Arthur alighted on the north bank of the great Pennsylvania Pike, and here took employment as night pumper in a modest Amoco station. Wearing the plain blue coveralls and friendly smile of his humble calling, he dispensed the golden fluid, wiped clean the insect-speckled windshield, kept track of the ladies'-room key with its giant tag. At night, between customers, he tilted back in his chair and listened to the highway. He knew he should resume his journey, should seek Nevada, yet it seemed to him that this highway had something to tell him. He felt a deep love for these broad humming lanes with their upping and downing, their easting and westing, their freight of fumes and destinations, and he sat and stayed and listened.

Years passed, and so it was at last that an ochre Caddy stopped at Sad Arthur's modest Amoco station and yielded up a bald old gent with low back pains and a large cigar. Sad Arthur looked on him and smiled.

"Sad Arthur!" cried the old gent. "Is that you? Are you here, only here? And all this time I imagined you at Nevada!"

"Yes," said Sad Arthur. "It is I, my old friend. Only I."

"What a gas!" cried the faithful Irving (for it was he), and then he laughed at his own foolish wit. "So neither of us made it to Vegas, eh? What a pair of losers!"

"Listen, my friend," said Sad Arthur, and he took Irving by the arm and led him closer to the highway's edge. "Listen to me, for I have learned the secret. The highway has taught me all. At one end of this highway, back beyond its beginning, is my father, the good banker. There too are the Illustrated One, the fair Lambie, the overturned diaper truck, my rusted old Kawasaki, and the lost size forty-two pants. At the other, beyond its ending and yet part of it as well, lies Nevada. At the same time, right now, they are all part of this highway, all one. This highway is everywhere at the same moment—the toll-taker and the toll-payer, the patient concrete and the headlong tire, the descendant swallow-dropping and the approaching open convertible, the totalled Pontiac and the greedy wrecker, the full box of Goobers on the dashboard and the emptied box of Goobers in the weeds by the roadside. This highway is the beginning and the ending, the cool and the uncool, learning and forgetting, the book revered and the book flung halfway across the room. There is no truth, no knowing, no wisdom, no Nevada, no nothing except, uh—well, simultanuity, like. So relax."

"Gosh, Sad Arthur," said Irving, "I never thought of it that way." He looked at his watch. "Well, Artie," he said hastily, "this has been real. Any time you're near Hasbrouck Heights—"

But again Sad Arthur drew him closer to the highway's edge. "Listen, faithful Irving," Sad Arthur said. "Listen to the highway. What does it say to you?"

"Well," said Irving after a while, "it sort of says 'Zoom!'"

"Yes," said Sad Arthur. He lifted his head in wonder. "Zoom!" he repeated. "Zoom-*zoom*!"

—*Roger Angell*

E.M. FORSTER
(1879-1970)

From The Mallomar Caves

'What is that?'

'It is I. It is only Aziz. Do not be afraid.'

'I meant the noise.'

'It is only an echo, Miss Quested. Nothing to worry about I assure you. Ah! Excuse me. I hope I have caused you no embarrassment?'

'What a funny way of putting it! I think the strap's broken, that's all.'

'The stone is so slippery. It is treacherous. May I assist you?'

'Oh, Aziz!'

'Merciful Heavens! What would the City Magistrate think?'

'Who's going to tell him? Don't worry. This must be the first really private spot I've found in India. Why are you giggling?'

'I am thinking of dear Mr. Fielding's face if he knew.'

'I like dark hairy men. You can call me Adela if you like.'

'Oh, Miss Quested—Adela... This is beyond the dreams of a humble Indian doctor like myself... To be in the arms of a beautiful English lady. I am dreaming.'

'Kiss me and see. Aren't I real? What's the matter?'

'Ah, what is real? I have a confession. I lied to you at the entrance. My wife is dead.'

'Silly! Ronny told me that days ago. You must be feeling very frustrated.'

—T. Griffiths

DAMON RUNYON
(1884-1946)

The Fable Of The Hare And The Tortoise

It happens I am around Joe's place and how I come to be around Joe's place is this way. There is a guy called Harry the Hare known to all and sundry as the fastest runner on Broadway on account of how he has done nothing but run from the cops since he was a kid in short pants. Now Harry the Hare is to race three times round the block against a guy called Tommy the Tortoise. So Joe's place is filled with guys and dolls anxious to place money on Harry, and maybe it is good business for Joe, and maybe it isn't as nobody who is wise to Joe's whisky will have any part of it, and most of Broadway is wise to Joe's whisky these days. Harry the Hare is drinking lime juice for training, but I get straight to the bar and slip a century on Tommy at twenty to one. Well, Harry gets away to a flying start, but in the second lap he gives a little moan and drops to the ground, and before the guys with money at stake can help him up Tommy has won. Upon which there is much argument, many citizens announcing their intention of laying into Harry the Hare more than somewhat for having sold them the old phonus bolonus. Personally I collect the two thousand smackers owing to me and disappear, saying nothing of how I have doped Harry's lime juice with Joe's whisky before the race.

—L. W. Bailey

P.G. WODEHOUSE
(1881-1975)

From Bertie and Emma

'I'm so unhappy,' Emma Bovary sighed, as she rested her head on Bertie's shoulder. 'I say, cheer up old thing,' he exhorted, patting her back with imprudent familiarity. He quivered as her warm flesh seared his trembling body. She raised her mouth towards his and Bertie snorted with undisguised passion. 'I'm not terribly good at this sort of rot,' he confided, before clamping his lips against her. 'Take me dearest,' she moaned helplessly. His knees buckled with excitement and he slithered to the carpet with Emma. Bertie closed his eyes discreetly as he glimpsed her bared shoulders, yet held on with the resolution of an unmitigated bounder. 'Now,' she insisted urgently. Bertie was engulfed by panic. 'Would you mind dreadfully if I phoned Jeeves?' he bleated.

—*Russell Lucas*

JAMES JOYCE
(1882-1941)

Early Morning Of A Motion-Picture Executive

. . . yes a quarter after what an unearthly hour I suppose they're just getting out on the lot at Fox now starlets combing out their hair for the day let me see if I can doze off 1 2 3 4 5 where was it in Jerrys memorandum yes oversimplify O I love great books Id love to have the whole of Hollywood filming nothing but great books God in heaven theres nothing like literature pre sold to the public the treatment and the working script by Dalton Trumbo and the finished picture in color and Todd A O as for them saying theres no audience interest in pictures based on great books I wouldnt give a snap of my two fingers for all their motivational research indie exhibs whatever they call themselves why dont they go out and make a picture I ask them and do a socko 21 Gs in Philly and a wow 41 in Chi ah that they cant answer yes in its purest form father searching for his son and son searching for his father chance for myriad boffolas there old man staggers out one door of pub where the beer and the boffola foam while kid goes in other O I love a good laugh Stephen Dedalus the intellectual we might try to get Paul Newman for the part hes a strong BO draw in Exodus certainly hed do very nicely too better soft pedal the egghead bit though make him a newspaper reporter have to shoot a lot of location stuff in Dublin by the waters of the Liffey by the rivering waters of we might fake it on the back lot and bring it in under three million or else knock up the budget and spot celebs the way Columbia did with Pepe it coined a huge fortyfive thou in its first week on Bway gives the property a touch of class I wonder could we get Bobby Darin on a percentage deal to sing Galway Bay I better have Sammy check in the morning where the hell Galway Bay is its somewhere around Dublin surely long color process shot of the bay at dusk cut to faces of old women in black shawls and the women in the uplands making hay speak a language that the strangers do not know a scene which it will knock them out of the back of the house in Terre Haute the alarmclock in the maids room clattering the brains out of itself better take another seconal and try to sleep again so as I can get up early Ill call a title conference at ten wait now who was it yes Kirk Douglas already made Ulysses the old story though this ones on three levels we might call it Pride Love and The Flesh that has a nice sound to it Ill have Sammy get ahold of Central Registry and see if the titles reserved Leopold Bloom the passive ill informed victim of habitual feelings problem on the religion bit though dont want Bnai Brith down on our necks well give him an Irish name in any case Leopold Malone and his loving wife Molly sensual carnal wholly natural she wheels her wheelbarrow through streets wide and narrow personally Id like to build the script around Molly and get Liz for the role so why am I after worrying we cant go wrong with Maureen OHara flashback to Gibraltar where she was a girl a flower of the mountain yes so are those bimbos all flowers of the mountain lap dissolve he kisses her under the Moorish wall we might send down a second unit to get some outdoor Gibraltar stuff cut in a flamenco dream sequence shoot it there and dub it on the soundtrack later yes chance for widescreen color background O the sea the sea there crimson sometimes like fire and the glorious sunsets and the figtrees in the Alameda gardens yes well have them bawling like goddam babies baaaawwaaaaaww at the world preem

ah well theres no talking around it were one of the smallest minorities in Hollywood nowadays us thinking that James Joyce Ulysses will be made into a superior movie TJ saying to me Harry youre one hundred per cent crazy him with his two dollar cigars and his Irving Thalberg award chasing those little chits of starlets and he not long married Mouth Almighty I call him and his squinty eyes of all the big stuppoe studio heads I ever met God help the world if everyone out here was like him yes always and ever making the same pictures showdownatshotguncreek whatever he calls the new one ah God send him more sense and me more money O he does look the fool sitting at the head of the conference table as big as you please he can go smother for all the fat head I care Im unabashedly intellectual and Ill make this movie or Im walking off the lot this day week Ive still got my integrity after all how long is it Ive been out here wait yes since 1923 O I love lying in bed God here we are as bad as ever after yes forty three years how many studios have I worked at RKO and Fox and Metro and Paramount where I was a young man and the day I talked to deMille when he was making the original of The Ten Commandments and yes he wouldnt answer at first only looked out over the set and the thousands of extras I was thinking of so many things he didnt know of yes how someday Id have my own swimming pool and go to Vilma Bankys parties and all the long years since Joan Crawford in Our Dancing Daughters and Richard Dix and yes the year Metro missed the boat on Dinner at Eight and Fred Astaire and Ginger Rogers and Asta rrrrrfffff rrrrrfffff and the andyhardy series and The Best Years of Our Lives and O all the Academy Award dinners yes Disney going about smug with his Oscars the Levant what year was it Gert and I took the cruise there I never miss his TV show and Rhonda Fleming with her hair all red and flaming and Sandra Dee and VistaVision and stereophonic sound cleaning up in the foreign market and Ben Hur and the night TJ asked me what my next project would be when was it yes the night they screened Psycho in Santa Monica eeeeeeeekkk its an Irish story I told him like The Quiet Man or shall we get Rock Hudson I was just thinking of it for the first time yes and I had Sammy give me a five page synopsis and the day in Romanoffs I asked Jerry Wald about it yes Ulysses by James Joyce which it is a highly controversial book and I asked him yes could out of it be created a picture as exciting as Peyton Place and yes he said yes it could yes but on a higher level Yes.

—*Thomas Meehan*

A. A. MILNE
(1882-1956)

From The Eeyore Gee

The first person he met was Rabbit.

"Hullo, Rabbit," said Pooh. "We're going to have an orgy with Christopher Robin."

"What is it when we're having it?"

"Something to eat, I hope," said Pooh. "Because Kanga said it would be a new Eggs Perients. She ate one before she found Roo and she says you ought to be very good at it."

"How can I be, if I've never eaten it before? It may taste Peculiar."

"Like honey, perhaps," said Pooh. "But there's to be a demonstration with Eeyore and Christopher Robin. Though I hope they'll leave enough for us."

"A demonstration?" said Rabbit. "Then we'll have to have banners. What shall we write on them?"

Pooh shook his head sadly. "I don't know," he said, "but we could ask Owl."

So off they went to find Owl.

—*Maude Gracechurch*

VIRGINIA WOOLF
(1882-1941)

From To The Lighthouse

As Mrs. Ramsay moved regally towards the sideboard, the crepuscular walls of her self-intimacy, most intense when she was thinking of Scott's novels and Balzac's novels, or of her friend Lily Briscoe's painting of her, clanged; and she knew that it would forever be so difficult to give him what he wanted—a testament of her love. She considered swimming to the lighthouse, her lower body encased in a slicker, for inducing comparisons, once her drowned self were found, with mermaids. She would be betraying her children, and the host of friends, some quite suicidal, who counted on basking forever in her effulgent charm. She smiled at herself in the mirror above the sideboard. Oh, how positively delicious the light up-turn of her lip! Her alabaster, plump forearms, turned as they were in the fashion of Madam X in the John Singer Sargent painting, were so attractive!

A small bi-plane flew past, bearing in its bosom the seeds of death. A wing nearly brushed the window, and she thought she saw Septimus Smith piloting the craft. What a booby! To fly so near the house. She was about to return the pilot's gesture of recognition when the plane nosed-down and buried itself nearly to the wings in the soft loam of the rose garden, where the gardener had been aerating the soil. "It is a triumph," thought Mrs. Ramsay, as the plane burst into flames. How could she tell the others what had happened, of this spectacle, as exquisite as the scent of olives and rose-oil and lime-juice, given to her alone by some enamored pagan god of death. No, though she had loved Mr. Ramsay, she would not destroy herself for him. She had not said it: yet he would know. She had triumphed. It was rich, tender, perfectly-perfectly cooked—the body, she meant, flame-seared, rushing away from the wrecked plane to a certain death in the rose garden. She was so glad to be alive, like a bird among cherries and raspberries, all the little rubbish of her charmed life. "My little strip of time," she thought, "lies still before me."

—Robert Peters

RING LARDNER
(1885-1933)

From The Young Immigrunts

Chapter 10

N. Y. To Grenitch 500.0

The lease said about my and my fathers trip from the Bureau of Manhattan to our new home the soonest mended. In some way ether I or he got balled up on the grand concorpse and the next thing you know we was thretning to swoop down on Pittsfield.

Are you lost daddy I arsked tenderly.

Shut up he explained.

At lenth we doubled on our tracks and done much better as we finley hit New Rochelle and puled up along side a policeman with falling archs.

What road do I take for Grenitch Conn quired my father with poping eyes.

Take the Boston post replid the policeman.

I have all ready subscribed to one out of town paper said my father and steped on the gas so we will leave the flat foot gaping after us like a prune fed calf and end this chapter.

Chapter 11

How It Ended

True to our promise we were at the station in Grenitch when the costly train puled in from 125 st. Myself and father hoped out of the lordly moter and helped the bulk of the famly off of the train and I aloud our nurse and my 3 brothers to kiss me tho Davids left me rarther moist.

Did you have a hard trip my father arsked to our nurse shyly.

Why no she replid with a slite stager.

She did too said my mother they all acted like little devils.

Did you get Davids milk she said turning on my father.

Why no does he like milk my father replid with a gastly smirk.

We got lost mudder I said brokenly.

We did not screened my father and accidently cracked me in the shins with a stray foot.

To change the subjeck I turned my tensions on my brother Jimmie who is nerest my age.

I've seen our house Jimmie I said brokenly I got here first.

Yes but I slept all night on a train and you didnt replid Jimmie with a dirty look.

Nether did you said my brother John to Jimmie you was awake all night.

Were awake said my mother.

Me and David was awake all night and crid said my brother John.

But I only crid once the whole time said my brother Jimmie.

But I didnt cry at all did I I arsked to my mother.

So she replid with a loud cough Bill was a very very good boy.

So now we will say fare well to the characters in this book.

—Ring Lardner

D. H. LAWRENCE
(1885-1930)

From Peanuts

The baseball mound!

And there stands Charlie Brown. A hotch-potch of yearnings for the little red-haired girl. But the game is a fulfilment. Baseball. The savage soul-conflict, gladiatorial, the *tlachti* of the Aztecs.

On his hand, a glove. One glove. It's an amputation. Why, even Wotan, giving up an eyeball, didn't make a sacrifice like that.

And Lucy, *She* lies in ecstasy against the piano, while Schneider batters away in an insanity of pure self-destruction. America. The piano is America and poor hopeless Schneider is trying to teach it Beethoven when all that will come is dissonances.

So Lucy sets up as a psychiatrist. The Doctor is In. She wants to forget Schneider and his queer mechanical outpourings. And all she gets is the poor sick soul of America, Charlie Brown, pining to be loved by the great cruel world.

—*John Dennis*

Schoolroom

Fricka Brandywine had suffered an horrendous morning in her classroom. Her collier-family charges, all foul-faced as they were, and uncouth in speech and manner, were entirely nonplussed when Hermione Starchworth entered the steamy room at ten o'clock, without warning, to instruct them (all by way of helping her dear friend Fricka) in the sexual behavior of catkins and flag flowers. In all her neurotic severity, wearing her mauve cloche hat and her mannish suit, in her deep male voice she had salivated as she separated the luscious, vaginal petals of the flag, thrusting her equine but noble nostrils deep into the blossom, emitting little oohs and ahs, stroking her own labial areas, quite oblivious of her own enormous needs. Snickers arose from a cluster of pimply boys, already themselves deep into puberty. "I got sumthin' 'ere for ye, madam," a brash voice said, startling Hermione out of her masturbatory reverie. "My dear! My dear!" she said, grabbing Fricka's shoulders. "I was carried off. I'm dreadfully sorry. I meant to be instructional." Without waiting for Fricka's response, she swept regally from the room, and disappeared towards a fogged-in lake a few hundred yards off.

Trying her best to pretend that nothing had happened, Fricka rapped with her ferule for order. Several minutes passed before the class quieted and returned to the solving of simple sums. The scent of nightshade hung in the air, mingled with the repellent odor of stale menstrual blood. "Oh," thought Fricka, "if only the world were less sexual." Unconsciously, she was drawn to the rear of the room, where she stood near a chunky, tall, black-haired youth who was chewing the nub of a pencil, entirely unable to solve his sums. Fricka's right thigh almost touched the lad's arm. Her flesh seemed to discharge racing electricity towards the boy's shoulder. He seemed jolted, pressed against the teacher's tweed-covered thigh, and suddenly thrust his face into her groin. "Mmmmmmm," he murmured. Fricka was unable to withdraw, and when a meaty hand ran up her skirt (she had forgotten to wear her undergarment that morning) she fell to the floor, quivering. In a moment, the young, blooded stallion was on top of her. As the other pupils crowded round, he threw off his pants and within seconds had inserted his tumescent organ deep between Fricka's thighs. Fricka endured scarlet waves of ecstasy, and imagined that she had been mounted by her father's polled bull. The youth's organ was long, hot, and sturdy. As Fricka reached orgasm, she felt that she was Leda, that the youth was Zeus in the guise of a swan. From his hot abundant sperm, which flashed and sizzled against her vaginal walls, she knew that either a god or a goddess would be born, the moment of conception witnessed and blessed by a host of pupil (tutelary angel) eyes.

—Robert Peters

SINCLAIR LEWIS
(1885-1951)

Shad Ampersand

A NOVEL OF TIME AND THE WRITER, TENTATIVELY
BASED ON 'CASS TIMBERLANE,' A NOVEL OF HUSBANDS
AND WIVES

Chapter I

The city of Grand Revenant, in High Hope County and the
sovereign state of Nostalgia, has a population of 34,567,
according to the official census taker, a vast and bumbling liar,
receiver of puny bribes and secret high acolyte of the poems of
Algernon Charles Swinburne.

Grand Revenant is 49.6 miles from Zenith and 99.2 from
Gopher Prairie.

It was founded in 1903, a year that also saw the birth, at
Kitty Hawk, N.C., of a strange boxlike contrivance that held
the bright seeds of death for Coventry and Nagasaki and other
proud cities half the world away.

Its pioneer settler was old Cornelius Ampersand, a
prodigious seducer of Indians along the thundering marge of
Lake Prolix and on the cold, improbable trails that lead from
Baedeker and Larousse to Mount Thesaurus. Corn was a He-
Man, a Wowser, a High Anointed Member of the Sacred and
Splendiferous Tribe of Good Scouts, and if his thin, despairing
wife often wept alone in the night, nobody knew—except
perhaps her two or three hundred closest friends.

In the years since old Corn raped his last squaw (and how
those golden girls would giggle in the dusk!), Grand Revenant
had grown like an angry weed in the fertile soil of the prairie.

Factories came—Wilson and Fadiman, who ravaged the
little firm-breasted hills for copper for moot points; Trilling
and Cowley, who made the smoothest, shiniest, most
astoundingly complicated little instruments for determining
tension and slack (it was hard to say what everybody did before
it was possible to determine slack to one-thousandth part of an
inch); Mencken & Nathan, who manufactured Hortex and
were said to have the seventh largest mangle in the state of
Nostalgia.

Stores were born—the Mad Mode Mart, Avis Cormorant, prop. (Miss Cormorant was a nymphomaniac and, very discreetly, a German spy, but her chic was the despair of her rival, Elsie Drear, who was a virgin and an Episcopalian); Blitberg's Department Store ("Nous l'Avons!"), which sold everything from needles to yachts, and if one or two salesgirls died each week from a strange and terrible disease called Dreiser's Botch, there was surely no kinder or merrier man in all Revenant than old Sam Blitberg; Dirge and Mouseman (Mrs. Mouseman, nee Birdie Jump, was that object of almost inconceivable grandeur, a former inmate of the Social Register), where you could buy, for very little more than it would cost to build supernal beauty or to stamp out Yaws, rare stones of devious and bloody history.

Other noble monuments—the Revenant Museum of Art, which boasted a Modigliani and a Dali and a whole roomful of Grant Woods, but which was chiefly notable for its swimming pool which was as deep and blue as a lake; Revenant Junior High School, which regularly and gratifyingly beat the upstart team from East Hemingway in the annual marathon, and if very few of her graduates could tell you who wrote "Thanatopsis" or even "Mantrap," they usually proved astonishingly nimble at selling not too aqueous real estate and beautifully shiny automobiles, which often ran quite well; and, always and most particularly, Mme. Moriarity's bowling parlors, where the nickering males of Revenant betook themselves for curious delights, which sometimes they even actually enjoyed.

Churches sprang up, to the glory of a Fat God, whose other names were Baal and Moloch and Ahriman and Samuel and Progress and Rugged Individualism.

Hotels and restaurants—the Revenant Inn, which travellers had been known to compare favorably with the glittering Bellevue-Stratford in Philadelphia, but at which there was no room for the Indians whose doomed camp-fires had once glowed where now its flying towers mocked the sky; Doung's Hotburger, where the cop on the beat, a cold and melancholy man, dropped in nightly to sigh: "Geez, you take my wife. A good woman, I guess, but no get-up-and go to her like some of these peppy society dames. And talk! Golly! One of these days maybe I'll have to shut the ole girl up." At six o'clock one bitter January morning, he did, very neatly and irrevocably, using the old .44 service revolver with which he had sworn to uphold the law; the Heyday Grille, where Doc Kennicott and George Babbitt and Sam Dodsworth and all the glorious he-male company of competent seducers (about once a year, Babbitt conducted a fumbling, inconclusive experiment with some derisive young woman in a canoe) and two-fisted drinkers (sometimes, uneasily, they had a cocktail before lunch) met every Friday to bumble cheerfully: "Well, I dunno what you other, uh, homo sapiensibuses think, but it strikes this not so humble observer that this lil ole burg is sure goin' straight to the twenty-three skiddoos." Solemnly, they agreed that Grand Revenant could not compare in splendor with Zenith and Gopher Prairie and Paris and New York; secretly they knew that she was strange and beautiful beyond all other cities of the earth.

Chapter II

Shad Ampersand, old Corn's grandson, lived in a neat $26,500 bungalow called Christmas Past, on Revenant Heights, overlooking the brisk, aspiring town. He was a tall, ramshackle, hayrick of a man of fifty-six, copper-red (a testimony, it was whispered, to old Corn's prowess with the squaws) and sad of eye, like a water spaniel or an early Donatello. An admirer of loneliness and rye whiskey and thin, hawk-vivid girls, who listened with vast politeness while he explained such recondite matters as Arbitrary Microcosm, Limited Frame of Reference, Elementary Symbolism, and Dated or Synthetic Idiom, about all of which they knew precisely nothing and most enthusiastically cared even less.

Sitting on his tiny porch on one of the brightest, briefest, and most poignant of all October afternoons, Shad was very weightily considering the profound mystery of Sex.

"I'm not one of these highbrow geezers like W. Somerset Maugham or John Q. Galsworthy," he pondered heavily, "and it sure gives me a pain in the old bazookus to hear some long-haired so-called intellectual claiming that love and marriage and kiddies and everything a dumb old roughneck like me has come to hold most sacred is nothing more nor less than something called the Biological Urge."

"Hey, you don't have to talk to *me* like that," said Trenda Boneside sharply. "I'm not the Pulitzer Prize Committee."

She was a small, fierce kitten of a girl, who lived for nineteen eager, sniffing years with her parents on a farm in Remnant, just across the state line.

"M? Nope. See what you mean," he said placatingly. She was a passionate white flame on a cigar-store lighter. He tried to imagine her cooking his breakfast. Tried and most conspicuously failed.

"No, you don't at all," she snapped at him, this brisk fox terrier of a girl. "You listen to me, Shad Ampersand. I'm not one of those old girls of yours—Carol or Leona or that awful Dodsworth woman, whatever *her* name was."

"Fran," he said humbly.

"Fran. Well, anyway. I'm not. Maybe that old hillbilly talk was all right for them, and even the *American Mercury*. But with me you can just talk like anybody else."

"M."

"That's another thing!" she cried furiously. "That 'M'! What the hell is that supposed to be? The name of a moving picture?"

"Gee, Tren," he sighed. "It's only an experiment in phonetics. You know, how to get something down the way it really sounds. As I was telling ole Doc Bongflap . . ."

Now she was really a tigress.

" 'Bongflap,' " she wailed. "I've known you for a long time, Shad Ampersand, and I've certainly heard some terrible names—Vergil Gunch and Roscoe Geake and Adelbert Shoop—but that's the worst ever. Nobody in the world was ever called Bongflap."

"Well, maybe not, but, drat it, when an author wants to suggest how a character . . ."

"I know all about that," she said, "and I know all about Charles Dickens, too, and you both make me sick. My God, even *Tarkington* wouldn't call anybody Bongflap. Or Timber*lane* either, for that matter. Timber*lane*. Timber*line*. Even Hansen and Chamberlain ought to be able to get that one, but I think it stinks. I keep thinking it's Tamberlane, or Timberleg."

"Aren't we getting a little off the subject, Tren?" he said mildly.

"I don't know. What *was* the subject?"

"Well, uh, love."

"Oh, *that*," she yawned. "What about it?"

"Well, uh," he fumbled. She was a laughing brook of a girl, cool, diamond-bright, a wanderer in secret loveliness. He dreamed of her in a gingham apron, cooking his breakfast. Golly! "Uh, I thought we might get married," he whinnied. It was so perhaps that Paris whispered to Helen before they came to the city of the Topless Towers, so the Roman gave his soul to Egypt's queen on the dreaming bosom of the Nile. She looked at him, and suddenly her heart was in her eyes.

"Shad!" she cried, and now she was a bell.

"Wife!" he clamored through their urgent kiss, and miraculously it was a word in nowise stained with use.

Chapter III

The little orange cat called Pox stretched langorously in Shad Ampersand's lap.

"I know you're lonely since your wife, Trenda, left you last November to join Blight Grimes, the polo player and nimble seducer at his hotel in Chicago, Illinois," she mewed. She was a very fetching device of a cat, an explanatory butler at curtain rise in a Lonsdale comedy.

Shad scratched her ears and thought: I should have known all along about Tren and Blight. The time they went away together for a week back in March and Trenda said—oh, she was very innocent and airy about it!—that they'd just gone up to Alaska to look at polo ponies; the time I found them upstairs in bed and they said they were just lying down because their feet hurt. I must have been pretty credulous, he decided, and Pox blinked her copper eyes in sardonic agreement.

"You're damn right," she purred, "but now, of course, she has delirium tremens and this Grimes character isn't exactly the kind of man you can picture running up and down stairs with paraldehyde and strait jackets. There's a strange streak of cruelty in him."

He nodded, but he was thinking despairingly: I must have failed her somehow. Maybe I was wrong to want to keep her here in Christmas Past pasting up scrapbooks for an old galoot like me—Blight, doggone his hide, was only forty-nine and lithe and puissant as a sword—when she ought to be running around with kids her own age, going to the movies and coming out with her head all full of stars and dreams (as a matter of fact, he knew she loathed the movies), having a soda with the gang at Bleeck's and feeding nickels into that juke box for "Smiles" and "Margie," maybe even being kissed, in sweet and childish innocence, in the back seat of a Chevrolet.

"Pope Hartford," said Pox, who was also a mind-reader.

"M?"

"Pope Hartford," repeated the cat irritably. "You might as well stick to the period. And while I think of it, you can lay off that 'M' with *me*, too."

Anyway, he had failed her, his lost and golden girl, and she was in Chicago with Blight. He looked at his watch. 11:46. Probably they were back from the theater now and up in their suite and Blight was slipping the little silver fox cape from her shoulders.

"His heart contracted," murmured Pox.

"M, uh, I mean what?"

"Don't keep making me say everything twice, for God's sake. 'His heart contracted.' That goes in somewhere. In parentheses. After the second 'and,' I should say. It's one of your mannerisms, though not a very fortunate one. Also you seem to have forgotten that she's on the sauce, if you'll pardon the expression."

Trenda spifflicated, swizzled, tiddly. He knew it was the truth, but the thought was a sharp agony, an unthinkable desecration, as if he saw the slender terrible beauty of the Samothrace deep in foul mud and marred with the droppings of obscene and dreadful birds.

"I think you're overreaching yourself there," said Pox. "Too many modifiers, and it's a pretty elaborate image. After all, you aren't Henry James."

"Golly, Pox—"

"Ah, the hell with it. Let it go. It's your stream of consciousness, thank God, not mine."

In his despair, his cold unutterable loss, Shad Ampersand began to think of all the world, and Pox looked at him sharply for a moment and then hopped off his lap and left the room.

Shad thought: Marriage. A man and a woman—him and Tren, Romeo and Juliet, Philemon and Baucis, Ruth and, and, drat it, who *was* that guy—anyway they fell in love—oh, Tren, sweet, we must have been in love the night we read "Gideon Planish" until the stars went out!—and they promised to love, honor, and obey—golly, the most beautiful words in the English language, except, of course, maybe some parts of Shakespeare—till death you did part. But then something happened. One day they woke up and the magic was gone. (He and Tren were having breakfast, Homogenized Virtex and Spookies, and suddenly, appallingly she cried, "Shad! I'm going away with Blight! Right this minute! He's going to take me to London, Paris, Berlin—Gee, I've always wanted to see the Taj Mahal and all those cute little Androgynes or whatever you call 'em—and we're going to take along a sleeping bag, you know, like in that book I read some of, and camp right out on the biggest darn ole Alp we can find." He had burbled, "Gee, that sounds mighty interesting, Tren. Yes, sir. Like to take a little trip sometime myself," but the Spookies were ashes in his mouth.) Anyway, it always ended—either in the hideous, clinging slime of the divorce court, or else—and this was unutterably worse—in the terribly, icy vacuum of indifference , the final shameful acceptance of infidelity. ("You ought to get yourself a girl, Shad," she had told him one night; as usual she was sitting on Blight's lap, knitting a new-fangled sock. "Why don't you call up Avis Cormorant? *There's* a cheerful little giver for you. Or maybe one of those Piutes you say old Corn was always talking about." He had almost struck her then.) It was this, this modern cynicism, this flat denial of marriage, not the Communists or the Fascists or the Technocrats or even the hot-eyed disciples of Fourier and Adam Smith, that was destroying America. In the ultimate scheme of things, the continuing marriage of Tren and Shad Ampersand, or, if you chose, of plain Helen and Robert Lynd, was more important than—

"Hey," said Pox, putting his head around the door, "I wouldn't disturb you, except you didn't seem to be getting anywhere in particular with that editorial. Anyway, she's back."

"Who?" spurted Shad, though his heart obliteratingly knew.

"Who the hell did you think?" said Pox scornfully, "Little Round Heels. With a hangover I could swing on by my tail."

She came in then, with a glad, unsteady rush, a broken cry into his waiting arms, and if she was damaged, if she was no longer the bright, imperious child his dreams had known, but something harder, wiser, and infinitely sad, he had no eyes to see.

"Tren, baby!" he whispered fiercely in her hair.

"Shad!" she breathed, and gave him the ruined glory of her smile. After all, she thought, stroking the remembered kindness of his cheek, you always have to figure that the old skeesix is practically indestructible, there ought to be plenty of books still batting around in him for all the endless years to come.

"Nice going, sister," murmured Pox, and most discreetly shut the door.

—Wolcott Gibbs

ELINOR WYLIE
(1885-1928)

Jenny Forlorn

Book One

<small>STEEL AND LEMONS</small>

The Honorable Gerald Boneyarde sat in a great arm chair in the attitude since popularized by the pencil of Maclise in his drawing of the senectuous and moribund Talleyrand. Upon his frustrate and osseous knees, bent at an acute and projecting angle, rested his astringent and maleficent wrists from which dangled his palmate and predatory hands, whose emaciate and prehensile fingers vied in macilency with his thin and bony nose. The elaborate and influential tracery on the Chinese brocade covering of the chair was plainly discernible through his attenuate and filamentous figure.

His hatchet face, frequently and lavishly maculate with freckles, was as yellow as a primrose. His eyes, of a pale and ceramic azure and of such singular and protrusive prominence as to merit the epithet pop, though lucent as nard, were closed. He opened them with a delicately damascened oyster knife, whose ivory handle was carven in amorphous convolutions redolent of Holland sauce and buttered rolls, and looked straight out of the window at a young girl, whom he now saw for the first time.

—Christopher Ward

EDNA FERBER
(1887-1968)

So Little

I

Selina Peake descended the bare wooden stairway. Her delicate nose, slightly pinched at the nostrils, but otherwise uninjured, was sensitive. She sniffed. Yes, there was pork for supper.

She had thought herself lucky to get the Dutch school at High Prairie and a boarding-place at the house of Swimmen Pool, the truck farmer, And now, on her first evening, there was pork for supper.

She was conscious of a thrill of adventure. "Life is just one damn thing after another," her dead father had told her. What other damn thing would there be for supper to-morrow night? She was yet to learn that her father was wrong. There would never be another damn thing but pork for supper.

Selina looked at Mrs. Pool. Holding a frying-pan in one hand, a knife in another, with a third and fourth she boxed the ears of the twins, Smaartje and Peertje. A fifth was adjusting her back hair, while the sixth milked the cow.

A feeling of unreality possessed Selina. Thus—thus were the demands of life met by these truck farmers' wives. This was their development. Would she become like that? Why, no! no!

Mrs. Pool thumped down upon the table a great platter of ham and eggs. Selina's beauty loving eyes, dark and soft, like chocolate cake, glowed luminous. Her fine sharp steel-strong clear-cut jaw-line vibrated. Her thick long fine hair stood all on end in a wonderful Circassian aureole.

"*Oh*," she cried. "They are *beautiful!* Like Burgundy and caviare! No! like—uh—oh, you know—porphyry and alabaster!"

Slowly as the lake mist drifts across the prairie, the idea entered into them. "Ham an' eggs is putiful!" they wailed in unison. "Og heden! Og heden! Og heden!"

Pool's round moon of a head revolved majestically on his great shoulders, eleven complete revolutions without stopping. The grizzled beard of Hoogendunk, the hired man, slipped slowly from its mooring and drifted up to cover his baldly blushing cranium. Mrs. Pool fell quietly, gradually backwards across the stove and relaxed into slumber, into the dreamless sleep of the overworked farmer's wife. The ham and eggs, hand in hand, tiptoed silently through the doorway.

But always to her ham and eggs were to be porphyry and alabaster. Life has no weapons against a woman like that.

—Christopher Ward

RAYMOND CHANDLER
(1888-1959)

Mr. Big

I was sitting in my office, cleaning the debris out of my thirty-eight and wondering where my next case was coming from. I like being a private eye, and even though once in a while I've had my gums massaged with an automobile jack, the sweet smell of greenbacks makes it all worth it. Not to mention the dames, which are a minor preoccupation of mine that I rank just ahead of breathing. That's why, when the door to my office swung open and a long-haired blonde named Heather Butkiss came striding in and told me she was a nudie model and needed my help, my salivary glands shifted into third. She wore a short skirt and a tight sweater and her figure described a set of parabolas that could cause cardiac arrest in a yak.

"What can I do for you, sugar?"

"I want you to find someone for me."

"Missing person? Have you tried the police?"

"Not exactly, Mr. Lupowitz."

"Call me Kaiser, sugar. All right, so what's the scam?"

"God."

"God?"

"That's right, God. The Creator, the Underlying Principle, the First Cause of Things, the All Encompassing. I want you to find Him for me."

I've had some fruit cakes up in the office before, but when they're built like she was, you listened.

"Why?"

"That's my business, Kaiser, You just find Him."

"I'm sorry, sugar. You got the wrong boy."

"But why?"

"Unless I know all the facts," I said, rising.

"O.K., O.K.," she said, biting her lower lip. She straightened the seam of her stocking, which was strictly for my benefit, but I wasn't buying any at the moment.

"Let's have it on the line, sugar."

"Well, the truth is—I'm not really a nudie model."

"No?"

"No. My name is not Heather Butkiss, either. It's Claire Rosensweig and I'm a student at Vassar. Philosophy major. History of Western Thought and all that. I have a paper due January. On Western religion. All the other kids in the course will hand in speculative papers. But I want to *know*. Professor Grebanier said if anyone finds out for sure, they're a cinch to pass the course. And my dad's promised me a Mercedes if I get straight A's."

I opened a deck of Luckies and a pack of gum and had one of each. Her story was beginning to interest me. Spoiled coed. High IQ and a body I wanted to know better.

"What does God look like?"

"I've never seen him."

"Well, how do you know He exists?"

"That's for you to find out."

"Oh, great. Then you don't know what he looks like? Or where to begin looking?"

"No. Not really. Although I suspect he's everywhere. In the air, in every flower, in you and I—and in this chair."

"Uh huh." So she was a pantheist. I made a mental note of it and said I'd give her case a try—for a hundred bucks a day, expenses, and a dinner date. She smiled and okayed the deal. We rode down in the elevator together. Outside it was getting dark. Maybe God did exist and maybe He didn't, but somewhere in that city there were sure a lot of guys who were going to try and keep me from finding out.

My first lead was Rabbi Itzhak Wiseman, a local cleric who owed me a favor for finding out who was rubbing pork on his hat. I knew something was wrong when I spoke to him because he was scared. Real scared.

"Of course there's a you-know-what, but I'm not even allowed to say His name or He'll strike me dead, which I could never understand why someone is so touchy about having his name said."

"You ever see Him?"

"Me? Are you kidding? I'm lucky I get to see my grandchildren."

"Then how do you know He exists?"

"How do I know? What kind of question is that? Could I get a suit like this for fourteen dollars if there was no one up there? Here, feel a gabardine—how can you doubt?"

"You got nothing more to go on?"

"Hey—what's the Old Testament? Chopped liver? How do you think Moses got the Israelites out of Egypt? With a smile and a tap dance? Believe me, you don't part the Red Sea with some gismo from Korvette's. It takes power."

"So he's tough, eh?"

"Yes, Very tough. You'd think with all that success he'd be a lot sweeter."

"How come you know so much?"

"Because we're the chosen people. He takes best care of us of all His children, which I'd also like to someday discuss with Him."

"What do you pay Him for being chosen?"

"Don't ask."

So that's how it was. The Jews were into God for a lot. It was the old protection racket. Take care of them in return for a price. And from the way Rabbi Wiseman was talking, He soaked them plenty. I got into a cab and made it over to Danny's Billiards on Tenth Avenue. The manager was a slimy little guy I didn't like.

"Chicago Phil here?"

"Who wants to know?"

I grabbed him by the lapels and took some skin at the same time.

"What, punk?"

"In the back," he said, with a change of attitude.

Chicago Phil. Forger, bank robber strong-arm man, and avowed atheist.

"The guy never existed, Kaiser. This is the straight dope. It's a big hype. There's no Mr. Big. It's a syndicate. Mostly Sicilian. It's international. But there is no actual head. Except maybe the Pope."

"I want to meet the Pope."

"It can be arranged," he said, winking.

"Does the name Claire Rosensweig mean anything to you?"

"No."

"Heather Butkiss?"

"Oh, wait a minute. Sure. She's that peroxide job with the bazooms from Radcliffe."

"Radcliffe? She told me Vassar."

"Well, she's lying. She's a teacher at Radcliffe. She was mixed up with a philosopher for a while."

"Pantheist?"

"No. Empiricist, as I remember. Bad guy. Completely rejected Hegel or any dialectical methodology."

"One of those."

"Yeah, He used to be a drummer with a jazz trio. Then he got hooked up on Logical Positivism. When that didn't work, he tried Pragmatism. Last I heard he stole a lot of money to take a course in Schopenhauer at Columbia. The mob would like to find him—or get their hands on his textbooks so they can resell them."

"Thanks, Phil."

"Take it from me, Kaiser. There's no one out there. It's a void. I couldn't pass all those bad checks or screw society the way I do if for one second I was able to recognize any authentic sense of Being. The universe is strictly phenomenological. Nothing's eternal. It's all meaningless."

"Who won the fifth at Aqueduct?"

"Santa Baby."

I had a beer at O'Rourke's and tried to add it all up, but it made no sense at all. Socrates was a suicide—or so they said. Christ was murdered. Neitzsche went nuts. If there was someone out there, He sure as hell didn't want anybody to know it. And why was Claire Rosensweig lying about Vassar? Could Descartes have been right? Was the universe dualistic? Or did Kant hit it on the head when he postulated the existence of God on moral grounds?

That night I had dinner with Claire. Ten minutes after the check came, we were in the sack and, brother, you can have your Western thought. She went through the kind of gymnastics that would have won first prize in the Tia Juana Olympics. After, she lay on the pillow next to me, her long blond hair sprawling. Our naked bodies still intertwined. I was smoking and staring at the ceiling.

"Claire, what if Kierkegaard's right?"

"You mean?"

"If you can never really *know*. Only have faith."

"That's absurd."

"Don't be so rational."

"Nobody's being rational, Kaiser." She lit a cigarette. "Just don't get ontological. Not now. I couldn't bear it if you were ontological with me."

She was upset. I leaned over and kissed her, and the phone rang. She got it.

"It's for you."

The voice on the other end was Sergeant Reed of Homicide.

"You still looking for God?"

"Yeah."

"An all-powerful Being? Great Oneness, Creator of the Universe? First Cause of All Things?"

"That's right."

"Somebody with that description just showed up at the morgue. You better get down here right away."

It was Him all right, and from the looks of Him it was a professional job.

"He was dead when they brought Him in."

"Where'd you find Him?"

"A warehouse on Delancey Street."

"Any clues?"

"It's the work of an existentialist. We're sure of that."

"How can you tell?"

"Haphazard way how it was done. Doesn't seem to be any system followed. Impulse."

"A crime of passion?"

"You got it. Which means you're a suspect, Kaiser."

"Why me?"

"Everybody down at headquarters knows how you feel about Jaspers."

"That doesn't make me a killer."

"Not yet, but you're a suspect."

Outside on the street I sucked air into my lungs and tried to clear my head. I took a cab over to Newark and got out and walked a block to Giordiano's Italian Restaurant. There, at a back table, was His Holiness. It was the Pope, all right. Sitting with two guys I had seen in half a dozen police line-ups.

"Sit down," he said, looking up from his fettucine. He held out a ring. I gave him my toothiest smile, but didn't kiss it. It bothered him and I was glad. Point for me.

"Would you like some fettucine?"

"No thanks, Holiness. But you go ahead."

"Nothing? Not even a salad?"

"I just ate."

"Suit yourself, but they make a great Roquefort dressing here. Not like at the Vatican, where you can't get a decent meal."

"I'll come right to the point, Pontiff. I'm looking for God."

"You came to the right person."

"Then He does exist?" They all found this very amusing and laughed. The hood next to me said, "Oh, that's funny. Bright boy wants to know if He exists."

I shifted my chair to get comfortable and brought the leg down on his little toe. "Sorry." But he was steaming.

"Sure He exists, Lupowitz, but I'm the only one that communicates with him. He speaks only through me."

"Why you, pal?"

"Because I got the red suit."

"This get-up?"

"Don't knock it. Every morning I rise, put on this red suit, and suddenly I'm a big cheese. It's all in the suit. I mean, face it, if I went around in slacks and a sports jacket, I couldn't get arrested religion-wise."

"Then it's a hype. There's no God."

"I don't know. But what's the difference? The money's good."

"You ever worry the laundry won't get your red suit back on time and you'll be like the rest of us?"

"I use the special one-day service. I figure it's worth the extra few cents to be safe."

"Name Claire Rosensweig mean anything to you?"

"Sure. She's in the science department at Bryn Mawr."

"Science, you say? Thanks."

"For what?"

"The answer, Pontiff." I grabbed a cab and shot over the George Washington Bridge. On the way I stopped at my office and did some fast checking. Driving to Claire's apartment, I put the pieces together, and for the first time they fit. When I got there she was in a diaphanous peignoir and something seemed to be troubling her.

"God is dead. The police were here. They're looking for you. They think an existentialist did it."

"No, sugar. It was you."

"What? Don't make jokes, Kaiser."

"It was you that did it."

"What are you saying?"

"You, baby. Not Heather Butkiss or Claire Rosensweig, but Doctor Ellen Shepherd."

"How did you know my name?"

"Professor of physics at Bryn Mawr. The youngest one ever to head a department there. At the mid-winter Hop you get stuck on a jazz musician who's heavily into philosophy. He's married, but that doesn't stop you. A couple of nights in the hay and it feels like love. But it doesn't work out because something comes between you. God. Y'see, sugar, he believed, or wanted to, but you, with your pretty little scientific mind, had to have absolute certainty."

"No, Kaiser, I swear."

"So you pretend to study philosophy because that gives you a chance to eliminate certain obstacles. You get rid of Socrates easy enough, but Descartes takes over, so you use Spinoza to get rid of Descartes, but when Kant doesn't come through you have to get rid of him too."

"You don't know what you're saying."

"You made mincemeat out of Leibnitz, but that wasn't good enough for you because you knew if anybody believed Pascal you were dead, so he had to be gotten rid of too, but that's where you made your mistake because you trusted Martin Buber. Except, sugar, he was soft. He believed in God, so you had to get rid of God yourself."

"Kaiser, you're mad!"

"No, baby. You posed as a pantheist and that gave you access to Him—*if* He existed, which he did. He went with you to Shelby's party and when Jason wasn't looking, you killed Him."

"Who the hell are Shelby and Jason?"

"What's the difference? Life's absurd now anyway."

"Kaiser," she said, suddenly trembling. "You wouldn't turn me in?"

"Oh yes, baby. When the Supreme Being gets knocked off, *somebody's* got to take the rap."

"Oh, Kaiser, we could go away together. Just the two of us. We could forget about philosophy. Settle down and maybe get into semantics."

"Sorry, sugar. It's no dice."

She was all tears now as she started lowering the shoulder straps of her peignoir and I was standing there suddenly with a naked Venus whose whole body seemed to be saying, Take me—I'm yours. A Venus whose right hand had picked up a forty-five and was holding it behind my back. I let go with a slug from my thirty-eight before she could pull the trigger, and she dropped her gun and doubled over in disbelief.

"How could you, Kaiser?"

She was fading fast, but I managed to get it in, in time.

"The manifestation of the universe as a complex idea unto itself as opposed to being in or outside the true Being of itself is inherently a conceptual nothingness or Nothingness in relation to any abstract form of existing or to exist or having existed in perpetuity to laws of physicality or motion or ideas relating to non-matter or the lack of objective Being or subjective otherness."

It was a subtle concept but I think she understood before she died.

—*Woody Allen*

KATHERINE MANSFIELD
(1888-1923)

From The Football Pools

But I didn't even *choose* them! shrieked Clara silently. A few random crosses on a piece of paper, and hey presto! a cheque for one hundred thousand pounds was pressed into her hand. ("No really—I must confess, I did it with my eyes shut!") Yet here it was, a real cheque, not to mention the fifty-three letters, the idiotic telegrams from people she hadn't spoken to for years, and heavens above! the newspapers—that awful, simpering photograph ripped out, of all things, from a *hockey* group! Surely the world had gone quite mad. She rushed into the window, fearing shattered houses and a people fled. . . . A milk-bottle squatted on every doorstep, and the black-and-white cat opposite was placidly laundering his chest. She felt it was all some terrible mistake. It's no use—her mouth opened—we must send it back! But before the words could escape, another thought winged out without so much as an excuse-me. Could we really, now, afford to buy a *whole* island? One hand, aghast, flew to her mouth, but she gazed enraptured across the breakfast table. Breathing a little heavily, totally absorbed, Bill had not heard her (perhaps she didn't really say it). He went on stroking the glossy pages of one of the seventeen Television catalogues. . . .

—Margaret Tims

ERLE STANLEY GARDNER
(1889-1970)

From The Case Of The Kangaroo

Perry Mason stood up at the defense counsel's table and announced, "I re-call Joe the Bartender. Now, sir," asked Mason, "tell the jury again about the last time you saw the deceased." "I was alone behind the bar when the deceased hopped in and ordered a vodka martini. I gave him his drink and his change, and then made a remark about not seeing too many kangaroos in there. He came back with a wiseacre crack about my prices." "Then what did you do?" "I shot him—he had it coming." "The defense rests."

—Joel Crystal

KATHERINE ANNE PORTER
(1890-1980)

Nobody's Fool

"The characters are all at sea," Mrs. Haverstick was explaining to them with her usual bitter charm, "and the reader is given the most vivid possible experience of being there with them. Yes, that will be the scheme of the book. I see that more clearly with each chapter that I finish."

Herr Gottschalk, seated beside her at the Captain's table, wondered only when she would finish the book. In one pocket of his coat was a radiogram from the publishing firm for which he worked, reading, "If you don't get it this time don't bother to come back," in the other a small phial of pills whose bitter taste was ever on his tongue, either in memory or anticipation.

He watched her pale hand—what exquisite hands she had, how many men in times past must have been struck by them—gesturing over her plate, then over his, as her description of the grand plan of the novel broadened out; it waved like a sea frond under his nose, mesmerizing him till his eyes crossed. He aspired to be her editor, therefore he sighed carefully, but the belt around his fat middle creaked like a ship's timber. What a symbolism! For ten years he had pursued her from one tropical paradise to another, each paradise a worse hell than the last, driven by the rumor that she was again at work on the book, lashed by the bitter dream that it might at last be his. He often saw himself as an Ahab on the track of a legendary whale. "There are times when I hate it," she said. As if he didn't!

"Our author, then," the Captain broke in. He sat with his napkin tucked under his pink gills, his fists on the arms of his chair, as though he were going to punch them all in the nose for having come. He had heard for ten days from their lips nothing but names like Nietzsche, Schopenhauer, Kierkegaard, and Weltschmerz—he knew the last was not the name of a writer but of some German dish, perhaps a good deal like sauerbraten. He did not want to hear any more about the characters in the book, for the time being, but he wished to give the beautiful English lady her head so that Herr Gottschalk would not start one of his lectures on the inherent goodness of man. "Our author then has mixed feelings about the human race?"

"Oh, yes. We cannot forever loathe. We must swing back occasionally to simple dislike. In this way a balance is kept."

Mrs. Haverstick's reply was designed not so much to answer the Captain, who was in any case a swine and in no need of conversion, as to torture Herr Gottschalk a little. Whom she now considered with a lazy malice, leaning slightly away from him in her chair. "Though every prospect pleases, and only man is vile. Eh, Herr Gottschalk?" she teased in her rather bitterly musical voice. Gottschalk was seized with the wish to rap her knuckles with the butt of his knife, but instead squeezed over them the juice of half a lemon intended, in point of actual fact, for his sole. That would teach her to deny the inherent nobility of man, his action seemed to say.

Almost instantly there writhed across his lips the apologetic smile for which he was in fact more famous than for such independent deeds. Mrs. Haverstick remained smilingly quiet, her tawny eyes, so like bees darting this way and that, took on a momentarily sated look. He had met her standards, for the time being.

Yet revolt was not entirely gone out of him. "I'm nobody's fool," he muttered, forlornly.

"You should find someone," Frau Hindendorf spoke up. She had finished gobbling her fish and was now ready to catch up on the conversation in a more intelligent fashion while she waited for dessert. She wore a plain blue linen dress and white beads, and on her arm an amorous bruise. "We all need someone to belong to in this world. To . . ."

The ship's saloon was filling up rapidly after dinner, and as Herr Gottschalk rounded the doorway into it his nostrils encountered the bitter smell of individuals. He hoped to find Mrs. Haverstick alone at a table. When he did his heart sank. "May I . . . ?" he began apprehensively.

"Of course. Please sit down."

Seated across from her, he felt a familiar dew gather on his brow. She seemed, herself, now, prepared to put him at his ease. She drew from her bag a bottle of Cointreau, unscrewed the cap, and began to pour the contents over her bare arms.

She let it trickle along her wrists to her elbows, rubbing it gently, pleasurably into her skin, at the same time inhaling its fumes with a lost air, her eyes voluptuously closed. Was she inviting him into the ornate privacy of her life, if you could call it privacy? But it was the book he wanted, he reminded himself sternly, the prize for which he had given up a decade of even the simple pleasures, let alone the exotic. Yet she was a woman and he a man, so that chase also had something of the bitter duplicity of love—about which no one knew more than this woman. He tried to affect a lover's nonchalance as he pressed the bell for the waiter. God, the energy that went into indifference!

The waiter came to take their orders. "Have you any cologne?" she asked. Herr Gottschalk became now quite terrified. He heard to his relief the waiter say no, with gratitude saw him go off with their orders for highballs—and return in two minutes with no further words spoken at their table. Herr Gottschalk raised his highball and with a flustered "*Adios,*" which was what the South Americans seemed to be saying all the time, drank it down as though it were a glass of water, he was quite parched.

Now he would make the pitch. It was all very well for the damned unwritten book to be a legend in her lifetime, but his was drawing to a close. Down the arches of how many years had he not followed her, not like the Hound of Heaven any more than a Captain Ahab, to be sure, but rather like some tireless meek mongrel trotting at her heels? The end of the book receded eternally before you like the horizon, and while she might be only forty-five and could wait ten more years, making it twenty in all, he was fifty-eight and could not.

Mrs. Haverstick, who did not miss a trick even with her eyes closed, had seen the flush go up his face and misunderstood his emotion. Seeing through people sometimes made her miss what was inside them, but that was the price one paid for the gift of penetration. She thought he was still smarting under the incident at dinner. Men never know when to quarrel, she thought: how to spare, against a hungrier day, the still uneaten portions of the heart.

"There is something I must say tonight," Herr Gottschalk began, his voice gaining an unexpected octave in pitch. She saw him fidget in his pocket. He was nudging the cap off his own little bottle with a thumb, so as to have in readiness one of the tablets which had so often saved his life and might be called upon to perform the same role tonight. "You are getting off at Port-au-Prince, they say, to finish another chapter."

"I hope to finish another chapter there," she said, kneading the aromatic liquid into her wrists, working it well down into the crevices of her fingers. "A page or two a day is all I can manage. Sometimes not that. It's slow going."

"Of course. It is so rich. How far through it are you?"

"Oh, a third. Perhaps a little less. Why?"

He cleared his throat hoarsely and, reaching between his thighs with his free hand, hitched his chair an inch closer to the table. "I am too old to make advances to beautiful ladies, but I am still fortunately in a position to give them." The dog's smile writhed across his face again as he joked. "I am in a position to offer you a check for ten thousand dollars for what you have of the manuscript."

She stopped kneading her hands and dropped them on the table, resting the undersides of her wrists against its edge. She looked at him quite blankly. "What manuscript?"

"The—the Book."

"You seem to be under some misconception, Herr Gottschalk," she said. "This is not a book I am writing. It is a book I am reading."

Herr Gottschalk sat like something molded out of cheese, staring at the table as if into a pool of sharks. His head went forward, slowly, like that of a man descending willingly into whatever it was transfixed his gaze, not falling helplessly.

"I'm a slow reader, and the book is long. And a masterpiece. One is sometimes discouraged, but one knows that what's there is worth staying with." She seemed to have forgotten Herr Gottschalk, and began to speak as though she were talking to another woman with whom she was gossiping about a third. "She's a genius, of course, and genius always has the right to bore us now and then, for the sake of what's up ahead. And why does characterization for a woman so often consist in having someone's number? Let me tell you about . . ."

His fingers relinquished the bottle in his pocket. It was the great, really quite blissful Letting Go that he had always dreamed it would be. Even before his head struck the table he had the sensation of sinking leagues through peaceful waters already far below the ship, into cool fathoms where he could rest forever among waving fronds and the great tides already tolling in his ears like a dim, delicious, distant bell. . . .

Mrs. Haverstick saw his head come to a stop among the litter of glasses, ashtrays, and spilled nuts on the tabletop. Rising, she reached across him and rang for the waiter.

"Clear these things away," she said in her most pleasant manner.

—Peter DeVries

PEARL BUCK
(1892-1973)

The Chinese Situation

It was the birthday of Whang the Gong. Whang the Gong was the son of Whang the Old Man, and the brother of Whang the Rich and of Auld Whang Syne. He was very poor and had only the tops of old Chinese wives to eat, but in his soul he was very proud and in his heart he knew that he was the son of Old Whang Lung who had won the Pulitzer Prize for the Hop-Sing-and-Jump.

Now Whang the Gong, although he was known far and wide among the local missionaries as a heathen, had read enough of the Gospels to know the value of short words and the effectiveness of the use of the word "and." And so Whang the Gong spoke, and it was good. Good for fifty cents a word.

Now Whang the Gong awoke on the morning of his birthday, and opened one eye, and it was not good, so he shut it again. And he opened the other eye, and it was worse than the first. So the young man shook his head wilfully and said, "I will open no more eyes until the harvest comes." Now the harvest was full six months away, which gave the young man a hell of a lot of leeway, and he rolled over again and slept.

But Rum Blossom, the wife of Whang the Gong, did not sleep. At four in the morning, before even the kine had begun to low or the water to run in the tub, Rum Blossom had rubbed her small hand over her small eyes, and it was not good. It was lousy. She arose, then, and went into the pump-house.

"Excuse," she said to nobody in particular, as nobody in particular was listening to her words, "excuse—I am going to have a baby." So she went into the pump-house, and, while the waffles were cooking, she had a baby, and it was a man. Which was pretty good, when you consider that it was born between waffles.

Now the winter wore on, and it was still the birthday of Whang the Gong, for Whang the Gong liked birthdays, for birthdays are holidays and holidays are good. And Rum Blossom, his wife, came to him and said, lowering her eyes as she pulled the stump of an old tree and threw it into the wood-box, "I am going to have another baby." And Whang the Gong said, "That is up to you." And he rolled over and shut another eye, which was his third, kept especially for shutting. So Rum Blossom went into the library and had another baby. And it was a woman, or slave, baby, which, in China, is not so hot.

"I will scream your shame to the whole village," said Whang the Gong when he had heard of the incident. "Yesterday you had a man child, which was good. Today you have a girl, which is bitterness upon my head and the taste of aloes in my mouth." And he repeated it over and over, such being the biblical style, "I will tell the village—I will tell the village." And Rum Blossom, his wife said, "All right. Go ahead and tell the village. Only get up out of bed, at any rate. And get your old man up out of bed, too. I am sick of seeing him around, doing nothing."

And Whang the Gong got up out of his bed, and got his old man up out of his bed, all of which made but little difference.

He went without reply then to the wall and felt for the roughness which was the mark of his clothes closet, and he removed the clod of earth which fastened it. "I will have my cutaway," he said, and went then back to bed. And Rum Blossom his wife came to him and said,

"I will get you your cutaway just as soon as I have had a child," and going into the clothes closet, she had a child and came out with the cutaway. "Here," she said, "is your' cutaway. Take it and like it." And Whang the Gong took it, and liked it, for it was a good cutaway.

It seemed as though once the gods turn against a man they will not consider him again. The rains, which should have come in the early summer, withheld themselves until the fifteenth of October, which was the date for Rum Blossom to have another baby.

And Whang the Gong said to Whang Lung, the old man his father, "How come? We have no rain." And Whang the Old Man said, "True, you have no rain. But you have babies galore. One may not ask everything."

And Whang the Gong was stumped. "A baby is but a baby," he said in confusion. "But rain is rain." All of which made no sense, but sounded good.

But the Old Man would hear none of his son's sophistry, and mouthed his gums, which were of tutti-frutti, and rolled in the grass, only there was no grass and so the Old Man rolled in the stones and bruised himself quite badly. But all this meant nothing to Whang the Gong, for three moons had passed since he had eaten nothing but spinach and his eyes were on those of Lettuce, the Coat-Room Girl.

There was a day when Whang the Gong awoke and saw his wife, Rum Blossom, pacing up and down the room, but, as the room was only three paces long, the effect was unimpressive.

"Another baby, I suppose?" said Whang the Gong, shutting both eyes.

"Not so that you could notice it," replied his wife, in extremest pique. "I'm through." And there was that in her pique which allowed no comeback, and Whang the Gong knew that she was indeed through, which was O. K. with him.

And when pay-day came, Whang the Gong arose and put on his finest silken suit with an extra pair of pants and married Lettuce the Coat Room Girl, making two wives for Whang the Gong, one, Rum Blossom, to keep the books, and one, Lettuce the Coat Room Girl, to be the mother of his children. Which made it very simple, so simple that everyone watching smiled.

—Robert Benchley

J. R. TOLKIEN
(1892-1973)

From The Spirit Of Middle Earth

Smirnoff was known as Smirrm's Knoff to the Red Dwarves of Voll-Gah, which lies far to the east of Eridor, where Smirrm, a fiery dragon over two miles long, dwelt beside Allko-Holl, the Liquid Mountain. It is said that the dragon made this delicious-tasting spirit from herbs gathered by the Elven folk in Elrond on the night of the first full moon after Mirkwyre Day. The Hobbits tell how the Goblins lusted after the recipe of the Knoff, and many times tried in vain to steal it, but it was lost after Smirrm was slain by Starlyn, a wandering Orc. After many moons the precious parchment came, no one knows how, into the hands of Andsorr the Bibulous, who gave it to Gandalf. Gandalf managed to decipher Smirrm's runes, and made the wonderful drink himself, and guarded its secret with more care than he gave to the Great Ring itself. But because he is wise, Gandalf has now made it available to the Men of the West. As Gandalf said: 'I could not tell an Orc from old Andsorr until I rediscovered Smirrm's Knoff.'

Smirnoff—the very spirit of Middle Earth.

—E. O. Parrott

DOROTHY SAYERS
(1893-1957)

From Scout's Honour

Lord Peter stared out of one window, Alleyn out of the other. Bunter and Fox entered noiselessly. The detectives spun round as one man.

"Whom have we here?" asked Wimsey "(as if we didn't know). They're comin' in this cabin, an' they want share o' them pickles an' that rum. Bunter, is it mutineh?"

"In a way, sir. We are finding our orders impracticable. We cannot shadow each other."

Fox added "It's because we can't shake each other off."

There was a silence. Alleyn suddenly took charge, somewhat to his own surprise.

"Lord Peter Wimsey, scout's honour, did you murder our host?"

"Detective-Inspector Roderick Alleyn, scout's honour, I did not."

"Well, then, scout's honour, neither did I. Si' down and prepare to detect."

—*Fergie*

ALDOUS HUXLEY
(1894-1963)

From Told in Gath

"Professor Pavlov has shown that when salivation has been artificially induced in dogs by the ringing of a dinner bell, if you fire simultaneously into them a few rounds of small shot they exhibit an almost comical bewilderment. Human beings have developed very little. Like dogs we are not capable of absorbing conflicting stimuli; we cannot continue to love Cleopatra after communism and the electro-magnetic field have played Old Harry with our romantic mythology. That characteristic modern thinker, Drage Everyman, remarks, 'Destroy the illusion of love and you destroy love itself,' and that is exactly what the machine age, through attempting to foster it through cinemas and gin-palaces, deodorants and depilatories, has succeeded in doing. Glory, glory halitosis! No wonder we are happier in the present! If we think of the 'Eastern Star,' in fact, it is as advertising something. And when we would reconstruct those breasts of hers, again we are faced with the diversity of modern knowledge. What were they like? To a poet twin roes, delectable mountains; to a philanderer like Malthus festering cancers; to a pneumatogogue simply a compound of lacticity and heterogeneous pyrites; to a biologist a sump and a pump. Oh, sweet are the uses, or rather the abuses, of splanchnology! No, for details of the pathological appeal of these forgotten beauties we must consult the poets. The ancients were aware of a good thing when they saw it, and Horace knew, for instance, with almost scatological percipience, exactly what was what.

"There are altitudes, as well as climates, of the mind. Many prefer the water-meadows, but some of us, like Kant and Beethoven, are at home on the heights. There we thermostatically control the rarefied atmosphere and breathe, perforce, the appropriate mental air."

—*Cyril Connolly*

J. B. PRIESTLEY
(1894-   )

From Apes and Angels

"I remember spending one very hot night in a London hotel. The place was full and I was a late-comer, so that I was given a tiny bedroom not far from the roof and looking out on nothing but a deep narrow court. I got off to sleep very quickly, but awoke about two and then vainly tossed and turned. There was nothing for it but to read, and I switched on my light. As a rule, I have a book in my bag, but this night I was completely bookless, and the only reading matter in the room was that supplied by two evening papers. I had already glanced through these papers, but now I had to settle down to read them as I have never read evening papers before or since. Every scrap of print, sports gossip, society chit-chat, City Notes, small advertisements, was steadily devoured. There I was, in my hot little aerie, reading those silly paragraphs about Lord A leaving town, or Miss B, the musical comedy star, making puddings, while the night burned slowly away. For weeks afterwards, the sight of an evening paper made me feel depressed."

—*X*

WILLIAM FAULKNER
(1897-1962)

Requiem For A Noun, Or Intruder In The Dusk

The cold Brussels sprout rolled off the page of the book I was reading and lay inert and defunctive in my lap. Turning my head with a leisure at least three-fourths impotent rage, I saw him standing there holding the toy with which he had catapulted the vegetable, or rather the reverse, the toy first then the fat insolent fist clutching it and then above that the bland defiant face beneath the shock of black hair like tangible gas. It, the toy, was one of those cardboard funnels with a trigger near the point for firing a small celluloid ball. Letting the cold Brussels sprout lie there in my lap for him to absorb or anyhow apprehend rebuke from, I took a pull at a Scotch highball I had had in my hand and then set it down on the end table beside me.

"So instead of losing the shooter which would have been a mercy you had to lose the ball," I said, fixing with a stern eye what I had fathered out of all sentient and biding dust; remembering with that retroactive memory by which we count chimes seconds and even minutes after they have struck (recapitulate, even, the very grinding of the bowels of the clock before and during and after) the cunning furtive click, clicks rather, which perception should have told me then already were not the trigger plied but the icebox opened. "Even a boy of five going on six should have more respect for his father if not for food," I said, now picking the cold Brussels sprout out of my lap and setting it—not dropping it, setting it—in an ashtray; thinking how across the wax bland treachery of the kitchen linoleum were now in all likelihood distributed the remnants of string beans and cold potatoes and maybe even tapioca. "You're no son of mine."

I took up the thread of the book again or tried to: the weft of legitimate kinship that was intricate enough without the obbligato of that dark other: the sixteenths and thirty-seconds and even sixty-fourths of dishonoring cousinships brewed out of the violable blood by the ineffaceable errant lusts. Then I heard another click; a faint metallic rejoinder that this time was neither the trigger nor the icebox but the front door opened and then shut. Through the window I saw him picking his way over the season's soiled and sun-frayed vestiges of snow like shreds of rotted lace, the cheap upended toy cone in one hand and a child's cardboard suitcase in the other, toward the road.

I dropped the book and went out after him who had forgotten not only that I was in shirtsleeves but that my braces hung down over my flanks in twin festoons. "Where are you going?" I called, my voice expostulant and forlorn on the warm numb air. Then I caught it: caught it in the succinct outrage of the suitcase and the prim churning rear and marching heels as well: I had said he was no son of mine, and so he was leaving a house not only where he was not wanted but where he did not even belong.

"I see," I said in that shocked clarity with which we perceive the truth instantaneous and entire out of the very astonishment that refuses to acknowledge it. "Just as you now cannot be sure of any roof you belong more than half under, you figure there is no housetop from which you might not as well begin to shout it. Is that it?"

Something was trying to tell me something. Watching him turn off on the road—and that not only with the ostensible declaration of vagabondage but already its very assumption, attaining as though with a single footfall the very apotheosis of wandering just as with a single shutting of a door he had that of renunciation and farewell—watching him turn off on it, the road, in the direction of the Permisangs', our nearest neighbors, I thought *Wait; no; what I said was not enough for him to leave the house on; it must have been the blurted inscrutable chance confirmation of something he already knew, and was half able to assess, either out of the blown facts of boyhood or pure male divination or both.*

"What is it you know?" I said springing forward over the delicate squalor of the snow and falling in beside the boy. "Does any man come to the house to see your mother when I'm away, that you know of?" Thinking *We are mocked, first by the old mammalian snare, then, snared, by the final unilaterality of all flesh to which birth is given; not only not knowing when we may be cuckolded, but not even sure that in the veins of the very bantling we dandle does not flow the miscreant sniggering wayward blood.*

"I get it now," I said, catching in the undeviating face just as I had in the prim back and marching heels the steady articulation of disdain. "Cuckoldry is something of which the victim may be as guilty as the wrong-doers. That's what you're thinking? That by letting in this taint upon our heritage I am as accountable as she or they who have been its actual avatars. More. Though the foe may survive, the sleeping sentinel must be shot. Is that it?"

"You talk funny."

Mother-and-daughter blood conspires in the old mammalian office. Father-and-son blood vies in the ancient phallic enmity. I caught him by the arm and we scuffled in the snow. "I will be heard," I said, holding him now as though we might be dancing, my voice intimate and furious against the furious sibilance of our feet in the snow. Thinking how revelation had had to be inherent in the very vegetable scraps to which venery was probably that instant contriving to abandon me, the cold boiled despair of whatever already featureless suburban Wednesday Thursday or Saturday supper the shot green was the remainder. "I see another thing," I panted, cursing my helplessness to curse whoever it was had given him blood and wind. Thinking *He's glad; glad to credit what is always secretly fostered and fermented out of the vats of childhood fantasy anyway (for all childhood must conceive a substitute for the father that has conceived it (finding that other inconceivable?)*; thinking *He is walking in a nursery fairy tale to find the king his sire.* "Just as I said to you 'You're no son of mine' so now you answer back 'Neither are you any father to me.'"

The scherzo of violence ended as abruptly as it had begun. He broke away and walked on, after retrieving the toy he had dropped and adjusting his grip on the suitcase which he had not, this time faster and more urgently.

The last light was seeping out of the shabby sky, after the hemorrhage of sunset. High in the west where the fierce constellations soon would wheel, the evening star in single bombast burned and burned. The boy passed the Permisangs' without going in, then passed the Kellers'. Maybe he's heading for the McCullums', I thought, but he passed their house too. Then he, we, neared the Jelliffs'. He's got to be going there, his search will end there, I thought. Because that was the last house this side of the tracks. And because *something was trying to tell me something*.

"Were you maybe thinking of what you heard said about Mrs. Jelliff and me having relations in Spuyten Duyvil?" I said in rapid frantic speculation. "But they were talking about mutual kin—nothing else." The boy said nothing. But I had sensed it instant and complete: the boy felt that, whatever of offense his mother may or may not have given, his father had given provocation; and out of the old embattled malehood, it was the hairy ineluctable Him whose guilt and shame he was going to hold preponderant. *Because now I remembered*.

"So it's Mrs. Jelliff—Sue Jelliff—and me you have got this all mixed up with," I said, figuring he must, in that fat sly nocturnal stealth that took him creeping up and down the stairs to listen when he should have been in bed, certainly have heard his mother exclaiming to his father behind that bedroom door it had been vain to close since it was not sound-proof: "I saw you. I saw that with Sue. There may not be anything between you but you'd like there to be! Maybe there is at that!"

Now like a dentist forced to ruin sound enamel to reach decayed I had to risk telling him what he did not know to keep what he assuredly did in relative control.

"This is what happened on the night in question," I said. "It was under the mistletoe, during the Holidays, at the Jelliffs'. Wait! I will be heard out! See your father as he is, but see him in no baser light. He has his arms around his neighbor's wife. It is evening, in the heat and huddled spiced felicity of the year's end, under the mistletoe (where as well as anywhere else the thirsting and exasperated flesh might be visited by the futile pangs and jets of later lust, the omnivorous aches of fifty and forty and even thirty-five to seize what may be the last of the allotted lips). Your father seems to prolong beyond its usual moment's span that custom's usufruct. Only for an instant, but in that instant letting trickle through the fissures of appearance what your mother and probably Rudy Jelliff too saw as an earnest of a flood that would have devoured that house and one four doors away."

A moon hung over the eastern roofs like a phantasmal

bladder. Somewhere an icicle crashed and splintered, fruits of the day's thaw.

"So now I've got it straight," I said. "Just as through some nameless father your mother has cuckolded me (you think), so through one of Rudy Jelliff's five sons I have probably cuckolded him. Which would give you at least a half brother under that roof where under ours you have none at all. So you balance out one miscreance with another, and find your rightful kin in our poor weft of all the teeming random bonded sentient dust."

Shifting the grip, the boy walked on past the Jelliffs'. Before him—the tracks; and beyond that—the other side of the tracks. And now out of whatever reserve capacity for astonished incredulity may yet have remained I prepared to face this last and ultimate outrage. But he didn't cross. Along our own side of the tracks ran a road which the boy turned left on. He paused before a lighted house near the corner, a white cottage with a shingle in the window which I knew from familiarity to read, "Viola Pruett, Piano Lessons," and which, like a violently unscrambled pattern on a screen, now came to focus.

Memory adumbrates just as expectation recalls. The name on the shingle made audible to listening recollection the last words of the boy's mother as she'd left, which had fallen short then of the threshold of hearing. " . . . Pruett," I remembered now. "He's going to have supper and stay with Buzzie Pruett overnight . . . Can take a few things with him in that little suitcase of his. If Mrs. Pruett phones about it, just say I'll take him over when I get back," I recalled now in that chime-counting recapitulation of retroactive memory—better than which I could not have been expected to do. Because the eternal Who-instructs might have got through to the whiskey-drinking husband or might have got through to the reader immersed in that prose vertiginous intoxicant and unique, but not to both.

"So that's it," I said. "You couldn't wait till you were taken much less till it was time but had to sneak off by yourself, and that not cross-lots but up the road I've told you a hundred times to keep off even the shoulder of."

The boy had stopped and now appeared to hesitate before the house. He turned around at last, switched the toy and the suitcase in his hands, and started back in the direction he had come.

"What are you going back for now?" I asked.

"More stuff to take in this suitcase," he said. "I was going to just sleep at the Pruetts' overnight, but now I'm going to ask them to let me stay there for good."

—*Peter DeVries*

From Sylvester The Cat

And get the hell on outa this kitchen! came with the hard rush of the maid's brush and a door banged and light from the kitchen got swept quick off the dusty yard and the two of them, the one tall and supple and black as molasses blacker than the night that held them there in its soft palpable grip blacker even than negroes, lisped with an almost feline intensity a curse incomprehensible and fleet and waved white palms in anguished yet unvanquished frenzy so that the other, the smaller longsuffering foil to and recipient of vicious and obsessional cruelty at last saw that a chance to alter the theme of their inexplicable and prime-time-honoured bondage from one of antagonism to one of complicity might be to say *They all so crazy in this country that you and me Sylvester we better team up fer pertection* so that *Yeth thir!* the first might say, long tongue fleering on the lips of his mouth *We gotta think of thom way of getting uth thom boidtheed, sshlurrp.'*

—*Derek Willey*

JORGE LUIS BORGES
(1899-   )

Don Antonio De Malvinas Takes A Bride

In the Rosado section of B.A. there lived, until some time ago, an aged rake of some means, Don Antonio. He had a palsied hand, and a withered dick, and his friends at the English club had long ago nicknamed him Pacho.

The family names were Quevedo Y Kipling, but he was called Don Antonio De Malvinas because he was known by all to be as stupid as a sheep, the source of his family's fortunes.

At age 68 Don Antonio decided to take a bride so he might produce a son to pass on his patrimony, but since no gentlewoman would have this "Don of The Indented Dong," as he was also called, he went to a nearby convent to offer his hand and so on and so forth to one of the Sisters.

"A son from a sister?" inquired the mother superior of the wealthy old reprobate.

"Indeed, yes. It is my wish. . . ."

"In the convent," she told him, "we have a saying: No brains in a *bicho*—how you say it—prick. But in your case I am likely to make an exception." Beyond her cowl she was comely, with fulsome cheeks: "I am still of child-bearing age and if you like señor I will leave the convent walls behind and bear your son for you, for, as I would not wish it on one of my novices, yet think it to be desirable, you may wish to spread my legs and enter what Quevedo called 'my mossy Ebro. . . .'"

"Indeed," Don Antonio said again.

And so it was done, much to the consternation of all the other sisters, and Mother Taka left behind her veil of Christ and chose to be the bride of the withered etc etc. . . . Their wedding nuptials were celebrated all over B.A. with public lewdness, drunkenness, and ribaldry. At the Feast, the Vicar proposed a toast: "To Machissmo, in whatever dress."

And the couple danced to the "Bang the Nun Tango."

Subsequently, they boarded the Red Arrow Express for Mar Del Plata to honeymoon.

All that we subsequently know we know subsequently, as it were, posthumously. The Wagon Lits attendant reported they were shown to their compartment and of their subsequent comportment he could report only overhearing harsh gutterals, and caterwaulings: "O in Christ I beseech thee etc. etc. . . ."

When Don Antonio's train arrived in Mar Del Plata he was discovered to be quite dead of a heart attack with his pants down at his knees, and every sign evident that he had been recently buggered.

A largish mound of human excrement was still steaming among the bed clothes.

Mother Taka had fled Don Antonio and his caca, and was never heard from or seen again, in B.A. or elsewhere.

To this day the street people in B.A. refer to a mound of shit on the curb as "Don Antonio's son," or even his "immaculate conception."

And in B.A. we have a song we all know which is composed in the manner of one of Gil Vicente's romances:

Caca
Taka
This or
That a
And how the sparrows fall
    Hola
Pretty little sparrow droppings

—John Howland Spyker

ELIZABETH BOWEN
(1899-1973)

From The Agatha Collaboration

Poirot bowed courteously. "It is *très gentil* of you to come and see me, Mademoiselle," he said.

Felicity felt glad she was wearing the stole; somehow its femininity defied those very male moustaches.

"I had no alternative," she answered.

"But surely, Mademoiselle, the alternative was—*ne pas venir, n'est-ce pas?*"

"*Non!*" she replied sharply, deliberately asserting her own linguistic powers. "You see—if I had refused to come, it would have been somehow, as it were, a confession of failure."

"Confession! Then you confess, Mademoiselle? You killed your lover, *c'est vrai?*"

"Confess, kill, lover," she murmured. "You use these words as though they only had one meaning. But think how infinitely many gradations of meaning there are to the word 'lover'——."

"Enough! Mademoiselle, I do not tolerate the equivocation. I, Poirot, ask you the straight question. Did you or did you not murder Roderick Spencer-Poumphrey?"

"Does it matter?" she sighed.

"Matter? *Mon Dieu!* Do you suggest, Mademoiselle, that Death does not matter?"

"Oh, it matters in a sense, yes. But compared with the slow weariness of life, with the subtle degradations of years in which illusions, faith, hope, are gradually stripped away—does it really, perhaps, so very much matter?"

—L. W. Bailey

ERICH MARIA REMARQUE
(1898-1970)

All Quiet On Riverside Drive

Chapter I

Aspic looked out over the sea of young female faces in English 37-A. I know the real hunger here, he mused, and it is not for thought. But how easy to confuse that base and primal instinct with the cold, asexual triumph of culture, how easy to sublimate the passion of the flesh, to rechannel it into a pure, thin love for surds and supines. In what a literal sense these virgins go to bed with books, he thought ironically.

The novel to be discussed that day was *Arch of Triumph*, by Erich Maria Remarque, previously celebrated, of course, as the author of *All Quiet on the Western Front*. It dealt exhaustively with the moral and spiritual anarchy in Paris immediately preceding the war, and at the last minute old Professor Garber had pleaded illness, as he always did when faced with an assignment beyond his waning powers. In desperation, they had called in Aspic, though he had no license to teach English at The Brearley, nor indeed at any school in America. Gritzman had seen to that. They had ways of handling recalcitrant authors in Hollywood. The papers had said that McHare had committed suicide, but it was suggestive that nobody had been able to find the gun or, up to that point, even a body. It had been a simple matter for them to drive Aspic underground, to condemn him to the life of a hunted animal.

On the way up to the school in the subway, he had underlined a few passages in the book and now, while the class was still busy with the written assignment, he reread them scornfully:

"There are more secrets in your hair than in a thousand questions." (This was on Page 161, a duet *con amore*, taking place in a taxicab.) "The hour is life, the moment is closest to eternity, your eyes glisten, star dust trickles through infinity, gods can age, but your mouth is young, the enigma trembles between us, the You and Me, Call and Answer, out of evenings, out of dusks, out of the ecstasies of all lovers, pressed from the remotest cries of brutal lust into golden storms, the endless road from the amoeba to Ruth and Esther and Helen and Aspasia, to blue Madonnas in chapels on the road, from jungle and animal to you, to you. . . . "

My God, how the fat collects on these successful writers, Aspic thought wearily, great, yellow layers of it, separating verb from noun, subject from predicate, stifling the clean brain with futile and superfluous tissue, clogging it with the pale suet of rhetoric. How many dinners at "21" and the Brown Derby had conspired to drape this unwholesome flesh on the once slender skull, how many soft beds and lazy hours in the sun had served to pad this style so fatally with adipose reference and fatty rhythms, how many enormous checks must have been swallowed to swell the belly of art to such astounding size. He turned the leaves with distaste.

"One could not escape it!" he read on Page 20. "The irony of nature. . . . The organs of ecstasy at the same time diabolically arranged for excretion."

Aspic grinned. Love and function. What an old friend *that* irony was, he reflected, and how it betrayed the awful naïveté of the literary mind that this reflection, comprehensible at sixteen, should come so blindingly to writers in their middle years. Maugham, Huxley, Hemingway, Farrell, Wolfe—a hundred of them in his memory had offered it in almost precisely the same words, always with exclamation points, always as a subtle, sardonic discovery of maturity. How writers must depress their wives, he thought, how much indulgence must be required to put up with these minds always triumphantly exposing the secrets of the nursery, ruthlessly laying bare the tiny scandals of the bassinet. The book was full of other ironies—the essentially bourgeois heart of the prostitute, man's simultaneous faith in God and high explosives, the specific and almost inevitable irony of a woman who carried death in her body, in the form of a disease, escaping by a hair's breadth a less agonizing death at the hands of the Nazis. It was Aspic's private opinion that *Arch of Triumph* was one of the most preposterous books he had ever read, but you had to admit that the critics had eaten it up. It was like catnip to them. How humbly they abased themselves before any talent capable of producing these high-school paradoxes; how they cavorted and leaped before it, like King David, with what obscene posturings; how they addressed it in unknown tongues, with what hyperpyrexial ardors. Well, it was no concern of his. He looked at his watch and saw that it was time for him to begin his oral examination.

"All right, Miss Abacus," he said, calling the first name on his list. "What is your opinion of this book?"

She was a tall, fierce girl, smoldering secretly, like an ancient fire in the bowels of a coal mine, like a dropped ash on a drunkard's mattress.

"Well, it ought to make an awfully cute movie, Mr. Aspic," she said.

Instantly, her words called up the searing past. "On the whole, I think you will find it wise to adapt *Cass Timberlane* for us," Gritzman had said pleasantly. "I make no threats, of course, but after all, there have been—ah—accidents." For six days and nights, he had stuck to his refusal, though they had burned strips of film under his fingernails and he had heard McHare scream when they lowered him into the vat of developing fluid. On the seventh, when they had left him for unconscious or dead, he had escaped, climbing down one of the artificial vines outside the window of Gritzman's office. Now he was in New York—finished, hunted, a never-resting corpse.

"I think it's *terribly* cute," he heard Miss Abacus murmur through the red and swirling mist. He fingered the revolver he always carried in his pocket these days, but some instinct stayed his hand. No, that was for Gritzman, and then one final shot for his own sick and rebel heart.

Chapter II

"You know what you are?" Aspic asked Puberto, who had once been an equerry at the Italian court but was now in charge of the washroom at the Hotel Navarre, where the fugitives from Hollywood often gathered in the afternoon for gin and little cakes.

"A comet flaring out in hollow space," said the old man. "A gnat swirling above a stagnant pond."

"I'll handle any figures of speech around here," said Aspic. "No, you are a literary convenience borrowed from a man called Ernest Hemingway. The symbol of a disinherited regime, the articulate voice of an ancient disillusion, the wisdom of an older civilization respectfully supplementing the cynicism of the new. Your literary function is to lend the prestige of age and experience and a Continental background to my observations about life, to place my epigrams, so to speak, in the golden setting of an established culture. You are Count Mippipopolous in *The Sun Also Rises*, Count Greffi in *A Farewell to Arms*, Max in *The Fifth Column*, Pilar in *For Whom the Bell Tolls*. In effect, you are a straight man with an interesting accent."

"That's right, Aspic," said Puberto. "You care to wash your hands for a change?"

Chapter III

"Well, where are we going for dinner tonight?" asked the woman sullenly.

"Dinner tonight?" he echoed. "Where shall any man go tonight or *any* night, and for what doomed and inscrutable purposes? Between the womb and the grave, the open door and the earthen cell, the song and the silence, lie many rich and mysterious feasts, making men happy and sick; many strange viands, but all fuel to the small, inexorable flame of dissolution. How ironical to think intellectually about a piece of steak—life eating life to maintain the slow, fatal combustion that must end in death, and the body finally returned to the soil, fodder for an eternity of steaks."

"You kill me, Aspic," she said, without amusement, and reached for the bottle of gin beside the bed. "Drink?"

"How ironical that man should look for peace in poison," he said. "Well, only a short one. I've got a class in the morning."

"Listen, just what *do* you do all day, Aspic?" she said. "I've never been able to figure it out."

"I *was* a writer," he said, seeing again in his mind the high, appalling towers of Hollywood and the bright insanity in Gritzman's eyes as they chained another author to his desk. "There was some trouble—I wouldn't make a picture. They are cunning devils out there—but I'll spare you the details. Now I teach English at a girls' school. Without a license, of course," he added bitterly, and took another drink. "We are all snowflakes on the lid of the infinite stove," he said.

"The trouble with you, Aspic, is you know too many Russians," she said. "All this irony and doom."

Outside the window lay Riverside Drive, the trysting place for roofless love, an urban lane of ordered asphodel and geometric shade, where the dead hero of Vicksburg and Shiloh and Appomattox lay in granite majesty brooding over a polluted stream, while high on the other bank Palisades Park, the summer playground of so many hollow men, lay gaunt and desolate under the winter sky. Suddenly, a row of flaming letters marched across the horizon: "The time is now 8:41. Longines The World's Most Honored Watch."

"*Götterdämmerung*," he whispered. "The hour of the rat."

The woman got up from the bed and went to the window. She moved as if to the sound of secret music—the "Barcarolle," "Japanese Sandman," "Ol' Man River," a confused and dissolute medley. He knew that she was deceiving him with the man from the State Income Tax Department (it was hardly likely that she'd gone to Albany with him solely to discuss a rebate of thirty-seven cents), but his blood called to her, this Helen of the sunken ships, this hamstrung Salome, this Nike proclaiming only stale defeats. She looked at him, lost and shameless secrets in her eyes.

"You know what I want, Aspic?" she asked sombrely.

"No." The pulses hammered in his throat.

"Food," she said. "God, Aspic, I could eat an author!"

The pleasure of the table, he thought, that grossest of the appetites—how women cherish it, how like a god. How many fair bodies on the long march from Eden to Babylon, from Rome to Wilshire Boulevard, have been sold for lesser flesh, for tournedos and sturgeons' eggs and the livers of fat geese, how often has chastity been martyred in the pale, blue flame of crêpes Suzette or racked by the cruel pressure on the duck, from the tang of that first apple to the putrescence of the final cheese, the dark story . . .

There was a knock at the door and the woman looked at him inquiringly. He took the revolver out from under his pillow and motioned her into a corner. It had come, then. Well, they would never take him back alive. He raised the gun and flung open the door. He had expected Gritzman and the studio police, but it was only a bellboy with something on a tray.

"Telegram for you, Mr. Aspic," he gasped, his eyes bulging at the sight of the weapon. Aspic took the message from the boy and kicked the door closed with his foot. With trembling fingers, he tore open the envelope and scanned the yellow sheet. For a moment he stood transfixed and then the little room was filled with the sound of his mad and terrible laughter. The woman shrank against the wall.

"What's the matter, Aspic?" she said nervously. "Some bad news?"

"Bad news!" he echoed, still shaking with his awful merriment. "No. A joke. A superb, impossible joke, one to stagger the credulity of the gods."

"You and your jokes," she said sullenly. "The Little Caesar of the hotfoot and the exploding cigar."

"No," he said. "This is like no joke you ever heard. It is the cosmic and ultimate irony, the last, sardonic chuckle of the Fates." For a moment his wild hilarity threatened to strangle him, but then he spoke again. "I can go back," he gasped. "Gritzman says the hell with *Timberlane*. They've got another picture for me and they'll pay ten thousand a week."

"Ten thousand!" she cried. "For God's sake, Aspic, what have they got? The New Testament?"

"No," he said, shaking with his secret, terrifying glee. "A stranger, far more costly dream. They've bought me *Arch of Triumph*."

"Oh, God," she faltered. "And there's no escape this time? No possible retreat?"

"No," he said. "They've tracked us here. Perhaps they're outside now. Besides, I'm tired of running away. Good-bye," he said. "Farewell, my false Godiva of the henna rinse." He closed his eyes and raised the .45. Outside the night crept softly down the dreaming streets, and Grant lay cold and mocking in his tomb.

—Wolcott Gibbs

ERNEST HEMINGWAY
(1899-1961)

Over The River And Through The Woods

I

When the shooting stopped, I needed a drink. Do not think I needed a drink because I was afraid. I have been afraid several times, but never because of the shooting. I needed a drink because I was thirsty.

I took a pull from the bottle. The whiskey was good. It burned my mouth and felt good and warm going down my esophagus and into my stomach. From there it was digested, and went to my kidneys and my bladder and into my intestines, and was good.

Then I got up from the ditch and walked back to the Red Cross truck. The doctor was bandaging someone's groin. It looked bad.

"What's your problem?" he asked me.

"I've been hit," I said.

"Where?"

"Here."

"Let's see. Hmm."

"Is it bad?"

"Nipped the left ventricle."

"Damn."

He bandaged my heart and I got a three-week furlough. I decided to go to Paris and I went to Paris. I had not been to Paris since I had left it, and it was fine to be back. I walked down the rue Pensées, and turned off at the rue J'Accuse. On the rue François-Hardy was a café. I did not want to go inside it. It looked dirty, and poorly lighted. But I saw Lady Bob Ashton and her fiancé Steve inside, so I went in. Bob had sleek curves like a high-powered hunting bow, and her sweater held them very well.

"Hullo, Abe," Bob said. "Hullo."

"Hello, Bob. Hello, Steve."

"Hello, Abe. Join us?" Steve motioned for me to sit down. "I was just telling Bob what a splendid time we are going to have in San Cugat."

"Oh, rather. I say, Abe, we *are* going to have a fine time," Bob said. She put a cigar in her mouth. "Give a chap a light?"

"I say, Abe, why don't you come along?" Steve asked. "You can come with us on the train, and we'll do a bit of fishing. Oh, do come. Do."

"Buy a pint of beer?" Bob asked. I think she was tight. "Have a glass of wine? Drink a pint a milk a day?"

"You're tight."

"Don't talk like a fool."

"You're cock-eyed."

"Oh, give a chap a break."

"I say, don't, what?"

"What?"

"What?"

"What?"

"I said, I say, don't, what? What?"

"Will I not!"

"I say, do don't."

"What?"

"I say, do let's don't. Do. Don't."

"Oh, rather."

"What?"

"What?"

II

That night I walked along the rue Petit-Mal. I must have been tight, because my mind was jumping around, and I felt pretty rotten. I thought about Bob. I had met her at an Italian field hospital for anti-fascist bullfighters. I crossed the Pont Pilate and walked up the rue Nausée. I had told Bob about everything. I told her about the time I was a boy in Minnesota. I had been present when my father had tried to deliver an Indian baby with a can-opener and a copy of *A Sportsman's Sketches* by Turgenev. It had been bad. The Indian father had cut his throat with the book, and the mother had gone blind reading the can-opener. Well, that was all past. And Bob was such a swell friend. Oh yes, a swell friend. The hell she was!

I passed several poules lying in the street, but walked over them. I had a few drinks at a café on the rue Mauvaise-Foi, and arm-wrestled with a Cuban fisherman. "I have been fishing the obscenity big fish today," he said. He beat me, and suddenly I started to cry, and felt like hell. The old fisherman patted me on the back. "There, there," he said. "It is nothing. When thou hast lived much like I have, thou knowest that it is nothing. I was a soldier in the war. I have lived much. It is nothing."

I asked him what he did in the war.

"I was twenty-one years of old. By myself alone, with a single hand, I defeated a group of Spanish soldiers. They were disguised as a machine for thrashing the wheat, but I was not fooled. I have many scars." He took off his clothes and showed me his scars. They were all over his body. "Also, I lose both the eyes." He took off his glasses, and I saw his eyes. Moisture beaded on the glass. "Also the hair falls out, I lose the power of the sex. The hands turn into claws, I have no heart, my head is stuffed with straw, and I am talking to you through the aid of a ventriloquist." He bought me a drink. After we had drunk the whiskey he said, "So thou seest, my friend, because I have lived much I know how to have a good time." I shook his hand, and he left.

Then I walked back to the hotel, and went to my good room. I slipped my shoes off and went to sleep. Later that night, I woke up and heard the wind howling and the rain beating against the windows. It felt good to be warm and asleep under the blankets. One of the blankets was my favorite pink frilly flannel comforter with the blue bunny rabbits on it, and it felt very, very good.

III

The next day I met Bob and Steve at the Gare Eau Way, and we got a train for San Cugat. It was a good day, and we had good riding. Bob looked damned good. She wore her hair brushed back like a boy's and a man's hat and jacket, and a beard. Once we were alone in the compartment, I held her close to me and kissed her. Her eyes looked all the way into mine. She said, "Oh, don't!" and pulled away. I didn't. Then I sat back and thought about the war.

Oh yes, the war. Here's to you, war. I remembered the last battle I had been in. It had been bad. We had spent many nights in the foothills when Franco's men besieged our camp. The fascists had sent a large number of troops across the lake disguised as crippled mules. I watched them through the trees, stepping out of the mules' skins and washing each other of the blood and tissue. We had been pinned down, and were surrounded without food or water for three weeks. I had decided not to wait them out. I didn't mind. You paid for everything in life. It was a simple exchange of values. So I stood up and shot as many men as I could, the bullets cutting deep into the soldiers' muscle and bone, and lodging there with a good clean pain. Many of the men screamed and died. The sun was hot, and there had been good screaming and good dying. I threw the mule skins into the river, and with some of the leftover mule meat made a fine casserole. Then I waited behind a rock until the others died of boredom. That had been good, damned good.

"I say, bungo old sportbean chap old man old thing, Abe old classmate fellow bean. We're here." Steve said. We had arrived at San Cugat. We took a taxi to the hotel, and we each had a good small room and a nice bed and a glass of milk and a cookie.

IV

The next day Steve and I went fishing while Bob walked around the town. I bought four twelve-liter bottles of wine from a small shop that smelled of wine and liters, and we packed our gear and set off.

We arrived at the river, and Steve went upstream to fish flies. I stayed downstream to fish fish. I baited my line and waded out into the cold stream. Ahead of me there were woods, and a forest. There were trees extending north and south, and pine scrub birch timbertops to the left of a ravine. Down a canyon ran a ridge of maple log peatmoss bog bark, while just above the left of the front of the mountain face was a cliff of ravine-bottomed dune boulders and a gush of mulch leaves streaming through a gulley patch as a deer of goats ran through the cactus bush and parched the elm grove. Beyond the fringe was mountain laurel and beechnut spearmint, while over to the east were green moss-backed canoe-tops of lily-livered mountain lions, timber elks, moose, kiwanis, and neighborhood rotaries. I swam out into a pool of water. It felt good to swim out. I was reading a fine book, a story of a horse, and the boy who loved him.

Then Steve came back, and we took out the wine and drank. He showed me his fish, and I showed him mine. He let me touch his fish, but I would not let him touch mine. We drank some more. The wine was icy cold, and tasted faintly rusty, so I drank it out of the bottle and followed each swallow with a chaser of chrome cleaner. Then, of course, the chrome cleaner reminded me of when I was in Africa hunting the big game. I thought about it. I had good thinking. I thought about the native boys we had in our group, who carried the guns and set up the camp and did everything while we drank and thought about the war. There was a guide in our party, a man named Williams. He had seen a lot of action in the jungle, and had been killed three times.

One morning we all awoke early. We knew we were going to hunt for very big game that day. We parked our gear and set off through the savanna. We hiked through the veldt and the steppes, and marched across the tundra and Tigris and the Euphrates. We passed many ferocious tigers and pumas that morning, but we were not out after them. We passed lions and zebras also, but we were not out after them either.

"We are not out after these poor brutes," Williams had told us. "You gents want to hunt the big game, or spend your time killing animals?"

We hiked along into the afternoon, and soon came to the place where, Williams said, the big game came to graze. I checked my rifle, and double-checked the pump barrel, safety catch, telescopic sight, barrel bore, and flintstone. Each chamber held a Schnauzer .414 shell. They were very powerful weapons. We hid in the tall grass, and in a while we heard the sound. There was a rustling of trees, and a shaking of dice and very large plastic pieces. Paper money began drifting down through the jungle growth. Williams squinted off into the distance.

"M'boomi m'boomi m'boomi boo?" asked one of the boys, a young tent carrier.

Williams shrugged and spat. "Can't tell, lad. Could be Rich Uncle. Sounds like Careers. Too early to tell."

Suddenly the wind shifted, and Williams leaped to his feet and cried, "There! See it? Careful, now . . . easy, gents . . ." It was an enormous set of Monopoly, the largest I had ever seen.

It came charging directly at us. The natives scattered. Two were knocked unconscious by huge green plastic houses that the Monopoly flung left and right. I saw Williams dodge a large die. Suddenly, the fear drained out of me, and I stood very still in the field and aimed the rifle and squeezed off the two rounds. The noise was very loud.

I saw the board lunch backward, and topple. Then came a rain of paper money, of many different colors. There were many twenties. Then the board fell, and was buried under its own money as more houses and big red hotels with good small rooms and warm beds fell around us. Then something hit me on the head, and I passed out. They told me later that it had been a falling deed, maybe one of the orange ones to New York or Tennessee. The camp was pretty much destroyed by the falling deeds, but we did not care. That night we had a great feast and roasted all the Chance and Community Chest cards over a bonfire and ate heartily.

It was a good memory. Damned good. But the sun was setting, and Steve and I had to pack and get back to the town.

V

The next day the festival was really started. All over the town people were dancing and singing and having fun. We walked around the town and saw the signs: HURRAY FOR WINE! HURRAY FOR THE COCKS AND BULLS! YANQUIS GO JOME! "Let's go see the bulls," I said to the others.

We walked to a corral where the bulls were. Many men and boys were standing around the perimeter of the area. I saw a man whom I knew from many years of coming to San Cugat. His name was Marimba, and he owned a café. I walked over to him.

"Your friends, have they *aficion*?" he asked.

"Some," I said. "Not as much as I do, though." He nodded.

Aficion means passion. There are those who have it, and those who do not. The cock and bull fights are a special ritual in Spain and only those who have *aficion* can truly appreciate the spectacle. Without *aficion*, the fights are nothing. Those with *aficion* know much about the *bullfighters* and the *cock-fighters*, because bulls and cocks have *aficion* also. Men like Marimba would forgive anything in a bull or a cock with *aficion*; fear, nervousness, fibbing, incest, extortion, anything. Otherwise, though, it is nothing.

Soon, there was the running of the bulls. The gates to the corral were opened, and the bulls ran around the city. Some of them went to good restaurants and ate *paella* and *bifstec*. Others just joined us at Marimba's café and got tight. Then we went to the cock house to watch the cocks warm up. There were many old bulls there, bulls too old or weak to be good bullfighters, but who were useful as practice partners for the young cocks. The cocks were dressed in their sweatsuits, each with the name of his sponsor sewn onto the back. JAIME'S LIQUORS, ROBERTO BAMA AUTO PARTS, JULIO MORON, REG. PLUMBER. The cocks hefted their weighted pics, and unsheathed their knives. Then they went at each other for a few practice rounds, not trying very hard to score any cuts since after all it was only practice.

"It is sad," Marimba said. He shook his head. "When I am a young man, there are many bulls and cocks and the fighting is good. Today, however . . . it is nothing . . ."

After a few more drinks and a few more drinks we went to the arena. Steve was tight, and Bob was drunk, and I was cockeyed, and we had a good party. We sat in the sun and passed a bottle back and forth. We did this for an hour before we noticed that the bottle did not have any wine in it, and was empty.

"I say, Abe, we *are* enjoying ourselves," Steve said.

Then the procession started. First the judges and referees came out, wearing their long dark robes and striped shirts. Then there were musicians. The pipes and fifes were playing the *riau-riau* music, and the drums were making the boom-boom. Finally, the bulls came out, the large hump of muscle on their backs fitted with the cock-saddles. They marched out in a solemn procession, dressed in bright silks and deep red capes. Then came the cocks, carrying their special pics and holding at their sides the sheathed knives. They too marched slowly to the *riau-riau* boom-boom, and were very proud.

I sat beside Bob and explained to her what it was all about. We watched as the cocks mounted their bulls and settled into the saddle. Then Bob saw the cocks set with their pics, and unsheath the knives. The blades flashed in the sun, which was very hot on the yellowish sand. There were six cock-and-bull teams competing, and all over the arena the people were cheering on their favorite team. The six teams formed a circle in the center of the arena, and a referee stood in the middle with a yellow kerchief held aloft. There was a great silence. The flags around the arena hung limply in the heat. Steve passed me something to drink, but it was only chrome cleaner, so I didn't take much. Then the referee dropped the kerchief, and the fight began.

I explained to Bob that the object of the fight was for each cock to cut off the ears of the other bulls and finally to kill the other cocks with the pics. There were several rules that made the cock-and-bull fights a test of skill and courage, and not just a lot of animals running after one another. No cock could be killed until all bulls had their ears cut off. If any cock was killed before that time, he and his killer were eliminated, and the bulls also. Once all ears had been cut off, an umpire raised a green flag called an *andipanda*, and then the work with the pics began. Any cock who fell off his bull was, of course, in great danger, as was any bull who lost his cock. There was great power in the partnership between the bull and the cock, and people with *aficion* came from all over the world to see these fights.

It was becoming clear that the competition was mainly centering on two teams, with the other four barely keeping up. Already most ears had been cut, with the people in the stands crying "otro oido!" every time another ear fell bloodily to the sand. Marimba was sitting next to Steve, and I saw him shake his head and say, "It is nothing." It was true, because most of the cocks were clumsy with the knives, and the ears were cut sloppily and without grace. Soon many people sensed this, and began throwing old pig's feet onto the area ground and calling abusive things to the animals. They ignored the crowd.

When all ears had been cut and the green flag raised, the air became more tense. Not long after that, the first cock was killed, and his bull had to carry him off on a stretcher assisted by an old steer who was the trainer. The cock-and-bull teams ran around the arena after each other, and the sun grew hotter. I told Bob not to look at the bulls when they got hit, but she could not take her eyes off them. After a while all cocks had been killed except two, and they stalked each other warily. The bulls were very tired, but they did not stop. They circled each other, the cocks lashing out with the pics. The crowd was silent. The sun was high in the sky, there was no shade for anyone.

The cocks soon tired. Their pics dropped, and they slouched in their saddles. Soon the bulls had slowed to a kind of shuffle, and it began to look as if the two teams were doing a slow cha-cha. The few remaining people with *aficion* in the stands began to boo, then they too went to sleep. I looked over at Bob and Steve, and the three of us left the arena, picking our way past the sleeping bodies. Just before we left I turned back to the arena and saw one of the cocks run his pic through the other one. Some people cheered, and a young girl skipped across the blood-caked sand and handed the victorious cock the key to the city.

VI

After that we went back to Paris. I ran into Jay Scott FitzDiver on the rue Genêt.

"Abe! Old sport!" He looked like hell.

"You look like hell," I said.

"Oh, I know it, old sport. How's the writing?"

"All right." That set me thinking. The writing, oh yes. I remembered when I was up in Michigan. Whenever I would be unable to write, I would go to the window and look out and think, "Do not worry. You have always written before. You can do it. You are a big boy now. Now go to the mirror." I would go to the mirror and look at myself. Then I would say, "Every day and in every way, I am getting better and better." Then I would think, "Now go write one true sentence," and I would sit down and write: The quick brown fox jumped over the lazy dog's back. Then I would go to a fine bar and drink anisette. I would dip my big toe in the dark green liquid until it turned a cloudy amber, and my big toe turned a deep orange. The writing of that one true sentence was easy, and a bad discipline. But the drinking of anisette was good.

"What are you doing, Jay?" I asked him.

"Oh, not much, old sport. I'm just travelling. A week or two here, a week there. In about a month I thought I'd go back to the States, write some love stories for McCall's, go insane, and kill myself."

I said I thought it was a fine idea, and that was what he did. Meanwhile, I crossed the rue Bourée. By then it was night, and after a few drinks I went back to my hotel, took out the gun I had used to kill the big game, and cleaned it.

—*Ellis Weiner*

The Nose Of Killer Mangiaro

"If he don't show up soon, we'll go and get him."

The two fight managers had waited in the gym since early morning. Killer Mangiaro, a middleweight native of Florence, was supposed to tune up one last time for his fight with McPherson in the public arena across the town.

"What time you got?"

"We have to get him."

"We might as well go now. Where do you suppose he is?"

They walked through the streets of Florence. "Fuh-rinzy," one of them said.

"Fee-renzy," the other corrected. "Fee-renzy Eetalia." They crossed the Ponte Vecchio over the Arno running through the streets of Florence. They were miserable. If their man was in a bar, he would be difficult to get out. It is a lot like handling a wounded bull. A bull that has been wounded will not be moved unless you approach him too quickly. Then he will charge you and gore you and kill you. So it is best to be gentle with a wounded bull. So it is best to be gentle with Killer Mangiaro.

He was seated in Harry's Bar. The two fight managers saw him through the window. It was still early in the day. The bar did not seem crowded. "How's about you go in and talk to him, you see? You speak wop, don't you. You could calm him down."

"Sure. You wait out here. He don't like you."

"He don't like you either. But you baby him and he likes that. He don't like you either, you know."

"Sure I know." He walked inside the bar. His eyes adjusted to the light slowly. "Thou art a great and noble and renowned master of the boxing," he said to Mangiaro.

"I am tired," Mangiaro said.

"Thou hast the strength and the speed and the skill which God hath given thee. Come with me to the gymnasium and we will punch the heavy bag and skip the rope."

"I am tired."

"I know that. I know that thou art drained of thy strength."

"Not the weakness," said Mangiaro. "It is the fear. I am afraid. Another," he said quietly to the bartender.

"Always thou hath this fear."

"Always," agreed Mangiaro. "You know my fear and this Scotsman knows my fear also."

"MacPherson knows not of your fear."

"I am afraid." His glass arrived. "No, I shall not go back with thee this time." He raised the glass of bourbon to his lips and the manager punched him hard, once, between the eyes in the middle of his face. Mangiaro dropped the glass. His nostrils grew big, and his eyes unfocussed and his hands dropped down to his sides and he slumped down on the bar.

"Geez Chrise," the other manager came running into the bar. "You sucker punch him? He's not gonna like that. Geez chrise."

"He don't like to get hit in the nose. You ever notice that? He don't like anybody to know he don't like to get hit in the nose either. He'll be all right when he comes to."

"You want me to help move him? Geez Chrise, right in the nose."

—Steven Goldleaf

Jack Sprat

'Come in, Jack.'

'I d'wanta come in.'

'D'wanta come in, hell. Come in bright boy.'

They went in.

'I'll have eats now,' she said. She was fat and red.

'I'd want nothing,' Jack said. He was thin and pale.

'D'want nothin' hell. You have eats now, bright boy.'

She called the waiter. 'Bud,' she said, 'gimme bacon and beans—twice.'

Bud brought the bacon and beans.

'I d'want bacon. It's too fat,' Jack said.

'D'want bacon, hell. I'll eat the fat. You eat the lean. OK big boy?'

'OK,' Jack said.

They had eats.

'Now lick the plate clean,' she said.

'Aw, honey,' said Jacks, 'I aint gotta, do I?'

'Yup,' she said. 'You gotta.'

They both licked their plates clean.

—Henry Hetherington

Across The Street And Into The Grill

This is my last and best and true and only meal, thought Mr. Perley as he descended at noon and swung east on the beat-up sidewalk of Forty-fifth Street. Just ahead of him was the girl from the reception desk. I am a little fleshed up around the crook of the elbow, thought Perley, but I commute good.

He quickened his step to overtake her and felt the pain again. What a stinking trade it is, he thought. But after what I've done to other assistant treasurers, I can't hate anybody. Sixteen deads, and I don't know how many possibles.

The girl was near enough now so he could smell her fresh receptiveness, and the lint in her hair. Her skin was light blue, like the sides of horses.

"I love you," he said, "and we are going to lunch together for the first and only time, and I love you very much."

"Hello, Mr. Perley," she said, overtaken. "Let's not think of anything."

A pair of fantails flew over from the sad old Guaranty Trust Company, their wings set for a landing. A lovely double, thought Perley, as he pulled. "Shall we go to the Hotel Biltmore, on Vanderbilt Avenue, which is merely a feeder lane for the great streets, or shall we go to Schrafft's, where my old friend Botticelli is captain of girls and where they have the mayonnaise in fiascos?"

"Let's go to Schrafft's," said the girl, low. "But first I must phone Mummy." She stepped into a public booth and dialled true and well, using her finger. Then she telephoned.

As they walked on, she smelled good. She smells good, thought Perley. But that's all right, I add good. And when we get to Schrafft's, I'll order from the menu, which I like very much indeed.

They entered the restaurant. The wind was still west, ruffling the edges of the cookies. In the elevator, Perley took the controls. "I'll run it," he said to the operator. "I checked out long ago." He stopped true at the third floor, and they stepped off into the men's grill.

"Good morning, my Assistant Treasurer," said Botticelli, coming forward with a fiasco in each hand. He nodded at the girl, who he knew was from the West Seventies and whom he desired.

"Can you drink the water here?" asked Perley. He had the fur trapper's eye and took in the room at a glance, noting that there was one empty table and three pretty waitresses.

Botticelli led the way to the table in the corner, where Perley's flanks would be covered.

"Alexanders," said Perley. "Eighty-six to one. The way Chris mixes them. Is this table all right, Daughter?"

Botticelli disappeared and returned soon, carrying the old Indian blanket.

"That's the same blanket, isn't it?" asked Perley.

"Yes. To keep the wind off," said the Captain, smiling from the backs of his eyes. "It's still west. It should bring the ducks in tomorrow, the chef thinks."

Mr. Perley and the girl from the reception desk crawled down under the table and pulled the Indian blanket over them so it was solid and good and covered them right. The girl put her hand on his wallet. It was cracked and old and held his commutation book. "We are having fun, aren't we?" she asked.

"Yes, Sister," he said.

"I have here the soft-shelled crabs, my Assistant Treasurer," said Botticelli. "And another fiasco of the 1926. This one is cold."

"Dee the soft-shelled crabs," said Perley from under the blanket. He put his arm around the receptionist good.

"Do you think we should have a green pokeweed salad?" she asked. "Or shall we not think of anything for a while?"

"We shall not think of anything for a while, and Botticelli would bring the pokeweed if there was any," said Perley. "It isn't the season." Then he spoke to the Captain. "Botticelli, do you remember when we took all the mailing envelopes from the stockroom, spit on the flaps, and then drank rubber cement till the foot soldiers arrived?"

"I remember, my Assistant Treasurer," said the Captain. It was a little joke they had.

"He used to mimeograph pretty good," said Perley to the girl. "But that was another war. Do I bore you, Mother?"

"Please keep telling me about your business experiences, but not the rough parts." She touched his hand where the knuckles were scarred and stained by so many old mimeographings. "Are both your flanks covered, my dearest?" she asked, plucking at the blanket. They felt the Alexanders in their eyeballs. Eighty-six to one.

"Schrafft's is a good place and we're having fun and I love you," Perley said. He took another swallow of the 1926, and it was a good and careful swallow. "The stockroom men were very brave," he said, "but it is a position where it is extremely difficult to stay alive. Just outside that room there is a little bare-assed highboy and it is in the way of the stuff that is being brought up. The hell with it. When you make a breakthrough, Daughter, first you clean out the baskets and the half-wits, and all the time they have the fire escapes taped. They also shell you with old production orders, many of them approved by the general manager in charge of sales. I am boring you and I will not at this time discuss the general manager in charge of sales as we are unquestionably being listened to by that waitress over there who is setting out the decoys."

"I am going to give you my piano," the girl said, "so that when you look at it you can think of me. It will be something between us."

"Call up and have them bring the piano to the restaurant," said Perley. "Another fiasco, Botticelli!"

They drank the sauce. When the piano came, it wouldn't play. The keys were stuck good. "Never mind, we'll leave it here, Cousin," said Perley.

They came out from under the blanket and Perley tipped their waitress exactly fifteen per cent minus withholding. They left the piano in the restaurant, and when they went down the elevator and out and turned in to the old, hard, beat-up pavement of Fifth Avenue and headed south toward Forty-fifth Street, where the pigeons were, the air was as clean as your grandfather's howitzer. The wind was still west.

I commute good, thought Perley, looking at his watch. And he felt the old pain of going back to Scarsdale again.

　　—*E. B. White*

THOMAS WOLFE
(1900-1938)

Of Nothing And The Wolfe

There they were, two dark wandering atoms.

Uncle Habbakuk, though one of the legendary, far-wandering Gants, and full to the bung of their dark, illimitable madness, was of but average height, being only eight or nine feet high. He lifted his form from one of his characteristic disgusting, unsavory, and nauseating messes which he had been Wolfeing in the most extraordinary manner. It consisted of old iron filings, chopped twine, oats, and clippings *hachis* from the *Times* classified ads section. With his hard, bony forefinger he prodded Aunt Liz. Ceaselessly he prodded her, hungrily, savagely, with maniacal intensity. But she gave no sign. She was lost (Oh lost! lost, who shall point out the path?) in a dream of time.

"Phuh! Phuh!" howled Uncle Habbakuk, the goat-cry welling up like a madness out of the vine of this throat. "Phuh! Phuh! Ow-ooh! *Beep*."

In the telling phrase of Baedeker, the situation "offered little that need detain the tourist," but Uncle Habbakuk, with demonic, fore-fingered energy, continued to lift up his idiotic, wordless and exultant howl. It was monstrous, yet somehow lovely, not to say fated, this gaunt confrontation of these two lonely atoms. . . . How strange and full of mystery life is? One passes another in the street, or a face flashes past as the great huge train-projectiles of America hurtle by, in all their thrill and menace, over the old brown earth, and the soul fills with sadness and irrecoverable memories. Why is this? Is it because we are the sons of our fathers and the nieces and nephews of our aunts and uncles?

Who will answer our questions, satisfy our furious impatience, allay our elemental desires, soothe our tormented unrest, and check our heavy baggage? Who?

"Beep!" barked Uncle Habbakuk in his coruscation and indefinite way. "What is man that thou—*whah!*—art mindful of him?"

"Whoo-oop," chirped and sniggled Aunt Liz. Sly and enigmatic, she picked up a morsel of bread and hurled it savagely upon the table, with a gesture old as time itself, and secret with the secretiveness of a thousand secretive, lovely and mysterious women, all secret. Then she relapsed into her dream of time. She was entranced in one of her brooding and incalculable states** (O the States, the States of America, O Alabama, Arizona, Arkansas and California; O Colorado, Connecticut, Delaware and Florida; O Georgia, Idaho, Illinois, and Indiana; O Iowa, Kansas, Kentucky and Louisiana; O Maine, Maryland, Massachusetts and Michigan; O Minnesota, Mississippi, Missouri and Montana; O Nebraska, Nevada, New Hampshire and New Jersey; O New Mexico, New York, North Carolina and North Dakota; O Ohio, Oklahoma, Oregon and Pennsylvania; O Rhode Island, South Carolina, South Dakota and Tennessee; O Texas, Utah, Vermont and Virginia; O Washington, West Virginia, Wisconsin and Wyoming; and O! O! O! O! the District of Columbia!).

At this very moment, so pregnant and prescient with the huge warp of fate and chance, the dark, terrific weaving of the threads of time and destiny, there was heard one of the loveliest and most haunting of all sounds, a sound to echo in the ears of Americans forever, surging in the adyts of their souls and drumming in the conduits of their blood. The doorbell tinkled.

"A moment's—*beep!*—peace for all of us before we die," snarled, bellowed and croaked gaunt Uncle Habbakuk, prodding himself violently in the midriff with his hard bony forefinger. "Give the goat-cry!"

"Phuh-phuh. Owooh! *Beep!*" came the goat-cry from without, and Aunt Liz opened the door. It was he, the youth, of the tribe of the Gants, eleven feet, eight inches high, with slabsided cheeks, high, white, integrated forehead, long, savage, naked-looking ears, thirty-two teeth, one nose, and that strange, familiar, native alien expression to all the Gants, wandering forever and the earth again. It was the youth but no less was it Jason and Faustus and Antaeus and Dronos and Telemachus and Synopsis and all those shining young heroes who want merely to know everything, who have hungered amid the *gewirr* of life and sought their fathers in the congeries of the compacted habitations of men, hot for the alexing of our cure and amorous of the unknown river and a thousand furious streets.

With a loose and powerful gesture Uncle Habbakuk, in frenzied despair, luminous hope and frantic entreaty, welcomed the youth, snuffling.

"Where have you *been*, youth? Have you touched, tasted, heard *and* seen *everything?* Have you *smelt* everything? Have you come from out the wilderness, the buried past, the lost *America?* Are you bringing up Father out of the *River?* Have you done any delicate diving for *Greeks?* Tell me, have you embraced *life* and *devoured* it? Tell me! Open the adyts of your soul. Beep."

"Beep," chirped the youth somberly. "I have been making mad journeys, peril-fraught and passion-laden, on the Hudson River Day Line, eight journeys, watching my lost, million-visaged brothers and sisters. I have been lying (in my upper berth) above good-looking women in the lower berth on a thousand train-wanderings. They were all of them tall and sensual-looking Jewesses, all proud, potent, amber, dark, and enigmatic. I always felt they would not rebuff me if I spoke to them, but yet I did not speak. Later on, however, I wondered about their lives. Yet I have been with a thousand women, their amber thighs spread amorously in bright golden hay. After ten thousand others have I lusted, making a total score of eleven thousand. O hot amorous flesh of sinful women!

"Pent in my dark soul I have sought in many countries my heart's hope and my father's land, the lost but unforgotten half of my own soul. In the fierce, splendid, strange and secret North have I sought; and, on the other hand, in the secret, strange, splendid and fierce South. In the fatal web of the City strangely and bitterly have I savoured the strange and bitter miracles of life; and at N.Y.U. (Downtown Branch) have I wondered darkly at the dark wonder of man's destiny. Amid this phantasmagoric chaos, in a thousand little sleeping towns built across the land (O my America! O my!) I have pursued my soul's desire, looking for a stone, a leaf, a door we never found, feeling my Faustian life intolerably in my entrails. I have quivered a thousand times in sensual terror and ecstatic joy as the 5:07 pulled in. I have felt a wild and mournful sorrow at the thought, the wonderful thought that everything I have seen and known (and have I not known and seen all that is to be seen and known upon this dark, brooding continent?) has come out of my own life, is indeed I, or me, the youth eternal, many-visaged and many-volumed.

"Whatever it may be, I have sought it through my kaleidoscopic days and velvet-and duvetyn-breasted nights, and, in my dark, illimitable madness, in my insatiate and huge unrest, in my appalling and obscure fancies, in my haunting and lonely memories (for we are all lonely), in my grotesque, abominable and frenzied prodigalities, I have always cried aloud—"

"Whoo-oops," gargled, snorted and snuffled Aunt Liz from out her dream of time.

"What is it that we know so well and cannot speak?" continued the youth, striding a thousand strides across a hundred floors. "What is it that we speak so well and cannot know?" Why this ceaseless pullulation stirring in my branching veins, not to be stilled even by the white small bite and tigerish clasp of secret women, of whom I have had one thousand in round figures? Whence the savagery, the hunger and the fear? I have sought the answer in four hundred and twelve libraries, including the Mercantile, the 42nd Street Public, the Muhlenberg Branch, and Brooklyn—ah, Brooklyn, vast, mysterious, and never-to-be forgotten Brooklyn and its congeries of swarming, unfathomable life, O Brooklyn! I have read in ten years at least 20,000 books, devouring them twelve hours a day, no holidays, 400 pages to a book, or in other words—X and I am furiously fond of other words—I have read 33 pages a minute, or a page every two seconds. Yet during this very same period I managed with ease to prowl ten thousand wintry, barren and accursed streets, to lie, you recollect, with one thousand women, and take any number of train-trips (Oh! the dark earth stroking forever past the huge projectile!) This it is to be a Gant! Questing my destiny lying ever before me, I have been life's beauty-drunken lover, and kept women and notebooks in a hundred cities, yet have I never found the door or turned the knob or slipped the bolt or torn off the leaf or crossed the road or climbed the fence. I have seen fury riding in the mountains, but who will show me the door?"

At this point Aunt Liz, with broad, placid, harmonious strokes, swam up out of her dream of time, and, uttering no words, arose from her chair. Out of her dark pocket, pursuing characteristically her underlip, she drew a Key and with it opened, at the back of the room, a Door. The youth followed her within. Before him stretched, extended, and was a combined and compacted pantry, provision-chamber, larder, storage-cellar and ice-house.

From the ceiling hung flitches of bacon, strings of onions, and festoons of confetti. On the walls hung and depended the carcasses and bodies of rabbits, hares, sheep, lambs, chamois and gazelles. On smaller hooks and on shelves were stored partridges, grouse, plovers, geese, turkeys, pheasants, snipe, capercalzie, royal bustards, and three penguins designed by Walt Disney. On the floor at the rear lay sadly a small whale. Ranged on shelves were seasonings and condiments—serried boxes, packages, canisters, bottles and jars of salt (including Epsom, Kruschen, Enos, Seidlitz and Glauber), cinnamon, saffron, olive oil, palm oil, colza oil, ground-nut oil, castor oil, and just the old oil. In a tumultuous variety of bread-boxes were to be seen cornbread, rye, gluten, white, whole wheat, buns, pumpernickel, scones, bannocks, oatcakes, biscuits, *croissants* and *brioches,* and many cubic feet of permanently buttered toast. In the section reserved for *charcuterie* the youth's brilliant eye fell on quantities of ham, tongue, smoked eels, salami, pork, caviar, smoked salmon, bacon, pimentoes, gherkins, pickles, *foie gras,* anchovies, sardines, *liverwurst, cervelat, chipolata, mortadello,* and striking quantities of plain boloney. In an enormous icebox rested crates, boxes and cases of eggs deriving from the hen, the sparrow, the bantam, the duck, the turkey, the goose, and the bald-headed eagle. In another, nested in ice, lay, deliciously, salmon, trout, carp, perch, eels, pike, herrings, mackerel, and shark's-fins. The cheeses included Roquefort, Camembert, Cheddar, Cheshire, Stilton, Gorgonzola, Brie, Saint-Marcellin, and Snacks. Of fruit and vegetables there were too many for recounting in this volume, but the curious reader will find them in the sequel, "Eugene on the River in a Catboat."

Dazzled, astounded, bewildered and amazed, the youth, thoroughly surprised, surveyed these riches, then turned, in a paroxysm of joy, to Aunt Liz, forever brooding on her dream of time.

"*This,* then, was the Key," he ululated, "*this* the Door from which the Wolfe cannot be kept!" Triumphantly he snatched a few dozen forks, knives, spoons, and can-openers and set to, his long, weary and unfathomable quest at last over forever. "Beep," chuckled Uncle Habbakuk gauntly.

—Clifton Fadiman

JAMES GOULD COZZENS
(1903-1978)

By Words Obsessed

Lance Champion gazed in solemn, half amused (or was it perhaps three-quarters?) interest—interest long since dulled by constant use yet never quite dulled enough to let him sleep (perchance to dream)—gazed down fondly now, no longer solemn, no longer half amused (or whatever it had been) at his mother's cat, a cat once named Erwin but now called Grace; a nomenclatural change brought about by a long-delayed and too-long-overlooked (who can say how much we overlook in this life?) (not I) examination of his (her) various characteristics; Grace, who now rubbed half thoughtfully half anxiously against Lance Champion's tweed-clad (but not too rough tweed) left leg, set slightly ahead of his right leg (similarly clad) in a posture of semi-walking, as indeed he was.

From upstairs, Lance Champion's mother said: "Lance, dear, is the cat out?"

Is the cat out? Lance Champion smiled to himself and thought of the day at the lake when Ella had asked that same question; poor Ella, now long since out herself—not knowing then that she would go out before the cat (and not even for the same reason)—Ella, loose-boned and mannish in her chamois-seated crew pants (she had rowed bow at Wellesley, and had become addicted—infatuated, even—to (with) having chamois next to her skin)—Ella, who could recite the whole of "Hiawatha" or have a child with equal ease (and interest); Ella always thought of the cat first, even on that now too seldom remembered (a man can't remember everything) day when Dr. Waters had slipped his gleaming stethoscope down around his neck and had said to Lance Champion: *Skeptophylaxis is what it appears to be.*

Recalling now, recalling by pressing his temples until he could feel his brown, green-flecked (often red-streaked, from nights of poring over technical manuals) eyes bulge from their spheroidally round sockets; Lance Champion saw the scene again with startling clarity; clarity all the more startling because he was beginning to black out from the pressure on his temples; he saw Dr. Waters wipe the snow from his glasses (a heavy drinker, Dr. Waters had lost his office and most of his equipment in an ill-advised mining venture, and was therefore obliged to hold his consultations out-of-doors) and start to write out a prescription.

Ashen his face, Lance Champion said: "Skeptophylaxis? Do you mean a condition in which a minute dose of substance poisonous to animals will produce immediate temporary immunity to the action of the poison?"

Dr. Waters nodded, losing his glasses.

Stunned, but not so stunned as an ox (or a cow) poleaxed by the running, hip-booted, sledgehammer swinging giant in the yellow brick local abattoir (which had been dedicated to Lance Champion Senior, The Old One, in an impressive flag-draped ceremony held in honor of his return from Law School); still and all with his senses reeling and deep gasps his breath, Lance Champion Junior said: "I take it an antiserum may be obtained from an animal. Is that correct?"

Dr. Waters said: "All too true. There are many aspects which we could discuss, and will discuss, if it suits you, but at the moment I think our first concern is for the lady, here."

Gallantly, moving as an old man but still a man with his memories, he helped Ella up from the ground, where he and Lance Champion had pinioned her for the examination, and deft-fingeredly he brushed the snow from the back of her play suit. Smiling, responding, her feet once more on the ground—the ground covered with snow but nevertheless the ground—she smiled respondingly and said: "First things come first, you know. I have to go home and feed the cat."

How like her! Lance Champion thought. How like her! And yet, looking at it from another angle, how utterly and completely unlike her! That was the thing about Ella—one thing, at least (there were others)—there were always two sides to everything about her; she had depth. And she was a woman. Everyone in town knew she was a woman, and two or three people in the adjoining town knew it, too. Lance Champion could well remember the day (afternoon, actually) not too long since but long enough for the cicatrix to have commenced its inevitable time-induced hardening, when Judge Mealy had called him into his chambers—Judge Mealy, a friend and onetime wrestling companion of The Old One's, who would always see to it that Lance Champion Junior got the best of all there was to give—and having called Lance Champion Junior into his chambers, with softness yet with judicial firmness had spoken: "Lance, this may come as a shock to you, but Ella is a shoplifter. But I'm going to have her committed this afternoon, so you don't have to worry."

Lance Champion gazed down fondly now, no longer solemn, no longer half amused (or whatever it had been) at his mother's cat, who rubbed half thoughtfully half anxiously against Lance Champion's tweed-clad left leg. Stooping, gently, yet stooping with a purpose, Lance Champion stooped and scratched the cat, then led her toward the door. And to his mother, Lance Champion called:

"No, Mom, but I'll put her out."

—Nathaniel Benchley

EVELYN WAUGH
(1903-1966)

From Officers and Booksellers

Julian Grass-Verge became a bookseller as the result of a chance encounter in a Fleet Street bar. A slightly drunk Irishman with a ginger moustache had told him that, although there were many bookshops in London, none of them were south of the river.

'None at all?' asked Julian.

'Not one' said the man. 'It's all betting shops and bingo over there. You could clean up with a nice little bookshop and I happen to have premises for sale in Brixton that would just suit a literary gentleman such as yourself.'

The shop was in Coldharbour Lane, between a fried fish parlour and the employment exchange, and Julian stocked it with calf-bound sets of the classics, devotional works, and the entire *oeuvre* of an obscure French poet published at his own expense.

On the second morning after he opened, he had his first customer; a sparsely bearded youth with a bad stammer and frizzy, fair hair which reached to his shoulders. After a lengthy discourse on the imminent collapse of the printed word as a means of communication, the youth asked for something by Marshall McLuhan.

Julian, who had listened gravely, if uncomprehendingly, directed him to Woolworths.

—*Ian Ardour*

NATHANAEL WEST
(1904-1940)

From Miss Lonelyhearts

Since the tragic death of our mother and step-father my brother acts very strangely. He talks about three mysterious pursuers. This seems unreasonable. How can I help him?

Electra

Your brother is suffering from mild persecution mania which may be cured if he realizes that others do not see his pursuers. Take no notice of his strange behaviour. If this fails, pretend to make friends with the mysterious figures and convince him that they mean no harm—arrange little dinner parties for just the five of you. Or you might try reasoning with him. He apparently feels uncomfortable about your parents' death but you can show him that he is no more to blame than you are, so that there can be no cause for anyone pursuing him. Question him sympathetically about his boyhood—his feeling of guilt may be at bottom simply shame for some unpleasant habit.

—Peter Alexander

I have seen figures in the air and heard voices while sitting in fields. I feel that I want to dress like a man and do something for my country. Can you help me?

Joan

Eyes are vitally important. Check with your oculist and get a thorough going over from an ear specialist, though it may just have been too much sun. I suggest you talk to your Mother about wearing boy's clothes. She'll tell you just how chic one can look with a boyish outfit and a close crop! As for your last problem I suggest that you join one of the many splendid Youth Organisations in your neighbourhood. If you can't locate one right away ask your vicar—there are many fine Christian ones.

—Richard Clements

My husband is the landowner in our village. Appalled by the penury of his tenants, and in the absence of a rent tribunal, I accepted his sporting offer to reduce the rack-rents if I would ride through the village unclothed. Although I begged the men to look the other way I have since been inundated with fresh complaints about stagnant drains, leaking roofs, etc. Do you think I ought to use the same method for dealing with these new troubles?

With a problem of this kind I always hesitate to give advice without knowledge of the local conditions. If all villagers—including the policeman—look the other way on these occasions, this way of exhibiting your social feelings may prove most effective. You should, however, first consult your doctor and your psycho-analyst who can see the subject from different angles and may shed more light on it.

—*E.G. Semler*

I was very silly when I was younger and sold my soul to the devil in return for knowledge. I am respected everywhere for my varsity record, but I am not looking forward to the future. I keep dreaming of fires. What can I do?

Well, "Faust," I need not tell you that you did a very thoughtless thing, but my advice would be "Brave it out and make the best of it!" Try quietly pointing out to your undesirable friend that you prefer the company of more homely people. It might help if you were to get a job with UNESCO, though I'm not quite sure how far the immunity of their officials extends. I can't discuss the rest of your letter in these columns, but I have arranged for our Doctor Ethel to send advice privately to your friend M.

—*Edward Blishen*

Can you suggest remedies for (1) sleep-walking, and (2) stains that just will not come off my hands no matter how hard I scrub them?

Scottish Lady (Mrs.)

Dear Scottish Lady,—Your problems are quite easily solved. The root cause of chronic sleep-walking is nervous tension, so please *relax* and above all avoid fretting about domestic matters. Try long walks during the day, an aspirin or two at bed-time, and if the trouble persists, don't hesitate to call in your family doctor.

I cannot fully advise you on your other problem without knowing the precise type of stain that is bothering you. Details (together with a stamped addressed envelope) would be appreciated. Meanwhile, perhaps Hubby could help to save those workaday hands by taking on an occasional household chore himself?

—Jan Aeres

GRAHAM GREENE
(1904-   )

From Touching Every Base

The small room was hot. Glancing round, Guy sensed that all eight of his companions were strangers to each other as well as to himself. Why had he, and they, come? What was his Lordship's motive in inviting this heterogeneous assembly to Motley Hall today? Still, his search for the rational had ended with his conversion, he thought self-mockingly. The situation promised—like his faith—an absence of void. An odd crowd. *Huis Clos.* Was it proscribed? In a far corner a Homosexual promised a Coloured Immigrant: 'Certainly it'll be made legal before they deport you!' There was a pallid man standing exactly in the centre of the room who had earlier confessed to Guy that he was a Liberal; to the left of him a Regular Church-goer comforted an OAP (Below Poverty Level) whilst at their feet writhed an Alcoholic in an interesting stage of DTs.

Were they then slivers from a mirror of society? If he were the Catholic wedge, then there must be . . . yes, there was the House-Owner, admiring the far wallpaper. That left one irrevocable tenth . . .

The door burst open to reveal a swaying, tousled Lord Motley. He giggled as he removed the pin from the hand-grenade he carried. 'Ten per cent of the population has been, is, or will be under treatment for some form of mental disorder!' he cried.

—*Peter Rowlett*

ANTHONY POWELL
(1905-   )

From Little Jack Horner

Horner had got himself established as far as possible from the centre of the room and I was suddenly made aware, as one often is by actions which are in themselves quite commonplace, that he was about to do something which would give him enormous satisfaction. He had somehow acquired a large seasonal confection which he was beginning to attack with a degree of enthusiasm I had not seen him display since the midnight feasts we had enjoyed at school. Eschewing the normal recourse to eating utensils, he plunged his hand through the pastry and extracted an entire fruit, an achievement which was accompanied by a cry of self-congratulation and a beatific expression reminiscent of some of those on the faces one sees in the more popular of the Pre-Raphaelite portraits.

—Alan Alexander

JEAN PAUL SARTRE
(1905-   )

From This Little Pig

I, this little pig, am going to market, but it will only become real to me when I recount my experience to the little pig who stayed at home. He stayed away from market because he cannot face the unbearable reality of finding how alone he is in a crowd. As for the little pig who is tucking into the roast-beef with his detestable pale trotters, spilling drops of red blood into the yellow tablecloth: he makes me feel sick. I feel the Nausea swelling over me again. I pull myself together and sweep the menace of beef off my plate. I have none.

Now I don't even suffer. The Nausea has departed. There is nothing but an empty hole and I cry *wee, wee, wee,* through the squares and quays, all the way home.

—*Susan Premru*

C. P. SNOW
(1905-1980)

From The Two Yogurt Cultures

Paunceley was regaling us with the clarets of '56.

'This is very civil of you, Senior Tutor,' observed Mainwaring.

'Thank you, Pettigrew Professor of Palaeontology and Sometime Fellow of Jesus,' replied Paunceley. He seemed nervous, drawn, tense.

It was a languorous February night, heady with the rich evocative reek of sweet-william. The chrysanthemums blazed in the court, a Scotch mist draped the plane-trees and above, in the sky, shimmered the stars—countless, desolate, shining.

I felt increasingly uneasy about my tendency to fire off adjectives in threes. It was compulsive, embarrassing, ineluctable; but at least it fostered the illusion of a mind that was diamond-sharp, incisive, brilliant.

'I have asked you to come here before breakfast,' continued Paunceley, 'because I have a most unsavoury revelation to make to you about one of our colleagues.'

I glanced at Grimsby-Browne. He seemed suddenly immensely old, haggard, shrivelled. Had he committed the unforgivable and falsified a footnote? I studied Basingstoke, the Bursar. He too seemed suddenly bowed, broken, desiccated. Had he done the unspeakable and embezzled the battels? The scent of Old Man's Beard saturated the combination room.

'It concerns Charles Snow,' said Paunceley.

The tension was now unbearably taut, torturing, tense. The plangent aroma of montbretia seemed to pervade every electron of my being.

The Senior Tutor's tone was dry, aloof, Olympian.

'I have discovered that his real name is Godfrey Winn.'

—Martin Fagg

SAMUEL BECKETT
(1906-　　　)

LGA-ORD

Then, Beckett decided to become a commercial pilot....
　"I think the next little bit of excitement is flying," he wrote to McGreevy. "I hope I am not too
old to take it up seriously nor too stupid about machines to qualify as a commercial
pilot."—"Samuel Beckett," by Deirdre Bair.

Gray bleak final afternoon ladies and gentlemen this is your captain your cap welcoming you aboard the continuation of Flyways flight 185 from nothingness to New York's Laguardia non non non non non non nonstop to Chicago's Ohare and on from there in the passing of gray afternoons to empty bleak eternal nothingness again with the Carey bus the credit-card machine the Friskem metal detector the boarding pass the in-flight magazine all returned to tiny bits of grit blowing across the steppe for ever

(Pause)

Cruising along nicely now.

(Pause)

Yes cruising along very nicely indeed if I do say so myself.

(Long pause)

Twenty-two thousand feet.

(Pause)

Extinguish the light extinguish the light I have extinguished the No Smoking light so you are free to move about the cabin have a good cry hang yourselves get an erection who knows however we do ask that while you're in your seats you keep your belts lightly fastened in case we encounter any choppy air or the end we've prayed for past time remembering our flying time from New York to Chicago is two hours and fifteen minutes the time of the dark journey of our existence is not revealed, you cry no you *pray* for a flight attendant you pray for a flight attendant a flight attendant comes now cry with reading material if you care to purchase a cocktail

(Pause)

A cocktail?

(Pause)

If you care to purchase a piece of carrot, a stinking turnip, a bit of grit our flight attendants will be along to see that you know how to move out of this airplane fast and use seat lower back cushion for flotation those of you on the right side of the aircraft ought to be able to see New York's Finger Lakes region that's Lake Canandaigua closest to us those of you on the left side of the aircraft will only see the vastness of eternal emptiness without end

(*Pause*)

(*Long pause*)

(*Very long pause*)

(*Long pause of about an hour*)

We're beginning our descent we're finished nearly finished soon we will be finished we're beginning our descent our long descent ahh descending beautifully to Chicago's Ohare Airport ORD ORD ORD ORD seat backs and tray tables in their full upright position for landing for ending flight attendants prepare for ending it is ending the flight is ending please check the seat pocket in front of you to see if you have all your belongings with you remain seated and motionless until the ending until the finish until the aircraft has come to a complete stop at the gate until the end

(*Pause*)

When we deplane I'll weep for happiness.

—*Ian A. Frazier*

IAN FLEMING
(1908-1964)

From Dr. Nope

As the sinister purple light winked again, the enormous eunuchs dragged Bond towards the massive steel door.

'In there, Bond,' said the unseen whisperer, 'are creatures much more formidable than any you have ever encountered. I observe that you are quivering—with curiosity.'

The door opened silently.

'Take him in!' commanded the whisperer. 'Release him—carefully. He is a little—fatigued.'

Bond darted a swift glance round the luxuriously furnished chamber.

'Yes, Bond,' said the whisperer. 'Women. Twenty beautiful women. All nymphomaniacs. None has enjoyed a man for months. Some are naked, some dressed, some in déshabille, some clad as boys. Doubtless you will have your preference.'

A naked half-caste woman stood before Bond. From her sleek black hair to her scarlet toenails, she was perfect. In a sudden frenzy of lust she threw herself upon him, kissing, biting, clawing, sobbing. Bond seized her by the throat. His only hope was to strangle, say, 15 of them. But many soft, urgent, experienced hands were caressing susceptible parts of his body, and soon he fell to the floor, writhing helplessly.

—*A. L. Thom*

MALCOLM LOWRY
(1909-1957)

From Under The Volpone

Could 'doble vista' explain the *two* vultures in the washbasin, Geoffrey wondered?

'I have no bee shames for your . . .' Dr. Vigil hesitated, ' . . . indihestion.'

'Must have something.' They turned into the Pulquerla Mordida (Geoffrey was still unsure; did it mean dog-bite or policeman?). Inside, his mind blank, he gestured wildly, 'Tengo . . . dolor del estomàgo . . .'

The barman frowned. 'Turista?'

'Dammit, I've drunk away my life here!'

'It means diarrhoea, also,' Vigil whispered.

'Ah!' Geoffrey nodded at the now scowling barman. 'Revancha del Montezuma? Haha!'

The scowl deepened.

'What's that medicine, Vigil? Bar chains?'

'Bee shame; it's English.'

'Never heard.' Geoffrey asked the barman, 'Bee shames por explosion del estomàgo?'

The barman, uncomprehending, proffered tamales, lime slices, even mucous pulque in a bucket, then, shrugging, began shooing a turkey off the enchilladas.

Feeling ghastly, Geoffrey rushed blindly out of the back of the pulqueria past an astonished mordida (so it *did* mean policeman), and stumbled into the ravine, to lie amongst the street rubbish, the dead burros and the squabbling vultures.

Don't let a silly misunderstanding spoil *your trip*! Always carry Beecham's powders!

—*Moray McGowan*

LAWRENCE DURRELL
(1912-   )

Ivy

Landscape-Tones: thumbsmudged grays athwart the walls of the unswept corridor; fuchsine pink of the floorward-pointing arrow above the door of the awaited, chain-rattling elevator. Mudspatter tans and greens on the okapi flank of the evening taxi. Remembered lilac mauves in the flecks of her eyes as she lay, softly sighing over some imagined slight, in her charming accustomed attitude of exhaustion. Bruise-purples on the shoulders of the wheeling pigeons, short scimitars slicing the white sky of this too-Western littoral.

Copernicus, the milkman, has been missing for a week. His last delivery consisted of two pints of strawberry yoghurt, a gnostic warning of his disaffection. Another mystagogue gone from the Cabal.

Cat-dust afloat between the ramparts of the timeless, senectuous tenements, caught and made golden by a random sunshaft, and below, in the dry jungle of smashed hedges and stillborn philodendron, ravaged by the sneakered *fellaheen* of the quarter, the animals themselves, self-consumed by the yellow hunger of their ancient eyes. She used to watch them from our back window, my sweet voyeuse, her entire body quivering in sympathy for their loneliness, and I would sense myself abandoned again. Ivy, the Nefertiti-eared. How can I face her now?

Crumbie, the subway motorman, sensed the truth, or the lie, in our relationship. Once, asprawl in my sling chair, his vast belly comfortably between his knees, and his humorous, rheumy, jongleur's eyes alight with the inner wisdom, the thesaurian omniscience that all my acquaintances seem to possess, he waved one of his great cuffed gloves at her as she lay asleep beside me, her head on my lap. "You think she loves you, don't you, *mon vieux?*" he said, his voice rumbling out of the caverns of his chest like an onrushing E train. "Love is your obsession. Your old noddle whirls with it day and night, the needle scratching out the same meretricious *javas*. My poor littérateur, you confuse possession with passion, convenience with adoration. Mark my words, Aeneas, you will do your innocent Dido a great hurt one day." Titubating slightly in his chair, he reached down between his feet for his glass, which was characteristically empty (he had a great thirst for the native elixirs), and held it out toward me. "You got any more *phabst*, buddy?" he said, smiling wickedly.

He was right, of course. I knew it, though I denied it thumpingly; even at the height of my shrill recusance, I could hear a piquant, subterranean *scritch-scritch*! within me—the rat-gnawings of suspicion and betrayal. How could I doubt the love of one who lay so innocently beside me now, one who had often rewarded me with a trusting, housewifely snore as I read aloud to her from my annotated volumes of de Sade and Rider Haggard? But for every trust there is a countering suspicion within us, love's antimatter. I remembered mysteries, evasions. From whom did she obtain such a gift as that uncut, sanguineous, Persian-red *bifteck* I saw her carrying, wordlessly ecstatic, across the croquet lawn of the Summer Embassy in Katonah early one Sunday morning? I never dared ask her. I have even suspected that she and Cloya might love one another. A bat thought, brushing my face in the dark. Once I surprised Cloya proffering her a Necco wafer, and sometimes on winter evenings I have intercepted a look between them, a feminine arrow of understanding and commiserating sympathy. Ouf! What confusions, what ferberian profundities!

Crumbie was still watching me. Could he know what evil surprise I had planned for Ivy? Guiltily, I looked down at her seamed, dew-lapped muzzle, the beloved profile of *ma jolie laide*, and then I awakened her and she and I played gaily before him, as if to exorcise, with her rubber bone, the witch truth that we all recognized. I remember that as we romped together, two acolytes of love hurrying through the enforced rituals of our order under the wise eye of an aged archimandrite, Crumbie murmured, "How typical of you to own a bulldog. Especially a bitch. Outrage is your forte, as are antipodes. Thus your effininate battler, your womanish Hercules. Of course, she is far too good for you."

Even as he spoke, there fell a sudden bumbling of thunder from the flat, sullen sky without—an ominous throat-clearing of the gods preceding the passing of some awful sentence. And now the deed is done, the sentence executed, and I must go this afternoon to Dr. Balsamic's establishment and face Ivy, she who understood almost nothing (no more than the impatient reader of some significant palimpsest) of what the hell was going on between us.

Season of the stocking-ladder. Winter-clank in the starved steampipes. Faint effluvium of mixed vetiver and pot from the empty marzipan jar. Rain squalls in the West Fifties, dappling the roofs of the versicolorate sports cars clustered like rank, overripe fruit in their dusty orchards. Cloya's face seen upsidedown in her full Martini glass, an avid water-lily.

Pierrepont, the gharry driver, is dead, possibly by his own hand. He was found slumped over the wheel of his cab, the coils of his *narguileh* twisted tightly about his aristocratic, Hittite neck. He had been a great womanizer, but he had been forced to deny his appetites cruelly. He confessed to me once that he suffered agonies from couvade and that his analyst (his "psyche-twist," as he called him) had warned him that he might not survive another confinement. Sad.

Aleicester, the poet, has at last finished the mighty palindrome that has entirely engaged his attention for the past eight years. Cloya brought it to me at dawn last Tuesday and I read it through in six hours, all the way from its brave, Homeric opening statement "T. Eliot, top bard, notes putrid tang," to the great dying fall of its final line," . . . Gnat-dirt upset on drab pot toilet." Cloya tells me it will probably never be published; Aleicester, half mad with his vision, has already wrangled with his publisher, claiming that since the work can be read backward as well as forward he must receive double royalties. Ironic end to one so talented, so bored.

Did I say "too-Western littoral" earlier? Odd! Just this morning I received another communication from Pinchbeck, the novelist, in which he urges me to move eastward. Near the end of this typically assertive document—a high-heaped interlinear correcting certain literate but misconceived comments I had scrawled in the margins of a fugitive work by Rhodmek Kün, the old bard of this narrow, fluminose island—he writes: "Novelists, like horticulturists, must find the proper climate for their little crop of hybrid conceits. If you persist in planting your lush tropical blooms by the sidewalks of a Hyperborean stone city, you will not be entitled to the luxury of surprise or hurt when preoccupied residents turn coldly away from your finest blossoms muttering, 'They don't even look real.' Your own verb-garden, your overmulched nouns, require a feverish Levantine sun, the swollen profligacies of some Eastern delta. Plant your flowers there—in Smyrna, Aleppo, or Alexandria—let them burgeon in all their premeditated brilliance, and *then* watch the tourists trample your borders! See them sniff, note the shocked delight in their eyes as they ogle each purple stalk, each velvet petal, each naughty stamen, and listen to them as they exclaim, 'How lovely, how wicked, how *true!*'"

Pinchbeck is listenable, of course, but I must confess that I suspect him of jealousy. For one thing, he writes so much like me—implacably Gongoresque, logorrheac to a fault. And then, Copernicus has told me that Pinchbeck once indulged in a bitter public outburst against my concept of the novel as a five-sided continuum—the quincunx book, with four characters (or four volumes) spinning in orbit about the fixed center dot of events, like a die flung down on the green baize table of truth.

I must leave now; she will be waiting. The skin over my temples feels tautly stretched—a certain warning of the onset of *cafard*. It takes me forever to get going these days; one might even suspect me of wishing to inflate the meaning of each action, however trivial or fascinating, through cunctation and quiddity.

Out, then, again into the streets. I turn westward, toward the sun, stumping bravely toward Dr. Balsamic's antiseptic couloirs. Mica-sheen from the minarets of the Squibb Building. Below the conflagration of afternoon sky, below the great Weehawken Corniche, the seared, exhausted traffic-swarm, thrilling the belly with the blare of its impatient horns. Squadrons, platoons, entire divisions of pedestrians, package-bearing, newspapered, come clicking toward me, and I notice again how blurred, how impalpable they all seem in the ambient mistral that blows across this city at all seasons from the slopes of Mt. Simile. On the corner, Gepetto, the bearded convert, winks to me as he hurries past on his way to evensong—the Copt on the beat.

I come at last to the address, pass under the chaste, fly-specked sign ARISTOTLE BALSAMIC, D.V.M., and step into the white-walled foyer and the clean, masochistic scent of iodoform. The Dravidian receptionist ushers me into Balsamic's empty consulting room, where I sit briefly, listening to the yelps and bayings of hell that fall faintly here upon my abashed ears. Palpitant, I hear a step and a shuffle without, and they enter, Balsamic resembling a sleepy-eyed snowy owl in his sterile gown, and Ivy almost hidden behind him, her head low.

No bandage. I had expected bandages. My waif is thinner, etiolated by her experience, but when she sees me her gazelle eyes light up bravely. But she does not throw herself into my arms in her customary abandoned *abrazo*. It is as I had known it would be: forgiveness was too much to expect.

I must speak. "How is she, Doctor?"

"Fine," Balsamic says. "No complications. You can take her home now."

"But then what?" I cry out. "What will she think of me for putting her through all this? I mean, what about the *spirit*, the inner maelstrom? Isn't there danger of post-operative synecdoche?"

Balsamic regards me skeptically, looking like—well, like a skeptical doctor. "Listen," he says wearily, "it was perfectly routine. It's normal to spay a dog of her age. I recommended it, and I'm sure I was right."

I take the leash from him and make one more effort. "Doesn't it mean *anything* to her?"

"Not a blessed thing. Oh, if she seems to have any trouble sleeping tonight, you might slip her a Bufferin, but that's all. In a few days she'll have forgotten all about this." He must perceive some vestigial shimmer—could it be disappointment?—in my eyes, for he steps forward and places a friendly, scrubbed, Philistine hand on my arm. "Look, fella," he says in his emollient baritone, "you writers, particularly you vocabulary-enrichers, ought to go easy on yourselves. All this high-class suffering and speculating, I mean. You're so damned sure that everybody is chock-full of passion and guilt and memory and all like that, when most of the time—almost all the time, if you ask me—they're not thinking of anything but their next can of Ken-L-Ration. Keep that in mind—O.K.?"

I nod, and Ivy and I take our leave. Outside, darkness has veiled the aged face of the courtesan streets, and the buildings above us cast down an autumnal pollen of yellow lights. The leash slack between us, we turn automatically and prophetically toward the East, each wincing faintly from our interior wounds. We are both exhausted, and no wonder.

—Roger Angell

ALBERT CAMUS
(1913-1960)

From Diary of a Stranger

Monday
By chance, blew up Perpignan Airport killing 3,000 people including my mother. It was a gloriously sunny day and if it hadn't been for the fag of stepping over the mutilated bodies the walk back to the boat would have been quite agreeable. I whistled to myself, thinking about the way I moved my tongue to vary the notes, and my benign disinterest stretched on to the limbless corpses that were strewn over the runway.

Tuesday, Wednesday, Thursday
Stayed in bed reading *The Ecstasy of Indifference* by Claude who plays on the left wing. Got half way through but couldn't be bothered to finish it.

Friday
Went to the beach with Marie. Very hot. Saw cripple kicking mangy dog. I wondered whether to stop the cripple and talk to him about happiness and money. I wondered whether to kill him or not, but didn't really feel in the mood for that. Perhaps tomorrow, after a swim. I put my head in Marie's lap and fondled her breasts. It was almost as good as whistling.

Saturday
Too busy living to think.

Sunday
Played in goal for Algiers Wanderers instead of going to mother's funeral. Nice sunny day. Can't remember the score.

—*Roger Pellman*

THE CONTEMPORARY SCENE

1954: Golding, *The Lord of Pop Flies.*
1965: Kosinski, *The Painted Broad.*
1968: Mailer makes public spectator of himself.
1969: Roth, *Katherine Anne Portnoy's Complaint.*
1971: O'Donoghue, *Let Me Teach You How To Write Good.*
1982: Updike, *Flick Your Bech.*

TOWARDS A NEW MACADEMIC NOVEL
Asked to complete Melville's sentence,

> Begin with an Individual and before you know it you have created a Typee; begin with a Typee and before you know it you have created _____ .

a Modernist like Hemingway might have said "nada," and been right. But how would a contemporary writer—circus 1982—fill in Melville's blank? It is unlikely that the Postmodern writer—say, John Barf or others of that elkin—would resort to traditional fictional elements. Rather, Barf rejects fictional elements with passionate, almost hemorrhoidal fury. In "Life Studies," for instance, Barf mounts a widowing attack on such pedestrian elements as plot and character. The narrator no sooner begins his chronological account of the action than he is undercut by his own authorial omnivorousness. Try as he might, he cannot proceed very far before the paralysis of Eliot's fractured Adams sets in and his fiction turns into a monstrous hall of *miglior fabliaux*. It is as if Barf is acting out Eliot's assertion about the ancients: that we know so much more than they did, and it is precisely *that* which we know. Although certain writers do attempt to eschew surplus knowledge (I think of the public spectators of Norman Mailer and the urban wit of John Updike), always to feel it necessary to respond to their age of lost bargain values by "recapitulating them by puberty" (Edmund Wilson's phrase) is not easy.

MORAL FICTION OR INELUCTABLE QUASIMODALISM?

Is there anything on the horizon to fill the literary vacuum which followed on the heels of the *coup d'état* scored by the Post-post-modernists over the Post-modernists? I suggest that it may be John Gardner's watershed book, *On Moral Fiction*, which sounded the carrion call against which the works of his gerontion must be measured. Gardner's point in *On Moral Fiction* is that a violent skewering has occurred in literature at the hands of a pulseless genera of hollow men, alcoholics, shriekers, suicidals, maniacs, manics, and depressives such as John Barf, Herbert Coover, Isaac Bolshevick Singer, Katherine Anne Portnoy, Dylan M. Thomas, Joyce Carol Oles, and others who purport to be our spiritual reprehensitives. Art has been overrun by Ineluctable Quasimodalists such as William H. Gass (author of *Hilary Masters's Lonesome Wife*). Gass holds that the text—or for that matter, the work of poetry or fiction—is the sum of its verbal constructs and nothing more. This theory is anathenema to Gardner, who invokes the epic shades of Odysseus and Aeneas, writers whose use of mnemonic visual aids and rhythm-method were intended to inseminate (by oral means) examples of right conduct and virtue in the eye of the beholder. Gass retaliates by citing such authors as Jorgé Louis Borgia, Vladimir Nabisco, Marcel Prude (the stepson of Mallomar), and Rainer Maria Roethke (the German Dean Martin). From these writers Gass inherited the notion that the author gets the first line of "inspiration" not from the Muse but from Paul Valery. Through cerebral effort—the writer is *not* a jug—the author completes the verbal construct, then throws away the line by Valery. Gardner scoffs at this parable, and instead invokes the shades of such great writers as Tolstoy, Baryshnikov, and Gogol's wife. Gass responded by calling Gardner a jawless clothespin. Furious, Gardner dashed off his Beowoolfian novel, *Helen Grendler*, in which Gass, represented as a kind of thinking wodwo, is torn limb from limb.

ART IMITATING FICTION, OR FICTION ART?

And there the combatants stand. Caught between two worlds are Gardner and Gass, one dead and the other powerless to be bored. Representatives of the Post-post-modern, they are involved in a conflict as powerful as any in contemporary fiction. Is it art which imitates fiction here, or fiction art? If only the works of the past followed, rather than preceded, the present, we would know, because then we would be able to predict the future. Because we cannot predict the future, we must remember what literature teaches us: first, that conflict is the verb of fiction; and second, that despite what's denied us, we can still stand back and admire our lack of perspective from a distance.

WILLIAM BURROUGHS
(1914-   )

"Bull" Burrup

A MEMOIR

Toddlers are taking over. O-
ver! Sabbath belling. Snoods converge
on a weary-daring man.
            —John Berryman

Brk-n-brk-brk. Ko-ax, Ko-ax
            —Aristophanes

The first time I saw Bull Burrup (Wilbur Seukus Burrup III, Harvard '38) was when I was scheming to indite obscenities on the wall of the faculty lounge at Colombia University. Bull came lurching down the street. His arms and knees flopped akimbo like one afflicted with some form of muscular degenerative disease.

His knees finally gave out, buckled. He sank to the sidewalk. Fifty-seven apathetic New Yorkers gazed on in utter indifference as Burrup gasped out an agonized barely-articulate plea for help.

At first the sound reminded me of a mantra I had picked up on the West Coast. But then I was jolted from this revery by the fascinating cyanotic hue beginning to suffuse his shaggy visage. Deeper than cornflower blue, it reminded me purplish-blue in the watercolors of the Zen painter Hirogoche.

I hesitated. Then I quickly ascertained that Burrup was choking on what seemed to be a large piece of gray meat. Immediately I positioned myself behind him and performed the Heimmlich maneuver. After I had made a few hard compressions of his upper abdomen, something popped out of Bull's mouth. It fell with a distinct plop on the sidewalk, began to wiggle, turned upright and slowly hopped away. At the same time I felt something turn squishy, mushy in my hands, still clasped around Burrup's solar plexus.

I stepped back. Burrup regained his color. But to my horror, I saw blood on my hands. Thinking I had injured him, I shrieked, "Are you all right?" I had visions of endless litigation, and I yearned for the apathy, the cosmic indifference of animals who placidly ruminated in fields far from the crazy-making asphalt and concrete cacophony. They moo and they do not curse their fate.

Bull nodded gratefully, his eyes still watery and red. There was a peculiar albumenous stain on the front of his trousers and the remains of a dead toad, crushed by my efforts, leaked through his shirt.

"Don't let it get away," he drawled.

"What?"

"The toad, you idiot. The toad!" He pointed at the beast, now rapidly hopping down the gutter toward a storm drain. Burrup made a hearty lunge for the toad, but it got away, lost in the humid subterranean murk beneath the harsh city. (Who knows what strange mutants lurk there after all these years—half toad, half alligator. Talk about your recombinant DNA. . . .)

Bull was disconsolate. I had saved his life. But for what. What price survival. He had lost his toads.

I went back to his pad with him and we snorted morning glory seeds and ginsing. It was then that Bull disclosed he was hooked on Bufotonin—a rare drug secreted in the mucous of certain species of toads.

Bull described a life of fear and squalor, of dread and ennui, of scissors and paste as he trekked from Tangiers to Toledo, Ohio seeking toad connections.

I assured Bull I'd find him more toads. The man was a genius, had the soul of a poet. Better yet, I told him, I knew of a physician—a certain Dr. Sax—who had developed treatments for addicts of all kinds. Bull seemed disinterested until I told him about the parts of therapy that involved ritual use of jimson weed, while sitting in an orgone accumulator, and, at the same time, being carefully strangled. Afterwards, one became part of a follow-up group where progress was rewarded by calibrated flagellation by pretty vicious young boys.

"You're a good lad," Bull said, patting my knee. "And I've noticed you have a really callipygous ass."

Say what you will, Bull *was* a genius.

I squirmed as he bent me over the sofa. *Callipygous* ass, I thought. *Just the thing to scrawl on the Dean's wall.*

Out of the corner of my eye I saw Bull slip something into his mouth. The bugger had another toad. I felt him shudder. Then he gasped and fell back on the floor. He quivered and jerked a few times. And that was all. His blue eyes ogled the ceiling for all eternity.

Still there might be hope. I phoned emergency medical, described Bull's condition. And they dispatched a unit. As I waited nervously, I looked once more at his face. Two toad legs twitched from the corners of Bull's mouth. I thought of Galvani. I couldn't help it. I thought of Galvani and electricity of the nervous system. I giggled, barfed, woofed my cookies. Numb, I sat in a corner and watched my formless naked lunch seep into the carpet.

The emergency medical technician took one look at Bull and turned to me. "Toad O.D.?"

"I think so," I responded. "Bufotonin. He OD'd on bufotonin."

The technician pulled the toad from Bull's mouth, briefly examined it and dropped it on the floor. The toad lit on his back. Its legs waggled helplessly in the air.

The medical technician shook his head. "Not bufotonin," he muttered. "Blowdarts."

"What?" I said.

"What you have here, said the medical technician, nudging the toad with his shoe, "is *Dendrobates Tricolor*. This little fellow is just brimming over with an alkaloid, Toxin 251 D, I think it is. Natives of Colombia and Ecuador rub it on their blow darts. Affects the cardiac nerve."

"My God. How could he have made that mistake? He was a genius."

"Well," the medical technician said, "there's a lot of bad shit out on the street these days. And these toadsuckers—"

"What? What about the toadsuckers," I said defensively.

"You know." He winked. "They'll suck anything."

—*Mark Worden*

SAUL BELLOW
(1915-   )

Claus

If I am entirely imaginary, then who is the overweight *misnegel* in all of the Coca-Cola ads, wondered Santa E. Claus.

Some people believed that he did not exist and for a time he himself had doubted his own being. I think, therefore I apparently am not. Descartes (1596-1650) is stacked against me, he had thought, smiling morosely at the old joke from his University of Chicago days when, ignored and unseen by the other graduate students, he had painfully labored through his Ph.D. thesis—"The Pathetic Fallacy in Sartre's *Being and Nothingness.*" But now, alone in bleak early January in his big old house at the North Pole, bundled up in his WMCA Good Guy sweater, he felt a sudden new confidence in his own existence. After all, he thought, *someone* had driven the sleigh in Macy's Thanksgiving Day parade—let Martin Buber dispute that.

Nervous, excited, and certain for the first time that there must be a Santa E. Claus, and that he was almost surely it, he had fallen under a spell and was writing letters to everyone under the midnight sun. Hidden in the upper reaches of the Arctic, he wrote endlessly, fanatically, to friends, to people in public life, and even to the dead.

Dear St. John of the Cross, he wrote, *Admittedly, you more profoundly than I have experienced the dark night of the soul. But in the often tortuous search for the essential either/or in my own condition, I feel that when it comes to spiritual suffering I have been no slouch. And what of the torments of one whose dark night of the soul is six months long?*

Curiously elated at being for the first time a writer of letters rather than a receiver of them by the truckload, he stayed up half of one gelid night to carefully type out, and himself mimeograph, a reply to one of the questions by which he was constantly bugged. *As to your query on how I am able to cover so much ground on Christmas Eve,* he wrote, *I have only this to say–it isn't easy. Indeed, I would point out that the growing demands of an increasingly bourgeois and materialistic* industrial civilization have caused my (in esse) *Transcendental stunt (a kind of metaphysical Parcel Post) to become as de Tocqueville rightly predicted it would, less and less of a cinch each year.*

A week later, down with a case of the sniffles (the sickness unto death?), he lay in his bed writing feverishly to Clement Clarke Moore. *Sir*, he began, *Kindly go climb a tree. As you see, I make no attempt to hide my powerful hostility toward you, for I would argue that the piece of popular poetastery for which you are responsible ("A Visit from St. Nicholas") has over the years greatly contributed to the entirely erroneous and grossly sentimental image that the American public today has of me. I have tried to understand the origin of your oddly distorted views, and can only conclude that you must have inferred—as Barth and Tillich both also mistakenly inferred— that because I symbolistically represent altruistic Good I must therefore be conventionally Biblical—bearded, old, and not prone to give a damn about what the public thinks of me. But I can assure you that none of this is so—I do not normally wear a beard, I am not especially aged, and I care as much about my image as, say, U Thant, the Xerox Corporation, or Bobby Rydell. Nor, by the way, am I an elf, jolly or otherwise. I am five feet eight inches tall in my stocking feet, forty-six years old, and, you may be surprised to learn, Jewish.*

As one of the more prominent symbols of Christian romantic moralism, he himself frequently found it difficult to believe in the fact of his own Jewishness, but there it was, and there was little that he—plump, ludicrous, eternally middle-aged, a *baal-chor*—could do about it. Of course, he realized, being Jewish, as well as woebegone, an intellectual, and hopelessly long-winded, greatly increased his chances of becoming the central figure in any one of a dozen soon-to-be-written paralyzingly introspective American novels. But if, falling back into the old Berkeleian anxiety, he was an imaginary character, had he anything to gain in the shift from being a figure in the imaginations of succeeding generations of cheerful kindergartners to being the product of the melancholy Jewish subconscious of Wallace Markfield, Bernard Malamud, or Saul Bellow?

At his letter-writing again a few mornings later, he suddenly realized that for the first time this year he hadn't fallen into his annual January depression—what his psychiatrist, Dr. Himmelfarb only half jokingly referred to as his *post-Christmasum triste*. (It was Himmelfarb who had years earlier led him to understand that his compulsive Christmas giving had nothing whatsoever to do with any innate good in his character but was instead the product of a deep-seated and neurotic sense of guilt.) *Listen, Sid*, he wrote to Himmelfarb, *good news—I'm happy. Nonetheless, I would still dispute with you that it is rationalistic to turn a man (me) into a symbol of limitless and indiscriminate magnanimity (jolly old Santa, as popularly conceived), though I'm sure that we both agree, with Buber, that by means of a spiritual dialogue the I-It relationship can be transformed into the I-Thou relationship. At this point, though, Sid, things are not so I-Thou between us that I'm going to pay that bill of yours, which is, as usual, outrageous. (In any case, as you know, I'm inevitably caught a bit short this time of year, after the terrific expenditures I have to lay out at Xmas.) Nevertheless, thanks for being one of the few schlepps over the age of six and a half who believe in me, although at thirty-five dollars an hour, I suppose it's worth it to you. By the way, as to the discussion during our most recent session, I have to agree now that you were right—I have made a mess of things with the reindeer.*

Dear President Johnson, he wrote the following afternoon, *You speak frequently of the so-called Great Society, but do you honestly believe that such a society can be achieved as long as the fundamental hypocrisy in respect to this writer is permitted to continue unchallenged? That is, on the one hand, it is coyly pretended by the manufacturers of Barbie dolls, Hammacher Schlemmer floorwalkers, and similar types that I exist, while, on the other hand, (indeed, in the very next breath), these same people snickeringly deny my existence. For such blatant materialists, I am apparently some sort of mythic delivery boy who is to come running whenever they whistle. But I feel that it is time to cease this childish game of Heidegger (1889—) and seek. Either I exist or I do not.* Under the pressures of conformity to an essentially predestinarian Calvinistic society, I admit that I myself have at times had doubts on this question, but, on the other hand, Buster, here I am.

Having sent off this last missive by dog team to Nome, he was suffused with a weird tranquillity, and whatever had come over him during those days, the spell seemed abruptly to have passed. He stopped writing letters and told himself once again that he was almost certainly not imaginary, thus bringing things, in a circle, back to where they had started from. And somehow, reading over the carbons of all the letters he had written during his curious seizure, it seemed to him now that they proved almost nothing, other than the possibility, of dubious value, that he himself was an uninteresting man. Still, the letters did lend him claim to being, as far as self-indulgence goes, the world's long-distance champion. Perhaps he could put the letters together into a book, bearing a title he'd had in mind for some time—*Toward a Theory of Boredom*. With this thought in mind, he fell into a long winter's sleep, as visions of sugarplums, paperback rights, a six-figure sale to Joseph E. Levine, and *The New York Times'* best-seller list danced in his head. And, for the rest of that winter, to the relief of virtually everyone but Philip Rahv, he didn't write another letter. Nothing. Not a single word.

—*Thomas Meehan*

MICKEY SPILLANE
(1918-   )

From The Nun Runner

'C'mon baby,' I said, 'you'll just have to kick the habit.'

'Keeka de habit? No understan'.'

'You can do better than that, sweetheart,' I said. 'Shed the wrappers, show the goods, peel!'

She still played dumb. But she wasn't fooling me. She wasn't fooling anyone anymore. Not now.

'Okay, baby, if that's how you want to play it.' I tore off the starched white headgear and the familiar platinum blond hair cascaded on to her shoulders. There was fear in her eyes now. She tried to run but I got my fingers in the back of her robe. There was a harsh tearing noise and she spun round, backed up against the door with a pile of black cotton round her ankles. She was still wearing the same gold star transfers. In all the right places.

'Let's go, sister,' I said.

—M. J. Monk

DORIS LESSING
(1919-   )

From First Day

Already the sun was hot, working the earth into red dust, searing the jacarandas while a thin, slip-like dress she had made only the night before out of her mother's discarded dishtowel, stood at the doorway, waiting. Now she would meet them all, the anxious, bony, well-read Jews who would be the revolutionaries and expect too much of her, the stolid, giggling girls who, in only sixteen years, would give themselves up to babies and slight security, and the thick-legged, big-chested boys who would die badly in new but ancient wars. "This will never be enough," she said to herself and to the heavy, worn-out African morning.

—*E. Klein*

IRIS MURDOCH
(1919-   )

Amor Vincit Omnia Ad Nauseam

AFTER AWAKENING FROM *BRUNO'S DREAM* AND
FALLING INTO THE NURSERY

"Hey diddle—?"
    "Diddle."
    "You're thinking about God again."
    It was true. She had been. The cat had been thinking about
the fiddle. She had been looking at him. He had a long stringy
neck and a plump brown resinous hollow body. His voice had
vibrato. She had been his mistress for four years. It had been
ecstatic but not extremely. She was a small-boned calico with
high tender ears and a broad subdivided brow and a moist nose
and an abrasive triangular tongue the color of faded drapes.
She had been attracted by his voice. They had met at a benefit
concert being given for churchmice. A bow had scraped him
and he had sung. The cat had gone up afterwards and had
rubbed herself against him and in her whiskers, so decisively
parallel, he had recognized something kindred. He had sung
to her of Viennese woods and she had related to him tales of
her previous lovers. There had been a succession of toms
behind the Bromley gasworks. They had had terrible voices.
They had clawed her. They had bitten. As the palms of a
religious come to be indented by stigmata so the image slowly
formed itself upon her mind of a hairless toothless lover,
fragile and lean. He would have resonance. He would be
powerless to pounce. Her telling the fiddle all this in those
days had pleased and flattered them both. That had been in
those days. These were these days. All day she took a small
abrasive pleasure in licking the calico fur of her chest with her
triangular tongue while he failed to sing but instead leaned in
the corner and almost hummed. She looked at him, his shape,
his texture, his state of tension. One of her toms had been
made into a tennis racquet. Perhaps that had been the
attraction. She thought, I need a larger fate, warmer, kinder,
yet more perilous in its dimensions, coarsely infinite yet

mottled like me. Her vertically slit eyes, hoarding depths of amber, dilated at a shadow from her barnyard days as a kitten in the straw at Surrey. Something large had often been above her. Something smelling of milk. It had mooed.

The cow was in love with the moon. Throughout the first three quarters she had wept solidly, streams and streams. The moon had become full. Tears poured down her muzzle in an invincible tide.

"You are seeking," said the full moon, "to purify yourself by giving rein to impossibility."

"Oh, God—I can't—I don't—"

"Go on."

"When I first saw you, you were new—a sort of weak bent splinter of a sort of nibbled thing. How loathsome, thought I. I think even then I was protecting myself from the truth. I believe even then I deeply knew you were cheese. You began to grow. Mare Serenitatis showed, and one bluish blind mad eye, and the side of your lopsided leprous smile. At first I loved you in spite of your leprosity. Then I loved it because it was part of *you*. Then I loved the leprosity itself, and you because you were the vehicle whereby it was boldly imposed upon the cold night sky. I have never known pain so ungainsayable. I beg you, What—?"

"Jump."

"Jump?"

"*Jump.*"

"Jump—"

"JUMP!"

"Imagine the moon," advised a little dog who had been eavesdropping, "as only slightly higher than the Albert Memorial. Or consider the Albert Hall. It is round and deep and vast and many-entranced, like a woman's love. Oppositely, the Memorial is phallic. Between them there is only the Kensington Road."

The cow was jumping. Splendidly. Galaxies concentrically countervaulted. Sphere upon diamantine sphere chimed the diatonic music that mesmerized Jerusalem the Golden. Time and space were fooled at their own game. *Ab ovo*, lactogalactic. He was near, Him, ashy, awful, barren, lunar, luminous, Him. *He was Him.* They grazed. The hint of a ghost of a breath of a touch. The cow was descending. The cow was reentering Earth's orbit. The atmosphere sizzled. The cat's eyes dilated as the shadow gathered. She felt the ponderous loved thing close and warm above her.

"Is it to be—?"

"Can't stop. Gravity."

"Oh— how *right!*" Black ecstasy flattened the cat. Her ego was, if not eliminated, expanded beyond the bounds of dissatisfaction. She was ever so utterly content. The little dog laughed to see such sport.

The fiddle cleared his long narrow throat. "Er—when you laughed like that—I, er, *twanged*. Strange to say, I love you insanely."

"Too bad," said the little dog. "I love the cow. This fact was asleep in me until I saw her jump. Christ, what an august uncanny leap that was!" He was a beagleish dog. A history of bitches had lengthened his ears and bloodied his eyes. His forepaws however had an engaging outward twist. He yapped amorously at the cow. She stepped backward into the fiddle. Her glossy hoof fragmented the ruddy wood.

"Thank you—thank you—" sobbed the fiddle. He had been excessively pampered heretofore. It was bliss to be hurt. "Of course I love *you*." He of course meant the cow. She became haughty. Her high hot sides made a mist like fog off the Greenwich Reach. She indicated distinctly that she had consecrated herself to the memory of the cat. Or rather the cat had become the angel of death whose abiding iron presence it is the destiny of all life to worship. What else is love? Nothing else.

The little dog yowled. "I discover I was confused. It is the moon I adore, for having permitted itself to be so splendidly jumped." He yowled and yowled.

The moon beamed. "I love everyone. I shine on just and unjust alike. I give to all the gift of madness. That is my charm. That is my *truth*."

The fiddle lived with his wound for a fortnight, as one would live with the shifting shades and fluorescent evanescences of an unduly prolonged sunset. Then he found he could sing. He had sung once. He was again singing. He sang,

"A questo seno, deh! vieni, idolo mio,
Quanti timori, quante lacrime . . ."

And the dish ran away with the spoon.

—*John Updike*

J. D. SALINGER
(1919-   )

From The Grand Old Duke Of York

There was this goddam English duke for Chrissake—and boy wasn't he just so damn grand and all. Anyway, this crazy sonuvabitch has this bunch of ten thousand crumby West Point rejects who are about as much use to him as a hole in the head. So this crazy duke walks the ass off these jerks up and down this lousy goddam hill. And these GIs work it out that when they reach the top of this hill they're up for Chrissake and when they reach the bottom they're down for Chrissake—which is a pretty big deal. Anyway there's this real smart sonuvabitch and he blew everyone's goddam mind when he says that halfway up is not up and not down neither. But you know—I felt kinda sorry for the guy. I get like that sometimes—and when he spoke, I was damn near bawling. I really was.

—*Tim Hopkins*

JAMES JONES
(1921-1977)

From There to Infinity

We all have a guilt-edged security.
　　　　　—Moses

"Stark Romanticism" was the phrase that kept pounding through his head as he knocked on the door of Mama Paloma's, saw the slot opened and the single sloe plum that was Mama Paloma's eye scrutinizing him through the peep-hole. "Oh, you again," the eye grinned at him, sliding back the bolt of the door. "The girls are all pretty busy tonight but go on up." A dress of sequins that made her look like a fat mermaid with scales three-quarters instead of halfway up tightly encased the mounds of old snow that was her flesh. She glanced down at the must-be-heavy-as-lead suitcase in his hand as she closed the door. "I don't dare ast how many pages you're carting around in that by now,"she grinned.

He mounted the steps with that suffocating expectation of men who are about to read their stuff, the nerves in his loins tightening like drying rawhide, the familiar knot hard in his belly. Shifting the suitcase from one hand to the other, his head swam into the densening surf of upstairs conversation, above which the tinkle of the player piano was like spray breaking all the time on rocks. Standing in the upper doorway, he reflected how, just as there can be damned senseless pointless want in the midst of plenty, so there can be the acutest loneliness in the midst of crowds. Fortunately, the thought passed swiftly. The whores moved, blatant as flamingos in their colored gowns, among the drinking-grinning men, and his eye ran tremulously swiftly in search of Dorine, gulpingly taking in the room for her figure moving erectly womanly through it all.

"No Princess to listen tonight," Peggy grinned toward him. "The Princess went away."

He could have slapped her. It puzzled him to find that beneath that hard, crusty exterior beat a heart of stone. What was she doing in a place like this? He turned and hurried back down the stairs.

"Come back soon, there's listeners as good as the Princess," Mama Paloma laughed jellily jollily as she let him out into the street.

With Dorine not there he couldn't bear Mama Paloma's, and he didn't know another place. Yet he had to have a woman tonight. Another woman would have to do, any woman.

Colonel Stilton's wife, he thought. Why not? She was from Boston, but there was no mistaking the look of hard insolent invitation she gave him each time she came to the Regimental Headquarters to ask if he knew where the Colonel had been since night before last. He hated Stilton's guts, or would if he, Stilton, had any. Hated that smirk and that single eyebrow always jerking sardonically skeptically up, like an anchovy that's learned to stand on end. Why not transfer out, why be a noncom under that bastard? he asked himself. I'm a noncompoop, he thought. He tried to make a joke of it but it was no good.

He knew where the Colonel lived from the time he'd taken him home stewed. He got out of the cab a block from the house. As he approached it walking, he could see Mrs. Stilton under a burning bulb on the screened terrace with her feet on a hassock, smoking a cigarette. She had on shorts and a sweater. Her slim brown legs like a pair of scissors made a clean incision in his mind. He went up the flagstone walk and rapped on the door.

"What do you want?" she said with the same insolent invitation, not stirring. He was aware of the neat, apple-hard breasts under the sweater, and of the terse, apple-hard invitation in her manner.

"I want to read this to you," he said, trying not to let his voice sound too husky.

"How much have you got in there?" her voice knew all about him.

"A quarter of a million words," he said, thickly.

She came over and opened the screen door and flipped her cigarette out among the glows of the fireflies in the yard. When she turned back he caught the screen door and followed her inside. She sat down on the hassock and looked away for what seemed an eternity.

"It's a lot to ask of a woman," she said. "More than I've ever given."

He stood there shifting the suitcase to the other hand, the arm-about-to-come-out-of-its-socket ache added to that in his throat, wishing he wouldn't wish he hadn't come. She crossed her arms around her and, with that deft motion only women with their animal confidence can execute, pulled her sweater off over her head and threw it on the floor. "That's what you want, isn't it?" she said.

"You with your pair of scissors," he said. "When you can have a man who's willing to bare his soul." He gritted his teeth with impatience. "Don't you see how much we could have?"

"Come on in." She rose, and led the way inside. Nothing melts easier than ice, he thought, sad. He watched her draw the drapes across the window nook and settle herself back among the cushions. "I'm all yours," she said. "Read."

The female is a yawning chasm, he thought, glancing up from his reading at the lying listening woman. He found and read the passage explaining that, how she was the inert earth, passive potent, that waits to be beaten soft by April's fecundating rains. Rain is the male principle and there are times for it to be interminable: prosedrops into rivulets of sentences and those into streams of paragraphs, these merging into chapters flowing in turn into sectional torrents strong and hard enough to wear gullies down the flanks of mountains. After what seemed an eternity, he paused and she stirred.

"What time is it?" she sat up.

"A quarter to three."

"I never knew it could be like this," she said.

Each knew the other was thinking of Colonel Stilton.

"He never reads anything but *Quick*," she said, rolling her head away from him.

"The sonofabitch," he said, his fist involuntarily clenching as tears scalded his eyes. "Oh, the rotten sonofabitch!"

"It's no matter. Tell me about you. How did you get like this?"

Bending his head over the manuscript again he readingly told her about that part: how when he was a kid in downstate Illinois his uncle, who had wanted to be a lawyer but had never been able to finish law school because he would get roaring drunk and burn up all his textbooks, used to tell him about his dream, and about his hero, the late Justice Oliver Wendell Holmes, who in those great early days of this country was working on a manuscript which he would never let out of his sight, carrying it with him in a sack even when he went out courting or to somebody's house to dinner, setting it on the floor beside his chair. How his uncle passed this dream on to him, and how he took it with him to the big cities, where you began to feel how you had to get it all down, had to get down everything that got you down: the singing women in the cheap bars with their mouths like shrimp cocktails, the daughters-into-wives of chicken-eating digest-reading middle-class hypocrisy that you saw riding in the purring cars on Park Avenue, and nobody anywhere loving anybody they were married to. You saw that and you saw why. You had it all figured out that we in this country marry for idealistic love, and after the honeymoon there is bound to be disillusionment. That after a week or maybe a month of honest passion you woke up to find yourself trapped with the sow Respectability, which was the chicken-eating digest-reading middle-class assurance and where it lived: the house with the, oh sure, refrigerator, oil furnace and all the other automatic contraptions that snicker when they go on—the well-lighted air-conditioned mausoleum of love. She was a better listener than Fillow, a middle-aged swell who had eight hundred jazz records and who would sit in Lincoln Park in Chicago eating marshmallow out of a can with a spoon with gloves on. Every time he tried to read Fillow a passage, Fillow would say "Cut it out." Fillow was a negative product of bourgeois society just as Stilton with his chicken-eating digest-reading complacence was a positive one, whom his wife had and knew she had cuckolded the minute she had let the suitcase cross the threshold.

"It'll never be the same again, will it?" she said fondly softly, seeing he had paused again.

He read her some more and it was the same. Except that the thing went on so long the style would change, seeming to shift gears of itself like something living a hydramatic life of its own, so that side by side with the well-spent Hemingway patrimony and the continental cry of Wolfe would be the seachanged long tireless free-form sentences reminiscent of some but not all or maybe even much of Faulkner.

The door flew open and Stilton stood inside the room. His eyes were like two wet watermelon pips spaced close together on an otherwise almost blank plate (under the anchovies one of which had learned to stand on end).

"So," he said. The word sailed at them like a Yo-Yo flung out horizontally by someone who can spin it that way. It sailed for what seemed an infinity and came back at him.

"So yourself," she said. "Is this how long officers' stags last?" she said.

"So he *forced his way in here*," the Colonel cued her, at the same time talking for the benefit of a six-foot MP who hove into view behind him.

Realization went like a ball bouncing among the pegs of a pinball machine till it dropped into the proper slot in his mind and a bell rang and a little red flag went up reading "Leavenworth." He remembered what he'd heard. That an officer's wife is always safe because all she had to do was call out the single word rape and you were on your way to twenty years.

Why did he just stand there, almost detached? Why wasn't his anger rising from his guts into his head and setting his tongue into action? But what could you say to a chicken-eating digest-reading impediment like this anyhow, who with all the others of his kind had gelded contemporary literature and gelded it so good that an honest book that didn't mince words didn't stand a chance of getting even a smell of the best-seller list?

"This is my affair," he heard her say coolly, after what seemed a particularly long eternity.

The Colonel lighted a cigarette. "I suspected you were having one," they saw him smokingly smirk, "and since Klopstromer was seeing me home from the club I thought he might as well—" He stopped and looked down at the suitcase. "How long does he expect to *stay*?"

"I have something to say," he said, stepping forward. "Sir."

"I have something to say, sir," he said, picking up the suitcase to heft it for their benefit. "When Justice—"

"You'll get justice," the Colonel snapped as Klopstromer sprang alertly forward and bore down on him and wrested the suitcase from his grasp. "If you won't testify," the Colonel went on to his wife, "then Klopstromer at least will. That he assaulted a superior officer. It won't get him Leavenworth, but by God six months in the stockade will do him good."

"But why?" his wife protested. "You don't understand. He's a writer."

"Maybe," they saw the Colonel smirkingly smoke. The anchovy twitched and stood upright. "Maybe," he said, motioning to Klopstromer to march him out through the door to the waiting jeep, "but he needs discipline."

—*Peter DeVries*

JACQUELINE SUSANN
(1921-1974)

From Pornucopia: The Best Seller

Lean, tan, blue-eyed Noel Walgreen, idol of millions, sank back into the satin sheets of his round, lavish bed, stared up at the mirrored ceiling that featured his flawless body, and mused over the stunning women he had enjoyed during the last month. He could never forget:

Tracy—By the time she got her name up in lights, they spelled it S-L-U-T!

Lynn—The stormy starlet whose biggest picture was shot with a Polaroid camera!

Mara—Her husband found romance in the arms of another woman . . . and so did she!

Naomi—The only good impression she made on Hollywood was in Grauman's wet cement!

Ellen—Star of stage, screen, and psycho ward!

Adele—The gossip columnist who could hold the front page . . . but not the man she loved!

Suzan—Even the Greeks didn't have a word for what she was!

Vicky—She lived every day as though it was the last . . . and every night as though it was the first!

Melanie—The sex kitten who turned into a hellcat!

Dawn—The hoofer who would one-step her way into a guy's heart . . . and two-time her way out!

Irene—Her movies got good reviews from everyone but the vice squad!

Nicole—When her agent promised to make her the "toast of the town," she didn't know the town was Tijuana!

Joan—The sultry songstress who knew every 4-letter word . . . except "love"!

Louise—Fans could find her autograph in any motel register!

Consuelo—The Latin bombshell who went off . . . with another guy!

Pam—The kind of girl men put on a pedestal just so they can look up her dress!

And, of course, Wendy, his wife, raven-tressed film goddess whose icy beauty had made her the "Queen of Tinseltown." Ten years ago, when he was just a kid back from Korea, he had met her, when she was just a waitress slinging hash at a truck stop in Elbow River, Montana. They were married two days later. Those first years had been happy ones. But that was before they had become stars. Somehow . . . somewhere . . . something had been lost in that heady climb to the top. They had become puppets, mere pawns manipulated by shadowy, faceless magnates to further cartels of illusion, caught up in a savage web of greed, lust and power. Eyes that once sparkled with joy now reflected only the tawdry glitter of flickering limelight. Their souls had drowned in kidney-shaped swimming pools.

The bedroom door swung open and Wendy walked in, nude, her ripe, full breasts glistening with cocoa butter. She was smoking marijuana, or "gage," as the hopheads called it.

"I can't go on like this any longer, Wendy, watching you destroy yourself," he said.

"No man in the world is ever going to hurt me again. Not even you, Noel," she commented.

"I made the mistake of thinking we felt the same about each other," he observed.

"You're playing with dynamite! It just may blow up in your face!" she exclaimed.

"Do you know what you want?" he inquired.

"I did once," she answered.

"How could I have been so blind," he concluded and pulled her down onto the bed. His hungry lips sought hers. Together, they scaled the peaks of ecstasy.

When it was over, he carressed her face gently with his hands and whispered, "I love you."

Moments passed. The only sound was the haunting tinkle of their 12-tiered chandelier. Then she swallowed a handful of amphetamines or "goof-balls," as the jet-set calls them, paused, and replied, "That and a dime will buy you a cup of coffee."

—Michael O'Donoghue

KINGSLEY AMIS
(1922-   )

From Lucky Jim

Making his Sunday Times book reviewer's face (which tended to merge with his ape imitation) Dixon bent over the sheet of paper. Belching slightly, he wrote, "The Influence of Somerset Maugham on the Modern Novel," and then used his ball-point pen to deal with an itch in his ear. For one frightful moment he found himself actually thinking of Somerset Maugham. His stomach turned over at the thought of that professional story-teller forcing neat little stories to happen wherever he went. Was there anywhere he hadn't smoothly arrived—was there any place he hadn't milked for its ten-page "little masterpiece of narrative"?

Suddenly Dixon touched his toes three times with his forehead, howling like a hyena, and dashed to the telephone. "Is that Claridge's?" he piped a minute later in his Central Asian voice. "Maugham? Willie?" He scratched a buttock gleefully with the split toe of his left shoe. "You just listen this, Mr. Mum. Here come story you ain't never told. I tell you it." He broke off and clucked like a hen for thirty seconds, timing himself by his watch. "You sure miss plenty stories on account of you no come Afghanistan," he shrieked.

—Edward Blishen

JACK KEROUAC
(1922-1969)

On The Sidewalk

I was just thinking around in my sad backyard, looking at those little drab careless starshaped clumps of crabgrass and beautiful chunks of some old bicycle crying out without words of the American Noon and half a newspaper with an ad about a lotion for people with dry skins and dry souls, when my mother opened our frantic banging screendoor and shouted, "Gogi Himmelman's here." She might have shouted the Archangel Gabriel was here, or Captain Easy or Baron Charlus in Proust's great book: Gogi Himmelman of the tattered old greenasgrass knickers and wild teeth and the vastiest, most vortical, most insatiable wonderfilled eyes I have ever known. "Let's go, Lee," he sang out, and I could see he looked sadder than ever, his nose all rubbed raw by a cheap handkerchief and a dreary Bandaid unravelling off his thumb. "I know the WAY!" That was Gogi's inimitable unintellectual method of putting it that he was on fire with the esoteric paradoxical Tao and there was no holding him when he was in that mood. I said, "I'm going, Mom," and she said, "O.K.," and when I looked back at her hesitant in the pearly mystical United-Stateshome light I felt absolutely sad, thinking of all the times she had vacuumed the same carpets.

His scooter was out front, the selfsame, the nonpareil, with its paint scabbing off intricately and its scratchedon dirty words and its nuts and bolts chattering with fear, and I got my tricycle out of the garage, and he was off, his left foot kicking with that same insuperable energy or even better. I said, "Hey wait," and wondered if I could keep up and probably couldn't have if my beltbuckle hadn't got involved with his rear fender. This was IT. We scuttered down our drive and right over Mrs. Cacciatore's rock garden with the tiny castles made out of plaster that always made me sad when I looked at them alone. With Gogi it was different; he just kept right on going, his foot kicking with that delirious thirtyrevolutionsasecond frenzy, right over the top of the biggest, a Blenheim six feet tall at the turrets; and suddenly I saw it the way he saw it, embracing everything with his unfluctuating generosity, imbecile saint of our fudging age, a mad desperado in our Twentieth Century Northern Hemisphere Nirvana deserts.

We rattled on down through her iris bed and broke into the wide shimmering pavement. "Contemplate those holy hydrants," he shouted back at me through the wind. "Get a load of those petulant operable latches; catch the magic of those pickets standing up proud and sequential like the arguments in Immanual Kant; boom, boom, bitty-boom BOOM!" and it was true.

"What happens when we're dead?" I asked.

"The infinite never-to-be-defiled subtlety of the late Big Sid Catlett on the hushed trap drums," he continued, mad with his own dreams, imitating the whisks, "Swish, swish, swishy-swish SWOOSH!"

The sun was breaking over the tops of Mr. Linderman's privet hedge, little rows of leaves set in there delicate and justso like mints in a Howard Johnson's roadside eatery. Mitzi Leggett came out of the house, and Gogi stopped the scooter, and put his hands on her. "The virginal starchblue fabric; printed with stylized kittens and puppies," Gogi explained in his curiously beseechingly transcendent accents. "The searing incredible *innocence!* Oh! Oh! Oh!" His eyes poured water down his face like broken blisters.

"Take me along," Mitzi said openly to me, right with Gogi there and hearing every word, alive to every meaning, his nervous essence making his freckles tremble like a field of Iowa windblown nochaff barley.

"I want to," I told her, and tried to, but I couldn't, not there. I didn't have the stomach for it. She pretended to care. She was a lovely beauty. I felt my spokes snap under me; Gogi was going again, his eyes tightshut in ecstasy, his foot kicking so the hole in his shoesole showed every time, a tiny chronic rent in the iridescent miasmal veil that Intrinsic Mind tries to hide behind.

Wow! Dr. Fairweather's house came up on the left, delicious stucco like piecrust in the type of joints that attract truckers, and then the place of the beautiful Mrs. Mertz, with her *canny* deeprooted husband bringing up glorious heartbreaking tabourets and knickknacks from his workshop in the basement, a betooled woodshavingsmelling fantasy worthy of Bruegel or Hegel or a seagull. Vistas! Old Miss Hooper raced into her yard and made a grab for us, and Gogi Himmelman, the excruciating superbo, shifted to the other foot and laughed at her careworn face. Then the breathless agape green space of the Princeling mansion, with its rich calm and potted Tropic of Cancer plants. Then it was over.

Gogi and I went limp at the corner under a sign saying ELM STREET with irony because all the elms had been cut down so they wouldn't get the blight, sad stumps diminishing down the American perspective whisperingly.

"My spokes are gone," I told him.

"Friend—ahem—*zip,zip*—parting a relative concept— Bergson's invaluable marvelchocked work—tch, tch." He stood there, desperately wanting to do the right thing, yet always lacking with an indistinguishable grandeur that petty ability.

"Go," I told him. He was already halfway back, a flurrying spark, to where Mitzi waited with irrepressible woman-warmth.

Well. In landsend despair I stood there stranded. Across the asphalt that was sufficiently semifluid to receive and embalm millions of starsharp stones and bravely gay candywrappers a drugstore twinkled artificial enticement. But I was not allowed to cross the street. I stood on the gray curb thinking. They said I could cross it when I grew up, but what do they mean grown up? I'm thirty-nine now, and felt sad.

—John Updike

NORMAN MAILER
(1923-   )

From The Armies Of The Man In The Moon

So this was weightlessness, this tossed-about tossed-off feeling, all the aggressive male mother-fucking virility drained out of him; he even had to piss into a plastic bag and chuck it through the window to circle forever in space, his hot pressed-out fermented liquid frozen for eternity.

The reporter looked out of the space-craft Jesus, so that was the moon. The arid landscape was there like he had been told, the mountain ridges, the dried-up seas, the dusty valleys. But there was something else of which he had not been told; a stench that penetrated the frail walls of the vehicle, a sour, evil, vomity stench, the odor of a world without life, without hunger, without sex, without color—the supplement pictures had been full of color, but now he saw that there was no color, there never had been any color, the photographers had lied in space as they did all the time on earth.

He started to adjust his space suit before entering the module. Awkward if he wanted to run-out—or anything else. The first man—he looked at the moon again. 'You dirty stinking whore,' he said. 'I'm coming to get you!'

—*L. W. Bailey*

TRUMAN CAPOTE
(1924-   )

The Snows Of Studiofiftyfour

Studiofiftyfour, a converted movie theater fifty-seven feet above sea level, was said to have been the liveliest discotheque in New York City. Close to the top seats in the balcony was discovered a matchbook cover¹ bearing the White House seal. No one knows what the White House aide was seeking at that altitude.

It was morning, and had been morning for some time, and he was waiting for the plane. It was difficult to speak.

"Can you see all right?" the attendant from the Fat Farm asked as they approached the ticket counter.

"It's okay unless the bandages slip," he said. "Then it's all fuzzy."

"How do you feel?"

"A little wobbly."

"Does it hurt?"

"Only when I sit down."

He thought about the railway station at Karabük and the headlight of the Simplon-Orient cutting the dark now, and he thought about his enemies and how he wished he had them laid out across the tracks. They would make a long row. Perhaps a mile. Too many, maybe. But he had fought often, and they had always picked the finest places to have the fights. The tea place in the Plaza Hotel with the palms. The El Morocco with the zebra stripes. The Bistro in Beverly Hills. That was where Jerry Zipkin² came out of the dark restaurant gloom that time, blinking his eyes, and he had hit him right along the chops, twice, hard, and when the Social Moth—that was what Johnny Fairchild³ called him, wasn't it, old cock?—didn't go down he

---

¹"Snows," in this case, is apparently not the material that falls on mountains, but is a reference to a white powder that is arranged in a thin line by such a pusher as a matchbook cover and is then ingested up a straw into either nostril—a practice referred to as "snorting."

²A familiar social figure of the times, in later years referred to as the "Social Moth" for criticizing a party to which he had not been invited in front of a man who turned out to be the host and who threw Zipkin down a staircase, at the foot of which he was caught by Nan Kempner, one of the great beauties and Zipkin-catchers of the day.

³The publisher of a journal called *Women's Wear Daily*, now defunct.

knew he was in a fight. Swifty Lazar[4] broke that one up, and he thought of how clean and white Swifty's hands had been coming between them, and he wondered how many bars of soap had gone into keeping them that way, and he was thinking of asking Swifty, and would have if the Social Moth had not been screaming like the bombing officer that summer evening who had been caught up on the wire at Mons.

Swifty, about his size, too, a sawed-off Purdy,[5] though he had not read a book, had mixed it up with some true contenders, though probably not Turgenev. He had driven those immaculately clean hands into the chops of Otto Preminger, who was a movie director with a domed head with not much in it except a German accent. He wished he had seen that one, which was at the 21 Club under the Goodyear-blimp model and the eighteen-wheel rigs that hung from the grillroom ceiling though he wished it had been at El Morocco, which was a good place to fight, with the palm trees and the high ground off the dance floor where the band played. He liked Swifty's left hook. If you fight a good left-hooker, sooner or later he will get his left out where you can't see it, and in it comes like a brick. Life is the greatest left-hooker so far, though they say the cleanest ever thrown was Swifty Lazar's.

Do you have any bags to check?"

He came to with a start. The gauze head-bandages from the face-lift had slipped down on one side.

"I'm sorry about the one eye," he said. "But I have two bags. I will carry the smaller on board."

"All right," the flight clerk said. He was a fine desk clerk with high cheekbones and a plastic identification badge that read Farwell Smith. He had good hands, too, and it was with pleasure that through the one good eye-hole he watched the clerk tie the baggage check to the handle of the big Vuitton with one hand, as it was supposed to be done if the bag was to be dominated properly, with the good brusque motion of the *recorte* and the baggage check truly fixed. He thought about the baggage itself, jiggling down the conveyor belt, and how it

---

[4] The greatest of the short literary agents; often called "Of the great literary agents, the shortest." He was also known as a "great washer" for his fear of germs, a trait he shared with the billionaire Howard Hughes.

[5] An extremely expensive shotgun model made in England. Not to be confused with James Purdy, a Brooklyn-born novelist and short-story writer, who is 5'10".

would disappear through the leather straps that hung down like a portcullis and maybe he would see the bag again at the LaGuardia. The LaGuardia was not the same since they had built the rust-colored parking building that obscured the view from the Grand Central Parkway, but then we were not the same either. He would miss the bag if it did not turn up at the LaGuardia, and went instead to the Logan, which was in Massachusetts and had the fogs. He would sorely be troubled if the bag went to the Logan. He had always packed a neat bag. It was a fine experience to open the bag up in the hotel room and see everything laid out just the way he had packed it, with the knuckle-dusters next to the big Christmas stocking he liked to hang at the foot of the bed.

"Smoking or nonsmoking?" the flight clerk asked him. He answered through the bandages. He asked for a window seat. Just then it occurred to him that when the stewardess came by with the tray of steamed towels and the tongs to grip them, which was what he truly liked about first class, he could not use the fine hot face towels because of the bandages on his face. It came with a rush; not as a rush of water or of wind; but of a sudden evil-smelling emptiness.

He thought about being alone in the motel room in Akron with the big table lamps, having quarreled in Memphis, and how he had started his enemies list, and how long it was, and how he had used the Dewey decimal system to arrange it in the green calfskin notebooks. Under K there was Stanley Kauffmann, who had written forty unproduced plays and ten unpublished novels, which had wrecked him just about as much as any other thing had wrecked him, but it did not stop him from trying to wreck people who were writing true stories about Christmas in Alabama and how they hung the mule from the rafters. Under R he had Ned Rorem,[6] who had a head shaped like John Dillinger's, who wrote untrue and snide, and Tynan, under T, Kenneth Tynan,[7] who had worn the same seersucker overcoat since the year the dwarfs came out on the Manzanares along the Prado road, and who wrote snide about

---

[6] A distinguished composer of the era. Capote apparently felt that a discordant section of a fugue featuring a tuba, a bassoon, and a glockenspiel (known by musicians as the "breaking wind" passage) was directed personally at him.

[7] A drama critic and essayist whose work often appeared in *The New Yorker*, a publication that in 1982 was purchased by a lady from Dubuque and is now a seed catalogue.

his party in the Plaza where John Kenneth Galbraith[8] had danced the Turkey Trot. Under A, he had Dick Avedon, who had hung snide two portraits of him in the exhibition that had him young in the first and like an old goat in the other. He thought how good the notebooks felt to the touch, and how he could buy fill-ins at Cartier when the lists became too long, and how he could look in them when the time came. Vengeance went in pairs, on roller skates, and moved absolutely silently on the pavements.

He looked through the eyehole of his bandages at the standbys. They would begin to call them soon enough, and some of them would sit in coach. He had sat in coach once. But that was when he was beginning as a writer, and now that he was successful he liked the face towels and the tongs to grip them, and the crêpes with shrimp within and the tall green bottles of California Pinot and the seats that went back when you pushed the button. They had the buttons in coach but they did not have the hot towels and the other things. So when the time came and he had to work the fat off his soul and body, the way a fighter went into the mountains to work and train and burn it out, he didn't go into coach. He went to the Fat Farm where they took his face and lifted it, and took a tuck in his behind as well, and they put the bandages on afterwards. The sprinklers washed the grass early in the morning and the doctors had taken his vodka martinis away from him, and later on, up in the room, they took the cheese away from him, too.

He thought about the people in the notebooks he wished were not there. They were the ones who cut him the way Ford Madox Ford had cut Hilaire Belloc at the Closeries des Lilas. Except that it was a mistake and it was Aleister Crowley, the diabolist, Ford was cutting. Well, Ford said he cut all cads. But then he was not a cad. He wrote things simply and truly that he had heard at the dinner tables when he sat with the very social and listened with the total recall that was either 94.6 or 96.8 percent, he never could remember which. The very social liked to talk about each other, but they did not understand him when he wrote about this and wrote about

[8]A tall crane-like economist of the times who espoused the curious Keynesian theory that it is better to set high prices than to pay them.

what they talked about at the Côte Basque and about the bloody sheet that one of them wanted to hang out a window at the Hotel Pierre, where downstairs in the lobby they had the good robberies. So they cut him. Slim Keith, Mariella Agnelli, Pamela Harriman, Gloria Vanderbilt, Gloria Guinness, Anne Woodward[9] *cut him, and so did Babe Paley,*[1] *whom he loved and who called him "daughter." He knew he would never be invited to dine with Mr. Paley under the great tiger painting at the polished table which reflected the underside of the silverware. He tried not to think about that. You had to be equipped with good insides so that you did not go to pieces over such things. It was better to remember that the difference about the very social was that they were all very treacherous. Almost as treacherous as the very gauche were boring. They played too much backgammon. Lee Radziwill!*[2] *The Princess, who looked fine in jodhpurs, although she never wore them that he could remember at the backgammon table, had a fine nose and a whispery way of talking. She had told him how Arthur Schlesinger had thrown Gore Vidal*[3] *out of the White House onto Pennsylvania Avenue, which was the length of two football fields away from the front steps, a long toss for anyone, but which was logical enough if you knew what a great arm Schlesinger had and how he had gripped Vidal by the laces and spiraled him. He had remembered because it was a good story, and it told about Arthur Schlesinger's great arm and the proper way to grip Vidal if you had to throw him a long distance. So he had told the story in an interview in Playgirl which was not as good a publication as Der Querschnitt or the Frankfurter Zeitung, but had a substantial number of readers anyway, and so Vidal sued him. The Princess did not support him. She said she could not remember telling him such a thing, which meant that she was treacherous, either that, or that she had a recall of .05 or 1.6, he couldn't decide which, which was not a great talent. He decided he would not take her to Schruns that Christmas where the snow, which he had never skied, was*

---

[9]The lesser-known of this group would include Mariella Agnelli, a member of the powerful Agnelli family, which controls the Fiat auto empire. Not to be confused with Mary "Fats" Agnelli, the present light-heavy-weight contender; Gloria Vanderbilt is a designer of blue jeans whose former husbands on occasion did not recognize her.

[1]A great beauty of the '50's and '60's, not to be confused with Babe Pinelli, a former major-league umpire.

[2]A reader since 1978 of *U.S. News & World Report.*

[3]His most recent book is a *roman à clef* entitled *Roman à Clef* about an Eskimo family's attempt to settle in Old Westbury, Long Island. An absorbing treatment of a neglected theme.

so bright it hurt your eyes when you looked out from the Weinstube.

He hoped there would not be three nuns on the plane. That had been a superstition he had held to for as long as he could remember. It was involuntary, but then he was not a complete man. It was an inconvenience also. You could not dictate to the airlines not to seat three nuns. Once on his way by air to the chalet in Gstaad he had looked through the curtain into coach and three nuns were sitting in a row and he had called out, "Nuns! Nuns! Three nuns in coach!" It spoiled everything about that trip, but he knew he could not brawl with three nuns and ask them to defenestrate, even though they were over the Kaiser-Jägers at the time which had the sawmill and the valley above where it was a good place to walk the bulldog. Brawling with nuns was not part of the code by which he lived. Besides, if the nuns fought, the odds were three to one, and maybe more if the bishops sitting behind the nuns involved themselves.

He thought about the very rich, who were just the same as him, and how his talent started to erode. Perhaps it was because of the negrinos, and the cherry-pit taste of the good kirsch, and the margaritas with the salt around the rims, and the cool glasses of Tab the color of the Dese River above Noghera where the sails of the sailing barges moved through the countryside for Venice where off the Lido Beach he had sat on the bicycle paddle-boat with C. Z. Guest[4] and told wicked stories to her about C. Z. Guest. He could no longer write these wicked tales because he had the block, the writer's block, which with a wide snout like a hyena's, like death, had come and rested its head on his nice little Olivetti, and he could smell its breath. He had tried to send it away. He thought he would try to tell his stories in the styles of other writers, even Gerard Manley Hopkins, and then maybe he would write about the great fights if the breath no longer dominated the Olivetti. About the Hemingway fight with Max Eastman over the chest hair in the office of Max Perkins, who always wore his hat indoors and had the sweet smile, and he jumped up on his

[4]One of the famous Cochrane sisters of Boston who among other things danced in the chorus of the Ziegfeld Follies before becoming a successful syndicated gardening columnist.

rolltop desk at Scribner's to keep out of the way of the two of them on the floor. That was before Max Eastman went mealy in the soul and became a Reader's Digest *editor. Or maybe he could write about the time F. Scott Fitzgerald fought the six Argentinians. He would write about the Metropolitan Club when Sinclair Lewis let out a big Bronx cheer at Theodore Dreiser and accused him of plagiarizing 3,000 words from his wife's, Dorothy Thompson's, book on Russia, and Dreiser had followed him into the marble anteroom and hit him two good shots with the flat of his hand which had echoed. That was the time that Westbrook Pegler had suggested that feuding authors should use "ghost-fighters." He would write about the zebra cushions of El Morocco where Humphrey Bogart[5] had fought over the big stuffed Panda that they had tried to take away from him, coming for the Panda steadily and lumpily past the linen-clothed tables with the single roses in their thin vases, and the hatcheck girl had cried like a girl. He had once arm-wrestled with Bogart on the set of* Beat the Devil *and he had won that one although Bogart had said, "Sweetheart, you wouldn't do this to an old character actor." He was very strong in the upper chest then, and still was, and he could pick up the front end of a Hillman Minx off a child with the best of them. He had not written about the arm-wrestling or about the* Ginger Man *restaurant where Sylvia Miles, the actress, had heaped her plate with a brie cheese, a potato salad, a steak tartare, and a quiche, not to eat, but to lob into the face of John Simon, the critic, who was standing next to the director, Bob Altman, who possibly got some potato salad, or maybe even the quiche, on the sleeve of his jacket, because he never asked Miles to be in his film about Nashville. That was one story he wanted to write about. He wanted to write about the night that Norman Mailer[6] had hit Gore Vidal in the eye at Lally Weymouth's salon—the evening that Vidal had called "the night of the tiny fist." There had been the good remarks. Was it not Christopher Morley who said that a literary movement is*

---

[5]A movie actor who had a way of saying "Sweetheart" that brought him fame and distinction. Apparently, he fought his third wife, Mayo Methot, more than the other three. Above the fireplace in their Hollywood home hung a framed souvenir of a fracas between the two at the Algonquin in New York—a receipted bill for a considerable amount of furniture breakage.

[6]The author's latest book is entitled "Why Are We in America?" in which the author denounces Diana Trilling, Jose Torres, thumb-wrestling, divorce, large families, prize-fighting, and gives high marks to the Internal Revenue Service and tax-collecting agencies.

two authors in town who hate each other? Was it not Robert Browning who had described Swinburne as a monkey creature "who sat in a sewer and added to it"? Ayee, that was fine. He himself had called Jack Kerouac a "typist," which was clever but he was not sure it compared and maybe it would not get into Bartlett's Quotations.

The writer's block moved a little closer. It crouched now, heavier, so that he could hardly breathe.

"You've got a hell of a breath," he told it. "You stinker!"

It had no shape. It simply occupied space.

"Get off my Olivetti," he said.

And then the flight attendant said, "Will all those holding blue boarding passes board the plane," and the weight went from his chest, and suddenly it was all right.

It was difficult to get him into the plane because of what they had done to him in the Fat Farm operating room, but once in he lay back in the seat and they eased a cushion under him. He winced when the plane swung around and with one last bump rose and he saw the staff, some of them, waving, and the Fat Farm beside the hill, flattening out as they rose. He tried not to think about the hot towels and the tongs. He remembered that he was a new man again, his face lifted and perky as a jackal's under the bandages and his rear end tucked up and river-smooth. They had drawn him true and taut, so that his skin was as drumhead tight as the tuna's he had caught at Key West and eaten with long-tipped asparagus and a glass of Sancerre with Tennessee Williams[7] sitting opposite. *Qué tal?*[8] Tennessee, and he wished he had been named after a state, too, perhaps South Dakota, or Utah even, and not with a name shared with that peppery man who sold suits in Kansas City.

The plane began to climb and they were going to the East it seemed. They were in a storm, the rain as thick as if they were flying through a waterfall, and then they were out, and through the plane window he suddenly saw the great, high, shadow-pocked cathedral of Studiofiftyfour with the mothlike forms dancing, the hands clapping overhead, and the bare-chested sweepers, who built up their crotches with handkerchiefs, sweeping up the old poppers with long-

---

[7]Now a law-enforcement official in Key West Florida. [8]What ho!

handled brooms. And then he knew that this was where he was going. He thought about the smooth leather of the banquettes under his rear end and how he would look out and think about his enemies. We will have some good destruction, he thought.

—*George Plimpton*

FLANNERY O'CONNOR
(1925-1964)

A Hole In One

They both listened painfully: Wilma, who was eight and a half months pregnant and ready to give birth at any moment, and Beauregard, who had impregnated her on a golf course with a single shot of sperm. They were the laughing stock of the town. A hole in one, the joke went. And Beauregard, at the age of fifteen, decided that he would become a family man and settle down with Wilma.

"I do," Wilma finally replied to the minister's question, after which the minister was paid. Wilma's mother, years before abandoned by her husband and left to raise her only child, went out to the porch and wept. Beauregard was pleased with his new bride and the fatherhood she was bringing.

Barely had they set up house, when, one night, a week after they were married, Wilma woke up suddenly and asked Beauregard: "Will ya call the Doc, please Beau? I think the baby's comin'." Beauregard ran to the phone and asked Glenwene, the operator, to alert the doctor. Glenwene rang up Doc Fletcher and got him to go immediately to the house, located at the edge of town.

An hour later Doc Fletcher showed up at the house stinking of whisky. Beauregard shouted, "Hurry, Doc. I think the baby's comin' soon." Doc pushed Beauregard out of the way and weaved into the bedroom where Wilma lay. She was definitely ready to give birth, and Doc took off his jacket and asked Beauregard to leave the room.

"Oh, my merciful God in heaven what the hell is this!" The shout pierced the thin walls of the small house, and Beauregard rushed into the room to see his new child, just delivered, on the bed, a large ear. No hands, no arms, no legs, no feet, no head, no torso.

"Oh, my merciful God in heaven what else can go wrong?" Beauregard shouted, and he hung his head and wept.

The doctor put his arm on Beauregard's shoulder and with his whisky breath hissed, "He's deaf."

—*Warren Philips*

J. P. DONLEAVY
(1926-   )

From First Day

This glorious day of crisp yellow and blue suddenly red bricked around Blessingworth's small life. Mustiness in the nostrils. Shouldering through the older ladies of the sixth grade, rife with possibilities, foregoing a possible perfunctory tweak of a cheek. Noel Blessingworth, scholar, displaying detachment as I slide into this arse-polished seat. To glimpse Miss Pennyquick's hallowed ground as she places it desktop and crosses the legs. Picking up the golden rule. With which she lacerates a geography book. Angry chip of sound. For punctuation. To begin the first period. O, school days. / But my nights / Are still / Free.

—Ford Hovis

TOM WOLFE
(1930-   )

"Watts, Kalifornia"
"Huh?"
"Watts, Kalifornia"
"Hhhuuuuuuaah?"
"Watts, Kalifreakingfornia, for Christ's Sake"
"Oh, Yeah, Maybe It's As Far West As You Can
Go Before You Get Your (Clap Clap) Wet, Yet!!;*!"

Da da da da Dot (pause pause) Da da da da Dot (beat beat)
Doot de dadeda dadah dot de da dot Doot de dadeda delee dot
delee dot do DADA dan de dan boom de dit dit dot boom bam
boom toot toot. Watts. Da da da da Dot (bang crash) Da da da
da Dot (smash bam) Doot de dadeda dadah dot de da dot BAM
dede dot CRASH SMASH dede doom KER—BLUEEEEEEE
ping ping ratedah de da de dahdeah BANG CHASH SMASH
pop BOOM lat de dah de dah BLAM BLAM tha-
BOOOOOMMMMM dodedoe bop bop banG why you crASH
Boom-a-lack-a Boom-a-lack-a Boom-a Boom-a-lack-a BOOM
la la lah poc pOC Minnesota oranges ping poc ping Texas taxes
pop boc ting We'll burn this town just for practice krrUMPH
riiiip PHLuuuEEEEEEE depocITA depOCita dePociTA
BLANG faLOOOOOOOMMMMMM . . . . . . BaBAbabA-
BOOOOOMMMMM EEE AAA EEE AAA EEE AAA
Whoom crash fart theK arfarfarfarf DONK piNG Baarroomm
VA VLOOOOOOOOOMMMMMMMMMMMMMM BOC
SSSSSSSSSSSSsssssssssssssssSSSSSSSSSS VIT KER
BLOUGGGGGGGGGHHHHHHHHHHR zip zat pocpoc
bweeeeeee POWPOWPOWPOWPOWPOW OMIGOD
ggggrrrrrrrr barkbark arfarfbark BA BOOMM zzzZZZZZZ
tttTTT BLANGBLANG dePoCiTa crash bang BAATAAH
BOOTAHA DANGONG-GOON OOOPHCLUMPH (a
steamer trunk falling down a flight of stairs) Dum da dum da
diddie dum C L O O O O O I I I I E E E E GLUMPH tic
GLUMPH tic GLUMPH tic (a man with one peg leg like Ahab
had) riiiiiiiiiiinnnnnnnnnnnnnnnnnggg. . . . .
riiiiiiiiiiinnnnnnnnggggg (telephone) chuga-ita chuga-ita chuGA-

ITA CHUGA-ITA CHUGA-ITA CHUga-ita chuga-ita (stereo record of a railroad train) Batten, Barton, Durstine & Osborne (advertising agency) crash bang smash boom clink bop bash . . . and Governor Pat Brown is vacationing in Greece . . . pleasant spot!

Pat's drinking ouzo out of a nipple-tan conch shell. "What is this stuff?" Marilyn looks up from staring at her hands. "You know what, sugar? Your name sounds like a cookbook instruction: 'Pat brown until a thin crust forms.'" Pat numbs his throat, emptying the rest of the ouzo down and puts the shell to his ear. PIRATES. Pat thinks he hears pirates. Maybe something's gone blueee-yy at home. Pat looks like he needs some cheering up. Marilyn stands up and yoohoos him. "You want to see me do my female impersonation? You've only seen me do it once."

Marilyn, of course, is a female, but she does a female impersonation. She moves her hips a great deal, wets her pinky and runs it along her eyebrows . . . cute. Bats her eyes like a strobe light and points at things palm up. She has it all down. It's easy. Anybody can do it but . . . Marilyn, well, she's the only *girl* that does it. Pat's not catching a bit of this . . . he keeps hearing unsympathetic pirate talk in that goofy conch shell. "Oh, DdddAAAAAAAAAA-ling, you're not watching a bit of my DE-VIIIIIne performance. Pay attention, pay attention, you cad." Maybe it would be better if Marilyn did *specific* female imitations like Marlene Dietrich or Emmanuelle Riva instead of this aggregate.

Pat's intuitive about trouble. This little harbinger crew in the shell is trying to tell him something and Marilyn over there is beginning to drown them out. Picking up his communications, he walks over to the rail of the terrace. Nice wood! His Vero-Cal belt buckle clicks against it as he begins to concentrate. "Watch me smoke a pretend cigarette, dumplin'. This is how a woman smokes a cigarette." Over comes Marilyn, long strides pitching and wafting and yawing and bunting into the rail of nice wood. And blows a big puff of imaginary silvery smoke in sugar's face. "That's good, Marilyn. Why don't you go into the hotel and get us both some cigarettes and order us another round of drinks." *Il faut cultiver nos jardins.*

He and California are like the Corsican Brothers. When California is being hurt, Pat feels the lashes. Californian born, Californian bred, and when I die, I'll be a Californian dead!! Humble beginnings breeds this. So it's understandable that Pat feels a little antsy right about now because a lion's share of Watts is doing a replay of what Alexandria got famous for. But he can't seem to put his finger on it. Dock strikes? Earthquakes? Ah . . . Okies . . . ah . . . Caryl Chessmans . . . the wine crop . . . all vague. Pat would put in a seventy-four-dollar phone call but everybody would be asleep and talk jibberish, but besides that, it'll come, it'll come.

Seventy-four dollars away in Watts, twenty square blocks are on fire. The flames are red and yellow and rise into grayish black smoke. The wooden buildings keep collapsing and it's terrible!!! There is so much smoke around that you can't see all the other colors. Just the red, yellow, gray, and black. A person in a white shirt here and there, but mainly it's just those colors. But something else is happening. There's a chant. It goes BURN, BABY, BURN . . . ALLITERATION. Fanfarkingtastic. Their own hymn of social sacrifice. BURN, BABY, BURN rhyme and all. Not bad, considering all of World War I produced only six decent songs and four poems! And this is only their second night. BURNBABYBURNBABY-BURN. Two more choruses. A New Year's resolution. They've put a torch to the old one. This paean's caught on. Nine-year-old drunks are singing right along. Burning down their own town set to their own music. BURN, BABY, BURN. And saying "baby" in there is just the right touch of hyperbole, or is it friendly cynicism or maybe expediency? A baby is a lovely hug . . . no one here is burning babies, of course, but to say BURN, BUILDING, BURN is a little too stilted. Who CARES, for God's sake, it works!!!

It's fourth-century Cyprus all over again. *Ubi nihil vales, ibi nihil velis.* Not this time. That World War II cake is still to be sliced. New money breeds new cultures. New traditions. It went without saying the first-born son, when he was of age, went to jail, the second danced and shuffled and hung around, and the next four played the vibes. The two following them worked in the button factory, the next joined the military, and served with distinction, and the last was hit by a furniture truck. Locked in to this as they were, burning your way out isn't too bad an idea. And with a "baby" and another "burn." Too MucH. It's being done with style. At last!

This thing is beginning to haunt Pat. He keeps looking down at his Zorrie sandals and waving his toes. Is it that the Dodgers are going to lose the pennant? Maybe it's that sneaky Nixon up to something. . . probably writing a book. What about Yorty, where's Yorty, for God's sake? . . .

"I'm back, dumplin'. And your drink's here." Nobody asked her to, but Marilyn has gone and changed her dress. From her Dacron zip-front double-knit alligator-insigniaed-navy-emerald-green size ten to her David Crystal ribbed neckline reversible tie-sash wrinkle-proof washable mesh-weave triple-monogram size sixteen. It fits like a cassock but Marilyn's been thinking of including fat-female impersonations in her act.

Pat turns around and stares at honeybunch like she was a fireplace or sea view. Transfixed. Incapsulated process. . . what the hell is it? Maybe it's just an Alaskan earthquake and we're getting a little too sensitive with these vibrations. His eyes fix on the ouzo-filled conch. Shall we give those pirates another listen? Pat forgets the empty shell he has with him and walks over to the filled one. He never takes his eyes off of it. Locked-in rays from his 20-30 eye bulbs. He sits down and picks up the shell like he was answering a phone. Reception, please hold all calls, we're going into conference here. Looking at Pat, Marilyn begins wondering why he wants to pour it in his ear instead of drink it. This water-colored juice is flowing down the jugular route and satiating his Mr. Timmy shirt, turning it the shade of palm wine. Pat's aware that something is happening, but he tends to believe it's psychic. A specter grin begins pinching at his lip corners. Taking the unintended cue, Marilyn smiles and pats the top of Pat's hand. "That's funny, darlin', I want to try that. But I'll do it as a fat woman. . . a fat woman who pours a drink down the side of her head." It finally dawns on Pat. Jesus. All over him! This is supposed to be a vacation. What a stinking vacation!!! Who needs this sort of crap?

Maybe the man who has a little of everything needs this sort of crap, Pat. Someone who is . . . well, George Plimpton, of course. George is running along with the jam in Watts. Running along and tagging along, mostly tagging along. George went a little overboard on the makeup to keep his identity hush. His charcoal face and marshmallow lips make him look like he was sired by Buckwheat out of Emmett Kelly. George is having a bit of trouble keeping up with the crowd because they have him carrying chunks of pavement, which they earlier had him rip up. Every once in a while, though, they give him a break and let him try his hand at throwing a brick. George throws a brick like a girl and they all keep yelling at him, "Spread your legs more keep your head straight other elbow tucked into the waist follow through watch the follow-through hold the stance!!!

Then they all laugh like hell except the guy he managed to konk. Then there's George's pie-eating grin, and he dashes back to pick up his chunk of asphalt and wait smiling puppy-dog-style till Team A decides to go on the run again. George isn't exactly sure why he's carrying this, but if he plays his cards right, he'll have plenty of time to think about it later. As soon as George graduates to bricks he hopes to go into this BURN, BABY, BURN business.... There it is again, beautiful. The *tres* penny opera flaming theater onomatopoeic hoedown crackling away that unfortunately can't be seen too clearly through all that goddamn smoke!

George, George. Where's George? George has run on ahead to tell his new pals a joke he knows. Be careful George.

"I don'ts know if'n yous-all had ebba heard this'n. What's da one thin yous gotta remembah when you is habben sexual intercourse [God, George] wif a female go-rillah?"

"What?"

"She's not ready until you is."

"Huh?"

"Oh, excuse me. I meant to say... ah... I dun said de wrong answeah. De right answeah is 'You is not done until she is.' HEE HEE."

George is pointed in the direction of his ceeeement luggage, around which is now standing a lurching, laughing, leering band of drunk children. They've had their little pink eyes fixed on George for a while now. George is sort of... well, you know... how shall we say... this image of... very, ah, circusy. Children will always be drawn to this, even during 175-million-dollar riots. They back up to give George plenty of room. They stagger along behind him for a while wondering about the asphalt. A few of them start shouting out suggestions. These kids are really cute, their soprano voices slurring out mischevous nonsense. George is having trouble making the ish bish dish fish gish out until a couple of these pygmy boogeymen run on ahead and begin pointing to the Mr. Saturday Nite clothier. They want George to liberate the cotton-velvet single-breasted peaked-lapeled purple jump-jackets with matching shirts, ties, and trousers, which retail for under $125. George finally gets the hint and goes into a jog, hoping to build up enough momentum so that he can just drop off and the hunk of asphalt will keep on traveling. And here he comes... winding down on it huffing puffing straining grunting lining it up... only one chance, the kids are so counting on this... here it is closer... make sure you let go, George, don't go through the window with it... step step DIVE... KA ZAAAKRRRRRRRAAAAAAASSSSHHhhhh. He did it. George did it. George begins screaming out "RIGHTARMRIGHTARM." A half-conscious mini-drunk tugs on George's sleeve and tries to set him straight. "Fight on FIGHTONFIGHTONFIGHTONFIGHT," screams George.

The sirens are now making this all official. Everybody out of bed, slap yourselves awake... THIS IS IT, GODDAMNIT. The Third Estate cordially invites you to attend the raising of an issue. And a block here and there cal-eee cal-aaa.

In case anyone is keeping count this is Pat Brown's first real vacation in quite a while, because you really can't count those junkets to Paris, Cannes, Monaco, and Casablanca, because those were fact-finding missions to find out... well, all you could and... of course not to forget mass transit. But this time it's really a vacation. Pat doesn't have to see a soul. He's supposed to be really relaxing but this... this *je ne sais quoi* is really booting things up. Pat Brown is truly the governor and not for one minute is he able to forget it. Marilyn. Sit down, Marilyn. Marilyn stands up and announces that this is what a fat female waitress working the Greek restaurants for the summer looks like. Pat lowers his eyes and decides to give the pirates another try. But he just hears the sea this time, big breakers folding over the sand, chasing, then beckoning sandpipers along her shoreline. No sign no warnings an empty calm sea bare of prophets, the vain blue horizon unbroken by any objects.

They've come and gone and don't wait around. Marilyn is

clumping around the table knocking into Pat. Fat people are too fat to bend their joints, figures Marilyn, so she's doing a female Frankenstein, mumbling the names of soups. Pat squeezes his eyes tighter shut and pans the distance for any traces that they must be out there.

The hotel desk gets a long-distance for Pat. The captain goes out to get him, but sees him there with his eyes squeezed shut and his ear in a conch shell and this . . . woman, this lady with her joints locked cheeks ballooned out doing the scarecrow walk around the table. . . . Well, it *is* their vacation, and whoever it is, they'll call back.

Da da da da Dot (beat beat) Da da da da dot (bang smash) Doot de do DOT de da dot de da dot Doot de do de da dot de da Doot Crash smash de do de do fart BOOM BOOM KrrrrrUMPH baggoooooph neg POC poC pOC POC TheeeeWACK bang pang Ark Da da da da dot (wack crumph) da da da da dot ping bic da da da da dot mumph ta de de de pop poot clink tinc   nng op teet pinc o   gg tt m ssss blump!

—Brian McConnachie

DONALD BARTHELME
(1931-   )

The Great White Swan

1. The swan is an ancient, enchanted symbol taken more seriously than war or famine or religion.

2. I am searching for my inspiration; the swan has stolen it.

3. The crowd cheers me on.

4. "Do it, do it, you shithead."

5. The swan is losing interest.

6. The broken bodies of those who have tried and failed lie strewn in the mud and slime and the swan tramples them with its webbed feet.

7. It could be dangerous.

8. I peek under the tail feathers—the crowd goes wild with excitement.

9. Traditional means of mounting are as follows.

10. I rise from the water.

11. Naked.

12. I crouch, singing, among the bushes and hope.

13. The swan gooses me.

14. And lets me go.

15. I swim after it, stab it, drag it back to shore, bleeding.

16. I decide we need a new enchanted symbol.

17. I roast the swan.

18. Feeding the giblets to the crowd who deserves them.

19. It's only a swan.

20. Nor does it particularly make sense.

—Vicki Armour-Hileman

CARLOS CASTANEDA
(1931-   )

Appointment In Mazatlan

I was hiking along the Pacific Crest trail when I smelled an unusual aroma of quixotol berries, jasmine, frankincense and myrrh. The hair stood up on my arms and I shivered as the old norepinepherine kicked in, and I felt the blood throb madly in my temples.

Don Junquero: I recognized the odor as one he carried with him like a familiar miasma. It was a fragrance which portended adventure, excitement, risk and doom. How did my mentor, the roguish Don Junquero, know to find me here, high in the Cascades, miles from town and technological impedimenta?

"It was easy, little brother Skunk," he said. "I tied a rock to myself and threw the rock in your direction." His laughter seemed to come simultaneously from three great ponderosa pines. The old trickster was testing me. Testing my will, my judgment and endurance, my fortitude. Testing my very *cojones*.

Of course, he was not behind any of the trees. Don Junquero was projecting his voice. At last I located the old sorcerer beneath a massive boulder of volcanic origin. He was dressed in immaculate LL Bean camping togs, and his expensive pack lay open beside him, its silver-plated frame gleaming in the evening sun.

Don Junquero beckoned me to sit. I did, and I watched with awe as he prepared bits of bark, moss, twigs and pinecones and lit the material with a match. The matchcover said Harrah's Club, Lake Tahoe. Much later Don Junquero told me that the little ceremony he had performed was called "lighting a campfire," and he promised to teach me one day when I had conquered my fears and become truly a Warrior. He also promised to take me to the land of enchantments called Harrah's Club, but that is another story.

Don Junquero instructed me to feed the "campfire" while he reconnoitered the forest. Shortly he came back with water and a bagful of berries, desiccated and wrinkled. Don

Junquero said, "Soon we shall have some special tea, and the instruction shall begin."

"How did you know I craved instruction, old one?"

He replied wisely, "The teacher knows a thing or two that are not in the books." He winked one of his crafty eyes. "A woman's not always a woman, little Skunk, but a good cigar is a horse of another feather."

Wow. I nodded at this ancient apothegm and wondered when he was going to teach me about what he called "the books" and "woman."

"You will know when the time comes, little Mugwump," Don Junquero said.

I resolved to be more cautious in my thinking.

The tea was delicious and we sat long and thoughtfully before the flickering flames of the "campfire." It made me think of Zane Grey. Riders of the purple sage. Fly fishing on the Umpqua. Cabin on the Rogue.

Don Junquero interrupted my revery. "Warriors do not let their thoughts dwell on fairy tales, little brother Skunk. But the special tea will facilitate transitions."

The tea? Oh lord, he had done it again. What was in the tea this time?

"A mixture of dried *Drosophila melanogaster*, left over from an ethanol inhalation experiment. Fungus buds, fruit of a rare night-blooming mushroom, a succulent devil unknown to mycologists. If you could 'see', little Skink, you would know."

"Skunk," I said foolishly. "Little brother Skunk." I longed to be able to "see", but Don had told me repeatedly that I could only "see" when I had become a Warrior and imbued with all that being a Warrior entailed.

It was night. Don Junquero's eyes gleamed greenly in the dark, and I could see his phosphorescent white teeth shining like a toothpaste commercial. His voice began to echo in my skull. As it reverberated, I also heard familiar footsteps clomping loudly down the dark path. Pirandello, I thought and the thought frightened me. How did my pet lizard Pirandello find me here?

Off through the mountain mist Don Junquero laughed, "I tied a rock to him and tossed him up."

Pirandello had grown to a huge monster, a great hissing

antediluvian beast. What a transmogrification! My pet lizard who used to gambol with me on the lawn was now an atavistic Komodo dragon with reeking foul cod liver breath and incandescent eyes.

I tried to remember whether I had fed him before I left on my hike. I had. I breathed a sigh of relief and Pirandello began to shrink. Before long he was hardly any bigger than Kareem Abdul Jabbar, and he was lounging against the log beside me reading a "book" and gazing now and then into the "campfire".

"When you have learned to control the dragons, you have centered, you have gotten to the nexus. You have gotten in touch with the hypothalamus-pituitary-adrenal axis." Don Junquero's voice came from deep inside my skull and every syllable burst with intense rainbows of color.

Pirandello deftly rolled a funny cigarette. Instantly I knew it was a special blend of cucumber leaves and squash stems. He puffed on it and passed it to Don Junquero. Don Junquero looked at the funny cigarette and giggled, "Lizard lips." What seemed liked hours later, the smoke came to me and I participated in the ritual without thinking.

When I did think again, I noticed the ornamental squash-blossom necklace dangling ostentatiously around Pirandello's neck. Designed by Joe "Ursus" Bearfoot, the necklace had been handcrafted in a Mexican assembly line. Suddenly I realized with great sadness that my pet lizard Pirandello had been deceiving me. His name was really Axolotl and he was descended from a long and distinguished line of Aztec lizards. He gave me a reptilian smile of confirmation. I knew it would be all right. I had the Power.

I reveled in the Power. I toyed with it. I took the words in my brain back etymologically to obscure Indo-European roots, and I saw how everything fit together. Everything except Iberian and Basque. But then I knew the Basque were descended from ancient astronauts.

Then Death came down the trail and stopped by our "campfire." When he looked at me an expression of astonishment came over his face.

I had the Power and confronted Death without fear and trembling. "Death, why do you look surprised?"

Death shyly looked at the ground and replied meekly. "Oh, little Skunk, it just amazes me to find you here high in the

Cascades. Because I have an appointment with you tomorrow in Mazatlan."

When I awoke the next morning Don Junquero and Pirandello were gone. Death had vanished. My Power was no more, and the "campfire" had gone out.

Cold and miserable, I hiked as fast as I could to the nearest town. It would have been much faster if I could have tied a rock to myself and thrown me there. But that was out of the question now.

With cold shaky hands, I called Mark Miller at the University of Oregon Drug Information Center.

"Hey, Dude," Mark said in the patois of the seventies.

I recalled the special tea of phantasticants, the smoke, the strange behavior of Pirandello. I thought of Don Junquero. I thought of Death. With quiet desperation, I said, "Mark, please enroll me in your next Drug Consumer Safety Education class." I thought for a second and added, "As long as it's not in Mazatlan."

—Mark Worden

E. L. DOCTOROW
(1931-   )

From Kangaroo Rag

In 1902 Father opened a saloon on Fairview Avenue in Yonkers, New York. It had a big front window and a large mirror behind the bar. Mother's Younger Brother was the bartender. One day Kangaroo walked in. "Here are ten dollars," said Kangaroo. "I would like a vodka martini." Mother's Younger Brother said nothing. He felt he should listen. President Theodore Roosevelt's third cousin was there. He said, "I have never seen a kangaroo here before." Emma Goldman stepped up to the bar. She said, "You never will again at these prices."

—Andrea Joline

JOANNE GREENBERG
(1932-   )

A Fever In The Phalanges

The explosions of shrapnel-filled, zinc-content, oxygen-fused bombs in crowded third class railroad cars at rush hour was always upsetting to Mary. Her gumdrops, her cherry drops, her licorice drops, her life savers in five flavors did not calm her, gave her no ease. The railroad car, its top gone, its sides shattered from previous explosions, crawled through the blue gloom of the towns and villages surrounding the city. Her ticket read Bendover; that was where she was going, where she would stay.

Most lower class Ladino women are not named Mary. Mary (Marianne) is an Aramaic name, although Jewish people tend to use the names prevalent in the circles in which they find themselves; thus, in Rome's Jewish community, we find women named Aurelia and Prudentia; in medieval England, Reine and Claire (not Saxon names, dummy, Norman names, because the Normans had won the war). God knows what Ladinos name their women, but Mary is unlikely.

Mary was not to be described. You'd do that anyway, wouldn't you, putting what you know about Ladinos (which is next to nothing) together with the way you want to see her, to make her look. I'd make her stout, you'd make her tall. I'd make her plain, you'd make her pretty. There's no percentage in describing her; you can see it's a goddamn waste of time.

Mary worked as a ruching seamstress in a small coffin factory in Bendover. Because she was Ladino, she had few friends. The three Chicanos in Bendover were Puerto Ricans, and didn't understand her Spanish. Bendover's four Jews were Ashkenazim from Russo-Poland, and they thought that she was trying to pass. She had been befriended, however, by the manager of the coffin factory, a blind man named Clon Frate. That is not symbolic.

Clon had managed the factory so well that in three years it was the largest and most successful one in Bendover. He knew all about fine woods, and joinery, and with his sensitive hands could feel the minute differences in the finishes his workers applied. He liked Mary because he could feel how even her stiches were, and because she never used rayon and told him it was silk.

When a person dies and is buried, it's important to get a good tight coffin so that the person's contents will not find their way into the environment. Except if you are Jewish. God told the Jews that their contents should be in the environment very quickly, the quicker the better, in order to get earth to earth. Then He put us in the desert where things are preserved for hundreds of generations. There is a lesson in this.

Clon knew this. This was why he used kapok and not polyester batt under the ruched and upholstered lining of his coffins. But kapok is almost impossible to sew. It is desperately hard on the fingers. It causes blood blisters and tears in the soft, padded flesh covering the ventral surfaces of the distal phalanges. Mary had been to see the doctor four times already. It was the reason for her riding on the bombed train. Kindly Doc Tudgut had left Bendover to go into the Peace Corps and Dinker the chiropractor had joined a religious commune. That is not symbolic.

The doctor had told Mary that she would never be able to sew again. She had cried out, "Ruching is my only trade!" But he had no time to listen to her complaint. Outside his office, the city's poor were lining up for the day. With all the bombings and urban terrorism of recent months, he had all he could do to take care of a day of amputations, and what he and his colleagues laughingly called gizzard groping.[1]

Alienated, Mary had left the clinic and wandered back to the train.

*   *   *

Fourteen years later, Mary and Clon were married and had five children. Their names were Ferdie, Millie, Emil, Letitia, and Shoshonah. Shoshanah was the Jewish one. She had a Litvak intonation. Clon was still using kapok, but they had gotten machines to sew it, and Mary's fingers were almost healed. She had sewn all the children's clothing, saving the family lots of money, but the children were laughed at in

[1] Exclude torrid sex scene.

school because the clothing all looked like coffin lining. This is symbolic.

—*Hannah Green*

JUDITH KRANTZ
(1932-   )

My First Day at School

April Rane shuddered into the clinging Pucci and turned to appraise herself in the full-length mirror. "Perfect," she thought, "the body of a twenty-year-old." She held the large gold hoops to her ears. "Too much," she decided. No sense diverting attention from the sleek chestnut hair caressing her shoulders. Once more she twirled before the mirror—a flick of mascara—and smiled at her reflection. April tiptoed across the bedroom (Brick was still asleep), picked up her pencil box, and with a soft click the door closed upon summer. "P.S. 501 look out," she breathed, "here comes April Rane."

—Mary Ann Madden

JOHN UPDIKE
(1932-   )

Big Chicken's Blues

RABBIT REBARBATIVE

Big Chicken Henderson scoops and whittles at the space beneath his chin with the checkout-counter razor; the blade will not grip the fold of skin, the wattle that has given him his name, and skates upon suds. A footfall upon the tiles behind him, a shadow condensed upon his mottled slab of mirror, and Big Chicken turns, impatient motion. Flamboyant in her nakedness she waits at the door; her eyes, he sees, shuttered with reproach. He notices for the first time the slow collapse of flesh over its frame. Her body is a garment much too big for her; the splendors that have seared him this night, are baggy, like an old wino's Salvation Army pants. Globes of ether, pure anxiety, slide down his legs; her nipples remind him of the wrinkled brown plugs of bathtubs in sleazy motels, he thinks of faucets that clank as they are turned and give no water, but beetlewings and rust. Womanhood! Big Chicken turns shuddering to the mirror, its passionless reflection, his face condor-ruffed with curds of foam, stubborn quills protruding beneath the jaw. She is scaly with his sperm: oh yuck.

His fingers twitch, the plastic razor snaps, brittle as his patience.

"Fuck this shit!" yells Big Chicken.

RIGHT ON, RABBIT

Frail tongues of juvescent grass probe aside the sooty crust of the vacant lot. Big Chicken's eyes pursue the twinkle of denim cutoffs. The sweet fat dimples the fringe does not quite hide. He has always been an ass man—she's young, skinny as a whippet, he likes the way she walks. Thighs of silver, he will scald her, quench her with his brand! Or dick. Later, though. Sun and moon, day and night, Big Chicken has a way to go just yet, he reminds himself. And yearns! Yearns. Ah: yearns.

FUCK LIKE A

He has barely time to wilt, a trembling pearl depending from the tip like a nosedrip on a winter day, when she is at him.

"You pig! Dumb prick!" Her eyes, superb olive wrath, dark with outrage. "You big schmuck. A dick on wheels is what you are. A human spittoon is all I am to you—"

Big Chicken feels his resentment pang and fade: sadness, a pallor, now chills the web of veins about his heart, a scrotum-shrinking melancholy. She is too shrill: a tinsel-toy let drop back in the gutter, after all; smeared, stunned, shopsoiled with his lust. Globes of ether, desolation, creep up his spine.

"Can it, sweetheart. Give it a fucking rest."

"But you:" he hears her words as he lies back, cradling the cigarette, fuse of his dejection, and hears the awe in them, that some presence has reached out and touched them both. "What is it about you, Barney. I don't know. Why I even bother with a jerk like you."

Her voice is dusky with tears. *Nor I baby, nor I,* he says to himself.

"You are . . . well—somehow—*life-enhancing . . .*"

"Yeah, well, no sweat," murmurs Big Chicken.

Globes of ether, sheer boredom, bloat his lungs. He hiccups. Up. Gotta go. Get out. Urk. So that legs will move, chickenshanks, among soothing ferns, and leaf-mould will be pliant to his tread. Urphf! He'll go. O.K.?

—Ian Duncan

RICHARD BRAUTIGAN
(1933-   )

Going to See the Guru

The troubled young man went to the Guru and asked for help in his life which was full of poverty, loneliness and misery. In the vernacular of the latter quarter of the 20th century U.S.A., the troubled young man was not "making it."

The Guru gazed impassively at the young man and almost imperceptibly nodded as the young man spoke. And then, when the troubled young man had finished, the Guru went into himself as Gurus do and came back and said "I can help you with many things in our joint pilgrimage through this stark and lonely life. We will share our tales, struggles, and in sharing grow to be more fully human, more aware of strengths and weaknesses, more able to seek the life experiences which nourish and do not stunt our growth and stultify our senses. Let us begin by filling out these forms."

The troubled young man looked down. He said, "I cannot write."

The Guru gazed at the troubled young man for a long time, then his eyes glanced heavenward. "Then this is the help I will give," the Guru said. "You do not need a Guru. You need a technician. I will make a referral."

—*Mark Worden*

JERZI KOSINSKI
(1933-   )

From The Painted Broad

I was living now in an S & M highrise with an inflatable balloon named Gert. She had once belonged to Lech, who lost her to me in a wager. It was a silly wager, made while Lech was siphoning the contents of his waterbed into the downstairs apartment through a knothole in the floor. I bet him that Gert was sensitive and capable of true aesthetic appreciation. In a rage, he withdrew the siphon from the knothole and plunged it deep into my eyesocket. He replied that he had been living with Gert for six years but never once had she evidenced one iota of aesthetic appreciation. I told Lech that if he would lift me off the railroad spike upon which he had impaled me for safekeeping I would prove it to him. I promised that the expansion of Gert's breasts would be scientifically measurable. Lech lifted me off the spike, setting off a commotion of predatorial insects among my dried scabs. Wiping gore and viscera off the spike with his handkerchief, he vowed that if I lost the wager I would pay for it by being made to suffer.

That evening we rode up seventy floors to the roof. I sat Gert in a collapsible chair. Lech unlocked the cage where the homing pigeons salivated in anticipation of the rats Lech fed them for snacks. Soon they were flapping and beaking viciously in the direction of my privates, waiting for Lech's command to tear me limb from limb. I motioned to Lech to keep his eyes on Gert's breasts while I pointed out to her the beauty of the New York skyline. Sure enough, Gert's breasts had expanded already; before long, her bra-snaps gave with two pings. I removed her size 36 and replaced it with a full 40. Lech's jaw dropped out of his mouth and there escaped an immense oath to the effect that he had been tricked by a simple physical law: air, especially hot air, expands in proportion to the elevation of one's highrise.

As if drunk with disbelief, Lech staggered to an open homing pigeon cage and fell in. Instantly the din of carnivorous birds filled the air. Soon Lech's body was plastered with droppings and wallpapered with little homing pigeon messages. I plucked one from his body. *Prepare for Hollywood,* it read. Suddenly it was as if an imperative of the universe was made clear to me. I crawled on my hams to Gert, waving my arms in front of her painted rubber face. She was uttering love coos and her already ample breasts were again expanding.

—*William Zaranka*

PHILIP ROTH
(1933-   )

Hello, Columbus

I don't know why I'm doing this. There's the money, of course, but how much am I going to keep of that three hundred thou anyway? Figure it out. It's no secret what bracket I'm in with my last two books. One-point-seven million, taking in the paperback, the book clubs, this movie.

And not only going to Hollywood to write the script of *Too Near The Sun* but *driving* there! Three thousand miles! Yes, it's a pleasure to drive my Mercedes 380 SEC coupe, listening to my own tapes, but all those *miles*. Well, I know why I'm doing Route 70 coast-to-coast. Who am I kidding? I'm doing it to be *alone*. I'm driving to be by *myself*. I'm doing it this way so that I can reacquaint myself with Arnold Shepler during all the solitary hours. Not the Arnold Shepler of *Too Near The Sun* and *My People, My Enemy*, but the Arnold Shepler of *Teaneck Revisited* and *Flying Free*.

But if I'm going to be truthful, I might as well go all the way. I'm going because of that Hollywood creep, Sam Winkleman. There is one sonofabitch that I truly despise. In a long list of antipathies, it's amazing how quickly this cockamamie has shot to the top! That lilac-colored Dior shirt! That nosegay of chest hair peeping out of the V of that shirt! Even the way he slips his fingers into the back pockets of his designer jeans. Quoting Rod McKuen, for crap's sake! The man's an apotheosis of pose!

It's not so much the pose itself but the consciousness *behind* the pose. If you catch him at the right angle, you can see a gleam of it. The mirrored travesty. I knew that first time we met at Herb Hockfleisch's penthouse party that it was a complicated game the man was playing. I knew that it was directed at something or someone. It took me a little time to figure out the target of his jape. Yes! Ridiculous as it seems, Sam Winkleman's parodic mortar shell is lobbed at taste, at intellect. He is saying: *"You don't like vulgarity? Well, get a load of this! You like the fine, the recherché? Well, eat my mummery!"* Of course he knows what good taste is! Of course he has literary discrimination! He uses that taste and discrimination as models to design himself into the outrageous opposite!

Why else would I have accepted that challenge—which came to me indirectly, incidentally—through my agent, that ten per cent *gonif*, Pushy Perlmutter? Pushy had told me that Sam had said to him that he understood why I was being chicken on that script-writing offer. I was afraid. Pushy told me Sam had said I was afraid to move out of my fur-lined eastern cult and play in the big league of mass entertainment. I had no choice, you see. You can't allow a person like Sam Winkleman to live out his snide fantasies. He's got to be shown there's a hate in this world to match his own. He's got to be shown there's a man who will take his three hundred thou and laugh all the way back to his fur-lined cult in the east.

God, how I hate people like . . . where the hell am I? Columbus. Columbus? Who do I know in Columbus? I think I gave a talk there once. At the university. Yes. I remember that. I gave a talk on *The Writer As Golem*. Aunt Sadie was in the audience. My God, Aunt *Sadie* lives in Columbus! I've got to stop here and say hello. I know what I'm letting myself in for, but this is a base I've got to touch. In fact, if it's Arnold Shepler I'm trying to rediscover, who better to talk to than Aunt Sadie?

There's a turnoff. God knows where she lives in Columbus. I know they had a house here while Uncle Max was still alive, but I seem to remember my mother telling me that Aunt Sadie had moved to an apartment after . . . Sadie *what?* . . . Max *what?* . . . Don't tell me I've forgotten my aunt's married name! . . . Max, Max . . . *Plotkin!* . . . Whew! Of course! Max Plotkin! That *grobyon!* That thick-wristed butcher! . . . Well, *de mortuis* . . .

Aunt Sadie with her upside-down peach cakes. For some reason, I remember only summer. We used to drive out to Aunt Sadie's place on torrid Sundays, and Aunt Sadie would serve her summertime specialties. God! Tuna fish salad, smoked white fish, lox, cream cheese, bagels, corn on the cob, sour cream and blueberries, upside-down peach cake. A light meal! A summer meal!

Now here's a funny thing. Here's a very strange thing. Do you know that I miss it! I have often thought of those summer Sunday lunches at Aunt Sadie's with *fondness!*

"Hello, Aunt Sadie."

"Arnie! Well, what a surprise! Come in, come in. How's the great writer? What are you doing here? Are you going to give another talk at the university?"

"No, I'm not going to give any talk. My goodness, look at you, Aunt Sadie! What's that you're wearing? A headband? A warm-up suit? Jogging shoes?"

"You'd have come five minutes later, you wouldn't have found me in," she said. "Yes, on Tuesdays I jog. Yesterday I bicycled. Tomorrow it's aerobic dancing. A little something every day."

"I didn't know that."

"Of course you didn't know that," Aunt Sadie said, looking at me with a smile I can only characterize as *sardonic*. "What do you know about me? You stay in touch? You ever inquire? Never mind, I'm glad to see you. How's your family?"

"They're fine. You know, getting older."

"I know. And you, Arnie? You still haven't told me what you're doing here."

"Passing through," I said, still trying to orient myself to this new Aunt Sadie. She was my mother's younger sister, but she was at least sixty—and apparently as many pounds lighter! She was actually *slim!* Some bagginess around the face, naturally, but here was a woman who had undergone a metamorphosis! I said, "I'm on my way to Hollywood, Aunt Sadie. I've been asked to write the movie script of my last novel, *Too Near The Sun.*"

"I know the name," she said, with that small smile.

I followed her into the living room of the apartment. Huge sofa. Suede? Yes, I believe it is suede. And those lamps! Was that a DeChirico reproduction? What was going on here?

"You look wonderful," I said. "You've lost weight?"

"Depends where you're counting from," she said. "Actually I've put on a couple of pounds in the last few weeks. But since Uncle Max died, I've taken off about fifty."

"How?"

"By not eating. By exercizing . . . So you're going to do the movie script, huh? I hope you'll make some changes."

I looked at Aunt Sadie from where I sat in the Swedish leather chair to where she sat on the suede sofa, her legs tucked up. Two things occured to me at once: one, that I had been in Aunt Sadie's presence for at least ten minutes, and she hadn't offered me a cup of coffee, a cup of tea, *anything;* and, two, that I was in for another racial scolding.

"You've certainly undergone changes, Aunt Sadie," I remarked.

"Fifty pounds."

"I don't mean only weight."

"Yes, I know, Arnie. I know it must seem like a tremendous change to you, but in reality it's not. Since your Uncle Max died, I've become more myself."

"This may sound trivial, Aunt Sadie, but it surprises me that you haven't offered me anything to eat or drink."

"Excuse me! I didn't mean to be impolite. Food doesn't occur to me the way it used to. But would you like something? I have some instant coffee, if you don't mind that. Tea I don't think I have. I was assuming you had lunch."

"I didn't," I said. "It's not important. As a matter of fact, I was remembering those summer Sunday lunches we used to have at your house in Jersey. The sour cream and berries. The upside-down cake."

Aunt Sadie laughed and shook her head. "You know, I don't blame you some of the things you wrote," she said. "You certainly remembered those details very accurately. It surprised *me* a little that you would use them so disparagingly—"

"Disparagingly!"

"Not disparagingly?"

"No, I mean, the *word!* Where did you get a word like 'disparagingly?'"

"Where? Where do *you* get words like that? You read it somewhere and you look it up in a dictionary. I read too, and I happen to own a dictionary. Listen, would you like me to make you something to eat. I made some gazpacho soup yesterday. Would you like some gazpacho soup?"

"Gazpacho? No, thanks. This is a very stylish room, Aunt Sadie. Did you decorate it yourself?"

"Yes, I decorated it myself. You're surprised?"

"No, not exactly surprised. A little bewildered. Things are so different from what I expected. Forgive me for saying so, but all this has the look of money. I'm delighted to know that Uncle Max left you so well off. I didn't think you could make that much money as a butcher."

"If you're the right kind of butcher, you can," Aunt Sadie said, with that strangely off-putting, almost *condescending* look in her eye. "Your Uncle Max didn't come out here to hack lamb chops. He was offered a big job with a meat distributor. He did business with all the finest hotels and restaurants."

"Uncle Max?"

"Before he died, they made him a partner."

"Uncle Max?"

"He left an estate in the seven figures."

"Uncle Max!"

"Hanging over his bed right now—I can show it to you—is the Salesman-Of-The-Year Award. National. The trouble with you, Arnie... never mind... you don't need amateur criticism, right?"

"No, no, I'd love to hear what you have to say. You've already dropped a couple of hints. You said before that you hoped I'd make some changes for the movie of *Too Near The Sun*. What kind of changes?"

"Come on, I'll pour you a bowl of gazpacho. Do you like it cold?"

"I don't want any gazpacho soup, Aunt Sadie. The damn stuff gives me gas. What kind of changes?"

Aunt Sadie shook her head and murmured, "Arnie, Arnie." It was getting distinctly annoying, this embarrassed, foot-shuffling *treatment!* This deprecating, superior *sufferance!* And from Aunt Sadie! My mother's sister! She of the Sunday lunches. The one who clapped her hands every time she saw me, *shepped noches* thirteen to the dozen over my career, faced her own children in my direction so that they could bask a little in reflected glory! Who could have anticipated something like this! I wonder why my mother didn't tell me that Aunt Sadie had gone off her trolley. I'm sure they communicate. I'm sure something must have come through in letters, in telephone conversations. This woman is *menacing!* I didn't have to make this stop in Columbus! I'm antsy enough about this whole friggin Hollywood deal. I didn't need a fate-figure at the crossroads on Route 70.

"What's with the 'Arnie, Arnie'?" I asked. "If you don't mind my saying so, you're being very mysterious. Are you by any chance connected with somebody?"

"Connected?"

"I don't know. Some magazine. Some critical group. People are always trying to do a hatchet job on me. It isn't exactly uplifting to find your own aunt in their camp."

"Please don't talk nonsense, Arnie. You're still my favorite nephew. I'm proud of you. But I wish you would grow up."

"Oh, I like that! That I like! That's what I need to fortify my confidence—a little patronization from my Aunt Sadie! And may I ask in just what way you find me immature?"

"All this petulance," she said. "Family petulance, sexual petulance, Jewish petulance. I know it's hard to get over being Jewish, but others have made it."

"I think you've got it on backwards, Aunt Sadie," I said, just about ready to throw respect to the winds. If this pathetic old broad thinks she's got the *zeitgeist* by the balls just because she puts on a pair of Nike shoes, she's going to have a rude awakening. "I'm not the petulant one. I write what I think and what I feel. *Others* pass out from coast to coast."

She shrugged. My God, I really believe she thinks she's got some overview of my *oeuvre!*

"You're setting up straw men," she said coolly.

"Don't give me that, Aunt Sadie. What do you know about it?"

"Nothing, nothing. Only what I read."

"What do you mean by 'straw men'?"

"I mean, *mein kind*, that once you were genuinely angry. You wanted perfection, or at least better behavior, from your fellow Jews, from everybody. It was a juvenile anger, but you made something of it. You had the talent. Nobody ever denied this. The youthful wish for perfection is an admirable and healthy thing. When it's well done, everybody recognizes it, everybody appreciates it. . . . Listen, Arnie, I can make a omelet if you'd like. I have eggs."

"I'm not hungry, Aunt Sadie," I informed her truthfully. I *wasn't* hungry. I don't think I would have enjoyed one of her upside down peach cakes. Why was I taking this so seriously, this razzing from one of the family's bleacher seats? I thought I was thoroughly immune by this time. But this was a *different* razzing. It came at me like a cold draft in a room where I had thought all the windows were shut. Mysterious. And from Aunt *Sadie*, of all people! Aunt Sadie *had* her role in life! Why was she stepping out of it like this! That was the eerie thing.

The one-time, thick-waisted wife of thick-wristed Max Plotkin! That cold draft was bringing with it a sibylline whisper. I said, "So what are you trying to say? I'm no longer angry?"

"Listen, Arnie, you need advice from me like you need a hole in the head," she said. "Six figures to write a movie script."

"One-point-seven million between my last two books."

"Who can argue with success?"

"*You* can!" I pointed out to her. "You're doing it. What did you mean by 'straw men'?"

"What did I mean? I meant that I don't believe in your people anymore."

"Did you ever believe in them?"

"Yes. In the first couple of books I believed."

"And why don't you believe now?"

"I'll tell you why, Arnie. Sometimes, when your Uncle Max was sitting at the dinner table, after a meal, when he was peeling off that paper band from his cigar, ready to light up, he'd tell me something about the business, about the people he had to deal with, and I'd believe him. But when he began to get red in the face, I didn't believe a word he was saying. The people in your books, Arnie, have been getting redder and redder in the face."

"Maybe they're angrier."

"No, they're not angrier. Neither are you."

"So what am I if I'm not angrier?"

"Richer."

"So?"

"So nothing. So *mazeltov.*"

"Seriously, what's the objection?"

"Nothing, nothing. Forget it."

"Why did you say I should make changes for the movie?"

She sighed, my Aunt Sadie, my Madame de Staël. She said, "All right, Arnie, this is my last word. After this, no more. When you told me you were going out to Hollywood to make a movie, I felt uncomfortable. I didn't think it would be nice, all that childishness for millions to see. It's time, Arnie, it's time you got over all your grievances. It's time you stopped stamping your feet. Who are these people you're talking about? I don't recognize them. Just as you never recognized

Uncle Max, or me, or, to tell you the truth, anyone in the family. Where's the heart's truth? That's where I thought you were heading. Instead you began stamping your feet. You made a fortune stamping your feet, but isn't it time to stop?"

"So why do millions buy my books?"

"They like the show."

"Do you know how many paperbacks have sold of all my books?"

"A lot."

"Eleven-point-five million."

"I'm impressed."

"Do you know in how many languages my books have been translated?"

"I have no idea."

"Sixteen! Sixteen different languages!"

"That must be something, to look in your own book in a language you can't read."

"People recognize me in the street."

"I recognized you. You haven't changed much. Lost a little hair, but essentially the same Arnie."

"Four foundation awards! Prizes!"

"Hmn!"

"There isn't a day the mailman doesn't bring a minimum of fifty letters."

"Arnie, I completely forgot! I got some blintzes in the freezer. I'll put it in the microwave, it'll take five minutes. I don't have sour cream, but I have yogurt. Come in the kitchen. It'll be like old times."

"All right, Aunt Sadie. I am a little hungry. But it won't be like old times."

"You're right. It won't be like old times . . . thank God!"

Who? That's the paramount question. Who could have gotten to Aunt Sadie? One person. Pushy. At one time or another, he's met everyone in my family. I can't remember the occasion, but he must have met Aunt Sadie. Maybe she wrote to him, asking him could he use his influence before we had a holocaust in America. Maybe they've had a correspondence for years. Maybe they had an affair.

Pushy was the only one who knew I was driving across the country. He probably figured I would make a stop in

Columbus. He might have gotten in touch with Aunt Sadie and told her to put the screws to me. But *why?* He was the one who set up this whole deal. Ten per cent of six figures is five figures. Maybe he's afraid this will be a block-buster and I'll stay out in Hollywood and write movies. No more ten per cent. He just wanted a one-shot deal. Make sure I do a lousy job on the script and come back with my tail between my legs and go back to writing novels. Sounds crazy, but so does Watergate.

I mean, can you *believe* Aunt Sadie! Immature! Stamping my feet! Somebody must have coached her. I don't believe in miracles. No person is going to change like that. Particularly Aunt Sadie, with the upside-down peach cake. No, Pushy got to her. The whole goddam thing was a carefully worked out, ten per cent plot, and Pushy's going to hear from me when I get back east.

Where the hell am I? Still in Ohio? My God! I got all those plains ahead of me, the Rockies, the deserts! Who do I know in all those states I'll be passing through? No one. And even if I did, I'd be afraid to stop. God knows what kind of plant has been set up in Illinois, in Missouri, in Kansas, in Colorado. Do they sell books in Kansas and Colorado?

That sonofabitch, Winkleman! How I hate the man!

—*Seymour Epstein*

ERIC SEGAL
(1937-   )

Sob Story

16

It's not all that easy to make a best seller.

Ask Ernie Hemingway (a Princeton man). Ernie Hemingway never made the top of the *New York Times* Best Seller List. Ernie Hemingway could take a lesson from Mrs. Naomi Greenbaum Oliver Bartlett XV.

We were sitting down over dinner. We had bought great Jap sterling steel silverware.

"If they want to laugh," she said, "they watch Red Skelton. If they're gonna shell out four ninety-five for a slim book with short sentences, you gotta give them something to cry about."

I shoveled another forkful of cocktail onions into my mouth and masticated thoughtfully. Sure enough, the tears started coming. Before I knew it, I was bawling like a baby.

"Don't just sit there, Preppie," Naomi yelled, "get to that typewriter!"

I did just that. Two hours and three hundred cocktail onions later, I had finished the first twelve chapters.

17

Naomi took a job in a cannery while I tried to finish the novel. I say tried because after a hundred pages, I still didn't have the grabber. I scoured back issues of *Modern Romance* until my fingers were stained with ink and the pulp was soggy with tears. Still, I didn't find the plot twist I needed. Then, one night, the answer came to me.

Naomi had come home from work and I decided to have some fun with her.

"Thought you were packing sardines," I said.

"Preppie, I am," she replied. "Who told you different?"

"My nose," I said. "It tells me you're packing smelts!"

Naomi laughed. Then she collapsed.

"Love is all you need," she gasped. "But just to make sure, get a big advance."

18

I took Naomi to the hospital. Her doctor (an alumnus of the Famous Surgeons School) took me aside and laid it on the line.

"She's cashing in," he told me. "We think it's an Oriental disease. Pressure on the eyeball. The Chinese call it pressed duct."

He told me something else: I was the one who would have to tell Naomi.

The next day, I hocked Naomi's high school ring and bought two plane tickets to Atlantic City. When I returned to the hospital, I told my young bride we were going on a vacation.

"But, Preppie," she said, "one of these tickets is round-trip and the other is only one-way!"

I watched the smile fade from her lips and the roses turn ashen in her cheek. I stood there like a big dumb jock and watched. There was nothing else I could do. Except cry. And write it all down.

19

She didn't die that night. She didn't die the next night.

In fact, it took four whole chapters before we reached the end. I was on page 127 when I heard her moan.

"Preppie," she asked, "wouldja hold me tight. Wouldja?"

"Of course," I answered, swilling a bottle of Gypsy Rose before hopping into the deathbed with her. Naomi looked scared and I gave her something to hold. My wallet.

"There's something I must know, Preppie," she said. "Who do you see for the movie?"

"Ryan O'Neal and Ali MacGraw." I said.

Naomi groaned and handed back my wallet. It was empty. My God, that girl had spirit.

"She's dying," I cried. "She's young and beautiful and she's dying. Oh, Lord, what is the answer!?"

"Tax-free municipals," Naomi said.

Those were her last words.

20

Marcel Greenbaum was in the waiting room. He was waiting. That was like him. He tried to stop me as I rushed past.

"How about Jack Lemmon for me?" he said.

21

I was crazy with grief when I walked out of the hospital. All I took with me was my love for Naomi and my completed manuscript. Suddenly, there was nowhere I wanted to go. Nothing I wanted to do. I decided to call my agent.

I put a dime in a parking meter and started to dial (I told you I was crazy). Then I saw him. He was standing in front of the hospital watching me. He was my father.

22

"Irving Oliver Bartlett XV," he said, "you should have told me."

"Irving Oliver Bartlett XIV," I said, "you wouldn't have heard."

I looked at the man who was my father. My thoughts traveled to the future. A future without Naomi. A future with nothing to comfort me except money and fame, sex-crazed groupies and guest shots on late-night talk shows. Not knowing why, I repeated what I had learned from the beautiful girl now dead.

"Life's like the pants business," I said. "Everything's on the cuff."

And then I did what I had never done in his arms, much less in his pants. I cried.

All the way to the bank.

—Robert Goldman

RAYMOND CARVER
(1938-   )

Could You Just Keep Talking?

Merlene wanted to go out. The kids had been screaming all day and she was tired of the noise and the house. She sat down on the couch and propped up her feet. The bottle of "Fire Drops" nail polish was on the coffee table. She picked it up and began painting her toe nails. When she had finished three toes, she leaned back to catch her breath. When Carl came home she was working on the left foot.

"Look at this Carl," she said.

"Look at what?" He said.

"My toes," she said. "I haven't painted my nails in god knows how long," she said.

Carl carried his lunch box to the kitchen and put it down next to the sink. He looked out the window. Sylvia, their neighbor, was sitting on a chaise lounge. She was wearing a two piece bathing suit with the straps down off her shoulders. He turned back to Merlene.

"What's for dinner?" He said.

"You take a shower and we'll talk," she said.

In the bathroom, Carl rolled the louvered windows out and looked through the hole at Sylvia. Then, he undressed and turned on the water and stepped into the shower. Merlene carried a beer into the bathroom and handed it to him. She reached around the plastic curtain and held the beer until he took it from her. Then, she sat down on the seat of the toilet.

"Let's go out tonight, honey," she said. "Let's go dancing."

"I don't want to go dancing," he said.

"Then let's go over to Mickey's for a drink," she said. "The kids have been driving me crazy."

"Don't they have dancing at Mickey's" he said.

"Yeh," she said.

"Well, I don't want to go to Mickey's" he said.

"Listen," she said. "Let's take some beer and stuff and go over to Mike and Cindi's."

"What about the kids?" he said.

"They been driving me crazy all day," Merlene said. "I can't stand any more of it."

"No, who's going to take care of them?" he said.

"I'll ask Sylvia to keep an eye on them," she said. "She won't mind."

"Yeh," he said. "OK, if she don't mind."

"She won't mind."

Jerry and Rita were running in the hall. Jerry was chasing Rita with his Louisville Slugger.

"Stop it," she said. "Your father's home and he don't like you running in the hall," she said.

"He tried to hit me," Rita said.

"Would you just shut up," she said. "Your dad and me are going over to Mike and Cindi's and I have to talk to Sylvia about watching you kids."

"Can I come with you?" Rita said.

"If you remember what I said and shut up," she said.

"Me too," Jerry said.

Carl watched Merlene and Rita and Jerry walk the distance between the two trailers. Jerry was carrying a plastic gun and when Merlene wasn't looking he would poke Rita with it. Carl closed the windows and wrapped a towel around himself and walked to the bedroom and dressed.

"Sylvia said no problem," she said.

"Let's pick up some beer on the way over," Carl said.

At the Pic-A-Pak Carl bought three six packs of Millers and some corn curls. At the check out he saw some Necco wafers and bought four rolls to go with the beer.

Mike and Cindi lived in a two bedroom ranch house. They lived in a development of two bedroom ranch houses. In back of their house they had put up a plastic free-standing swimming pool; they had painted the house Latin Sunset Tan. Their son Dennis had drowned in the pool two years ago. Since then they didn't use the pool, but kept it up so that their house would be easy to spot.

"Let's surprise them," Merlene said.

"Now how are we going to surprise them?" Carl said.

She said, "We can sneak around back and go in the back door."

"Don't be dumb," he said.

"Come on let's sneak around," she said. "We can make faces at the window or something."

"Ok," he said, "But I don't want the beer to get hot."

Carl parked two houses down and they started for the house. They crossed the neighbors yard and were heading for the side of the house, when the neighbors dog started barking. The dog was a big mixed breed mutt and it headed straight for Carl.

"Jesus Christ!" he said.

Merlene picked up a stick and threw it. The dog ran after the stick.

"Be quiet Carl," she said.

They tip-toed up to the living room window and peeked in.

"What are they doing?" Merlene said.

"Don't you have eyes?" he said.

"Maybe I better look again," she said and laughed.

"Quiet," Carl said. "Let's go around to the front," he said.

"Why don't we ever do that in the living room?" she said.

"Yeh, and let the kids watch?" he said.

They rang the doorbell and waited.

Cindi opened the door and yelled, "Hey, look who's here. Come on in." Cindi was flushed and her hair was messed up. "Carl and Merlene are here," she called.

"We brought some beer," Merlene said.

Mike took the beer into the kitchen and opened four. "Do you want glasses?"

"Don't embarrass me honey," Cindi said.

Mike carried out the beer and glasses.

"We were going to go dancing but decided to stop by instead," Merlene said.

"We were not going dancing," Carl said.

"Come on, don't be a grouch. Carl is a grouch tonight, he doesn't want to go dancing," she said. "Ever," she said.

"We brought some corn curls and Necco wafers," Carl said.

Cindi stood up and began to fidget with the record player. She took a long time in selecting a record. Mike looked at his shoes and then finished his beer in one long swallow.

"They were Denny's favorite candy," Mike said.

"How about another beer?" Cindi said. "Come on let's all have another beer and some Neccos."

"Sure," Carl said.

"God, that music makes me want to dance," Merlene said.

"Don't start that," Carl said.

"Come on Merlene, I'll dance with you," Mike said.

Carl went into the kitchen and brought out more beer and he and Cindi sat on the couch together and drank the beer.

"Beer goes right to my head," Cindi said.

Mike and Merlene were dancing in the corner near the hallway. Carl could see that Mike had his hand on Merlene's breast.

When the record ended, Carl said, "Let's go home Merlene."

"Oh honey, I'm having fun. The kids will be Ok" she said.

"No kids to worry about here," Cindi said.

"I'll get more beer and the corn curls," Mike said.

"Beer goes right to my head," Cindi said and began to laugh.

Merlene started to laugh. "Don't be such a grouch Carl. Have some fun," she said.

Mike put on another record and led Merlene to the corner. Carl opened a pack of Necco wafers and spread them out on the coffee table. "I don't like the licorice," he said.

Merlene had both hands on Mike's ass. Carl could not see Mike's hands. "Want some Necco wafers" he called to them.

"Let's go for a walk," Carl said to Cindi.

They walked through the kitchen to get more beer. Cindi turned on the pool lights and they went out the back door into the yard. Carl walked over to the pool and balanced his beer on the rim while he lit a cigarette. The bottom of the pool was covered with algae and bits of trash.

Cindi opened her beer and threw the ring into the pool. "That's where we found Denny," she said. "Over there by the ladder."

"Over there by the ladder," Carl said.

"Yeh," Cindi said.

"That's a lot of water," Carl said.

"Ten thousand gallons, I think," Cindi said.

"Nice pool," Carl said.

"You and Merlene should have brought the kids with you," Cindi said.

"They were driving Merlene crazy," Carl said. "You know how kids are," he said.

"Yeh," Cindi said.

"Next time we will," Carl said. "Bring the kids."

"Mike can clean the pool and we can all go for a swim next time," she said.

"Yeh," Carl said. "It would be nice to get wet in that pool."

Cindi threw her beer can into the pool. "Let's go see what they're doing," she said.

They walked around the house. At the corner of the house the neighbors dog came out of the shadow of a bush and caught Carl by the ankle. Carl yelled and kicked the dog. The neighbor turned on his porch light and shook his fist at Carl.

"Let's peek in the window," Carl said.

"I'm too drunk," Cindi said.

Carl walked to the edge of the window and looked in. Merlene was against the wall with her dress up around her waist. Mike had his back to the window and was rocking against Merlene.

"What are they doing?" Cindi said.

"Dancing," Carl said.

At the front door Carl tried to kiss Cindi but she pushed him away and laughed.

"Here we come," Cindi called as she opened the door.

Merlene was sitting on the couch eating Necco wafers, Mike was not in the room.

"Had enough dancing?" Carl said.

"Sure," Merlene said.

"We better go home," Carl said.

"Ok," Merlene said.

Mike came out of the bathroom and sat down next to Cindi. He picked up the licorice flavored wafers that were left on the coffee table. "These are my favorite," he said.

Cindi started to laugh then Merlene started to laugh then Mike and Carl started to laugh.

"Next time we'll all swim," Cindi said.

"Yeh, I want to swim with you next time," Carl said.

Driving home Merlene said, "Too bad about Dennis."

"Yeh," Carl said.

"They don't know how kids can drive a person crazy though."

Carl parked next to the trailer. "I'll get the kids," he said.

The light was on at Sylvia's. Carl took his time crossing the yard, then knocked. When Sylvia opened the door she was wearing a shorty nightgown and panties.

"The kids are sleeping," she said.

"Can I come in?" Carl said.

"No, I'll get the kids," she said. Carl could see through the nighty when she walked toward the bedroom. He carried the kids back to the trailer and put them to bed. Merlene had gone to bed. Carl opened a beer and turned on the T.V. When he finished the beer he turned off the T.V. and went into the bedroom. The lights were off and he undressed in the dark. When he got into bed he could feel that Merlene was naked.

"Did you have fun tonight, honey," she said.

"Sure," he said.

"I think I'll paint my nails more often," she said. "I think I'm more attractive with painted nails," she said.

It started to rain and they could hear the rain falling on the roof of the trailer.

"It's nice to be all warm and cozy and out of the water," Merlene said. "It feels safe to be out of the water."

Carl started to cry.

"What's the matter honey?" Merlene said.

"Could you just keep talking?" he said.

—Kenneth McMurtry

Aren't You Kind Of Old For This?

The two of them stop at the end of the drive and stare at my sign. There isn't much wind, so the plastic flags I strung up last night just droop. I miss the way they flapped last year. The kid across the street, who's since moved away with his parents, said it looked like a rainbow waving bye-bye.

The two of them are still there, talking it over. The one in the rumpled, baby-blue cotton suit digs into his pants' pocket, pulls out his fist, opens it and counts. He nods to the guy in the plaid shirt who looks like he sells used condoms. Here they come.

I look away. The elms remind me of a girl I knew. Or maybe it's the clouds. Under my tee-shirt, a drop of sweat's crawling over my ribs. I think of the lady who came down the drive last year, how the hot wind plastered her peach-colored dress to her thighs.

"Kool Aid," the cotton suit says.

"Yeah," I say. I squint up at him. Just under his jaw there's a maggot-colored scar. It reminds me of my mother.

"Just strawberry?" says plaid shirt.

"Cherry," I say.

Cotton suit counts his loot. "Twenty cents," he says. "Pretty steep."

"Inflation," I say. He's got a grease stain right by his zipper. Probably mayonnaise. He looks like the mayonnaise type.

"Don't worry, Mort. I'll pay you back," says plaid shirt. He makes a wheezing sound, as if he's got asthma or a bad case of gas. "I'll pay you back," he says again.

Mort shrugs. "It isn't that, Al. I just don't like cherry," he says.

Al wheezes again. "It's all the same damn thing," says Al. "I *need* it, Mort."

Mort's breathing shallow now. His upper lip's wet and his black sideburns glisten. I feel my face growing damp like Mort's. Al definitely has gas.

"Two," Mort says. "And hurry."

I pour two Dixie cups full from the pitcher. The pitcher's sweating, too. Al reaches for one, but I cover the cups with my hand.

"Forty cents," I say.

Mort slaps down three dimes and two nickels. The two of them drink.   "Ah," says Al, wiping his lips. "How do I spell relief? K-O-O-L A-I-D."

"Damn," says Mort. His eyes are all teared up.

I could use a good cry myself.

"It's the heat," says Al.

"There's no damn wind," says Mort.

My eyes wander to the crack in the drive. The ants are skittering in and out of their mound. "Wind," the woman said last year, trying to pluck the peach dress out of her crotch. My eyes wandered to the crack in the drive and the wind whirled her smell up into my face. It was nothing like Al's. "Ants don't get thirsty," she said. The Kool Aid had turned her white teeth pink. "Set me up again." She held the cup to keep it from blowing away while I poured.

"I said, 'Hey,'" says Mort.

The two of them are staring down at me.

"Set you up again?" I say.

"I *said*, 'Aren't you kind of old for this?'" says Mort.

"Yeah," says Al. "What are you, thirty? Thirty-five?"

I look back down at the crack. I scratch my beard. It reminds me of a girl I knew. Or maybe it was a girl I wanted to know.

"Get the fuck out of my yard," I say.

"Hey," says Mort.

I look Al in the eyes. They're a stale grey color. It reminds me of my jockey shorts. "You're a stinker," I say.

They leave right after they beat me up, pour Kool Aid over me, and take their money back. I lie quiet awhile, head heavy on the anthill's breast. I'm sweating and bleeding. My face is crawling with ants. And now there's a wind, but it's vague and directionless, like prose.

Maybe I should lie here until it rains. Then, at least, I'd be clean.

—Joseph Hutchison

JOYCE CAROL OATES
(1938-   )

The Pose

Then what, they asked her?

WHAT? WHAT? and... and... then (was he looking at me?? how was my hair... my nails were bitten... did he see my nails bitten??) It was a policeman... a cop.

A COP. A REAL COP...

Yes, no... I don't know... We were at the beach and this photographer was there. Three shots for a quarter. You know?

And then? And then?

Then. Then. Then. Wait. Wait. I said, sure. I'll do it. Why not? What the Hell? Who cares? The gulls were screaming. The laundry flapping. My nails were dry. The guy I'm with has big shoulders that keep heaving with merriment. With merriment. He thinks I'm funny but he's only a mechanic at the Texaco station. He knows I will give myself to him. Yes. Yes. Let him wrench my virginity. Then. Yes.

But. But.

My face was flaming. Everything's flaming. I could feel his hands before they touched me. Touch me. Then. But. And. He could have been from the Gulf Station. The Sunoco. The cheapie Brand-X. I don't know any more. Does it matter?

Then the cop said, the REAL COP SAID, look do we need another story like this? Do we really need another story like this?

Then what. What. Then.

This photographer started taking pictures saying, Jeez, you look good like that. Turn this way. Turn that way. Hey. Boy.

But all the time, I'm writing this letter to you, Henry, all the time Mr. Goodwrench is saying things to me, whispering things like who won the series in '48? In '64? In '70? And it was like a Louisville slugger thumping homeplate. Thumping and thumping. I kept reciting everything I could remember... all the names... George Sisler... Rogers Hornsby... Joe DiMaggio... Maury Wills... Ty Cobb... Bob Feller... Lou Gehrig... but I knew none of these guys. I didn't even know this guy from the Texaco station or this photographer but they kept saying turn this way, turn that . . . my cheeks are now burning. Everything's burning . . .

I write this letter and do this with everyone looking at me. LOOKING AT ME. Dear Henry, you thought you'd get it but I'm giving it to this guy from the Texaco station but I'm thinking of you the whole time. THINKING OF YOU. What does he matter, his lust is ignorant, but he knows his baseball. What do I know? I'm a dumb kid that people laugh at . . . LAUGH AT . . .

Wait . . . wait this is the real cop talking. THE REAL COP . . . Let's see the pictures.

Later, I stand on Broadway and 104th. I see this guy with the camera. He looks at me. Hi, kid, he says sourly. You remember, I say. Sure, I remember. He keeps walking. Walking. There are people on the street. ALL AROUND US. Did you develop the pictures, mister. His eyes close down to f. 64. Naw, they were all overexposed. Know what I mean? Over-exposed. I knew . . . I thought I knew. SOMEONE KNEW . . .

—H. T. Masters

ANN BEATTIE
(1947-   )

Pals

Henry and Joyce sat by the edge of the pool. Shirley lay on the *chaise longue* and Bill stretched out flat on the hot tile that had been put around the edge of the pool by Shirley's father, George. Henry was taking Joyce's picture with a Pentax while she made goo-goo eyes at him through the 50mm Schneider lens.

"Where did you get those earrings?" Henry asked. He liked Joyce's earrings. They were long, dangly and made of green glass.

"I got these at Woolworth's in White Plains but not at the jewelry counter. More near the yard goods."

"I had earrings like that once," Bill said. No one said anything. John Klemmer started tootling "Touch Me" and the other personnel included Larry Carlton, acoustic guitar, John Guerin, drums and Echoplex, flute.

"Who put the shit on?" Shirley asked.

"Mary Beth put it on," Henry said, turning Joyce into a different pose. "Turn this way. Turn that way."

"Did you put that shit on?" Shirley asked Mary Beth who just came out of the house. Mary Beth was holding a large ceramic flower pot.

"Yes, I put it on. Doesn't anyone want to look at my pot? I just took it out of the kiln."

"It looks just like you," Bill said, sorry that he had seen it. He had wanted to sleep with Mary Beth but now that he had seen her pot, he didn't feel that he should. "Don't you get cold posing for those things all the time?"

The needle scraped across the record. There was silence. Then Lenny Kay Connection and the Nitecaps took over.

"Who did that?" Shirley asked.

"It must be Sybil and Jake," Mary Beth answered. "They are in the basement, messing around."

"Or it could be Agnes, Phil and Ramona," Joyce reminded us. "They were in the dining room polishing up the first act of their play."

"Gosh, we're artistic," Bill said. "Photography, pottery, play writing, messing around."

"How long have you been in Connecticut, Bill?" Mary Beth wanted to know.

"Am I in Connecticut? I've been in New Jersey, Vermont and Pennsylvania but I didn't think I've been to Connecticut."

"Hey!" We all turned. It is Alex who has just come through the sunporch. He had left, a while back, to get pizza, some with peppers and some without. "You know what that little jerk, Raymond did? He stole my Zippo lighter."

"Where's the pizza?" Henry asked. "Turn that way, Joyce."

"As I was giving the order to the guy at the counter—you know, some with peppers and some without, Raymond picks up my Zippo and disappears around the corner. They're out of Tab and Mountain Dew. I got Dr. Pepper. Who's playing Lenny Kay Connection and the Nitecaps?"

"Call the cops," L. C. said.

"Not in my house," Shirley said. "No cops in my house."

"Okay," L. C. agreed.

"Who's that? Where did he come from?" Shirley said sitting up. She held up the front of her swim suit with her right hand, and pointed at L. C. with her left.

"That's L. C.," I said. "I just put him in."

The doorbell rang.

—H. T. Masters

IAN McEWAN
(1948-   )

From The Garden Party

Chapter One: I Grow Up.

When Uncle Ron bought the chainsaw my big sister Adela was pissed off. "You great burk," she told him, "What did you want to go and waste money on that for? There's no trees around here." "These things can come in useful," said Uncle Ron, getting all huffy as he always did when Adela was snotty to him, "you never know." He had bought it from a mate of his at the garage and didn't want to admit that he had wasted his money. Still, discouraged by Adela's attitude, he never said anything about it for a month or two, and just left the thing standing in the coal-shed, where little Ernie and I would creep in and stare at it in awe.

Then one afternoon while I was at school Uncle Ron took Ernie off in his van and they drove around picking up all the stray cats in the neighbourhood. When I came home, they were in the back yard. Ernie would toss one of the moggies high up in the air and Uncle Ron would buzz it with the saw on the way down. I went into the kitchen for my tea, where Adela was washing up. She was really pissed off at the mess they were making. But that wasn't the real cause of her irritation, as I soon found out. "Now don't you go out there," she said, "I'm not having you ruining your school things like those two daft idiots. Look at him, a grown man!" She fetched me my hot milk and beans on toast, and I reached up her skirt, but she shoved me away. "Not now," she said. "And how many times have I told you not to pick your pimples while you're eating." She began to complain about how hard it was to look after us all and make us behave right. Today she was upset because the neighbours had complained about Mum again and Mr. Purvis from the Social Security was coming round to speak to Uncle Ron.

"How is mum?" I asked.

"Bit blue round the edges," she said, and began to cry. "But she's all right, she's all right, I keep telling them she's good for another month, at least until her birthday!" She hugged me and I slipped my hand into her knickers to comfort her.

Just then the doorbell went. It was Mr. Purvis. I didn't like him because of his funny voice and the way he looked at me and Ernie. Uncle Ron wouldn't get his name right, kept calling him Mr. Pervert and said he was a fairy, but however hard I looked I couldn't see where Mr. Purvis kept his wings. Maybe folded up under his coat.

"Ah, well well, the happy family at home, a touching sight," said Mr. Purvis. He looked out of the kitchen window and a lump of cat's guts slapped the pane in front of his nose. "Fresh air, fresh air, yes, that's what they need," he mused.

Then him and Adela started arguing about Mum. I went outside to fetch Uncle Ron. When we went back in, Adela had fetched Mum out from her room and was crying over her.

"I don't care," says Mr. Purvis, "She'll have to go to the dump, she's a hazard to public health. Don't worry, the corporation will pick her up for you."

I looked at mum and suddenly a strange wild fondness and grief welled up in me, a feeling I had never had before. It was my first intimation of bereavement, of loss. Mum wasn't looking too good. The rats had got to her again and she was missing an ear and another two fingers.

"Bugger me backwards," said Uncle Ron, "she don't half pong."

"No!" cried Adela. She knelt by Mum's barrow, lifted a corner of the sheet. "It's a bouquet, a garden—she's our garden. Look!"

And, it was true, and wonderful to see, how Mum had changed; whereas last time I had seen her she had been sort of dirty yellow-grey now she was mottled all over with blue and green blossoms of mould, pale violet posies, delicate foliations of yellow and mauve.

"Well then," said Ron, "we'll have to have a garden party for her, won't we. Have the neighbours round, soak her in paraffin, have a bonfire."

I saw him smirk, and wink at Mr. Purvis. Adela ran sobbing from the room. Only little Ernie giggled and clapped his hands at the prospect of a party with a bonfire. As for myself, I was stricken to the heart with a strange, wild, desolate feeling, a feeling that I was young and innocent no longer, but witness and party to the unique deceptions of adulthood. It was my first intimation of the ways of the world. Sadly, I slunk upstairs to masturbate, knowing that this childhood consolation would never again cure the bleakness in my heart.

—*Ian Duncan*

The Elements Of Friction

Chekhov is supposed to have said that if an author hangs a gun on the wall at the beginning of a story, he had better fire it to signal the end. In this antidote, Chekhov was addressing the problem of *natural selection* in fiction. While real life may be cluttered with all manner of wall-hanging, it is unlikely that the count's mistress will murder the count by shooting him with a moose-head. For argument's sake, however, let us examine such a story. It is "The Count's Mistress," where author Horror de Balzac has ignored a fundamental principle of *natural selection,* and hung a moose-head on the wall instead of a gun. Because of this, the count's mistress faces some almost insurmountable difficulties. According to the *plot*, she is supposed to leave the verandah, tiptoe up the marble stairs to his study, and secret the gun in her bosom:

> Emplumada scanned with her eyes the wall for the count's dueling pistol. Instead, generations of the count's ancestors—he came from deep soil in which to write—stared down at her mockingly. Frustrated, she tore from its place the great moose-head whose hindquarters she had always imagined a part of living nature on the other side of the wall. Down came the immense bust with a crash, followed by the moose-head itself. Only with great difficulty could she lift it to her bosom.

If Emplumada can scarcely lift it, how on earth will she hide it? Clearly, one important element of fiction—*realism,* or *fidelity to hormone experience*, first introduced by Samuel Butler Richardson in *Shamela*—will be immeasurably weakened if she is unable to hide the weapon with which to murder the count.

Through sheer Balzacian ingenuity, however, the count's mistress *does* succeed in hiding the murder weapon on her person. What other fictional difficulties does she face? Balzac writes:

> Opening the screen to the verandah, Emplumada eyed the count bending over the dying poodle. She exhaled in a rush and felt her nerve-ends knock against her bladder. In one motion she drew the moose-head out of her bosom.
>
> "You swine," she whispered, aiming down the tic-infested neck with her chin.

Here another fictional element has been brooched. The element is *verysmellytude*, that quality of fiction which convinces the reader that the author is maintaining proper *fidelity to hormone experience*. Although Balzac tries his best to convince us of his *verysmellytude*, we simply don't believe him. He even goes so far as to add the *realistic detail* concerning the "tic-infested neck" to persuade us to believe him—yet it is not pestilential infestation of the moose's neck which disturbs us. But let us grant that the count's mistress may, by dint of sheer athletic exertion and strength of will, manage to draw and aim her weapon. How, pray, is she to fire it? —Attention to detail is very important in fiction!

On the other hand, let us mention a few things at which Horror de Balzac has succeeded. First, he has succeeded in involving the reader in a *conflict,* which is *the verb of fiction.* Presumably, the count has done something to offend Emplumada. Perhaps he has wounded the poodle; more likely, he has just finished leaving her for another. We are not sure. What we *are* sure of is that the two of them are enmeshed in a powerful *verb of fiction.* Furthermore, we are kept in sufficient *suspenders* to wait breathlessly on the outcome. The author continues:

> A loud report filled Emplumada's ears as the count whirled. The large caliber of his wound had torn a hole in the pretty ruff at his waist where it exited. It was a report heard round the small world of poodle and meadow, where Emplumada had first played with the pale phylacterie on his zipper. She remembered the malaise of his thighs, as she slipped the murder weapon through the boards of the porch.

At this point in the story, nothing would seem more natural than that Emplumada should seek to rid herself of the murder weapon. Yet who could blame the knowledgeable reader who asked how a 500-pound hunting trophy can be "slipped" through the boards of a porch?

On the plus side, however, it should be pointed out that Emplumada is here undergoing the modern experience of *time as vertigo* (first introduced by Joyce in "Arabesque," where Gabriel Conway relives his wife's flatulence for a dead lover). At the very instant Emplumada is murdering the count, she is also reliving a childhood *fleshback* in the adjacent meadow. Like most of Lawrence's *fleshbacks*, this one is accomplished more or less *in medias wreck* (cf. the "beginning, midwife, and wedding" of Aristotle's *Odious Rex*), through the miracle of *personal point of view*, whereby the author drops his *omniscience* for a kind of Godlike overview of the whole panatella of humid experience:

> But as sometimes happens, dropping through the boards of the porch was not easy for the murder weapon. Watched by the vast eye out of *Spiritus Monday*, the enormous firearm bounced from this board to that, burdened by its freight of taxidermist's stuffing and the innumerable glimmering points of its antlers.

It is to the author's credit here that he recognizes the problems of scale involved in slipping an object of such tremendous size through a narrow gap, and that he follows a casual chain to its realistic conclusion (much as Kafka does in *The Metamorpheus*, where a cockroach is posited and then followed to its final *denudement* and death). In the next line, Balzac, freed from the fritters of personal *omniscience*, chooses instead to zoom in for a closeup of his character:

> But with each ricochet, each carom of the majestic thing off the boards of the porch, Emplumada became visibly more distressed, and the mole on her neck—the one near the mastoid wen below her earlobe which the count so loved to caress with his tongue—that mole began to weep.

Here the moose-head seems a little better integrated into the *action* of the story. The sound of its clatter sets off an associative daisychain which fulminates in Emplumada's grieving mole. Rather impressive is the telling *juxtapollution* of the *tiny microcosm* of the mole against the *huge microcosm* of the "vast eye out of *Spiritus Monday*," so reminiscent of Twain's Calaveras and Faulkner's Yucknapoocaca.

In any event, the mole becomes a powerful *cymbal* of the *Trocomarian Libido* of D.H. Lawrence. Its power derives not so much from context but from the *tone of vice* of the author. Furthermore, because we have been so well-prepared by the author's painstaking development of Emplumada's *motiveless malignity* (which she no doubt learned from Coleridge's *Ancient Mallomar*), the *climax* which she undergoes at *the pinochle of rising action* does not come as too much of a surprise:

> Suddenly the great *schnozole* of the murder weapon rolled smoking to a stop and the verandah was silent past all hearing. Across the meadow a rook stood stock still, a bitten crawdad hanging from its beak. Now Emplumada saw herself as a creature driven and derided by vanity. Irritated, she wondered who it was coming over the rise, whistling "le style, c'est l'homo." Was it the chief inspector of their district, or was it her *dopplegänger?*
> —It was her *dopplegänger*, and she died.

Finally, with the loss of momentum by the moose-head, the *complication* set in by the author's choice of the wrong wall-hanging has been resolved. Disburdened at last, Emplumada is free to experience the Joycean *epiphany*, which is quickly followed by a *sudden flesh of insight*. The *epiphany* may be said to redeem her, while the *sudden flesh of insight* takes from her her life. Or is it the other way around, as the author's use of the *dopplegänger* (a kind of *deus ex meshugena*, or *fallen archetype* of oneself) seems to suggest? Here a cunnilinguistic *ambiguity* asserts itself, and is left for the reader to judge.

A final *paradox* is worth considering. Death generally signals the end of life in the real world, yet the death of Emplumada here does not necessarily signal the end of this story as a *fricative experience* (Barbara Herford Herrnstein's term). While the *climax* of the story occurs at the very *pinochle of rising action*, we still have to undergo the letdown of the story's *denudement*. In Balzac's "The Count's Mistress," this *denudement* just happens to coincide with the story's great freshman themes:

> As her *doppelgänger* hasted gingerly past without greeting, Emplumada sank to the pavement next to the count. Day faded from view and night came; the stars in their perfect orbits around the sun stared down but without tears on a careless universe, full of limp victims. Nor did any pureness of purpose evidence itself in the dumb glaze of the great moose lying senselessly where it had been strewn also.

Echoing Camus's point in "The Myth of Syphilis" and Pirandildo's in "A Cat, A Goldbarth, and the Stars," Balzac quite clearly invites us to peruse his *themes*, which have to do with our humanity's place in Sagan's *Cosmos*. The author himself seems to draw attention to this point by accomplishing *closure* in a highly metaphorical *style* which comprises *frigative language* and *epic-smellies*–a *style* all Balzac's own and, like any good *style*, identifiable by the author's fingerprints.

And so, almost despite itself, Balzac's "The Count's Mistress" succeeds as a work of *fiction*. The reader forgives its sins against *natural selection*, its clumsy use of *traumatic irony*, and its rather *flat-chested characterization* of Emplumada (as opposed to the preferable, *round-chested characterization* of E.M. Forster), because the story reminds us, as art always reminds us, how unimportant we are, and yet how crucial it is to us all. Perhaps the poet W. H. Dryden said it best when, in another contest entirely, he wrote that, like poetry, fiction "makes nothing happen," but that

> . . . it survives,
> A way of happening, a moose.

Index